UNDESIRABLE

LAURA STAPLETON

DEDICATION

This is for all my Beta readers. I owe you.

.

CONTENTS

ACKNOWLEDGMENTS

So many people to thank! My husband and daughter for their massive support. My readers because without you, all this would still be hanging out on my computer. The intrepid pioneers who kept journals because without them, I'd have few facts to check. Phil Lacasse's patience in reviewing my tourist level French helped improve this book and the next. Finally, there's Julie Mason, my wonderful editor. Her patience and enthusiasm knows no limits. For that, I'm beyond grateful

.

CHAPTER 1

"Can't you go get Mrs. Warren?" Samuel Granville asked while scanning the sea of covered wagons from his horse.

"I don't have time for her games today. I've already been to the fort." Charles Warren crumpled the paper. "Do you know anyone who needs to go again?" He glanced around as if searching for his own answer. "Maybe they can find Marie in the saloon and tell her to come back here."

Shocked, Sam asked, "She's where?" He stared at the man, not sharing his calm demeanor. There was no telling what sort of trouble the fur traders passing through would give a nice, proper woman like Mrs. Warren. His heart pounded at the thought. He didn't like losing people to accident or sickness. Death by mischief, though, he could prevent or stop. Looking at the sun, he judged enough time remained in the day to get across the river to Laramie and back. Some patrons might be drunk, but not enough to harass her, he hoped.

"If you can think of someone to go get her, I'd appreciate it. On the other hand, I ought to leave her there all night. It would teach her a lesson about trying this sort of thing again further down the road." Charles leaned against his wagon, arms crossed. "Now that I think about it, I like the idea of her spending all night in a saloon. It would serve her right for leaving camp."

The very idea angered Sam, so he adopted his betting face from the force of habit. He smiled at the man and thought how the attractive face of the older gentleman must not extend the handsome past the skin. While his brown eyes seemed friendly and trustworthy enough and the silver white hair suggested wisdom, Sam suspected otherwise. "No need for that, I'll visit the fort." He wanted the instructions where the man was to meet his wife. No telling how long she'd been expecting her husband. "Does her note say if she's in the saloon proper or in one of the hotel rooms?"

"Here," Warren said as he passed the wadded paper to Samuel. "If you're sure about bringing her back, this is what she wrote." He shrugged, "I'm too busy and too tired to fool with her.

1

Marie is lucky I don't just leave her there for good."

Sam looked at him, angry. Warren couldn't know what had happened to his sister-in-law, Beth, in this area. How she'd been left here. Alone to die. The man didn't know the fear-filled days of waiting to hear from Sam's brother, Nicholas, as he searched for either her or her grave. Yes, their story had a happily ever after, but the same might not be true for Mrs. Warren. He couldn't let her stay there overnight alone. She waited in a place known for its harassment. He gritted his teeth and forced a grin. "Again, no need for that. I'll make sure she's back here before dark. If you'll excuse me."

Not happy with the entire situation, Sam went to his horse. He sat atop Scamp before rereading the message. She wanted Warren to meet her at the 101 Tavern, room four as soon as possible. He took a deep breath of the dusty air, glad she didn't wait in the main bar but in a private room instead. Knowing this, he didn't fear as much for her safety.

She'd written "Love, Marie," and kissed the paper with rouged lips. Mrs. Warren had interested him far too much from the moment they'd met. He'd worked to keep his distance from her in the last couple of months since they'd left Independence, Missouri. When Sam had learned her last name, he'd hoped she was anything but the man's wife, but eventually, he'd pushed aside the lingering regret over it. Glancing again at her lip print, he grinned and folded the note, putting it in his shirt pocket. Warren may be blasé about his wife's lips, but he couldn't be. Nothing wrong in treating another man's trash like his own treasure.

He clicked at Scamp and headed south. Having been at Fort Laramie and this particular establishment a time or two, Sam knew exactly where to find her. She waited for him, or rather, her husband, in one of the buildings adjacent to the actual fort. As he neared the fort, he paused for the lowering of the American flag for the night. Sam removed his hat for the ceremony, and once the last bugle notes sounded, he put his hat back on and continued to where Mrs. Warren waited. Reaching the saloon, he tied his horse to the railing and went inside.

Sam tried to pass by the bar, but the bottles of whiskey looked awfully inviting. He paused, considering her reaction to his appearance instead of her husband's. Smiling, he'd found his justification for sitting a while. He needed the liquid courage to tell

2

a woman her husband didn't want to be seduced. Maybe a drink or two might soften the pain she'd inflict on him. He'd not seen her angry so far. In fact, now that he thought back, Mrs. Warren seemed like a good natured woman. Looking again at the selection behind the bar, he thought it prudent not to take any chances. Sitting on a stool, Sam put down two bits. "I'll need a shot of your best."

The barkeep grabbed a bottle and hollered to be heard above the piano and rowdier customers. "You're in luck; we just got a fine whiskey in today. One of the wagons headed west had this and someone traded a bottle for a room tonight."

He recognized the label and frowned as the bartender poured. Sam had seen the brand in the Warrens' personal wagon. It seemed Marie had traded Warren's best for tonight. "That's interesting." He sipped the whiskey a little to taste the flavor.

"Yep, I'd have given two nights, but the person said they only needed one." The man lifted his chin at a customer's raised glass. "Wanted me to be discreet."

Sam tipped his head back, drinking down the remainder of the whiskey in a gulp. Stifling a laugh at the man's lack of discretion, he lifted the empty shot glass. "Well, I'm going to need one more, please."

"Two bits covers two shots," the man replied and refilled the small glass before attending other customers.

He downed the drink in a gulp. A shame to not savor the smooth, liquid heat, but he had a member of his party to retrieve. The alcohol swam through his veins, warming his body. The sensation was as pleasant as the taste. Tonight, his money had bought far better than the usual rotgut common on the plains. Setting the glass down, he stood, wanting to get on with the chore.

Working ladies called out to him as he climbed the stairs, earning him catcalls from the other patrons. He fought the urge to deny why he was there. He didn't know anyone and no one would believe him, anyway. Continuing on to the hallway, he counted to the fourth room but then hesitated. What if this hurt her feelings, he wondered, instead of making her angry? Sam often saw the affection she held for Warren by her expressions, words, and actions. The woman seemed to be a devoted wife. He dreaded the wounded look he might see in her eyes after telling her of her husband's refusal. He took a deep breath and knocked, determined not to put off the task any longer.

"Come in, please."

Marie's request through the closed door took him aback. She expected her husband, but how did she know for sure who was at the door? Shame on her, he thought, for being so careless with her safety. He'd need to give everyone yet another lecture once back at camp. Sam opened the door, stepped in, and closed it with one quick and fluid motion so no one observed who he met in the private room. When he saw her, his pulse pounded in his ears right along with her shriek.

Mrs. Warren's hair, released from the usual French braid, fell over her shoulders in ebony waves. Her dark eyes glittered in the lamplight, the same light giving her skin a golden glow. She wore a dancing girl's dress that Sam figured was likely brought from New Orleans. Her black bustier pushed her breasts high and together, and her short red skirt left most of her legs bare. Not completely undressed, he noticed. She also had black stockings that nearly reached the bottom of her ruffled skirt. With two steps and a shove, she'd be back on the bed with him following. A thin sheen of sweat broke out over his skin. "I don't think this is right."

Her lips pressed together, her chin quivering, Marie turned to a decanter. She replied, "Of course it isn't. I thought my note was very clear. Where is Charles?" After pouring a liberal amount of whiskey, she drank it like water.

"Who?" When she glared at him, Sam remembered why he was there. "Mr. Warren remained at camp. And is busy. Or so he says. He asked that someone tell you. I needed to visit the fort one last time. So he asked me. I mean, asked for me to attend to you. Um, I mean, retrieve you." He paused, unsure of what he'd just said to her. The woman glared at him, unsettling Sam with her intensity. He didn't want her angry at him, so he continued, "That's why I'm here. And to bring you back to our camp. Tonight." He babbled, of course. What else could he do in such close quarters with a woman dressed so provocatively? His throat too dry to swallow, he asked, "Might I have a drink as well?"

Marie sighed. Pouring another glass with hers, she asked, "So he won't be here at all, and I've wasted my time? And yours as well?"

Sam didn't want to mention how her words echoed her husband's, not when seeing how angry tears shimmered in her eyes.

4

Instead, he responded, "No, I don't think he will be here after all. I'm supposed to bring you back for him." While Sam spoke, Marie swirled the liquid before gulping it down as before. He couldn't remember the last time he saw such a small woman drink so much at once. "Mrs. Warren, you might not want to imbibe all your whiskey tonight."

She laughed and set down the glass. "Oh? Will it make tomorrow more unpleasant than it already will be?"

Putting himself in her place, he'd not like such a personal rejection from a spouse, either. "I know you must feel embarrassed, but I won't tell anyone."

Marie gave him a smile not reaching her eyes. "You can't know how I feel. Embarrassed is the least of it." She pressed the back of her hand to her forehead for a moment until she began braiding her hair. "I'm sure Hester knows by now. Both she and Charles, I assume, are already chattering about it in their twin speak."

"I've heard them talking and wondered at the language," he said, glad she'd explained a little of the mystery Sam noticed between the brother and sister.

Marie sighed, saying, "Most children outgrow it, but not them. They'll reassure me they don't gossip about me, but I'm not sure that's true."

"You don't believe them?" he asked, taking a drink.

"Not when they talk, look at me, and laugh."

"I see." Sam felt the need to reassure her and offered, "Your husband didn't know how you're dressed. He might be amused in my place, but not laughing."

She looked at him as if taking in every detail. "You're very kind." Marie sat and patted the bed next to her. "Since you've been sent on a fool's errand, I feel I must explain to you why I'm here. Come here and have a seat."

Sam didn't want to pull away, but to be near anything comfortable with her worried him. "Are you sure that's wise?"

Frowning at him, Marie retorted, "Stand, then, if you're afraid I'll attack you like I would have Charles."

He smiled, surprised she didn't see the problem with her request. The examination Marie just gave him must have reassured her of his honor, and he felt an odd urge to be the man she thought he was. Taking off his hat and putting it on the bedpost,

5

Sam sat next to her. "Now, then, what did you want to tell me?"

"Just so you know, I never need constant rescue from places of ill repute." She drank the remaining alcohol in her glass before continuing. "But that doesn't answer why I'm here in this dress. To please Charles, since he was, or is, older than I am, I befriended some ladies in New Orleans."

Sam kept his face expressionless. If Warren frequented *these* women, no wonder Mrs. Warren felt the need to go to such lengths to interest him. In an even tone, he asked, "They knew him?"

"Not him, personally, but they knew men. I would go to various brothels, in a back way, of course, and pay them to tell me their professional secrets." She faced him, eyebrows raised, and added, "Now mind you, this was only for my husband's benefit."

Thinking of how Marie knew things most ladies didn't, Sam took a deep drink before asking, "These women told you what they did with their clients?"

"When I paid them for their time, they did, yes." She shrugged. "As a result, I know everything, but Charles being the way he is, I've not been able to practice anything. So I hardly know if what I've learned from the women I consulted is useful or a farce."

"I see." He wondered if her husband knew of her skills. Most likely not, else how could Warren remain indifferent to her current request? In his place, Sam might have moved mountains to honor an appeal from Marie. He glanced at her, seeing how as she looked down at her empty glass, the middle part in her hair mirrored the cleft of her bosom. Desire began coursing through him like the warmth of his drink. Indicating the whiskey, he asked, "Could you pour me more, please?"

"Of course." Marie gave him a generous amount. "I'd rather hoped he'd be here tonight, and I could ensure us some privacy."

Yes, Sam thought, she had indeed provided some privacy. She added more to her own glass, and he looked at her. He felt her body heat from her arm through the fabric of his shirt. Marie reminded him of the tropical flowers in Panama. He'd always expected, with her exotic looks, for her to smell like anything but the traditional rose perfume of her skin. The subtle scent urged him closer to her. She intoxicated him far more than any alcohol. Sam stopped his examination at the thought. "Mr. Warren is a very fortunate man. If my wife had arranged such a meeting for me, I'd move heaven and earth to attend."

She laughed, saying, "Thank you, sir. I'll be sure to tell him so". Marie blinked a couple of times as if her eyes were cloudy. Tilting her head as if getting an idea, she suggested, "You might help me with something since you are here, and we're alone."

Feeling himself close to the edge of a cliff, he asked, "What might that be, ma'am?"

A pink blush spread across her face as she responded, "This may sound odd, but I would like an impartial opinion and possible accounting of something."

He grinned. Opinion and accounting? The words seemed safe enough, and he responded, "Certainly. It sounds simple, what do I need to assess?"

Marie turned to face him, and looking into his eyes, she said, "I need you to kiss me and let me kiss you back. When we're done, you can tell me what I'm doing wrong and how to improve."

"You want me to do what?" His heart thudded, desire giving way to fear. Sam searched his mind for clues he might have given of interest in her. She seemed so earnest and sweet, yet, had this all been an odd game? "No. Out of the question." He stood, adding "I need to get you to camp right now. We must leave in the next few minutes."

Her eyes glistened as if tearing. "Very well. In fact, you go ahead. I'll follow later, so there's no talk or suspicions."

"You'll be directly behind me?" At her nod, he took his hat from the post. "Thank you ma'am, and I'll check to make sure you arrive soon after I do." Sam left the room, careful to close the door behind him. He waited for a moment, hoping to hear her lock it. When hearing a reassuring click, he turned for the saloon. Various girls standing in their own doorways hollered at him, teasing. He ignored them, his pulse still hammering. He had already faced enough temptation for one day.

Passing by the first barstool, he wanted to drink the place dry. Anything to numb the dull ache from seeing the shame and hurt in her eyes. "Barkeep?" Sam sat down and put two bits on the bar, gaining the man's attention.

"Couple more fine whiskeys, or will four of the rotgut do ya?" he asked, wiping out a glass.

"Two of the fine. Tomorrow's a busy day."

The man palmed the coins, placed the sparkling glass on the

counter, and poured. Most times, Sam liked starting a conversation with people he met. Asking questions intended to draw out a man or woman's interests seemed to be his forte, he thought. But right now? From the moment he entered Mrs. Warren's room until the second he left had been an ordeal. He took sips, enjoying the tingle of alcohol. Her face had shown anger, curiosity, amusement, sadness, and at last, hurt. Staring at the remaining swallow of amber liquid, he knew he had been short, maybe even cruel with her. Mrs. Warren didn't know Sam had reacted more to his own desires than her request.

After waving off another inquiry for a refill, Sam left the saloon. He refused to be impaired at any time during the journey between Missouri and Oregon. Sam liked the taste much more than the effects, and once outside he took a deep breath, letting the fresh air clear his head. He untied his horse and sat in the saddle, gazing out toward his camp. A line of fires flickered in the distance, some his responsibility, many others not. He sighed and shifted in his seat. Sam wanted to hurry through this part of the trail. The next few days promised to be difficult due to the overcrowded campsites, skimpy creeks, poor grass for the livestock, and little rain.

Overall, he considered this trip a good one. Two months in the journey and only a couple of people had died. He'd heard of entire companies gone before reaching Fort Laramie. Unless something catastrophic happened, he'd have nearly everyone alive at Willamette Valley. He looked back at the fort, seeing if Mrs. Warren followed. Spotting her off in the distance wearing one of her work dresses, Sam went on north and into their camp.

He glanced around at the various wagons in their group. This party was larger than the one he led a couple of years ago but small enough to get along well. The greater the numbers, the more potential he had for personality conflicts. He dismounted at his own camp, giving a nod to the men gathered around the fire. After seeing to Scamp's comfort and tossing his hat into the wagon, he joined the rest of his crew.

"We already ate, boss," Lucky said, nodding at another one of his men. "Saved some for ya, though."

"Thank you." He grinned at the younger man and took the clean plate Lefty held out with his good hand. Sam sliced off a hunk of cheddar and scooped out some beans. He worked to get

pieces of ham into the ladle, too. "I appreciate you all not waiting to eat."

"I saw you ride over after talking with Warren," said Arnold. "I mentioned to the others you might be a while."

Sam swallowed his bite of cheese before replying, "Yes, I had to do an errand for him."

Lefty nodded. "Figured as much, sir."

He ate, listening to their chatter. Sam didn't bother asking about the livestock in their care. His ironclad policy was animals received care first. He'd picked good men for this trip. Sam knew Lucky from earlier travels, while Uncle Joe, Lefty, and Arnold were recent hires. He'd hated to see Monsieur Claude go. Considering the lovely woman le Monsieur married. However, Sam understood his reasons. He stared down at his spoon, thinking of Chuck and the illness taking him. The young man hadn't deserved his fate. Cutting a too large piece of meat in half, he wondered about Larry, too. He'd disappeared just as he'd appeared, here one moment, a mystery the next. Sam missed his quiet cheer most of all.

Unwilling to spend the rest of the evening morose, he asked, "So, gentlemen, are we set for the night's watch?" Sam continued after their affirmative chorus, "Excellent. Cooks don't wash up, so I'll take care of the dishes." He stood and collected their dishes, grinning at how scraped clean each plate was.

He walked to the Platte, glad the full moon hovered over the eastern horizon. The air hung heavy with the scent of heated vegetation now cooling in the night air. As he drew closer to the river, he saw and heard others doing chores after the evening meal.

Sam paused when he saw Marie already at the river. He'd wanted to put off any casual chatting until later, or at least until the sight of her didn't recall today's incident. He watched as she knelt, working to clean the Warrens' dishes. Maybe her effort kept her too occupied to notice him, he hoped while approaching the bank.

She glanced up at him, frowned, and returned to her scrubbing. His welcome smile faded as he said, "Mrs. Warren. I'm glad to see you this evening."

Not facing him, Marie responded, "Likewise, Mr. Granville."

He squatted next to the water, rinsing each dish and utensil. "Lovely evening, am I right?"

"It is." She scooped up some sand, using it to scrub off the crusted food.

Sam snuck a peek over at her. Seeing her frown as she worked, he asked, "I trust your meal was as good as mine tonight?"

Not pausing, she laughed, retorting, "It will be, I'm sure."

"You've not eaten?"

She rinsed off the sand from the clean plate. "Not yet. That's why I'm here, cleaning up something to hold our food."

He'd not noticed if Marie was the only person in the Warren group to cook. Sam shook his head at his lack of knowledge about the detail. The new men in his crew needed training and his attention more than he'd expected. "I'm sorry to hear that."

"So am I." She began work on the third plate. "I've received a stern lecture on-"

"Marie!" Charles and Hester walked up to them. "Are you not done, yet? We're hungry."

"So am I, dearest." She smiled and held up the dishes. "I'm almost finished and am ready to eat, too."

"Granville!" The older man took Sam's hand to shake, clapping him on the shoulder at the same time. "Thank you for retrieving my wife, and sorry she was such a bother."

He glanced down at her still cleaning, saying, "Mrs. Warren couldn't be a bother if she tried, sir."

Hester Warren shook her head while crossing her arms. "Passing notes and clandestine meetings in a saloon are vulgar."

Charles slapped him on the back. "Still, the next time she pulls a prank like this-"

Marie stood, shaking water from the last plate. Her smile seemed strained to Sam as she said, "I've already promised to never do so again, Charles."

As if she'd not spoken, her husband continued, "As I was saying, next time we'll be better prepared. One of your men can drag her back to camp, instead of you bothering to do so yourself."

Much like the idea of leaving her behind at the fort, the thought of any other man seeing Marie in such a dress infuriated him. "No. Absolutely not." Sam felt like a water jug full of nothing but jealousy. "If it happens again, I'll handle it myself, once and for all." He looked at Marie, her eyes wide in her face. "But I won't have to worry about another occurrence, will I?"

Her eyes narrowed at him when she retorted, "Of course not, Mr. Granville. I've been scolded quite enough to have learned my lesson."

Warren spoke up, "Enough, Marie. We're all hungry and will say things now we'll regret later. Tell Granville goodnight."

"Goodnight," she said, frowning as she left the group.

He almost tipped his hat from the force of habit. Instead, he smiled, saying, "Ma'am. Sleep well." Sam watched her walk away, as did the other Warrens.

Once Marie moved beyond earshot, Warren asked Sam, "Did she give you any trouble today?"

Hester interjected, "Beyond the obvious of course."

Sam didn't care for the older woman's remark about Mrs. Warren. He looked from one to the other. The siblings appeared very similar. But where Charles kept a constant smile as an expression, Hester looked as if always displeased. He felt the need to defend her actions to these two. "Mrs. Warren was no trouble at all. I met her in the room. She was understandably disappointed I wasn't you, and we left at separate times so as not to arouse suspicions."

The siblings had looked at each other before Charles said, "I don't know if I can believe you, sir."

A red haze of anger swept Sam. He forced a smile before responding, "I don't know if your approval matters, sir. I speak the truth."

The elder man laughed. "You're far too kind to my wife. I've been at the blunt end of her temper."

Sam lifted his chin as understanding hit him. He'd meant Mrs. Warren had caused a fuss and not the unsavory insinuation Sam reckoned in its place. "She was a perfect lady."

"Hmph!" Hester snorted.

At her noise, Charles glanced over and smiled. "Now, now, Hess. She does try."

Ever striving to be diplomatic, Sam refrained from arguing with them over Marie's actions. Instead, he wanted to excuse himself. "We'll be on our way tomorrow. If your animals are struggling to pull the load, now is a good time to discard unnecessary items."

"Everything is necessary," Hester retorted.

"Maybe so, but with no oxen left alive, could you continue onward while pulling your own wagon?" Enjoying her shocked then surly expression, he smiled at Warren and tipped his hat. "It's completely at your discretion, of course. Good evening." Sam left for his own campsite, glad his group of men respected his authority.

"Hey, Granville," hollered Arnold. "We mailed your letters."

"Thank you," he replied, settling to sit by the fire.

"You got something, too." Arnold hopped up and went to his saddlebags. "Looks like a letter from some lady." He handed the envelope to Sam. Once seated, Lucky hit him on the arm. "Ow! What's that for?"

"You don't look at a man's letter when there's a woman's name on it."

"I didn't read it. I saw the name on the outside." He rubbed his arm. "Don't hit that hard unless you want some back."

"Thank you, Arnold. Appreciate it." Looking over the envelope, he winced at the sender's name. Sam didn't want to read anything from Anne now. He'd hoped his mother had sent the letter to say that his brother, Nick, had a new son. Sam would rather hear news of a nephew any day over some mea culpa from his former fiancée'.

Lucky hollered at him, "So, Mr. Granville, did Jenny happen to see anything she liked at that Indian trade today?"

The other men all teased him for his question. After they had quieted, Sam replied, "I noticed her lingering over a couple of things."

"You might have to show me what they were, just in case."

He laughed when his hands chimed in again, causing Lucky to turn an even deeper shade of red. "I can do that. Before we leave Laramie, you and I can break off and see what's available for her."

"Much obliged." Lucky bowed his head over his dish, still receiving catcalls from his friends.

After a quick meal, Sam tore into the letter. Anne had written an apology, much as he'd suspected. The second half, telling him of her new daughter, hurt more than he had imagined.

Arnold asked, "What's the matter, boss?"

Larry looked over at Sam's expression. "You look like someone cooked your last chicken."

Sam smiled at Larry's comment. "It's fine. My former fiancé has had a girl with her new husband. She and the baby are well, and all are happy."

"Should I have lost the letter?" asked Arnold. When Uncle

Joe nudged him, he protested, "What? Next time he gets something from her, I can have something happen to it instead."

"It's fine, Arnie. If I get a letter at one of the forts, I will want it no matter who it's from."

Arnold smirked at Uncle Joe and said, "Will do, boss."

Sam put the letter among his personal belongings, saying, "We should begin watch and bedding down for the night."

Used to the procedure, his men began their nightly duties. Later, Sam lay in his bedroll and watched the embers. Marie had captured his attention so entirely. While he'd not forgotten about Anne, his former fiancée had become less important as the weeks passed. The two women didn't match up to each other. They did look similar, but he'd known Anne most of his life, while Marie remained a mystery. Comparisons between the two women dominated his mind as he fell asleep.

The new day started hot and humid despite the night's cool air. As the sun rose, Sam sweated with the least little effort. He'd become used to dry days, and now his shirt clung to him, increasing his discomfort. People and animals plodded along. They made their way along the rocky road and through the thick air. He'd not been hungry but stopped the group at noon, feeling the sick, and young needed the rest. He didn't want anyone to have a reason to climb up or jump off a moving wagon just for food or water. Better to halt altogether than have a child crushed under a wheel. After being witness to such an event once before, the horror haunted him still.

He kept watch on the sky. Little puffs of clouds had been gathering all morning. By noon, they'd amassed into rainclouds. A couple of massive thunderheads won the race for moisture in the mid-afternoon. He let all of them drive into a refreshing rain, cold, but not as much as showers in the past. The storm ended as they entered the Black Hills.

Later that day, helping the Warrens over an unusually wide creek was grueling for Sam. The old maid sister kept giving him the come hither look, while Charles frequently offered unsound advice, and Marie was just herself. He vowed no matter what it took, someone else would help them next time.

Before he could ride away, Marie waved to him. "Mr. Granville, Ellen read to us from the guidebook about how even though illnesses decrease on our journey, the amount of poisoned water we encountered would increase. Has this been your experience as well?" she asked.

"Sadly, yes," he replied. "A few people will die from various causes, but in my experience, accidents and illness are the main reasons. I've heard of Indian attacks and murders, but have been lucky to not experience them first hand."

"I'd hoped to see fewer graves as we went west." She shook her head. "We've walked past so many along the way." They watched the children for a moment until she asked, "How many of us will die too soon, do you suppose?"

Sam stared at her, feeling like a weight crushed his chest. He'd never considered losing Marie to illness or injury. "Us? I'm counting on not losing anyone else." He preferred she go back home to New Orleans today than die on the trail at any time in the future. He looked at her, knowing his expression showed his feelings but unable to stop the display.

Marie broke their stare at each other, her cheeks flushed. "I've expected deaths from childbirth, old age, and Indians. There are much more ways in the American desert, I'm sure."

He grinned at her. "You personally might need to worry about childbirth before Indians."

She'd stopped smiling at him, instead frowning while watching the children play. "You'd think so, wouldn't you?"

Sam couldn't read her expression. "We can worry later. Right now, we need to get these youngsters back to their families for travel."

Marie helped him with ensuring every child was counted and ready to go. He'd relied on his men to get the adults ready. As families finished gathering together, their wagons began rolling. When Hester joined them, Sam nodded to both Warren ladies and left for the front. He wanted to discuss campsites for tonight with Arnold, Uncle Joe, and Lucky. Lefty and a couple of the group's men brought up the rear this afternoon. They'd have their turn picking campsites tomorrow night when they led the party and enjoyed the day without breathing in the dust clouds.

Trying to pay attention to the tasks at hand, Sam still couldn't focus on what needed doing. Marie and the request he spurned back at Laramie took over all his thoughts. He'd thought her pretty enough when they'd first met. The fact that she was a little older than him and married, not to mention Anne's betrayal, had distracted him from what now seemed all too clear. The woman appealed to Sam in a basic, carnal way. A way he wanted to shake like a dog would water from his fur.

He thanked God his hands had everything down to a fine art by now. Duties were fast becoming habits, the way Sam liked it. Stopping for noon, helping decide the evening's camp, they knew what to do. When people in his party did their tasks and kept a routine, any problems showed up sooner rather than later. An inconsistent schedule might mean people were left behind to wander the land on their own. Every mile west also brought them closer to the Sioux Indians who roamed the area. The Sioux he'd dealt with were friendly despite how he'd heard others found them hostile and prone to stealing everything in sight. He shook his head, not agreeing with the assessment. At the kernel of every bit of gossip had been a white man's mischief.

Sam moseyed around the camp later in the night, trying to stay sharp. Scamp snorted, and he patted his horse in reassurance. He didn't want to be on night duty, either. Still, he couldn't ask his men to do what he wouldn't. Looking around in the darkness, he didn't expect any varmints or bandits to wait for daylight. At least, he figured, the smart ones would use the cover night provided. Hushed voices caught his attention and Sam realized with a start he'd ridden next to the Warren's wagon. Despite knowing it was wrong, he couldn't help listening.

"Please, Charles, I need you."

He couldn't hear what Mr. Warren replied, but he heard Marie's plea. "Please love me, dearest. Hester's asleep and I promise to be quieter this time."

Living amongst married people meant accidentally overhearing couples' intimacies. Still, randomly listening didn't mean being rude by continuing to listen in on private time. Sam gave couples the same courtesy he hoped others would give him if he were married. He also insisted his men did the same. None of those who crossed the line and gossiped continued in his employ. His body stirring in response to the thought of her making noisy love, he moved on instead of lingering, keeping his emotions in check.

A couple of things about Marie were now clear to him. She

wasn't frigid by a long shot, and she desired her husband. Sam imagined how in her husband's place, he might cover her mouth with his own as he satisfied her, to keep down the noise. She'd not have to request a second time if he were in Warren's place. Sam shook his head, knowing how dwelling on Mrs. Warren might mean he'd need a dip in the Platte until the desire eased.

Tired from last night's lack of sleep, Sam yawned before scanning the sea of noontime activity from atop his horse. The wagons lined up in rows along the thin creek, letting everyone take advantage of water for themselves and their animals. He dismounted and led Scamp to the water. While the animal drank, a familiar voice caught his attention. He looked downstream, seeing Marie and Jimmy take advantage of the flat part of the sandy creek bed.

"No odds for you, young man!" She laughed, "You missed all ten pins fair and square." Marie threw the ball back to the boy, so it'd roll to him, "I'll give you another try." The ball went past him, and Jimmy scrambled to catch the ball before it hit Sam's feet.

The boy almost ran into him before stopping and said, "Hello, sir." Scooping up the ball, he added, "My turn!"

Marie walked up to Sam, smiling as she said, "Oh! Mr. Granville, please excuse us!"

He returned her grin even as his heart thumped. "Of course, I will, ma'am. If you'll excuse me as well. I wouldn't want to interfere with your sport." He saw her cheeks flush as she turned to watch Jimmy's roll and the result.

"I've already lost this round anyway." She tucked her hair behind her ears and continued, "Your interruption is welcome, in fact. I'm very glad you stopped to chat with us." She flushed an even deeper shade of pink, crossed her arms, and drew a line back and forth in the dirt with one foot. "With Jimmy and me, I mean, but then, probably mostly Jimmy. Of course, since you're both men and all, you'd want to talk about men things with him. Or not, I'm not sure." Her cheeks grew redder as the seconds passed.

Sam tried not to laugh at her fluster. "Losing that badly, then?"

"Sadly, yes. His prior bad throw didn't do enough for my score." She turned to the boy. "We'll have to play again in the evening." Over his protests, she added, "I know, but I promised your mother, so please take your game back to the wagon."

The young man ambled to them, reluctance showing with his every step. In what must be a routine, Marie held open a cloth bag while the boy dropped the ball. Sam dismounted, wanting to do anything to regain her attention. He helped Jimmy add pins to the bag. "Does the loser owe the winner anything after a game of this?"

Jimmy's face lit up like a full moon. "Yeah, the loser should owe the winner something!"

"Not exactly," she laughed with a mock frown at Sam. "Winner gets bragging rights; loser gets to practice for later."

"Great, since I get to take these for practice and get to brag." Jimmy had a smirk before leaving at his mother's holler.

The lady shook her head, saying to Sam, "That boy is too corruptive. I'm supposed to be preparing lunch, not playing games."

"Persuasion will get him far in life. Influence always worked for me."

She laughed, "I can imagine so." Taking a step back, Marie added, "A pleasure chatting with you. Take care."

The smile felt stiff on his face. Considering his more pressing tasks, he needed to move on to his chores. Instead, Sam grinned in response to her shy glance. She returned his smile, leaving him wanting to ignore whatever else needed doing for the rest of the day to spend the time with her.

"Granville!"

His focus wrenched from Marie to Charles Warren standing behind her. A hundred thoughts raced through Sam's mind, most dealing with giving the man a distracting chore so as to resume his chat with Marie. He smiled, schooling his features into an impassive mask. "Good day, Mr. Warren. I'll be with you in a moment."

Warren continued, seeming unaware, "We're camped a few wagons down the way. Follow me, and I'll show you where."

Sam took his horse's reins and smiled at Marie, "I do hope to see-"

Addressing Marie, Warren interjected, "Hessy's at the river, washing up from noon dinner. I assume you had better things to do, else you'd be helping her." He turned and walked away.

Marie scowled, and then smoothed her expression as she

followed. "I didn't leave until everything was done."

Charles's eyes narrowed. "I don't think you need to say anything more in front of Mr. Granville and show him your ill manners. Go help Hester while I conduct my business. I insist."

Marie stood in front of him, silent, her hands clasped behind her back, her expression surly. "Very well, I can table this discussion for the moment." She reminded Sam of a rebellious youngster as she stared at his boots. "Mr. Granville, a pleasure. Good day." Not even stealing a peek at Sam, she walked to the front of their wagon, then down to the river. Her body seemed to quiver with irritation.

"How about that?"

The question jolted Sam back to the conversation he was supposed to be having. What had the man been muttering? Sounded like something to do with the livestock, possibly. "You'll have to excuse me. An item you'd mentioned earlier led my thoughts down a tangent."

"Am I keeping you from other duties? I'm afraid to ask anything more about the prairie at the moment, for fear of keeping you too long."

"Sad to say, there are items I must attend to before we leave." Tipping his hat, Sam swung up onto his horse. He cantered away, his mind swirling with ways to end his attraction to Mrs. Warren. Yet, her request for a kiss made him want to see her often during the trip. "Damn." He had a lot more empathy for Nick. If his brother had been this smitten with his new wife, Beth, it's a wonder Nick waited before claiming her as his own. Sam's sane mind knew his feelings for Marie weren't rational. He also knew infatuations were temporary. The woman had to have an undiscovered character flaw; maybe she was an ice maiden. He remembered her saloon dress and laughed at the idea, knowing he'd have to keep searching for another reason to dislike her.

The day dawned slowly, gray drizzle obscuring last night's tracks. Unable to boil up any coffee, Sam and his men growled more than spoke to each other. Sodden blankets dripped early morning rain from the ribs holding up the canvas tops. He hoped the skies would clear and their bedding dry by nightfall.

Packing up, he saw some of the sickest in his group struggle a little less than they had yesterday. They were leaving some of the worst country for cholera. If he could keep everyone uninjured and healthy, they'd reach Oregon with energy to spare. By midday, the sun peeked from behind low clouds. The light mist hadn't been enough to turn the dirt to soup. It had merely settled the dust. The further they rolled away from Ft. Laramie, the more hills and rocks they encountered. He grinned, full knowing what complaints he'd hear at dinner. Usually, it would be about the never ending plains. Now, it'd be the pull and brake of the hills. He chuckled to himself, trying to feel sympathy for them. This was still the easiest part of the journey.

Later in the morning, Sam spotted Marie. She gathered purple and orange wildflowers from among the prickly pears. Her blue calico had picked up mud and dirt around the bottom third of the hem. He'd noticed her being the first to wash clothes every chance they had. Sam made a note to make camp a little early this evening. From between the wagons, he spotted Larry as he rode over to him.

"It's my turn to bring up the stragglers, sir."

Sam nodded, "Fine. We will have noon at the next decent creek." He snuck a look at Marie, who had stopped searching for flowers and watched them, instead.

He trotted over to her and hopped off his horse. "Good morning, Mrs. Warren."

"Good morning."

Sam felt shy as she stared openly and smiled at him. Having a loss of words puzzled him, but for the moment, he concentrated on keeping her attention. "That's a nice handful of flowers, there."

"Thank you, I think so." She buried her nose in the petals and smelled before adding, "I had second thoughts about picking them. Now I'll attract bees in addition to all those mosquitoes."

Staring at him instead of the ground, she didn't see the prickly pear cactus like he did. Sam grabbed her elbow, stopping Marie in place. "Whoa!"

"What?" She looked at her feet, exclaiming, "Oh, mercy! That would have hurt!"

"Especially if you're not wearing boots."

"I'm not." She let the toe of her shoe peek out from under the hem of her dress.

He chuckled, trying to behave and unable to do so. "Maybe I should carry you."

Marie grinned while shaking her head. "You shouldn't, even though I'd like it."

"You would?" Her bold admission first surprised and then worried him a little.

"Of course." She shuddered, facing another cactus. "Who wants to step on one of these? They're horrible."

"I don't know about that." He smiled at her frown. "With a little butter and salt, they remind me of okra."

She grinned from ear to ear, "Really? No, you can't mean these things. You're joking with me. No one could eat around the needles."

He stopped next to a prickly pear bush and squatted. "See here? Pulling this out isn't as bad as messing with these." He indicated the smaller stickers growing from each needle's base. "They're like tiny fishhooks, and you can barely see them individually."

Bending over to look, Marie examined the plant. "Hmm, and yet you eat these?"

"Yes, and they're good." Her disbelief amused him. Sam liked her arguing with him and chalked up the enjoyment to infatuation. To teach, he added, "After the large stickers are gone, you can burn off the little ones. You could also cut them off, but the inside is juicy like okra, and those tiny spines get stuck in there. I've never taken the chance."

"Can't say I blame you." She narrowed her eyes, pinching the fleshy part of the plant while avoiding the stickers. "Maybe I could try cooking these after all. I do miss fried okra."

He straightened. "I'll cook up some for you soon. If we stop as early as I'd like, I'll call you and your family over tonight for dinner."

"If it's not too much trouble, I'd like that." She smiled at him, her cheeks a little flushed. "In case Charles and Hester can't accept, you wouldn't care if I were the only Warren there?"

Sam followed. "Not at all." Although at a loss for what else to say, he scanned the horizon. "We're about to see a lot fewer trees than before, leaving us with burning the sagebrush for fuel."

"I'm glad. The idea of using buffalo chips was horrible." She picked another flower for her bouquet. "Since I get to have dinner with you and the boys this evening, how about y'all come over for coffee tomorrow morning?"

"Are *y'all* sure it's fine for us to drink all your good coffee?" he teased.

"All right, I slipped up and didn't say *you all*." She frowned and shook her head. "I was doing so well in not sounding like a spoiled Southern belle, too."

Sam didn't know what to say. He'd thought it endearing. They walked for a few moments in quiet before he said, "I like the way you talk no matter what you say."

She watched the ground as she strolled. "You're kind, and I appreciate it."

He leaned over to her. "I'm not so much kind as I am honest. Everything I've heard you say is charming and attractive." Sam grinned when her cheeks reddened. "Besides, from what I've seen, your behavior on this trip has been anything but spoiled."

"You've traveled this route enough to know, I suppose?"

He nodded. "I've been here a couple of times before now. Once as a boy and again after I graduated back east. Nick stayed behind another year after finishing his schooling so we could leave together."

"Nick?"

"My older brother." Lost in remembering, he continued, "Then, I went east by steamer ship for legal experience, and came back west a couple of years later. Finally, I forced Nick to return to Independence with me and lead another team to our home. Doing so stopped him from living as a mountain man."

Her mouth fell open as she exclaimed, "Your brother was a mountain man? Was he a bona fide hermit living in a cave and everything?"

He glanced at her to see if she was teasing. At the serious expression on her face, Sam laughed. "No caves, but he had an impressive beard."

"What made him choose to live as a hermit? He has you as a brother, and I assume a family." Marie paused as if sizing him up before continuing. "And then, I'd like to know why you've gone back and forth over land so many times. You seem to have the means to travel by steamer ship. Why go by wagon when a ship is so much faster and less dangerous?"

Grinning, he retorted, "This is going to take a while to answer. Should I write an essay instead?"

"Fine, you're right." Marie smiled. "I'm much too intrusive, but there are no new novels to be had out here."

If he'd packed anything more than a couple of favorites, Sam would loan them to her. Wanting to help, he asked, "What about chatting with the other ladies? Would they want to share stories or books?"

She gave a shrug. "We've already traded and are back where we started. As for chatting, I know everyone's story, as they know most of mine. I'm sure they didn't tell me everything because I didn't tell them everything."

He tried not to chuckle at her sly smile. "Good. Otherwise, the ladies would be pestering me for kiss critiques, too."

"You're mean!" She glanced at him at him before adding, "Do they not already pester you? Both Hester and Ellen talk about you on a near-daily basis."

"They do?" Noticing how Marie hadn't picked any new flowers in a while, Sam looked ahead. The land grew less grass, rocks and dirt taking over the ground. They'd need to stop at the first water with any sort of grass growing nearby. He looked at her walking with him and wondered if she considered talking about him to anyone else. "I don't mind Ellen knowing my business, but Hester would be happier with someone like Uncle Joe."

Marie laughed. "That's a nice way of saying Hester's past a certain age." She bent and picked a small, stray flower. "Ellen is very pretty, too. A lot of the young men at the trading post were shy around her when we visited the store."

Sam took the chance to tease her and said, "I don't know. I think Miss Warren was a handsome woman in her youth. She'd be a great wife for a young man who didn't want children hanging around."

Marie stopped, hands on her hips. "You must be joking! Oh! You are!" She tapped his shoulder with her bouquet. "If she weren't such a sour thing, you'd be right about Hester." Shaking her head, she continued walking.

Liking her little flash of temper, he almost wanted to antagonize her further. Sam didn't want her truly angry at him, though, and decided against any more teasing. They walked along, the hour growing closer to evening with every step. He liked being around Marie, even while silent. All the talk of wives, women chatting about him, and the letter from Anne made Sam think. Maybe his fiancé had done the right thing in not waiting to be married to him if his heart was so fickle.

He stole a glance at Marie. Because of her, Anne's letter stung, but it didn't have the heartbreaking impact it would have a few months ago. She walked arm's reach from him. Wanting to shake off the rush of desire for her, he needed to focus on someone or anything else. Marie was unavailable, her husband healthy, and Sam knew he didn't stand a chance. Who else had she said asked about him? "Ellen is a lovely girl. She and I talked a little after visiting the trading post. Do you know if she is interested in anyone?"

Her gaze cut to him, eyes narrowed. "No." She shook her head as if shaking off the expression on her face. "No, I mean, maybe. I've heard her mention you a few times, how interesting you are and all." She pointed at the wagon party. "Looks like it's time to camp for the night! We should catch up, shouldn't we?"

"We should." He stifled a smile. She was jealous. Sam tried not to be pleased with her reaction. Neither one of them had any right to their feelings. Still, he liked how she reacted and wanted to see how possessive of him she was. "I find Ellen's views on the natives to be very intriguing."

"Um hm."

"I wonder what it is about me she finds, interesting, you'd said. Maybe she and I could talk later."

"I'm sure you could. You might want to think about whether or not you wanted children."

The even tone of hers seemed a little forced so he asked, "Why is that?"

She continued as if measuring her words. "You'd indicated Hester being an ideal wife for men who disliked children."

"Ah, I see." Thinking of Anna's letter prompted him to reply, "Hester would be a bad choice for me since I do want a child someday. Actually, I'd like one or more of each. Nick has a son; I'd like to have a daughter." He glanced over to see her reaction. For some odd reason he needed to ponder later, her wanting children mattered to him. When he looked at her, Marie seemed intent on watching for prickly pear.

After a while, she said, "I think Ellen is a very nice person. She's not as old as Hester and is probably not barren, either. You'd be able to have all the children you'd want."

Understanding clicked in his mind like tumblers in a safe. No wonder she and Warren had only his sister with them. While Sam knew Warren had at least one son his wife's age or older, Marie wasn't old enough to have grown children. She had to be barren. The nearest fresh buffalo chip was miles away, and yet Sam felt as if he'd stepped in one. The reassuring replies racing through his mind all sounded trite right now. He kicked a rock, more than a little frustrated. They walked, growing ever closer to the circle of wagons. Finally, he said, "Wait, Marie."

She stopped, surprised, "Yes?"

He took a deep breath before saying, "I don't know how it would feel; being unable to raise a family with the one I married." Sam looked away from her face, hoping he accurately said what he thought. "For me, if I were married to the right person, well, we could get through any hardship if we loved and cared for each other through the heartbreak."

"That's very lovely, Mr. Granville." She patted his arm. "Ellen or whomever you choose is already a lucky woman. She just doesn't know it, yet."

CHAPTER 2

Marie Warren scanned the area, wondering where Charles and Hester had run off to so close to dinnertime. She'd planned on them eating soon and wanted to join in as various people gathered for music and dancing. Despite her husband's disinterest in attending, he always allowed her to go and visit with other ladies. She dished out food for Charles and Hester, impatient and a little angry at their inconsideration. They knew she wanted to eat, clean up, and enjoy the evening music.

She waited a little longer, her food growing cold in the night air. Marie said a quick grace before the meal under her breath and ate. Finished in a hurry, she stood and stretched before walking around their wagon to where the last of the day's light faded. Not seeing either him or her sister in law, she drummed her fingers on the wooden frame. Even allowing for the night watch on duty, she wasn't comfortable leaving the wagon alone.

"Hey, Mrs. Warren!" Jimmy and a few of his friends ran up to her. "Are you going to tonight's dance?"

Snapped out of her musings, she shook her head. "Not just yet, I'm afraid." Marie decided to clean up her mess. She placed her dishes in the pail and lay handkerchiefs over the duo's meals. "I may have to miss the entertainment tonight, so go on and enjoy."

They ran off, the boy yelling over his shoulder, "Tomorrow for sure!"

She waved, "For sure." The little group disappeared among the wagons. She sighed, already hearing the music. Marie rummaged in the wagon for her sewing, figuring she might as well accomplish something in the waning light. The sun set in a clear, but dusty sky, giving her an orange glow in which to work. The mending from various brush snags needed the attention she'd been giving the nightly gatherings. After spotting all the repairs to do, Marie sighed, thinking it just as well the other Warrens kept her waiting here.

"Hello, my darling."

Marie looked up when Charles and his sister joined her at the ebbing fire. "Hello. I'm glad to see you."

Hester pulled back one of the napkins covering a dish, her nose wrinkling at the food. "You might have waited until we were here to begin cooking. This looks terrible."

Glancing down at her work, she didn't want the irritation to show in her expression. Marie had no sympathy for either of them. They knew by now when mealtimes were. "I have to admit everything looked and tasted better earlier."

"I see you didn't wait for us before eating your dinner."

"No, I had mending to do and wasn't sure if you two dined with someone else."

The subtle reminder of how often the twins ate their evening meals with another family without informing Marie quieted Hester. Now, she ate her food, casting sullen looks at Marie whenever she glanced up.

Disliking the tension, Marie introduced a happier subject. "Everyone is saying we will reach Independence Rock before July 4th. We may find our new home sooner than expected. Isn't that exciting?"

Hester grunted a humph while Charles held a bite of fish over the fire. "Don't get too excited," he said. "We have to have our home built first. Nothing is waiting for us out in the wilderness just yet."

She paused her sewing. Even now in late June, the high altitudes kept her feeling frozen most of the time. Some days, only the promise of a roof and walls kept her moving west. "Where will we live?"

He gave her a scathing look. "Oregon, of course. What have we been talking about for the past two months or so?"

"Have you learned nothing since we left home?" As if to a child or slow adult, Hester continued, "We are traveling to the Oregon Territory for land and to capitalize on new industry out west. We've sold everything in Louisiana and have the money ready for new investments." She turned to Charles. "How many more times do we need to tell her?"

Marie took a deep breath trying to be calm. "I know all that, of course. However, I've never heard if you have a particular place in mind. I'd like to know if or when we'll arrive at a real home with a real bed."

Hester stood, tossing her dish and cutlery in the pail with a clatter. "Of course, he has a place in mind, don't you, Chas? He wants to settle us in Oregon City."

"How long will we live there?" Marie asked. She took her husband's dishes from him and put them in the pail after her sister in law's.

Hester laughed. "How long? You're full of smarts today. I thought you'd have better sense than this. We're not making this trip again."

"No, we're not, unless it's to visit family," her husband added. Charles stretched his legs and relaxed by the fire while the two women set up the beds. "I expect to do so well at farming and shop keeping in the territory that we'll be able to find passage on a steamer to the Isthmus, across, and then to our New Orleans whenever we choose to visit."

Marie struggled to keep from frowning or arguing. Prior discussions about her husband's expectations in the new land had led to horrible rows with Hester taking his side every time. Charles knew very little about either farming or running a store. She'd learned a little from her father on the plantation, yet relied on their slaves to work the land. Marie wondered if Oregon Territory allowed slavery. Even so, they couldn't afford a simple serving girl now, never mind the men needed for plowing and such. Learning everything possible to help him make a living at their destination seemed something she needed to do before they reached Oregon City.

Animals and people rustled around their campsite. During the two months on the trail, she'd learned how to block out the nocturnal sounds. She waited until Charles slid under their blankets before settling in close to her husband. Marie liked this time of night between dozing and sound sleep the best. Charles, almost asleep himself, didn't seem to mind her touch. She snuggled close to him, enjoying his body's warmth. He smelled like sunshine and a little sweat, but not overly so. The scent of honest work clung to his skin, despite the probability he'd only done minimal labor earlier.

Her drowsy mind drifted to Samuel. She loved her husband, a fact the charming Mr. Granville wasn't going to change. Marie smiled. Still, he was very easy on the eyes. She'd thought so from the first time they'd met. His eyes, legs, hair, mouth; everything about him tripped her triggers. Her cheek resting against Charles, she smiled, remembering how the other man smelled like leather and starch, the latter from his ironed stiff shirt. How he kept it white in the camp's dust was a mystery. Maybe he had a gaggle of washerwomen obeying his every order. She almost laughed, imagining a herd of females all batting eyelashes at him while scrubbing his clothes. It's a wonder the man wasn't already married several times over. Her eyes popped open at the notion. Married? Mercy, she thought, Samuel was probably married for sure. A gentleman such as him must be. Her cheeks burned in embarrassment. No wonder he refused her kiss. She wondered how to tell him she'd only needed an honest opinion, not an affair.

Yet, a shiver swept through her. She suppressed a sigh of disgust with her body's desire. Guilt nudged her insides. No, she'd not needed anything from him. Since seeing the flash of hope in his eyes at the saloon, Marie pushed aside any answering desire in her body. She'd spent sleepless nights wondering the outcome if he'd indulged her request. Her conclusion circled back to his refusal was for the best.

She knew her feelings for Sam already ran too wild. Hester had blathered to Charles on and on about setting her cap for Samuel had he been even a few years older. Every time she said his name, Marie grew more irritated with her. For her to carry on for such a younger man was unseemly, she thought. Sam had his pick of young and pretty women. Neither word described Hester.

Smirking, she thought of the haughty looks her sister in law gave her daily. Hester could want Mr. Granville all she liked. Wishing on an outcome wouldn't make it so. When a man didn't desire her, nothing a woman did changed his mind. Marie learned this for herself less than a year after marrying Charles. She snuggled closer to him, enjoying how warm he felt in her arms. He'd been so kind to her all these years. With just a little bit of passion and a lot less of his sister traveling with them, he'd be perfect.

Early next morning, she cuddled her tin cup of coffee. The sun struggled to shine on a cloudless and frosty day. Her eyes didn't want to stay open. She took another long drink of the cooling liquid. She'd spent most of the night unable to sleep. Marie tried first to think of those sick in their company, then the various gossips, and even pondered how long they had before Indians attacked. All this did nothing to end her thinking of Samuel.

Now at the end of her drink, Marie sighed, and still drowsy, she checked for more coffee. None remained, and the last of their buffalo chips burned low. She glanced at Hester, surprised the other woman still loitered near camp. The woman always disappeared when the chip gathering chore needed doing. Charles didn't seem to know or care. He was always off taking care of the oxen when his sister slipped away. Despite knowing the answer, Marie asked, "Hester, do you think we could gather chips after washing up breakfast dishes? We will need more for noon, and two makes the work go faster."

"You'll have to excuse me." After standing, she gave her cup to Marie. "I have things to do this morning that helps Charles. Doing your work for you will take too much time."

She smiled, gritting her teeth at the other woman's haughty tone. "Very well, I'll take care of fuel after I clean up from breakfast." Marie wasn't afraid of the work. She only resented how often the woman found more important things to do. Watching her walk away, she thought of how much Hester would complain without hot coffee in the morning or warm food at dinner. "Not important, my eye," she muttered under her breath.

Marie finished her chores just before hearing the order to move. Hester sat on the wagon seat, perched rather like a vulture, she thought. Charles waved to her, and Marie walked over to him.

"Good morning, sweetheart," he greeted, kissing her forehead.

"Good morning." She smiled, walking with him ahead of the wagon as it rolled. Careful about eavesdroppers, Marie glanced around before speaking. "Darling, I'd like to ask you something."

Distracted with nodding to others as they noticed him, he said, "Of course, what do you need?"

She willed herself to not be bothered by his lack of attention. "I'd like to know why you sent Mr. Granville to fetch me last week instead of doing it yourself."

He gave her a glare. "I've said before now, I don't think the subject is appropriate for public conversation."

"I agree. However, the only time we could have a private moment is when nature calls one of us, and the other follows." His continued inattention by how he looked everywhere else but her irritated Marie. "Now would be a good time to discuss this.

He sighed." Very well, I'll tell you what you are really asking. I sent Granville because I knew he'd point you back to camp without harm. In case you hadn't noticed, we're not alone in this journey. We won't be like newlyweds and embarrass ourselves with nightly romps."

"We couldn't visit a safe area once in a while?" she blurted in a voice too loud. At his warning expression, Marie lowered her tone, adding, "I rather like the idea of doing so with you."

Charles shook his head. "If we did, some child could find us. It's best for everyone if we wait until Oregon."

"What!" She shrieked at the idea then covered her mouth with a hand. Recovering, Marie laughed, "You are such the prankster! Wait until we reach Oregon, indeed."

He smiled at her. "You're right, Oregon, indeed. We will resume our relations once there. Out here is not appropriate."

The grin faded from her face. His paternal tone infuriated her. Being almost young enough to be his daughter didn't make her a child, not so close to her mid-thirties. She struggled to keep her own voice light. "Goodness, isn't our journey four or five more months?"

He nodded. "We'll be on the trail about that long, yes. We'll want to wait until we're settled and Hessy has her own home."

Marie said under her breath so anyone nearby didn't hear, "Do you realize the time building her house may take? Are you willing to wait over a year for me?"

Putting an arm around her, he gave her a half hug. "It's for the greater good."

She recalled the temporary insanity of asking to kiss Sam Granville. While blaming the whiskey gave her an easy excuse, Marie knew alcohol alone wasn't causing her feelings for him. She wanted to be tempted only by Charles, but the distance he kept between them made it increasingly difficult. "We are married, so some lovemaking is allowed, I'm sure. I enjoy loving you very much."

"How unfortunate, because waiting until we reach our new home is perfect for us." He shook his head, slapping his riding gloves against his thigh. "And for Hessy, too. She's a sensitive woman and wouldn't like knowing we sneak around to escape her."

Marie stared at her husband. His constant reference to Hester angered her, and defiant, she said, "I don't mind telling her outright why we're leaving her behind during berry picking or hunting." She smiled at his angry face, now looking at her. Even when negative, she liked having his full attention. "Hester is a grown woman, isn't she? I'm sure she'd understand our actions."

His brow furrowed so much his eyebrows almost met in the middle. "We don't need to discuss this further. I'm your husband, and I've decided. I'm also tired of your arguing." He tipped his hat to her. "If you'll excuse me, I'm in need of more pleasant company."

Gritting her teeth to keep back a sharp retort, Marie watched him walk back to their slow rolling wagon. She shook her head. If he chased any other skirts, she'd assume his disinterest had everything to do with her own lack of appeal. He hopped up with a natural grace that denied his age. Seated next to his twin, he and Hester chatted quietly enough so Marie couldn't hear. She didn't want to walk alone this morning, not wanting the time to think. The road wound around the rocky cliffs so much yesterday, it seemed as if they'd traveled mere feet in an hour. Every so often, the land flattened, allowing better grass to grow. Upon coming to such a treasure, the party stopped and let the livestock graze until full. With today promising to be as slow as yesterday, she decided to find the other ladies.

The oxen kept Charles busy, and Hester wouldn't budge from her perch. Their preoccupation left her lonely, leading her to spend more time with her new friends. She caught sight of Ellen and Jenny at the Platte River. She and the two women were the only younger females without children and could pass uninterrupted time together. They'd become fast friends in the past couple of months.

Marie judged from those crossing on horseback that the river looked the perfect height for swimming in some places. In others, the water ran shallower. Recent rains churned the bottom so much that even the animals only drank the smallest amount. Hoping the dirt might settle before dinner, she grabbed the water pail and started for the river. As she approached, the two girls saw Marie. They waited midway between her and the Platte while she caught up to them.

"Did you hear?" Ellen asked while pushing her glasses back up to the bridge of her nose. "One of the trains going east yesterday afternoon lost more than half their passengers. The rest of their group just wants to reach civilization again."

31

Jenny exclaimed, "I'll bet Indians attacked, scalped, and killed most of them!"

Ellen shook her head. "Indians didn't kill them. At first, it was cholera, and then poisoned water killed more people, animals, too."

"Who would do such a thing?" Marie asked as they reached the riverbank. Water was so precious, ruining it seemed insane.

"No one poisoned the water," replied Ellen. The tallest of the three, she knelt first to fill her bucket. "The soil is such an alkali, the guidebook says don't allow your animals to drink from any source other than a flowing stream or spring."

"That's interesting. I wonder why?" Jenny asked. "Water is water unless it's smelly and full of crawly things. I wouldn't drink it."

Seeing Ellen's shrug, Marie offered, "Maybe flowing streams bring it in from better sources than the alkaline areas. I know the Mississippi brought us water from Canada and the Great Lakes." She stepped as close to the water as possible without falling in and scooped a full pail of the muddy liquid.

"Sounds reasonable and makes perfect sense," Ellen replied. "Marie, did you happen to see the wagons going east? The survivors looked puny. Mr. Granville was gone, so Mr. Lucky took it upon himself to give them fresh food and drink."

"They said they saw all sorts of wild animals, but no one had the strength to hunt," Jenny added.

Marie shook her head. "Those poor dears. No, I didn't see the wagons or the people up close."

"I'm sure Mr. Granville will be glad Lucky helped them." Jenny retrieved her pail of water with a thoughtful expression. "He is such a fine man. Mr. Granville, I mean."

She smiled at the blush reddening Jenny's face. The color contrasted with the girl's blue eyes and pale hair. Marie agreed with her opinion on Sam but was not so bold as to admit it. When he'd sat next to her in the saloon, his body heat through the fabric of his shirt had warmed her arm. He'd smelled like leather, whiskey, and soap, a combination she'd not thought appealing until associated with him. "He seems to be, certainly."

"Does Lucky know you're developing feelings for Mr. Granville, Jenny?" Ellen smirked at them.

"That's foolish," snorted Jenny. "I might care for Lucky, but Mr. Granville is far too old."

"Goodness, Jenny!" Ellen laughed. "He's not so ancient as to be gray-haired already."

"Oh, no, there is nothing wrong with an older man." She smiled at Marie. "Your Mr. Warren is a very handsome man, of course."

She smiled, feeling odd at the comparison. Even with him belonging to her and her to him, Marie thought Charles held more power than she. "Yes, you're right. I try not to let him out of my sight when there's a tavern full of women within walking distance. I do find him handsome as well."

The other two ladies giggled. Marie looked at them again, thinking of how free Sam truly was. Either young woman could attract his attention. Ellen, almost as tall as Sam, had a ready smile, hazel eyes, and auburn hair. She wore glasses most of the time, treating them like treasure. Jenny was Marie's height, but willowy and very fair. Jenny's blond hair often escaped her bun and curled around her face. Imagining how Sam might prefer either lady to her left Marie oddly unhappy. After his rejection over a silly kiss and her husband's continued denial, she wanted to be appealing in some way.

She tried to listen to them talk about the other people in their wagon party. Almost every woman's heart fluttered when Samuel Granville focused those clear blue eyes on her, even her own. His clothes looked posh, and yet, he was a rugged trail leader. What man of means worked as such, she wondered. While pondering over Sam's history, Marie realized she knew nothing about him other than the fear in his eyes when threatened with a kiss from her. She felt a flush sweep her face. *There was that,* she conceded.

Marie tried to listen as they walked until stopping at each of their wagons. She ate a quick noontime meal of extra food from breakfast. At the signal, she stood, brushed crumbs from her skirt, and reluctantly continued. Ellen and Jenny soon found her, and they spent the afternoon talking as they walked along with the wagons. Choking dust kept them a little ahead of the stretched out line of oxen. She tried to keep pace with the others' conversation. After a while, she stopped paying attention to the girls' chattering and more to her own thoughts. Her mind kept drifting to Charles and his chaste rejection of her.

She hated how first Charles's inattention bothered her, and Sam's refusal later angered her. Had they been married long enough for her husband to be tired of her? Maybe so. Her smile felt strained as she waved to the young ladies as they left to camp for the night. To have asked a young, single man like Mr. Granville for a kiss? She still wondered what had possessed her, but shamefully knew the answer. Desperation. If Sam lets her give him a little kiss, maybe even a hug, he'd be a valid critic of her appeal. He could accurately tell her how Charles could start withdrawing affection. Although, Marie conceded, her husband did allow contact while sleeping.

Upon reaching their wagon, Marie liked seeing how Charles had taken the livestock for water. That particular chore wasn't her favorite. Instead, she walked to the south, following a dry stream bed to a stand of trees. After gathering up as much wood as possible, she returned to their camp. She began building a fire from the cedar, glad to not have Hester fussing around her. The woman's absence gave her time to focus on cooking without a constant critique. Instead, she cut up the onion, potatoes, carrots, and turnips the way she preferred. As the food simmered in the pan, she saw her husband and sister in law approach. Standing, Marie said, "Good evening! How was your day?"

Charles gave her a friendly hug, "Good, all things considered. Did you have fun chatting with the girls?"

"Yes, they're excellent company." She looked at Hester. "You're always welcome to join us, of course."

"Thank you, but no. They are children and seem to gossip far too much." After exchanging a glance with her brother, she added, "You're kind to ask."

She didn't quite know how to reply. Hester's benevolence caught her by surprise. "I appreciate your saying so. Dinner is almost ready if you are."

"Good! I'm starved," he said while spreading out blankets for them. By the time they settled on the padding, their food was ready. Hester took charge and dished out dinner.

As the night fell, like other evenings when they camped near another group of travelers, the people gathered together to socialize. Those with musical instruments played and the young singles danced. Married people traded off watching their children. Marie managed to chat with a few of the mothers during the women's turn around the bonfire.

While she searched for her friends and a little bit for Samuel, Charles startled Marie by sitting beside her. She greeted him with, "There you are." She looked around the circle, smiling. "They started without you."

He grinned back at her. "So they did."

Marie watched as people enjoyed themselves. The setting sun cast brilliant orange rays across the sky's deep blue. The mountains to the south, the highest she'd ever seen, came alive with color. She nodded toward the others. "Seems everyone finished evening chores in double time tonight, doesn't it?"

Charles gazed over at the dancers. "Everyone who isn't ill, that is."

"Hester is still feeling poorly? I did notice she ate a little, but just." She tried to be more concerned about his sister despite not caring for the woman.

He smiled his approval at her. "She is and decided to turn in early if the music will let her."

Clouds, now flattened with evening cooling, glowed as if made of burnt gold. The music sounded across the prairie as she glanced at Charles. "Such a beautiful end to the day, isn't it? The moon is new tonight, so I doubt they'll be doing much past dusk."

"I hope you're right for Hessy's sake."

The mention of his sister by her nickname hit her the wrong way. She licked her lips, trying to keep back the irritation. "I don't suppose we have anything to talk about except Hessy, do we? You've spent every minute of today with her." Her shrewish tone surprised Marie as the words poured out of her.

Before she could apologize or recant, Charles glared at her. "Do you have to talk? Can you not be quiet and listen to the music for a while?"

"I can, yes." Anger bubbled up in her like fermented fruit in a jar. Unable to stop, she added, "However, I've had to agree to your postponing relations until the Territory. The very least you could do is visit with me after dinner."

"The very least I could do?" His eyes narrowed. "As in caring for the livestock and being responsible for your health and wellbeing isn't enough? I want our privacy to preserve your good name. I suppose that means nothing to you."

Her husband had a reliable way of making her feel like a spoiled child. She agreed, "It means something, yes."

He remained silent for a few minutes. After a while, Charles said, "I can't enjoy the music anymore. Goodnight. Try to act like the lady you're supposed to be." He stood and began the walk back to their camp.

"Good night, then." She stifled a sigh. Twice in as many days, she'd irritated him into leaving. Marie needed to have more care in how she treated him. She wanted a husband, not a resentful keeper. She gave a reassuring smile to a too curious gentleman seated nearby. He grinned back at her and continued watching the mêlée.

The sky's warm hues gave way to all sorts of blues as she watched and listened to the songs. She let her gaze travel along the cloud tops as the last bit of color faded from light to dark.

She needed a distraction from being too close and too far from her husband for the next few months or she'd cry with frustration. She wanted to laugh and talk with her friends, not be angry at her husband the entire way to their new home. While scanning the group for Jenny or Ellen, she saw Sam and glanced twice at him. Her body tensed when he gave her a knowing grin from her unintended compliment. She focused on everyone else, trying to ignore him. His stern refusal to kiss her had stung her ego. She'd not asked due to desire, after all. He didn't have to be a child about her query. She'd prefer not seeing him again for a very long while.

Back in Independence, she should have fought harder to stay until late April, doing anything to not be in this particular wagon train. She frowned upon seeing Sam's seat empty. Marie avoided Sam somewhat since the whiskey had loosened her morals at the fort. She half listened to the music played around the fire. She stared into the flames while vowing unless she faced the loss of a limb or her life, there'd be no more whiskey and no more begging for kisses.

Tired of thinking about the entire mess, Marie stood. She swayed a little, her feet tingling from being sat on for so long. A voice at her side startled her as did a hand on the small of her back. She turned to see who touched her. "Hello?"

"Hello to you, too." He held out his arm. "I'm assuming you're ready to retire?" When she nodded, he continued, "Take my elbow in case you stumble."

"Thank you." She let him walk her back to the wagon, liking how his warm scent drifted to her in the night air. As they walked further from the fire, a slight child went through her and Marie shivered.

"You're cold," he whispered. "You'll warm up under a blanket in no time."

She liked his consideration for those sleeping. When they arrived at her family's wagon, the Warrens seemed to be asleep. She didn't want to allow for impropriety even if both slept like the dead. Marie stepped back from her escort. "Thank you for seeing me here, Mr. Granville. I'm sure my husband will appreciate your thoughtfulness."

The campfire embers gave a brush of light to his face. "You're welcome, ma'am. It's my duty after all."

As he turned to leave, his hand gave hers a squeeze before letting go. She watched him disappear into the dark, feeling torn. Still angry at Charles, Marie gave their bedroll a contemptuous look. They always slept close, but now she felt uncertain.

Charles stirred. "Why do you wait? Come to bed. You need the sleep."

"Very well." She slipped off her shoes and crawled in under the blanket. The thin goose down mattress softened the ground.

Snuggling closer to Marie, he murmured, "I'm glad he walked you here this evening."

"He had to. You heard him say it's his duty. I think he takes getting everyone to Oregon very personally." She enjoyed the warmth despite her irritation at her husband. "I did stay a little later than planned. I was enjoying the music and lost track of time."

Giving a snort, he retorted, "Nightfall didn't give you a clue?"

She didn't take offense to his jibe. He teased her, Marie knew, and she grinned. "You'd think it would have, wouldn't you?" After yawning, she added, "Next time I have too much fun, I'll be sure to do it during a full moon."

"As if you could behave for an entire month," he snickered.

She smiled slightly as his retort. Marie did enjoy his wry sense of humor. She grew drowsy while enjoying the warmth. "Charles?"

"Um-hm?" he rumbled.

Marie turned her head back to him and asked, "Can we kiss?"

"Hmmm, I'm tired."

Not surprised by his answer, she speculated, "When we reach the homestead?"

"Um hm."

"Very well." She faced front and rested her head on a pillow. Marie tried to be grateful for what affection he managed to give her at the moment. Still, she'd not been a real wife to him in months and missed the love. She blinked back frustrated tears, wondering how to change his mind before Oregon. Any other woman would take Charles's declarations as a challenge to seduce him, but from previous attempts, she knew better. Making him act like a husband was easy; motivating him into wanting to be one was near impossible.

After a restless night of futile planning, Marie spent the morning with Jenny and Ellen. She tried to pay attention to the conversation, but her head seemed full of cotton. The girls talked about the prior night's activities. They compared viewpoints on the music as well as on the people. She nodded at the right times, made the correct noises, but felt as if she were sleepwalking.

She wanted a nap more than food during the lunch break. Fear of being left kept her from any sort of rest. Instead, Marie shook out the picnic blanket, folded it, and then stored it away. She watched as the twins took their usual places at the front of their wagon. Maybe due to her exhaustion, but it seemed today's midday exclusion from the duo bothered her more than usual.

She picked up the bucket of dirty dishes and rushed to clean them. Marie had the goal of being ready before hearing the order to move. She washed in a hurry and put the bucket back just as Lucky's horn sounded. Following the Platte river bottoms as they did for the rest of the afternoon meant a smooth road. She enjoyed the walk and how the air stayed hot and humid. Marie missed the sultry days and warm nights of Louisiana. Until today, the journey so far seemed like a never ending winter without the benefit of snow. Not seeing anyone she knew nearby, she picked wildflowers while walking. The corn puffs of clouds on the horizon seemed to expand as she watched. Some looked like large columns, rising and then hitting an invisible ceiling. By now, she knew to expect late afternoon storms with this sort of sky. She breathed in, smelling the promise of severe conditions before nightfall.

The weather didn't disappoint her expectations. Samuel and his hands rode along the group. Each man stopped at a family, then went on to another. Marie hadn't seen much of Arnold, so he surprised her by riding to her with a greeting, "Ma'am."

"Hello. Is there trouble?" she asked.

The young man frowned, replying, "Afraid so, we're stopping early to lash down everything."

Marie nodded. "I thought as much. Thank you for telling me."

"You're welcome, ma'am." He signaled to his horse and went to inform others.

She saw as Samuel stopped the young man, they talked before heading in different directions. The wagons slowly moved into their customary circle. The men on horseback backtracked a half mile hoping to caution any stragglers about the impending storm. No one needed a warning when the cold gust smelling of rain hit them. The afternoon turned dark as midnight, lit only by flashes of lightning. She and Hester double checked the cover's fit against the ribs holding up the canvas. Meanwhile, Charles first hobbled their oxen, and then helped others with their own.

He hurried up to them, shouting above the wind. "I hope we're ready. If it's as bad as the hands make it out to be, we'll sleep in here tonight."

As he spoke, a couple of riders galloped by, stirring up even more dust and noise. Marie coughed before asking, "Should we get the bedding ready for sleeping there, then?"

Hester wrinkled her nose. "I think that's what he said, didn't he?"

"How foolish of me. Yes, he did." She forced an agreeable expression on her face. Marie preferred routine much more than this unexpected event. She didn't like doing things the wrong way, thus inviting Charles to correct her like one of his children. Hester did the same, and her censoring seemed worse than her brother's.

Spying the water barrel, Marie took it out of the wagon. She paused, thinking the winds might blow it away before the rain fell enough to weigh it down. Unwilling to lose their only large container, she tied it to a wheel and crawled into the wagon, satisfied the barrel would catch the most water.

Charles hoisted himself into their shelter just as huge raindrops started their drumming. "Looks like everyone's hatches were battened down and ready just in time."

Each minute ticked by slowly as everyone waited for the storm to end. As the afternoon wore on, the flashes grew brighter, the thunder sounded louder, and the rain fell harder. The constant din made any sort of talking futile. To Marie, it seemed as if hailstones caused the noise until true hail hit against the wagon. Horses protested with whinnies, and she wanted to join in the complaining.

She winced as a clap of thunder shook the wood underneath them. Years of living through hurricanes with Charles and Hester trained Marie what to do. Or rather, prior storms had taught her the other two didn't like entertainment while waiting out bad weather. She rested her chin against her palm and tapped her fingers on her cheek, much preferring the plains' harsh but short storms. Days of hurricane weather left her feeling crazy from boredom afterward.

Charles took her hand, patting it on the mattress and blankets. Marie understood. They might as well try to sleep. By the time the storm ended, the three would be exhausted. She lay down on the bed next to her husband. He was right. The rain eased to a gentle fall, lulling her to sleep.

The next morning, the Red Buttes to the south reflected vibrant reds. They'd been warned by Sam's men that they'd be leaving behind the Platte soon. The dry stretch between the now familiar river and the new Sweetwater worried everyone. Secretly, Marie liked the idea of rolling away from the water. Maybe then the mosquitoes would leave her alone. Despite the long sleeves on her dresses, she seemed to always have a new bite to scratch.

She loved the Red Buttes. By noon, they'd neared enough for Marie and Jenny to walk over to see if they were as colorful up close. Dust from the bright rouge dirt and shale comprising the buttes stained their shoes. Later at dinner, Marie told Charles and Hester about her discoveries. Seeing their bored and distracted expressions, she didn't try to lure them into the conversation. Instead, Marie left to find her friends, seeing Ellen first at the Platte, washing up from lunch.

After a wave, Ellen came over to Marie. "Did you hear? Mr. Granville and the other men have decided we'll camp here tonight."

"I'd hoped we would! All but my Sunday dresses are stained brown now, no matter what color they used to be." She followed her friend to the Winslow campsite. Marie shied away from the family, the father ill-tempered and the mother too accepting of his bad behavior.

Breaking into Marie's thoughts, Ellen said "Mine, too. I'll like having color in my clothes again." While piling laundry onto a sheet, she said, "I also heard a group of men shot a couple of buffalo this morning."

She watched the girl tie the corners into knots, making a carry all. "I thought I'd heard something like a gunshot."

"Yes, and they stayed behind to dress both." Ellen put the bundle on her shoulder and followed her friend to get more washing.

Marie asked, "Do you think they'll sell some to anyone?"

"No, not sell. Jenny told me that Mr. Lucky was in the hunting party. She said they're distributing the meat since no one is sure who fired the shots that killed them."

"They're very considerate, then." The good news disappointed Marie since she knew Charles hadn't been hunting with the others. They'd not had fresh meat since leaving Fort Kearney, and she missed it. Still, the Warrens weren't sick like other families. She was glad they had plenty of root vegetables, certainly. "Did your father manage to go along?"

"Not this time, which is a pity, but Jenny's did." Ellen chuckled and leaned in toward her. "Besides, as sweet as Mr. Lucky is on her, I'm sure he'll see she does well in the division."

At her own wagon, Marie smiled at her friend before gathering the dirty clothes. "I'm certain he will. Knowing him, he'll give her most of his share."

The younger woman laughed. "He is a little overanxious, isn't he?"

"A little, yes, but he is sweet nonetheless." Marie asked, "Shouldn't we stop by to ask Jenny if she'd like to wash clothes with us?"

Ellen slowed. "Let's do. It'll make the work go faster."

Later, with Jenny accompanying them, they made their way to the Platte. It seemed every woman camping at Bessemer's Bend, even the younger girls, clean clothes, blankets, and linens. The men were absent, working on various chores left undone while on the road. When the boys started swimming while wearing their dirtiest clothes, the youngest girls cried off of their responsibilities to join in the fun. Soon, nearly all the children played in the water downstream.

Once back at camp, Marie draped the wrung out garments to dry. Clothing and bedding covered every part of their wagon able to support them. Alone, she supposed Charles was off hunting or some other such task. Hester had disappeared soon after lunch, too. Marie gritted her teeth, putting her hands on her hips in frustration. The woman did as little as humanly possible on a trip like this. She'd find out, sooner or later, that Marie had not washed any of Hester's clothes. How could she, when her sister-in-law had ordered her not to snoop in her belongings?

"It's a shame to see an angry face on such a lovely day."

Samuel's voice startled her into first shrieking then laughing for the noise. "I was lost in my own thoughts and didn't hear you walk up."

He chuckled. "I can tell."

He wore a crisp white shirt and dark denim pants. She wanted to pop one of his suspenders in mock annoyance. "How is it you're so clean without washing a thread of clothing today?"

His expression darkened. "The secret? My wagon is full of nothing but clean clothes."

She didn't believe his boasting and narrowed her eyes. "I'll bet it is."

"I'm honest," he said, holding up a hand as if giving an oath.

"So, in case a Sunday accidentally occurs, you're ready?" she teased.

"Absolutely, I'm prepared for anything."

She sighed and leaned against the only uncovered wagon wheel. "Even supper? Because I'm not, although my stomach is."

"I'm always ready for supper, even when it's not ready for me." He seemed shy all of a sudden, examining the dripping blankets. "I'm thinking, after the success of this afternoon's hunt, you might want to have dinner with us."

"I might like that, but am not sure how Charles or Hester would feel." She glanced around. "In fact, I don't know where they are."

"Do they often leave you with all the washing to do?"

Marie nodded, "She more than he, certainly, but yes. We had to either sell or free our household help before leaving home. I'm afraid Hester is still very resentful." Looking for something to do, she squeezed water from a sock. "I don't know why. They were mine long before they were with Charles. We moved her into the guest house, and I suppose she became spoiled." She smiled at him in reassurance and not wanting Samuel to think of her as always dour. "At any rate, we're here now on an adventure. She forgets this at times."

"She probably does." He took a step back. "Please see if they'll join you tonight at our campfire. The men are hoping to share our buffalo stew since you shared your coffee with us."

"How kind of them, since it was only coffee. I don't mind sharing." She leaned in, "Will I like buffalo? I've never tried it before today."

He grinned over at her. "You'll love it, I promise."

"About when will it be ready? I'd like to wash me since I'm the only thing not clean around here."

"Give it a couple of hours. Maybe the other two will be back by then." He put his hand in his pockets and took yet another step backward.

Marie tried not to smile at his reaction. He didn't need to run away; she'd not planned on attacking him in broad daylight. "I'm sure they will. Last time I saw them, Charles was walking upstream, while Hester went downstream with a bucket. But, that was at noon. They could be anywhere by now."

He shrugged. "If they're not back in a while, I suppose missing supper tonight will improve their work ethic around here."

She laughed at the notion. "Don't give me an excuse to attend dinner without telling them anything, Mr. Granville, because I might do just that."

"By all means, Mrs. Warren. You're always welcome." He turned and walked back to his camp.

She watched Samuel, enjoying how he moved. The man was certainly in fine form, Marie thought. She liked how he seemed strong without being bulky and sinewy without being stringy. Stifling a girlish sigh, she gathered the necessities for bathing. Cleaning herself in the late afternoon meant changing out in the wagon for privacy's sake. The cramped effort of struggling out of wet clothes would be worth the clean feeling afterward.

By the time Marie had returned from the creek, Charles and Hester were in camp, starting supper. Hester had been in a snit over her clothes remaining unwashed and reminding her of her own rules hadn't helped. She looked angry enough to spit, something Marie tried not to enjoy. Charles just waved her away when Marie told him of their dinner invitation. She went alone; glad to be away from such grouches.

A small group sat around the cook pot. No one was eating. She walked up to them, suddenly shy with everyone looking at her. "Good evening."

Mr. Lucky bounded over to her. "Mrs. Warren! How are you? Come over here and sit next to me and Jenny. It would be best since you are friends and all. Mr. Granville says this will be your first meal of buffalo, is that right? How have you missed out so far?"

She was seated between Jenny and Samuel. Smiling at both her neighbors, she answered, "I'm fine and hope you are, too. It is my first taste of buffalo, so I'm rather excited. I don't know how I've not had some before now."

The young man settled in between Lefty and Jenny. "Probably Mr. Warren hasn't tried hunting one, because if he shot at any sort of buffalo, he'd hit one. They're big."

Marie nodded. "I've seen them. They are very big."

"Lucky," Samuel said, "Why don't you dish up you and Miss Jenny some dinner?" Quietly to Marie, he added, "He can wear you out with questions."

"I've noticed." She smiled at him. "Maybe he'll settle down as he gets older."

Samuel grinned. "I hope so since I doubt he could be more energetic."

Lucky gave a meal to Jenny and Marie first since they were the only ladies present. For the men, it was an organized scuffle. Afterward, everyone stayed quiet while eating. The meat was so good that she hated having the last bite.

"I guess you like it," said Sam.

"I did! You're right. Buffalo is a lot like beef."

Lucky interjected, "Boss! Tell her about the Indians today. Miss Jenny says she doesn't know."

"Were there Indians at camp today?"

"You brought it up, Lucky. You tell the story." To Marie, he added, "The youngster goes to sleep sooner if he speaks all his words out during the day."

She laughed. "Youngster? He's what, a couple years younger than you?"

Grinning, he placed a hand over his heart. "Madam, I'm hurt. Lucky is a child."

Fidgeting, the man in question piped up. "Come on, am I going to get to tell about the Indians or not?"

"Neither one of you are children, but you're certainly close to the same age, aren't you?" she asked.

"I'm a mature twenty-eight. Mr. Lucky is nineteen."

"And I want to start the story of what we gave the Indians today, so they wouldn't attack."

"Yes, please do," Marie said with a chuckle. She struggled to keep the disgust from her face as Lucky described the bloody buffalo hunt.

Samuel was younger than her by four years. She felt far past her prime, and yet she'd been a little calf-eyed over a man who wasn't in his, yet. A little dagger of betrayal pierced her mind. She knew marrying a much older person meant a lifetime spent with a man who was more a father than a spouse. Half listening to Lucky, she nodded as he described searching for a nearby Indian village. Marie mentally shook herself. She had no reason to dwell on age differences between her and anyone else. In five months when this trip ended, she and Charles would have their home, and Samuel would be back in his own life.

She glanced at him, wondering what life he led when not on the trail. She'd been so focused on pleasing Charles that she hadn't considered what people did when the journey was complete. When Samuel smiled at her staring, she grinned back, embarrassed, and looked at Lucky.

"Then, while we wanted to invite them over for dinner tonight, Mr. Granville decided against it. Most of you have seen Indians before now, but he didn't want to chance any misunderstandings. So, we traded them sugar, tobacco, and whiskey along with the rest of the buffalo."

"Whisky?" she asked Samuel, trying not to smile.

"Not mine," he replied. "It's a keepsake."

Jenny tapped Lucky's arm to get his attention. "What did you get in trade with them?"

He shrugged. "We didn't get goods so much as safe passage through their land."

Shuddering in revulsion, Jenny said, "I don't think we'll be safe until they're all dead."

Before the other man could reply, Samuel interjected, "Lucky, let me answer her, please. I figured since we're using their land and resources, they deserve payment. We'd pay any other landowner. Why not them?"

Marie saw a glint in his eyes and knew the girl hit a soft spot with Samuel. He cared about the savages. How strange. "But still, they attack."

"Some do, yes. Before you become alarmed, you should know they usually just take what they want without asking. We also take what we want without asking, and in some cases, more than we need. No matter if they were forced or willingly gave it up, we're traveling through the lands of their ancestors without every tribe's permission. In any other part of the known world, that would start a war."

With a mulish look on her face, Jenny said, "Maybe so. They could still clean up a little and wear decent clothing."

Marie piped up to dispel the rising tension. "Wearing our clothes sounds good until practiced. I think Indians would look as ridiculous wearing pants and dresses as we would in buckskins."

Indicating his other hired hand, Samuel said, "I can't completely agree. I think Uncle Joe looks dashing in his buckskins."

She smiled as everyone else nodded. "I think so, too. He's also very well groomed."

Jenny added, "Grooming is what I miss most about civilization. When we get to Oregon, I'm having father find the largest bathtub possible for a proper bath with warm water."

"I have to admit, it's something I miss as well." Samuel stood, holding out his hand for Marie. "Lucky, would you walk the ladies back to their families? You can tell them all about Soda Springs." He pulled her to her feet. "Meanwhile, us unfortunate men will wash up and bed down for the night."

Lucky held out his elbows for the ladies to take. "It'll be a pleasure, sir." Marie and Jenny each took an arm. "The water there is bubbly from boiling, carbonation, or both. It's interesting and easy to be poached if you fall in."

Marie listened with half an ear to the stories of various geysers they'd later see while resisting the urge to look back at Samuel. She wanted to offer help with cleaning. A blatant effort to spend more time with him, she knew, but even chores sounded fun if he were there.

The walk to her camp wasn't far, and as she left them, the young couple spoke almost in unison, "Good night, Mrs. Warren."

"Goodnight, Marie."

"Goodnight Lucky and Jenny. See you tomorrow probably."

As they walked on, she readied for bed. Such an exciting night with all the talk of Indians, age, and naturally boiling water. She slipped into her bedroll next to Charles. He and Hester had missed a fun time. She felt bad for them, thinking the buffalo made a welcome change from salt pork.

So Samuel was only twenty-eight. No wonder Charles bristled at the younger man's orders. Samuel and Charles' first two sons were around the same age. Marie sighed. Thinking about those boys and their sister could keep her awake all night. The family was a mess before she ever married into it. Nothing she'd done improved the relationships, while leaving Louisiana helped a little.

Frustrated with how her thoughts buzzed in her mind, Marie imagined how a bath in soda water might feel. She drifted off wondering if the bubbles tickled.

A short rain woke everyone with its damp chill. Coffee made the Warrens bearable to Marie, but without it, she found it best to avoid them. Skipping breakfast entirely, she walked along the grassy and sandy hills, picking flowers. Little minnows darted in the crisp and clear spring. The water tasted as crisp as it looked. She smiled a greeting when seeing others on the opposite bank taking the chance to fill their water barrels and cooking pots. Meandering back to camp, she saw the first of their group boarding the ferry. Panicked and trying not to be, she hurried to find her own family, hoping they'd not crossed yet.

Charles saw her and yelled, "There you are! Where the hell have you been? Hester is out looking for you."

"I am so sorry, dearest!" She hurried to where he stood. "Everyone said to be ready by this afternoon. I didn't expect…"

"I don't care." His voice rising, he continued, "We have to contend with you either being in the way or not available for us on a daily basis. I don't know how many times we've had to sit and wait on you, or hurry so you are not bothered." A whistle from the ferryman caught his attention. "Damn it all," he muttered before turning back to her. "I'll search for Hessy. You make sure the oxen and rigging get across. Keep to the right, and we'll catch up to you yet again." After digging around in his pocket, Charles handed her some money. "Here's the fare. Give it directly to the ferryman and try not to drop it. We need every penny."

He left before letting her reply, so Marie closed her mouth without a squeak. Charles had never been violent, rarely became angry, and she was never actually scared. Yet, as she handed the gentleman their fee, her hand still shook. The oxen followed her up the ramp, onto the ferry, and remained docile while afloat. The short trip ended almost before it had begun, and she led the animals away and to the right as Charles had instructed.

More and more people crossed, the Warrens not among any of them. She waited for a while, growing more restless along with the animals. Their stock had swum over, she'd noticed, a half hour or so ago, by Granville's men. They continued to work the small herds across as each family joined the others on the southwest bank. When she thought the last of their group had joined them, the twins walked up, both frowning.

"I'm sure Charles already spoke to you?" Hester asked.

"He did. I'm sorry." Lucky's bugle sound stopped Marie for a moment. "I'll try to do better at being available."

She walked to the front of the wagon without a reply, leaving her brother to say, "At least you're here, now. Thank you for that."

"You're very welcome." Marie stayed back a little as the wagon lurched forward. She should have gone ahead to avoid the choking dust. Sighing, she instead walked to the side of everyone, hoping to find fresh air to breathe.

The hard ground stretched barren for miles. Even the sagebrush and cactus thinned to sparse, and the grass disappeared. Looking ahead, what she considered mountains seemed so close yet took days to reach. Every so often, the livestock scattered, and she'd see Sam and his men scramble to retrieve them back into the herd. The afternoon lasted forever and all uphill.

They stopped late evening at last. Willow Springs, while crowded with others, had the last fresh water until Sweetwater River. Marie went to the creek with a pail, dismayed to see how muddy and churned the water was from all the activity. She'd hoped they'd have a good drink tonight without grit. Too tired to complain, she let the silt settle a little before starting supper.

Marie tried to appreciate the sunset but couldn't keep her eyes open. Reluctant to talk with the Warrens or be social with anyone else, she readied for bed. The dishes could wait. She'd be good with Hester leaving them for her just so she'd get to sleep right now.

Waking up to a beautiful morning, she smiled until trying to walk. While washing last night's crusty dishes, she learned that yesterday's roads had bruised everyone's feet. She saw others use pebbles and sand for scrubbing their breakfast plates and did the same. By lunch, she'd regret not eating now, but with the bugle sounding and Charles's lecture yesterday, she didn't delay.

Along the rocky trail, Marie and the others passed various grave markers. Most had wooden crosses, others discernible by nothing more than a mound of rocks. Each one, no matter who they'd been, saddened her. The person started with a hope for a new life, she imagined, only to have it end far short. All the reminders of death had disturbed her, but none as much as the eight in front of her now. The graves looked weathered by a few years. She wondered how long ago they'd passed and what happened. After a while she continued on, still full of questions with no answers.

The train had moved steadily since Willow Creek. She noticed later in the morning the ground seemed covered in ashes. Samuel had said this would happen since the soil was rich in alkali, so much so, the standing water was poisonous. She'd heard second hand how he wanted people to wait until after Poison Creek to drink the available water. What the various marshes and pools held could make them ill. Samuel's instructions were to drink milk instead of water from the stagnant pools of alkali.

Despite this, she'd seen several people ignore the warning. The animals wandering to the seeping spring water she understood, but she had no sympathy for those ignoring the advice to wait until the river. They drank from the trickles of old rainwater standing in the dry creek beds. Protesting the water tasted fine and that Granville was an old woman about the matter, no one became sick right away, seeming to make Samuel a liar. Marie glanced at one of the wagons, most of the family members now ill.

The party went along single file down the dry creek's ridge until nearing the top of Prospect Hill. At the most level ground, she heard Lucky's signal to stop for noon. She hurried to catch up to the wagon, so the Warrens need not look for her. Busy getting the cold lunch, she didn't bother to try and chat with her husband or his sister.

Charles broke the silence between them first. "Darling, I may have spoken too roughly yesterday. Since then, you've been doing well with being near when we need you and out of the way when we don't." He smiled at her, leaning in to kiss Marie on the forehead. "Thank you."

Smiling from the appreciation, she responded, "You're welcome. I wasn't aware I'd been such a bother and plan to do better in the future."

He gave her a warm look. "I'm glad. Granville said the next couple of days would be rough. The water might continue to be either bad or poisonous, meaning scarce grass for the stock and not much fuel for mealtimes. We'll want extra biscuits and bacon cooked, too."

A rider galloping up to them stayed her reply. She saw Samuel approach and swing off his horse.

Before either Warren could greet him, he said, "Warren, we'll need your help. Another family's wagon lost control, and the wheels rolled over someone and one of their animals."

"I'm not a doctor. I don't know how you expect me to help," Charles retorted.

"You're able-bodied and have a good shovel. That's all the help we need to dig a grave for the poor soul." Tipping his hat to her, he said, "Ma'am, a pleasure to see you," and got on his horse. "It's ahead a mile or so."

The gray of Samuel's face bothered her so she asked, "Is it one of ours?" When he nodded, she understood his demeanor and asked in a quiet tone, "Who?"

He pursed his lips together as if unwilling to say aloud before answering, "Jimmy."

CHAPTER 3

Sam crawled into his bedroll in what seemed like days past sunset. The stricken expressions on everyone's face as he'd spread the news of Jimmy Marshall's accident kept him awake. He tried to shake off the sorrow, knowing many other children died along the trail, too. From helping bury the child to staying the night at a waterless campsite, the day had been one of the worst he'd experienced in a long time.

He tried to get comfortable on the rocky ground. Restless, he squirmed to lie face up again to stare at the star filled sky. The fire nearby had burned down to embers long ago. Sam let his gaze follow his favorite constellations for this time of year. He adored Marie. She'd comforted Mrs. Marshall and the smaller children while him and the other men did the somber tasks. Mr. Warren's back gave out at around five strikes of his shovel against the near bedrock ground. Just as well, Sam thought while smiling a little. They'd really only needed his shovel. His men could handle everything else.

He woke with a start to the sound of Lucky's bugle. While regaining consciousness, Sam saw the sun midway to noon. He groaned at the time. Heavy low clouds hung overhead and spread to the west, darkening the morning. He got out of bed, intending to follow his nose downwind toward the heavenly aroma of boiling coffee. The nearest water had to be at least five miles away, though. Either the wind was stronger than he'd thought, or someone had made a ten mile round trip without waking anyone else. He frowned at the idea; his men knew better than to let the crew sleep much past daybreak. As he passed various campsites, Sam noticed nearly everyone in camp had overslept. He approached the Warrens and grinned. All of his hands and a few others sat around their fire, enjoying the strong brew Marie had made.

Walking up to them, he chided, "Here's all my help, sitting around like it's Sunday church."

Mr. Lucky, seated a little too close to Jenny, spoke up first, "Yes, sir. If you had ever tasted Mrs. Warren's coffee, you'd be sitting here with us. It's the best in camp."

Marie shrugged, her face flushed from Mr. Lucky's compliment. "I let the dirt in the water jug settle to the bottom overnight. I'm sure that's the only difference."

Frowning, Sam asked, "You've been carrying water stores up Prospect Hill?"

"Not stores so much as a large jar for emergencies like this." She held up the empty glass. "You can't be angry at the weight; it's empty now."

Sam grinned at her smile, unable to be irritated with her. "Would you have an extra cup for me?"

"Of course, I would. There's a little more coffee left, but no cups. Let me wash mine out for you." She stood to do just that when he held up his hand.

"I can't take the coffee away from a lady. My cup is sitting idle back at the wagon. Let me get it and rejoin everyone." He walked away before she began to argue.

He hurried back, seeing Mr. Lucky entertaining the group with his next tall tale. Jenny hung on his every word a little more than everyone else. Next to Marie, Sam asked, "Ma'am, may I have some of your superior coffee?"

She laughed and poured him a cup. "Superior? I'm hoping you find it tasty at least."

He breathed in. "Hmmm, smells good so far." After a sip which turned into a longer drink, he said, "I was going to order us rolling on after this cup, but I might wait until I've had two. This is good."

"Thank you, I'm glad you're enjoying it." Marie poured herself a little and stood, giving more to those who held up their cups. She placed the coffee pot back over the embers.

While listening to Lucky, Sam looked up at her still standing. "Mrs. Warren?" Catching Marie's attention, he patted the ground next to him. "Have a seat, please."

She smiled. "I think I will. At least, until you need your second cup."

Shaking his head, Sam said, "As much as I love your coffee, I'll have to pass today. We need to get rounded up and going."

"I agree." After a nod to the horizon, she added, "It's later than we usually head, out and everyone is already very slothful. Everyone except Mr. Lucky, that is."

He grinned before taking a deep drink. "Chuck and Larry aren't too bad, but Uncle Joe is a slow starter. He's really best at night watch. I can count on him to never fall asleep while on duty."

"That's good." When Lucky jumped to his feet, Marie told Sam, "I'd figured Mr. Lucky to be the best night guard, considering his energy."

Sam chuckled at her observation. "Not at night since he's worn himself out during the day."

Bristling with nervous energy, Lucky asked, "We're about ready to go, aren't we, boss?"

"Yes," Sam replied and added, "as soon as I see the bottom of my coffee."

"Great, I'll get started." The young man nodded at Marie. "Ma'am," he said and strode off in a hurry.

Sam looked around the camp, frowning, and asked her, "Should we have saved some back for the other Warrens?"

Marie drank the last few drops before replying, "It's no matter. Hester might have minded none left, wanting the excuse to be here with you." She stopped, face flushed. "I mean, she enjoys talking about you. In a kind way, of course."

He struggled to keep a neutral expression at the thought of Hester showing interest in him. Not saying anything for a moment, Sam instead finished up his coffee. "I see."

She smiled at him, "Don't feel too cornered. Every unmarried woman in camp feels the same way about you as she does."

Feeling a little less uncomfortable, he stood and held out his hand to help up Marie. "I'm not surprised, ma'am. The Granville charm is very powerful on the fair sex."

Seeing the Warrens approaching camp, she chided Samuel in a quiet voice, "I'd have to see this so-called charm before believing you."

"I thought my appeal was blatantly obvious, yet, you don't see? Your harsh words hurt my heart, Mrs. Warren." He stood, addressing a sleepy Uncle Joe and quiet Arnold, saying, "All right ladies, coffee time is over. We need to start rolling if we're to make Independence Rock by noon."

As everyone hurried through their last chores before leaving, the campsite buzzed with activity. Sam helped those lagging behind tend their animals and get moving. Once every wagon wheel turned, no matter how slow, he could relax and keep an eye out for

Marie. He smiled when thinking of how she might enjoy Sweetwater River's somewhat flat riverbed. Walking, at a decline or incline both, was tough on people and animals.

He spotted her near the Warren's wagon, inching its way down the long hill. She'd been keeping close to her family lately, not on her usual explorations of whatever caught her eye. Sam didn't know why she'd neglected her curiosity in the week or so before yesterday. Today, though, he understood and shared her somber mood. She'd been fond of Jimmy, taking it on herself to fill some of the gaps his own mother was too sickly to fill for him. It was going to take her and a lot of others time to get over the boy's death.

Arnold stayed with Sam. Both men rode at the back and to the left of the group. Greenhorns rode behind just once before they learned to avoid the choking dust. He smiled. Arnold thought he knew everything right up until he needed help out of a mess. Still, the youngster had not made the same mistake twice in anything. Sam thought he'd made a fine hand in the past couple of weeks.

Independence Rock loomed ever closer as the morning passed into afternoon. Everything took extra time in a group, whether fixing a broken wheel or stopping at a clear spring for a drink. If alone, he'd just gallop over. Instead, he forced himself to be patient.

Arnold looked at him, eyebrows raised in a silent question. Sam answered by saying, "When we get to Sweetwater. Joe and Lucky already know." Hearing an exasperated sigh from the young man, he agreed with the frustration. They'd spent today on a vast barren plain. Low mountains lay all around them and seemed to recede as they approached, teasing the impatient travelers. After inching past Black Rock, Independence Rock grew larger every few miles.

His stomach growled in protest as they brought up the rear to the new camp. Many others also rested in the area, the cooking smells thick in the air. He'd be happy with a biscuit and hunk of ham at the moment. Settling everyone into place came first, and second? A duty he owed himself and his brother.

He rode past each family to ensure their welfare. Several others helped the Marshals set up, and Marie was among them. She gave him a slight smile and nod as he passed, and Sam tipped his hat in return. He dismounted at the Granville wagon when seeing Uncle Joe there. "How is everything? Under your control?"

"Yes, sir." The elder man grinned at him. "The boys are out helping others with the livestock while I unload for tonight."

"Very well, good job." Sam didn't need to glance at the sun to know he had plenty of time. This next task was one of his favorites on the trail. He unsaddled and staked out Scamp near some grazing before turning to Independence Rock. A chunk of granite seeming so small at a distance grew into a monolith up close. Grinning, he went to the far side, to the familiar climbing spot and dug in to ascend. When separated by circumstance, he and his brother Nick used this piece of the monument to communicate. He laughed when seeing Nick's last message to him ending with Nick and Beth Granville. Rather arrogant for him to assume Beth would accept his proposal, Sam thought, and yet, she had.

He cut in his name and the date below his brother's. Satisfied with his carving skills, Sam climbed higher to sit at the top. The view stretched in all directions. The mountain ridge to the south, he chuckled at calling them mountains, finally seemed large. The chilly wind blew more up here, making him glad for the warm day. The first time he and Nick had the idea to conquer this rock, a gust sent them tumbling. His blood still ran cold when remembering the loss of control he'd felt right then. In every climb since then, both men crept close to the surface.

Looking west, he shook his head when thinking of how he'd not planned to ever be here again. Yet, when Anne ended their engagement, the trail called to him. Sam wanted the isolation while the wheels rolled. He wanted to meet people, wanted to get out of his own mind. No sense in wondering what he could have done differently. She'd been unfaithful to him early last year and had a new child and new marriage as a result.

The heartache eased the further he went from Oregon. He'd expected it to return as he inched closer to the territory. But it hadn't, and he knew why. Examining those on the ground, he sought out Marie. The people seemed so small from this point of view. Any number of wagons, people, or even trees by the riverbank might be hiding her. He did see a few of his men. None of them seemed in a hurry or busy, so chores must be done for a while.

Sam leaned back on his elbows, legs stretched in front of him.

He had time before dinner to daydream about Marie and smiled. She seemed to be a sponge, absorbing the ages of the company she kept. He enjoyed visiting her when she spent time with Jenny and Ellen, or Jimmy, but not so much with Charles and Hester. She always had a ready smile for Sam, and her eyes sparkled more when he saw her with the youngsters.

He knew the pain of being betrayed and wouldn't wish it on any other man. Yet, he couldn't help but want to spend more time with her during the day. She had an open friendliness to everyone, not just him. He liked her demeanor, but wanted more from Marie and disliked the needy feeling. Sam sighed and lay down upon the rock full length, putting his hands under his head as a pillow. She'd been kind enough before asking him to kiss her at the saloon. He thought her lovely, charming, and a client to get from one town to another in the next few months. Until Fort Laramie.

Closing his eyes, he still saw her beauty that evening in the lamp's glow. Every campfire he'd seen her at since reminded him of how close he'd been to kissing her. He'd watch her from his peripheral vision, not wanting to stare. She'd glance at him, but not often enough for him to think her request for a kiss had been more than what she'd claimed. A quick experiment? He shook his head. Not for him, he'd be like a baby with candy. One taste and he'd be gone.

"Oh! This is lovely. Very much worth the effort. Good job, Mr. Granville."

Sam sat up as if poked in the back by an arrow. "Marie?" He turned to see her behind him, inching her way to where he sat. "What the hell are you doing up here?"

"Making biscuits. What does it look like I'm doing? I'm enjoying the view just as you are." Next to him, she sat and took in the surrounding countryside. "The girls said I was crazy to try. I think they're out of their mind for not."

Her sunbonnet hung down her back, her fingers rough from the rock. He took a hand of hers in his, examining for cut marks. "You're lucky you didn't fall. Getting up here is tough enough in trousers; I can't imagine climbing up in a skirt."

"It wasn't easy, no." She gave him her other hand to examine with a grin. "Trying to be modest and not get tangled up in several yards of fabric did add to the difficulty." As he traced her scratched palm with his fingertips, she said, "I'm not bleeding, so no harm was done."

Grinning, he looked up from her hand. "Have you given any thought to getting back down with modesty and body intact?"

She frowned. "No, and I should have. I might have to wait until nightfall and feel my way down."

The idea of her doing such a thing in pitch black terrified him for her safety. "No, I'll help you and need to apologize for my language just now." The faint beginning of freckles on her nose distracted him for a moment. She returned his smile until he added, "You're the last person I wanted up here."

Her smile faded. "Oh. Very well, I can understand you'd like some time alone. Everyone needs quiet time, especially in a group like ours. Plus, you're responsible for everyone and with Jimmy yesterday…" Her eyes grew watery. "I'm feeling the need to be alone, too, all of a sudden." She stood, a little wobbly from a gust of wind. "I might be back for help in getting down, if or when you're ready."

He got to his knees, reaching out a hand to her. "I'd prefer my alone time to be with you if you don't mind, ma'am." She held on to him when another gust threatened to topple her. "See? You're being told to stay put until the winds die down a bit."

With a frown, Marie sat next to him. "It seems so." She straightened her skirt, adding, "I appreciate you allowing me to interrupt your solitude until it's safer for me to leave."

Sam nodded, his glib charm failing him all of a sudden. Alone with her, but in plain sight of everyone else, he could say anything to her. Maybe do nothing, but no one would hear him speaking from his heart. "I might have been abrupt in saying you'd be last on my mind. It's truer that you're the first person I'd want up here with me." He glanced at her from the corner of his eyes. Had she thought of him as much as he did her? Or had he stopped being on her mind after a while? The part of Sam wanting her warred with the part knowing to leave her alone. He smirked, contemplating the ribbing he'd get from Nick at this, now that Sam had fallen for a married woman himself. Their mother would beat both of her boys if she knew and they'd deserve it.

"You're overly kind, sir. At any rate, I'm glad you're not angry I'm here," she said.

"How could I be, ma'am? I'm up here on a beautiful day with a lovely lady. Chores are done until dinner, and afterward is washing up in a clear river."

After a pause, she said in a quiet voice, "Now that no one else can overhear, I'd like to speak to you frankly about my ill-conceived request at the fort."

"There's no need if you choose not to."

"That's kind of you to want to protect my reputation, kinder than I deserve. I just wanted to apologize for putting you in an awkward position."

Sam took in a deep breath. "No need to. I hope you figure out why I had to refuse."

"I do, yes." She looked to the south at the mountains. "If not angry and desperate, I'd never have asked and still feel ashamed for doing so."

Two more words to make his pulse jump. An angry and desperate Marie could put him in any position she please, Sam knew, and he'd be good with her decision. Taking in a slow, calming breath, he then said, "No need to be ashamed. Nothing happened that night, and I did exactly as your husband requested."

"You're a good man, Mr. Granville."

Sam looked at her, the breezes ruffling the tendrils of dark hair around her face. "I try to be. Just don't ask for another kiss, please. I don't have the strength to refuse again."

She laughed. "No more requests, I promise." Marie fidgeted a little on the granite before adding, "Thank you, too, for the flattery. I don't have to believe your sentiment to enjoy it."

Long lashes and arched eyebrows framed her dark eyes. His heart pounded in his chest as he realized he loved her. "Ma'am, I don't mean to flatter you at all. I'm not sure I could stop with one kiss with you."

Her jaw had dropped a little before she recovered. Marie grinned, "You are a charmer. Very well, since you insist on pretending, I'll play along." She leaned back, her hands against the rock. "Thank you, sir, for fighting your baser instincts and not ravaging me in the saloon's private room. Such a virile man as you, when faced with such a delectable creature as me, well, that must have been near impossible for you to control yourself." Fanning herself with a limp wristed hand, she added, "My, my, I am so lucky you're a gentleman."

He noted how her southern accent thickened along with the sarcasm. Not sure what to think, Sam felt sure he didn't like the implication he had been dishonest. "You are lucky. Any other man might have taken advantage of a woman like you."

"Like me?" She shook her head. "No, I have no worries in that area. While you tease me mercilessly, I know for certain how men see me as something other than female."

Giving her a side glance, he wondered if she were teasing him or just fishing for compliments. "Excuse me? That's not possible, not with you."

Laughing at him, Marie continued, "They, you, Charles, all know I'm a woman, yes, but see me as a friend or sister more than a wife."

He shook his head, certain he didn't consider her a sister. "I see you very much as a woman."

"You're too kind yet again." She smiled at him. "Ellen and Jenny are the first female friends I've ever had. I played boys games, despite my mother's best efforts, until the boys turned into men. That's about the time I became invisible."

Sam laughed, "You did?"

With a sheepish grin, she said, "Maybe more ghostly, then." Marie looked ahead. "I shouldn't be talking about any of this with you. For some odd reason, you draw me out and make me say things I regret the next day."

Her confession bothered him. Sam patted her on the shoulder before saying, "I wouldn't want you to regret anything."

"I do." She looked at his hand and smiled a little. "I'm sorry for asking you to kiss me because it put you in a spot. And now I'm talking with you about my husband and how he hasn't seen me in a long time. Next thing I'll be telling you about how, well..." She looked at him in surprise. "About things I shouldn't ever tell another soul." Marie leaned over and nudged Sam. "Maybe we should talk about you for a while. You can tell me all your secrets."

"As if we were brothers and sisters holding misdeeds over each other?"

"Exactly!"

He wanted her as anything but a sister. Sam had a lot to think about, especially what Marie didn't say about not being seen by Mr. Warren. Glancing at her, he saw the worry on her face as she examined a small chunk of granite she'd picked up. Dark circles stained the delicate skin under her eyes. He knew she'd spent a sleepless night over Jimmy's death. Sam didn't want her remorseful about confiding in him. "I have a huge secret of my own. If I told you, my reputation and honor as a man would be ruined. So if I say it to you, I need an oath you'll never use this against me."

"Never?"

Searching his mind for possible loopholes, he found one. "You can tell if the situation is life and death. Otherwise, never."

She grinned and faced him. "Oh, then you must tell me! I know a lot of secrets, most of them not my own, and haven't told anyone. Not a single one to a single person, so you have to trust me."

Sam turned to her. The amusement in her eyes and the excited expression on her face told him he had to give her a real secret. Since she didn't believe his infatuation, he wanted to convince her his comments weren't idle flattery. "I have the note you gave Mr. Warren. The one you kissed."

Her face paled. "You do? Oh no! Where is it?"

"It's in my Bible." He chuckled. "Of all my books, I put it there."

"Why did you keep it?"

"Because your lips touched it, and I liked the idea of a woman asking for a clandestine meeting, even if not with me. Also, I needed to keep the note in case I forgot the room number."

Twisting and untwisting her sunbonnet strings she said, "You'd forget?"

"All right, no, I wouldn't." He stared into her eyes. "I wanted to keep a note sent from a woman like you. Later, when I tried to burn it, I couldn't. Not with your rouge on there, teasing me."

She licked her lips, nervous. "You're right. You've told a splendid secret."

He held out his hand. "Do we have a pact?"

"We do," she said while shaking his hand. "I suppose I should inch my way back down to camp. Charles is cranky when I'm not there as needed. I've not been wearing my bonnet, either, and he's not happy at how dark my skin is becoming."

His heart sunk, not wanting the afternoon with her to end so soon. He forced a smile. "I don't blame him for wanting you there. I've enjoyed my time with you. His opinion about your skin is a different story." She frowned at him as if puzzled, so he added, "A little bit of color looks good on you. Just enough to keep you from looking faint, but not so much you look in need of washing."

Laughing, she said, "As always, you're too kind." She gave him a sly glance before saying, "I think this time, though, I'll believe your compliment." Marie stood, a little unsteady in the late afternoon wind.

Sam stood as well. "Let me go down first, so if you fall, I can catch you."

"Are you sure? If I fall on you, we'll both tumble to our deaths." She rubbed her palms on her skirt. "My hands are sweaty just thinking about it."

"Don't even begin to be afraid. I'll go first, get grounded, and wait for you. You're a sensible, careful woman, and I have faith in you."

"You do?"

"Of course, ma'am." He gave her one last grin before climbing down the rock. Sam eased his way down, glad to be on flat dirt at the end. He looked up to see Marie still at the very top, waiting for him to be out of her way. Motioning for her to go, he watched as she tied her skirt together for the descent. Every minute or so, his body reminded him to breathe with a slight gasp.

She jumped the last couple of feet to the ground and turned to him. "I'm so glad that's done! Climbing up is always more fun than inching down, don't you think?"

"Always is." He didn't know what to say, here on solid footing. "Shall I walk you back?"

"I'd like that, yes."

He almost offered his arm for her to hold, but even a usual polite gesture seemed too intimate at the moment. They walked to camp in silence. Sam looked over at Marie, her face covered by the sunbonnet. He had said in a quiet voice before they neared the others, "Thank you for spending part of your afternoon with me, ma'am."

"You're welcome, and it was my pleasure as well." She paused before turning to her campsite. "I enjoyed explaining myself. Thank you for allowing me to do so, Mr. Granville."

"Anytime, Mrs. Warren." He tipped his hat and went to find his own wagon. When there, he saw how the men had been busy washing clothes. He grinned to see they'd added his shirts and pants in with the other laundry. Joe and Lefty played cards, Lucky polished his bugle, and Arnold read a book at the campfire's circle. "Thank you, gentlemen."

Looking up from his work, Lucky said, "You're welcome, boss."

Arnold also glanced at Sam. "It was in our own best interest, sir."

Sam laughed. "I'll bet it was. Looks like you all managed to wash up yourselves, too."

"We did," Arnold said. "Uncle Joe went hunting but didn't get anything."

"Game's scarce," added Joe with a shrug.

Sam went to the wagon for bathing gear. "I expected as much. A plain dinner is good. I'll go wash up so you girls aren't offended by me."

The men snickered and continued their activities. Meanwhile, Sam carried soap, a small blanket, and clean clothes to the river. He didn't expect privacy, and nearing the water, the various people assured him he had an audience. Examining the bank downstream, the crowd seemed to thin the further from Independence Rock they were. A stroll along the river might do him some good, he determined, and then headed down the bank to some open space.

The sun, halfway between noon and twilight, warmed his back. He breathed in deep, enjoying the marshy smell of wet earth and trampled weeds. Various women scrubbed their families' clothes. Their chatter on both sides of the water reached his ears, but the murmurs had no meaning for him. He wondered if Marie might need to wash anything. Sam couldn't remember her mentioning chores. Her admissions of her reasoning for wanting a kiss from him crowded out almost everything else she'd said. Except maybe the sentence about her husband not noticing her. He kicked off his shoes. A glance upriver showed too many women might see him, so he took off his socks and shirt, but nothing else.

He stepped into the water, still wearing his dirty pants. The cold took some getting used to, and while he worked to ignore the discomfort, he thought of how perfect being alone with Marie seemed to be. Her husband might well be blind to his wife, especially when Sam recalled how much he saw them apart, but he sure as hell wasn't. He soaped up his torso and put the bar back into his pocket.

Searching his memory, it seemed the Warrens had always included three people, the husband, wife, and sister-in-law. He eased into the river, gritting his teeth against the chill. Shivering distracted him from anything else on his mind. He scrubbed his white shirt, trying to get it closer to the original color. Once satisfied the stains were gone, he pocketed the soap, rinsed the sudsy fabric, and threw it on the grass to dry.

Hiding his lower half beneath the water, Sam slipped out of his pants, using the soap still in his pocket to get them clean. Tossing the soap onto the grass, he rinsed them free of suds. He wrung as much water out of them as possible before throwing them on the bank as well. The shallow water kept his modesty covered, and he grinned at the thought of standing upright. Embarrassing, but humorous.

His stomach growled as he went underwater and suppressed a yowl from the cold covering him. Once rinsed, he swam to his belongings and dressed. His clean shirt's tail reached far enough down to cover his backside. A quick shake of the new pants and they were ready to wear. He stuffed one sock and the soap inside the other for later washing. After another wringing, he folded his shirt and pants and headed for camp. The wind shifted direction and carried dinner smells to his nose. Sam picked up his pace as his stomach growled yet again.

At his camp, the only thing changed from when he left was now food cooked over the open flame. He glanced at the simmering pot of beans and rice. Tomorrow, he'd go hunt for fresh meat. It had been a full week since any sort of variety. He looked forward to getting further down the Sweetwater and catching trout.

Lefty greeted him with a nod. "Hey, boss. We're in line to cross first thing tomorrow."

"Good work." Sam hung his clothes up to dry. "I expect everyone knows to be ready?"

"They do." The younger man sat back, letting others pass around the plates Uncle Joe dished up for them. "I warned them all about being ready to go, no waiting around for picking up dry clothes left out overnight."

Sam nodded, dinner tasting better than usual. Had he missed lunch altogether? Seemed so, since he felt hungrier with each bite. He swallowed before saying, "Good."

The men all chewed more than they talked. Even during the sparse conversation, Sam enjoyed thinking about Marie and her slight confessional this afternoon. The evening slipped into night, people came and went, and still he thought of questions too improper to ask her. Part of him wanted to help her in what seemed like a quest to interest Warren in her again. The other part felt she shouldn't have to try when men like him were interested in her already. He paused at the sudden thought with the fork halfway to his mouth.

Seeing how he caught Lucky's attention, he smiled and continued eating. Interested was a strong word but apt. The entire Laramie fiasco predictably triggered his lust. The time spent with her since then drew him into caring for Marie with every second they talked. He went through the motions of cleaning, getting bedding ready, all the usual nightly tasks before the others came over for entertainment. Sam watched for Marie and the other Warrens, but they didn't attend. Distracted and hiding disappointment, he tried to focus on those around him.

When the last person left for the night, he caught himself sighing in relief. "Second watch, let's get some sleep. Tomorrow's an early day." He yawned, causing Lucky to do so, too. They settled into the bedrolls and fell fast asleep as Uncle Joe and Lefty began first watch.

The next morning, the bridge trembled under the weight of the wagon and animals. Had no one made repairs since the last time he'd crossed, Sam wondered. He held his breath with each step until landing on solid ground. Looking back on the rickety wooden structure, he added it to one more reason for retiring from guiding settlers west. He faced forward to lead the animals out of the way for the next group. Walking on to where Lefty held their horses, he nodded at the young man. "Thank you. Ours is the last of them."

"You're welcome, sir," Lefty acknowledged while hopping up on his horse. "I'll take the front with Arnold."

Sam nodded his agreement and sat astride Scamp. His insides felt light, having seen Marie and her family across already. Her smile and the flash of her deep eyes brightened the new day for him, the nagging ache of Anne's betrayal eased considerably by such sights. He grinned at his infatuation, counting on it to not last, but enjoying the feeling anyway. She and Mr. Warren loved each other enough to marry and soon enough they'd remember that, leaving Sam feeling foolish in his interest for her.

The air warmed as the sun rose overhead. They neared Devil's Gate, reaching the landmark at noon. He gave the call to stop for both food and the chance for everyone to marvel at how the river cut through rock like a knife through meat.

Walking Scamp to the water for a drink, he saw Marie already there and greeted her. "Good day."

She straightened with a full bucket. "Good day to you, too. Are we climbing up there today? I'll bet the view is lovely."

"No, we are not."

"Such a shame. Still, you must be busy, and I can certainly climb up by myself."

"No, you can't, Mrs. Warren." At her raised eyebrows, he continued, "We lost a young boy the first trip I made through here when he and a few of his friends climbed up to look down. A gust of wind caught him by surprise, and he tumbled down into the river."

"How very sad! No wonder you have such strong feelings."

"It is, and I do, ma'am."

"Very well, just for you, I'll only climb when you allow. I'd prefer to be alive for a while longer, and you seem to know all the ways to die out here."

"I do, don't I?" He grinned at her smile. "Experience is a great teacher."

"It is, and it's taught me if I don't get back, I shall have a couple of cranky family members to answer to." She backed away before turning back to her wagon.

As Scamp pulled at grass, Sam watched her for a while. She turned the corner of a wagon, disappearing from his sight and breaking the spell. He shook his head. Even the briefest of moments both pleased his heart and left him wanting more time with her. He sighed at his foolishness. With any luck, familiarity would soon breed contempt and end this budding infatuation.

Better to think about the afternoon ahead. The sluggish flowing river caused by a lack of rain meant mosquitoes. It also promised a dusty few hours until camping for the night. At the signal, he got back on Scamp and headed to the front of the group. The road, though rocky, stayed reasonably flat for most of the afternoon. As they neared Split Rock, everyone traveled in a wide band across the plains. He noticed how some of the ladies wore handkerchiefs like the men, like a bandit's mask. He grinned at their appearance, these delicate flowers of womanhood dressed as if ready to rob a bank. Considering how often Marie went without a sunbonnet, she'd end up oddly colored if not careful.

He'd never noticed her looking into a mirror, so she might never discover the uneven tones. Unless Hester or Charles told her. He shook his head, thinking of how often they made suggestions to her within his earshot. The Warrens wasted no time in pointing out imperfections to her. His good humor evaporated. Even his bossy older brother didn't henpeck him so much.

Spread far and wide to avoid most of the dirty air, Sam and everyone else didn't have much chance to talk. He regretted not talking with anyone since he enjoyed almost everyone's company. Being alone gave him too much time to think. Not what he wanted to do when his thoughts drifted to Marie too often.

Glancing around, Sam saw he'd ridden ahead of everyone else. He squirmed, unhappy at how little he'd paid attention to his surroundings. The Sweetwater, a few yards in front of him, had changed its course recently it seemed, giving moisture to the lush grass growing in its wake. He stopped Scamp and doubled back to tell his men he'd found a camp for the night. The river went in and out, almost creating an island with the loop.

By late afternoon, everyone had caught up and parked their wagons in a semi-circle around the riverbank. The Granville men swam the stock to the island after blocking off the narrow entrance so they stayed on the grassy stretch of land. The water was thigh high, not enough to keep the cattle corralled, but the animals didn't know that for sure. Some ventured out to drink, but not far, and they always came back to shore for more grazing.

The sun eased to the horizon, a few fingers above mountains in the far distance. He'd seen a few pronghorn antelope today. Nothing worth hunting, mostly nursing mothers and their babies. After dismounting, he unsaddled Scamp and staked him out for grazing. Sam hopped into the wagon, searching out his fishing supplies.

"Mr. Granville?"

Sam turned to see Arnold at the back, peering in. "Yes? What can I do for you?"

The young man looked at Sam's hands. "Hey! You're going fishing. That's great!"

"Don't be too sure." Arnold stepped back as Sam hopped down. "I've not been and back with anything just yet."

"Sure. Do you want us to wait supper on you?"

"Yes, do that. I'm feeling optimistic." Grinning at Arnold's disbelief, Sam left, strolling upstream and away from the others. He followed the bank until unable to hear most of the noise behind him. Shadows darted in the water, and he cast, hoping one of the fish snagged the line. He let the lure be caught by the current and drift downstream. The occasional nibble tugged his line, but none strong enough for him to set the hook.

A movement west of him caught his eye. He looked up to see Charles and Hester rounding an outcrop of rock jutting from the foothill. They jostled each other as if playing a keep away game. He grinned, having seen older people act sillier than this before now. It seemed to him that siblings never outgrew their relationships with each other. He focused back on his fishing, determined to have trout for dinner tonight.

He didn't notice their sour expressions until they drew close to him. He nodded, saying in a quiet voice, "Hello, Mr., Miss Warren."

Giving him a stony glare, Hester replied, "Hello, Mr. Granville. Charles, I'm going to the wagon. I trust you'll take care of this."

Sam's eyebrows raised at her command, and also a little at the volume of her delivery. The woman had seemed carefree only minutes ago. Now, she was loud enough to scare away his dinner.

"Mr. Granville, Sam, how are you this evening?"

He winced at the man's booming voice. Half a mile away from camp for the quiet and this yahoo seemed determined to yell his fish out of the water. "I'm all right, sir, if a little intent on catching something today."

"I see." Charles put his hands in his pockets. "I'm also wondering what else you might have caught."

Sam suppressed an annoyed sigh. He'd hoped Warren would pick up on the quieter tone he used, but the man seemed oblivious. Giving him an irritated glance before recasting, he tried to imagine what he meant by caught. "Nothing else, I'm afraid."

"All right, I'm happy with that for now." Charles nodded, "You're a good man, Granville. A good man, indeed." With that, he strolled off, whistling.

He looked at him, frowning. First the loud chatter and then the noise? Disgruntled, Sam rolled up his fishing line and went further downstream. If Warren was worried about being found playing like a child, he needn't worry. Sam didn't give a plug nickel for who did what as long as there wasn't blood involved. Moving away from the duo improved his luck and his mood. Soon, he sauntered back with a few small trout on the line.

After dinner, Lucky's bugle sounded the first few notes of a favorite tune. Sam grinned and leaned back, giving a "later" signal to Uncle Joe. The older gentleman gathered their dishes in the bucket and put it to the side, for later washing up by the full moon. All three Warrens entered the firelight's circle, and Sam nodded in greeting. With a bit of fuss, Hester sat near Lefty and patted the ground beside her. Charles settled in just as Jenny and Ellen sat next to Lucky. Marie looked around as if unsure what to do before deciding on a place near Charles.

Hester leaned over to Charles and said in a loud whisper, "The music is nice, much like it has been every night he's played this song."

"Sshh," Marie hissed.

"I'd gladly buy him a songbook when we finish this trip," Hester continued. "Or maybe he can find a discarded one along the way. Anything to help his repertoire." She raised her eyebrows at Charles. "May we leave, now?"

Her brother shrugged. "Of course, go ahead."

Hitting his arm, she growled, "We, Chas, meaning you may walk me to our wagon."

"Oh, right." He stood. "Everyone, good night. Marie? Are you with us?"

She shook her head. "I'd prefer not to since this is just the first song. If you don't mind, I'd like to stay a little while longer. Please?"

"Very well. I trust you can walk yourself the short distance to our wagon?" He frowned at his sister's glare.

Marie gave him a reassuring smile, replying, "Yes, I'll manage."

Sam grinned at how Marie seemed demure until glancing over at him with an eye roll. Before he could enjoy their silent communication, Mr. Winslow staggered over to the fire.

The circle of people blocked him from falling into the flames as he hollered, "Ellen! Yer mamma needs yer sorry hide to come help with the babies."

Sam narrowed his eyes at the drunk. So far, the man had behaved well, though inebriated. No one in his family had shown bruises or flinched when he moved suddenly, so Sam considered him mostly harmless. Rumor was Mr. Winslow never got over his first wife, despite remarrying and starting another family. He watched as Ellen didn't respond except to follow her father back to their camp. Looking east at the rising moon, Sam also stood. "I suppose now is as good a time as any to bunk down for the night."

Lucky held out his arm for Jenny. "Miss, it would be my honor to walk you back to your wagon tonight."

She locked arms with him. "Thank you, Mr. Lucky, I'd like that."

Marie eased to her feet. She straightened her skirt a little before turning to leave.

"Ma'am? Would you like an escort back to your camp?"

She paused before saying, "I don't need help in going such a short way."

"I could use a stretch of the legs." Sam worked to act like her answer didn't matter.

Marie smiled at him, her face a little flushed in the waning firelight. "By all means, do accompany me. I'd hate to think of you with nothing to do."

He fell in step with her, unsure if he should offer his arm to hold. Giving her a side glance, Sam decided against it. Wanting to make her laugh, he said, "It takes a tough old gal to walk herself home at night, you know."

"You're a brave man to use the word old in front of a 'gal.' But then, it takes a man with a little salt, vinegar, and a lot of bravery to lead greenhorns across a country that could kill them."

He was pleased she thought of him as such. "Thank you, ma'am, one might say it takes a courageous sort of woman to leave her home for rough country."

Shaking her head in disagreement, Marie stated in a quiet voice, "I'm not courageous at all. I've hated every minute. Each day has been an ordeal, and I'm tired of the constant freezing temperatures. Under the blankets at night is the only time I'm comfortable. Even then I'm asleep and can't enjoy the warmth. If I were a man, I'd be on my way back east or anywhere else that isn't here."

Charles turned the corner, and Sam felt Marie startle when her husband yelled, "No, you sure as hell wouldn't, young lady. Your family is gone, and my family doesn't want you burdening them, so forget you're going anywhere without me."

"And Hester." Marie said through clenched teeth, "We mustn't ever forget about her."

"Yes, and Hester. You should thank her every day for putting up with you." Turning his attention to Sam, he said, "Sir, we need to talk about how often you catch me by surprise, especially after today."

CHAPTER 4

Marie went for water with Hester first thing in the morning. She glanced at her sister-in-law. "I appreciate you helping me with this." After receiving a scornful glare, Marie renewed her resolve to stay silent. She also reiterated her commitment to moving the woman into a house of her own.

When seeing Samuel and his men with their horses at the creek's edge, Hester hurried over to them. "Why, Mr. Granville! How are you?"

Ignoring her, he continued saying to the others, "It's a six-mile round trip. There's no need to overload the horses but get as much as you can and get back here. I'll be along in a little bit." Finished, he addressed them, "Hello, ladies. How are you?"

Hester stepped in front of Sam, saying, "I'm all right, of course. With such excellent leadership on this journey, how could a girl be anything but wonderful?"

The woman's simpering both amused and nauseated Marie. To keep from groaning outright, she went up and petted Samuel's horse. After a while, she paused, lowering her hand. The animal took a step forward and nudged her for more. She chuckled and gave a sideways glance toward Samuel. He watched her as Hester continued to talk.

Feeling a blush steal over her face, Marie asked the first thing that came to mind, "Should we be gathering wood or buffalo chips today?"

"Such a foolish question, isn't it, Mr. Granville?" Hester snickered. "She is such a goose, never paying attention to her surroundings."

He turned to Marie and grinned. "Wood, since there's a lot of cedar growing on the bluffs."

Hester's meanness tied Marie's tongue for a moment. Struggling to ignore her irritation at her sister in law, she gave a little laugh. "Of course, we can use wood. I've been so accustomed to chips that I haven't considered anything else."

He leaned against his horse, seeming content to stand and talk for a while. "We'll need both types of fuel, and any more we can get. The chips are going to become scarcer as we go on, and the wood won't be plentiful after we're another two weeks along."

The lack of fuel disturbed her, as did the lack of fresh meat later down the trail. Hester's sour face, however, she found quite enjoyable. She said to the other woman, "I'm certain we're boring you, Hessy. Go on and I'll catch up very shortly." When Hester gave an eye roll and left, Marie turned back to Sam. "I liked the buffalo we had a few days ago. Do you prefer it to beef?"

"I do like buffalo, but have to admit I prefer beef any day. My family raises the best cattle. After too much bison meat, I get homesick." He winked at her. "Ask me again in a couple of months when there's been only deer and very little of that. You'll get a different answer."

"I can imagine!" She returned his smile. His clear blue eyes seemed to mirror the sky and see into her thoughts. In an instant, she knew why he seemed so attractive. The man focused on her in a conversation instead of through her. The attention intoxicated her, freezing her mind. Not the best thing when she needed to think up questions faster than he answered them. Marie tried to be casual. "Is it as beautiful there as people and Ellen's guidebook say?"

He nodded. "More than anyone can describe, though people living there don't want to tell anyone else."

"They want it all to themselves, I suspect," she said.

Sam stared into her eyes. "Yes, they do."

The unexpected intensity in his expression surprised her. Somehow, Marie sensed he didn't mean the Territory. Nervous at what he might mean, she smoothed her skirt. "I can see why some might be selfish and not want to share."

He returned her grin. "How about I loan you my favorite guidebook, and you can decide for yourself. I'll drop by your camp this evening." A whistle caught his attention. "Excuse me, I need to help my men."

The moment evaporated and Marie felt like she'd missed a subtle hint from him. "I'll take good care of your book."

"I have no doubt." He tipped his hat and rode away, following the hired hands.

Marie put her hands on her hips, wondering if their conversation was really about Oregon. Ellen and Jenny tended to think everything an unclaimed man said had more than one meaning. She thought the girls silly. After Samuel's statement about outsiders, however, maybe they had a valid point. She very much hoped so, anyway. Marie hurried to catch up to her sister in law, already halfway back to camp.

When she fell into step beside her, Hester said, "That man is a complete libertine. Did you see that wink? Well! He apparently feels safe doing such a thing to a married woman." Hands on hips, she added, "If he'd winked at a single lady like me, there might have been trouble."

After years of listening to Hester, she knew to not laugh outright. Marie instead struggled for an even tone before saying, "I'm sure he'd agree."

Narrowing her beady eyes, she asked, "Are you being sarcastic with me, young lady?"

Marie smiled. "Oh no, I'm certain you're right. You're single, and he's probably not to be trusted around single ladies." She kept to herself how she considered the two facts not related.

Hester seemed somewhat mollified. "I suppose. It sounds to me like his family is wealthy if they eat beef every day."

"I'm sure. That and the way he dresses would indicate as much." A fire burned in the pit at their camp. Marie made a mental note to thank Charles later.

Hester said, "A woman would be wise to set her cap for Mr. Granville." Her eyes narrowed as if considering the idea.

Turning a laugh into a cough, she asked the older woman, "Do you mean to do just that?"

She gave her a little sneaky smile. "Someone should."

Getting the breakfast pan, Marie stepped around her sister in law. "No doubt a lot of available girls have him in mind as a husband."

"Maybe even a few married ladies, do you think?" Hester settled in, sitting next to the campfire. "I'm sure there are plenty of wives wanting a wealthier husband."

"I never considered that. A few widows might, but those already married?" Marie shook her head. "Those women might like him, but are wrong to consider Mr. Granville as a choice."

Poking at the fire, Hester said, "I suppose so." She pouted while the food cooked, brightening only when seeing her brother.

While eating breakfast, Hester and Charles talked about Mr. Granville, how the sick were too dependent on others, and if cedar smelled better than pine when burned. While they barely spoke to her, Marie liked how they talked with each other in English versus their own language. French would have been better she thought, then corrected herself. She would be melancholy if anyone addressed her with her father's language.

She stood and brushed biscuit crumbs from her skirt. Dishes went into the wash pail. She watched, waiting for a break in the twins' conversation. Nature called her in a way Marie couldn't ignore as she stood there. Unable to wait any longer, she left without excusing herself and walked outside the wagon circle. Her sunbonnet was back at camp, and Marie wished she'd worn it now. Hearing hoofbeats drawing near, she kept her gaze on the clump of scrub brush ahead.

"Good morning, Mrs. Warren!"

Marie halted, her eyes squeezed shut for a moment from irritation. She loved Sam, truly she did, but not right now. Taking a breath, she smiled up at him. "Good morning, Mr. Granville, it's a pleasure to see you."

"Why thank you, ma'am. The sight of you always brightens my day as well."

Seeing him begin to dismount, she panicked. "Oh no, don't get down on my account. I'm off to take care of things, and I know how busy you must be, so good morning to you, sir."

He seemed puzzled, then grinned after catching on to what sort of things she needed doing. "I'm never too busy to chat with a lovely woman, Mrs. Warren."

If not so close to a critical and embarrassing moment, she'd have laughed at the mischievous glint in his eyes. "Yes, you are, and so am I." Marie took a couple of steps toward the shrubbery as Sam laughed.

"Very well, I'll be on my way." He tipped his hat while giving her a cheeky grin. "Ma'am."

She waved as he turned to leave and then all but raced to privacy. Finished, she walked back feeling much better and not so afraid of dust making her sneeze. As Marie approached the camp, she saw Hester walking up from the river with the wash pail in hand.

Catching sight of Marie, Hester glared at her. "You timed that just right."

"I did?" Marie fell in step beside the woman.

"Don't give me that. You always wander off during chores and leave me to do everything."

"No, I don't." Marie put her hands on her hips. "In fact, it's often just the opposite."

Charles walked up to them. "What is it now?"

"It's her." Pointing at Marie, Hester said, "She's always running off and getting out of doing anything useful. I thought you had a talk with her about that."

He held his sister by the shoulders in a comforting way, "I did."

Hester pulled away from him, pouting like a child. "Then why, when dishes needed doing and the livestock cared for, was she over there flirting with Sam?"

The accusation horrified Marie. "I was not!"

"I saw you, and you were," she hissed.

"You saw nothing of the kind!" Marie stared at first one sibling then the other. "She's not telling the truth."

Charles stared at her, scowling. In a growl, he asked, "Are you saying Hessy is a liar?"

His tone frightened her in its quiet ferocity. She stammered, "No, I mean Sam, Mr. Granville, stopped to say hello."

"Ha!" Wrinkling her nose, Hester added, "See? She was indeed flirting."

"It's not like that." These assertions angered Marie. "She's adding too much to the truth and is dead wrong about any flirting this morning. In fact, you should know how she…"

"Enough," Charles interrupted. "No more fighting. I'm tired of you always starting arguments with Hessy, Marie." He began walking to the front of the wagon, adding, "You're so tiresome some days. Very well, wander off and spend the day elsewhere."

"What?" Hester snorted. "How is that different from any other day so far and what's keeping her from sparking Granville?"

"Hessy, enough. We both know her better than that." He said to Marie, "We'll see you this evening and not until then." The siblings sat on the seat as Charles snapped the reins.

She watched as they rolled away from her. Her tongue hurt from biting back retorts to the accusations hurled at her. Marie shook her head, unsure of how she'd lost such an argument. After so many other fights between Missouri and here, Marie knew better than to defend herself. The odds were always two against one. She knew she pouted but couldn't help herself. At least Charles trusted her more than Hester did.

Stay away until this evening, though? His command was harsher than usual. Most times when she'd angered him, he didn't want to see her for half a day. During the noon meal, she'd have to find a way to avoid the Warrens without attracting attention. Anger and shame settled down hard in her stomach as she began walking. Unwilling to inflict her bad mood on anyone else, she stayed at a distance from Jenny, Ellen, and the other ladies. She took deep, calming breaths, focusing on the terrain instead of her emotions.

The crisp morning gave way to a pleasant afternoon. They stopped for the noon meal at the daytime shadow's shortest point and most people gravitated to their wagons to eat. Marie kicked at a young sagebrush, wondering if she should chance meeting up with the Warrens. The last time she'd done so after being asked to leave, Charles had been furious. Looking around, her sunbonnet blocked most of her vision so she let it fall behind her. Everyone seemed busy caring for themselves or the livestock. Marie decided to get a drink at the river. Better to do that than stand here looking foolish, she decided, and headed north.

At the river's edge, the soupy soil pulled at her shoes when she neared the water. She frowned at the thick goop covering the soles of her shoes, looking along the bank for drier ground. Disgusted, she hiked up her dress a little and walked carefully to the water. She stifled a yelp at the icy cold and scooted the soles along the bottom of the river to clean them. Marie walked upstream, looking for a rock or sand to stand on until her feet dried. She held the shoes away from her dress. No sense in letting mud drip all over one of her best dresses. An underwater stone caught her toe. She stumbled, clinging to the shoes but not her hem. Marie barely managed to recover in time to prevent a headlong dive into the water.

"Careful!"

She turned to see Sam dismount and walk up to the bank's edge. "I am!" she snapped. Cold wet on her torso distracted her. She looked at the mud smeared there and sighed. "Although, I suppose falling in here would be beneficial. Seems I could use a good scrubbing."

He grinned, leading Scamp for a drink. "We may have to make time for all of us to do just that."

"I don't suppose there's any privacy with this?" She indicated the river with a wave of her free hand. "The mountains are too distant to hide behind, the brush too short, and as for trees? I've seen very few close by."

He laughed, "You've summed it up quite well. I'm sure we can devise some solution. Especially since the conditions will worsen before they improve."

Pausing her mud scrubbing, she stared up at him. "Worsen? My goodness, Sam, how much worse will they be?"

"Ellen hasn't read that part and told you, yet?" He shook his head. "Never mind, I have my guidebook here." Retrieving the small book, Sam opened it to a little after the middle. "You'll want to start around here since you know everything before this page." He grinned at her still standing in the river. "After you're on dry land, of course."

"I agree." She watched as he thumbed through the pages. He needed a trim, his black hair unruly under his hat. His shirt, while still clean, didn't have the same starched appearance as usual. Sam's pants fit him well, too. The angle he stood in relation to her and Scamp showed off his hamstrings very well. She rubbed the shoe's soles together, lost in thought while looking at him.

He glanced up at her from the book and grinned. "Mrs. Warren? Are you well?"

"Yes." She scooped up her wet skirt in one hand and made her way to the riverbank. "I was wondering what could be worse than poisoned water and horrible mosquitoes."

"Longer stretches without water and bigger mosquitoes." He held out his hand. "Let me have your shoes, then I'll help you out of there." She complied, and as he pulled her from the river, added, "We'll have some steep inclines and declines to cross."

She took his outstretched hand for balance and held tight while she put on her shoes. "There's no way around them?"

"No, no way out but through." Lucky's bugle caught his attention for a moment. "Noontime is over, and I'd suggest you change into dry shoes if you have them."

"I will, Mr. Granville." She smiled as he handed her the guidebook. "Thank you for this as well. I'll read it as soon as possible and get it back to you."

"No rush." He mounted Scamp and tipped his hat. "I know it by heart. Good afternoon, Mrs. Warren."

Marie watched him ride away, saddened at his absence. She slipped the book into a pocket in her skirt, not realizing how alone she'd felt until talking with him. The line of wagons approached them, dust billowing out from behind. Did she want to stop Charles for dry shoes? She shook her head. Better to wait until later when it was his idea to pause. Unsure of which way to go, she waited until the group passed her before joining them. Marie walked upwind so she'd not need a bandana.

The pleasant afternoon lasted until she saw a line of Indians on horseback lining the ridge north of the river. Familiarity with savages left her wary, not fearful. The wagons crossed the shallow and wide river, going toward the onlookers. Marie held up her skirt as she followed. The cool water eased the sting of new blisters on her feet. She kept a grip on Sam's book through the pocket's fabric, careful to not slip and drop it into the swift current. Once on the other side, she saw the Indians continued to watch their progress. She shuddered. Maybe the guidebook held advice on avoiding a scalping.

Scrub brush and the rocky soil kept interrupting her reading as she walked. Exasperated, Marie gave up and watched as a trio of wagons approached from the west. They inched closer with each step. A single ox pulled each cart, making her frown. Didn't everyone need at least two if not four animals? She tried to not stare at the families but couldn't help herself. The few older people led the way with the children trailing behind them after the dust settled. Some of the youngest glanced at her as they walked by, but the others watched their feet. Unlike the ones in the Granville group, these children seemed lifeless and somber.

The sight of such beaten people tore at her heart. Marie searched for Sam or one of his men. Arnold intercepted the first eastern traveler. She watched as they talked for a short while. The hired hand rode to the southern end of the Granville party. How far the wagons had left her behind surprised Marie. She wanted to catch up to them, yet, she also wanted to see what Sam and Arnold would do now that they approached the sad little group.

She couldn't tear herself away from the drama. Sam talked with the two men and a woman, the children clustered around the adults. Both he and Arnold dismounted and looked in the wagons. She saw how Sam shook his head and knew their situation was dire. When he gestured to the westbound group, she figured he wanted them to join them. The yes nods and no shakes told her even at this distance they'd continue east.

Sam and Arnold went to their horses. Though his employee mounted, Sam stayed on foot and pulled his saddle bag from Scamp's back. He handed it to the oldest man, who declined to take it. Marie knew without hearing what Sam wanted when he gestured to the motley crew of youngsters. Seeming defeated, the man took the offered bags and shook Sam's hand. The second man shook his hand also, and the woman hugged him. He then sat astride his horse, tipped his hat to them in farewell, and began riding west. Marie smiled as he rode closer.

He frowned at her, the sternness not reaching his eyes. "What are you doing out here alone, young lady?"

She laughed. "I've not been alone for long."

"Are you sure?" He indicated the wagons in the distance. "They're up there a ways."

Her stomach tensed seeing just how far they'd gone ahead. With optimism she didn't feel, Marie said, "I'll catch up, they're bound to stop sometime before dinner."

"Come on." Sam held his hand out to her. "Hop up here and let me get you back to your family."

When Marie hesitated, he made a hurry up motion with his hand. She glanced again at the wagon train, now small against the vast horizon. They'd gone fast enough to give her no choice now. She put her right foot in the stirrup he vacated and, with a jump, sat sidesaddle behind him. The breath whooshed out of her at the close contact of her chest and his back. She'd not realized how cold she was until so close to him and his body heat. Marie wanted to lean into his back and absorb his warmth but didn't dare. She held the back of the saddle for support. Leaning a little bit away from Sam for propriety's sake, she still caught his clean leather smell and felt small next to him. "I assume your saddlebags had provisions?"

"Some, but not enough. I had money in there and a couple of meals for one person."

"Oh." She didn't know what to say, knowing most of the eastbound group would still sleep hungry tonight.

He took off his hat and ran a hand through his hair. "I know it's not enough. As soon as we find your place, I'm getting Uncle Joe to help me deliver them enough food to reach Independence Rock. They can buy or trade there for more, if necessary."

"Can I help?"

He turned back to face her. His examination of her expression seemed like a caress. "Thank you, but no. We have extra provisions for this."

"We can always spare food for hungry children, Sam. Do let me know if we can help."

"I will." Sam leaned toward her just a little before facing front. "You're a good woman, Mrs. Warren."

Her cheeks burned from the compliment. "Thank you, Mr. Granville." Her head felt full of cotton, and she enjoyed how they rode in silence until reaching the others. Quiet time spent with him lacked the undercurrent of disapproval that silence with Charles had.

She glanced ahead, surprised to see the Warrens' wagon in front of them. Her riding with Sam could make Hester's accusations more credible. When adding in Charles' order to stay away until dinner, she tapped Sam's shoulder. "Don't drop me off here." She scanned the landscape for her friends. "Maybe with Ellen and Jenny, if they're..."

"Dearest!" Charles walked up to them. "We've been missing you today."

At first hesitant, Marie let him help her down instead of Sam. "Oh? I've been making myself scarce as you'd asked this morning." Her feet touched the ground, sore from wet shoes rubbing in the wrong places. "Surely you've enjoyed the quiet my absence provided you and Hester."

"Don't be difficult. You're here now, and that's all that matters." Charles turned to Sam. "Thank you for retrieving her, Samuel. Hessy has often suggested putting my wife on a rope to keep her safe."

"Hessy?" Sam asked, his voice sharp. "Who is she to suggest such treatment of Mrs. Warren?"

Disliking the anger on his face, Marie wanted to explain. "He means his sister, Mr. Granville. It's a childhood pet name."

"Don't speak for me!" Charles sneered at her. "You can barely speak for yourself."

Angered, Marie swallowed a retort, instead saying, "Gentlemen, if you'll excuse me. I have chores to do." She turned, walking to the wagon on uncooperative legs. Her feet hurt, and mortification drove her every step. Marie could almost feel their eyes watching her. She picked her way around the sagebrush to join the others as they rolled on toward the horizon. She looked back to see where her husband was and saw he walked alone a short distance behind her.

In what felt like days later, the call to camp for the night sounded through the group. Marie sighed in relief. No one had stopped since lunch. Having missed the noon meal, her stomach had kept up a constant growl for the past couple of hours. Caring for the animals and cooking couldn't happen soon enough. She searched the usual spots in their wagon for anything left over from prior meals. Hearing her sister in law's sigh, she paused. "Is something wrong, Hester?"

"Nothing more than usual. Chas wanted me to tell you we're doing chores, and you're to fix supper tonight."

"I see." Marie turned back to the wagon's contents and saw no spare firewood. Expected, since she'd not gathered any at noon, having relied upon them to do so. "Very well, I'll get started."

Hester left after giving a sneering grin, and Marie sighed. Frustration and anger would solve nothing. She leaned against the wooden wheel, not remembering passing any firewood. The only chips for burning today had been dropped by their own cattle. She shuddered at the thought of even trying to pick up one. Sagebrush, she decided while walking away from the riverbed to find the driest and thickest to burn.

The arid land made finding dead brush quick and easy. Marie soon had a fire burning, augmented by discarded wood found down from the main trail. Seeing the empty water pail, she made a quick trip to the river and greeted others in passing as they went about their own chores. Not finding Ellen, she spotted Jenny walking with Lucky. She smiled, thinking of her own courtship with Charles. He'd been younger and more agreeable back then, much like Sam is now. The mean thought bothered her conscience. The arduous trip west turned even saints into sinners. Charles had every right to be unhappy at times, they all did. Given enough time, even the charming Sam would turn into a Charles someday.

Dinner cooked on the fire, its aroma made her stomach hurt with hunger. Shadows stole over everything except the campfire as the day ended. Marie ate without Charles and Hester, unwilling to wait until the food burned to the bottom of the pan. She poured a little water into the cook pot, hoping the moisture improved the taste. Her dirty plate and fork went into the pail, and she began laying out the bedding for sleep.

"Good evening, darling." Her husband walked up to her, his sister trailing behind him. "Smells wonderful."

"Have you eaten, yet?" she asked.

Hester brushed past Marie and said, "Of course not, we've been busy with the animals." After taking a spoon, she began loading up her plate.

Charles gave her a weak smile and began dishing his own food. "I'm sorry we're so late to dinner."

Marie frowned when seeing the smirk Hester flashed her brother. She ignored her irritation. "It's fine. I assume the food is still good?"

"Very, thank you. You're actually getting better at this."

Surprised at the compliment, she glanced up at him and smiled. "I'm glad you enjoy it."

She didn't watch as the two ate. They talked using their twin language so Marie couldn't eavesdrop if she'd wanted to do so. She felt for and retrieved Sam's guidebook. Reading about the landmarks already passed was fun. She paused when learning about Prospect Hill. Jimmy had been buried there, poor boy. Her heart hurt for him. She stared at the page without seeing, wanting to remember all the games they'd played. Hester had called her a child back then, and Marie had tried to ignore what the crabby woman said. Having fun with the children made the boring and scary parts bearable. Her eyes watered a little, and she blinked back the tears over Jimmy's death.

Hester dropping their plates into the metal pail startled Marie. The sour-faced woman said, "I'll wash these. I'd prefer to not wait until morning like you do."

As she left, Charles asked Marie, "What's that you're reading? I don't remember seeing that book before now."

"It's Mr. Granville's guidebook. He's loaned it to me for a short while." She ran her fingers over the leather cover. The gold embossed letters retained their indentions, if not their shine.

"I'm not sure how I feel about our leader not having his guidebook."

She smiled away her irritation at being spoken to like his child. "I won't keep it long. Since we've traveled halfway, the first part was an easy read."

"Just make sure you get it back to him unharmed."

"I will." Staring at the page, she struggled to concentrate on the words. Weariness set in, and she decided to stop reading for the night. Instead, she opened the front cover and saw his full name suffixed by "Esquire." Had she known he was a lawyer?

Marie looked up into the fire, reviewing conversations with Sam in her mind. She didn't remember him ever saying so, though he might have. Her heart beat a little faster at the thought of him being so educated. Adding intelligence to charisma, handsomeness, and a strong body made the man nearly irresistible. She sighed. The brief moment they'd contacted while on horseback still gave her goose bumps. With a grin, she imagined a kick in the right spot on Scamp might have goaded the horse into a trot. She'd have had no choice but to squeeze Sam around the waist. A shudder traveled her from head to toe. Marie closed her eyes, unwilling to let them betray the sudden rush of desire filling her.

"If you're tired, go to bed already."

Hester's strident tone acted like a splash of ice water. Marie smiled, grateful for the distraction. "That's an excellent idea." She slipped off her shoes, nestled between the mattress and blanket, and slipped the guidebook under her pillow.

Morning came far too early and left just as soon. The twins seemed in better moods than usual, Hester doing chores on her own initiative. The woman's help gave Marie more time to spend with her friends. Ellen's father's health had improved, reducing her responsibilities. For the next two days, rocky hills added to the livestock's misery. Some cattle grew lame from the jagged stones, their hooves cracking. Abandoned animals lay scattered along the trail where they died, one every couple of miles or so. She couldn't get used to the smell and gave each carcass a wide berth.

They didn't reach passable grazing fields until late the second day. No one brought surplus cattle and felt desperate to keep alive every one they owned. The high bluffs along Sweetwater caused them to cross the river twice, losing a cow or two each time. From a distance, she watched a heated exchange between one of the men with the most animals and Sam. The halt order went around the group soon afterward.

Marie unhitched the oxen before Charles could. He nodded when seeing her bringing the animals to the water's edge. "Thank you," he said. "I'll let you take them for water and grazing while I build the fire for dinner."

She nodded at him as he went past her toward the back of the wagon. Charles' even temper felt like a small reward to Marie. Considering all the barren earth they'd passed in the morning, she enjoyed leading the hungry animals to a patch of good grass. She noticed Sam driving a few cattle toward her. He'd been on her mind far too much since she rode with him on his horse. Unsure whether she wanted to avoid him or not, Marie slowed her pace to a near stop while trying to decide. She snuck a peek over her left shoulder, wondering how close he was. When nudged in the back by the animals' noses, she chuckled and continued taking them for food and drink. By focusing on the distant hills, she could keep her back to Sam and avoid conversation.

"Mrs. Warren?"

She startled with a yelp, surprised at Sam's voice to her right. "Yes, Mr. Granville? What may I do for you?"

"For me?" His eyebrows raised. "Nothing at the moment. I just wanted to point out the snow on the peaks over there."

"Snow this time of year? I thought it were some sort of gypsum or maybe the source of all the alkali in the area." Putting her hands on her hips, she examined his face while asking, "Are you sure it's snow? I'd hate to tell Hester and have her think I'm an idiot again."

Sam's smile faded into a frown. "No, it truly is. I've been there and back on other trips. I'll tell her so myself."

His defense of her warmed Marie more than any shawl she wore. "If we were home right now, I'd send someone over to get some for a mint julep or two."

"I'd go if you had the fixings." He dismounted.

"If I did, I'd certainly let you." She smiled, trying to ignore how his pants fit him so well. "I've never seen snow up close."

"Honestly? I can't imagine."

From his expression, Marie thought he seemed worried and wanted to reassure him. "I've seen frost and a few flakes, but not enough to make a snowball. I've always imagined them to be like shaved ice."

"They're something similar, maybe softer."

"I suppose that's good if you're in a snowball fight."

"It is since my brother has a vicious arm." He took a step

closer. "If we had more time, I'd ride up and get you your own bit of snow to see up close."

Sam seemed boyish all of a sudden, and she enjoyed the expression on his face. "It's very kind of you to offer." They stood in silence for a moment. She felt self-conscious standing there alone with him among the animals. "I've read a lot of the book you loaned me. There'll be plenty for me to throw at you in a few weeks."

Grinning, Sam swung up onto his horse. "Ma'am, you have no idea what sort of expert you're challenging." Uncle Joe rode up to him, asking about the watch schedule.

She tried to not listen in as they talked. Instead, she led the oxen away slowly to not attract attention. Marie looked at the white-topped mountains. Even if impractical, she liked how he'd offered to show her real snow. Glancing at him, she saw him looking at her while Uncle Joe talked. Shy, she went back to tending the oxen. By the time she led them to the river for a drink, Marie had looked back to find Sam gone. The other man watched the cattle in his place.

It was just as well. If he'd stay any longer, she'd have been tempted to flirt even more. When out of eyesight, Marie could think clearly. Snowball fights indeed. Between playing games with the children and now getting into hijinks with Sam, she found it difficult to be a real lady.

She shivered while bringing the oxen back to camp. The air was turning cooler with every hour. Charles walked past her with the water bucket, giving her a nod as he did so. They'd barely talked in the previous two days, something she thought for the best. Less chatter meant less arguing. With a smile and a wave to Uncle Joe, she finished staking out the animals and walked back to cook dinner.

A campfire burned with a pot of food sitting in the middle. She stirred the mix and soon after the beans and salt pork simmered in the pan. She heard someone rustle behind her and said, "You're back so soon dearest?"

"I tried to hurry, sweetheart," a man's voice answered jokingly behind her.

She stood and whirled around to see Sam behind her. "Oh! Hello." Marie's face burned with embarrassment, while her stomach did flip flops of excitement.

"Hello to you, too."

Seeing his smile reminded her of how much she'd missed him in the past couple of days. "I mistook you for Charles. He's supposed to be bringing back water soon, I think."

He shrugged. "One of the boys fetched up our water, or I'd be out there, too." Sam kicked at a rock before saying, "It seems I've broken a promise to you, and I'm not sure how to fix it."

She tried to remember such a thing and shook her head. "No promise that I can recall..."

"I wondered how you could forget after passing all those cactus fields."

"Goodness, Sam," she said in a quiet voice. "You're busy enough without my pestering you for a treat."

"It's a treat for me as well. I'll make a point to fry some up soon and have you over to try it." He nodded toward the west. "The official reason of why I stopped by is just beyond the mountain range and headed this way. My bet is on rain, but as cool as the air is today, I can't rule out flurries."

"We're to have snow here in camp?" She liked the idea but not the reality. "I suppose we might as well have the beauty since we're suffering the cold."

He smiled at her. "You'll want to keep handy any extra blankets. I can't have you freezing to death out here."

"Hey, Granville, what's going on here?"

Sam turned to Charles, "Hello. I'm letting everyone know about possible snow tonight."

"Snow?" He barked a laugh, "Ridiculous! It's July, young man, and we're hardly in the Arctic."

"Nevertheless, snow is possible, so humor me and be prepared."

Giving him a withering look, Charles said, "Very well."

She had noticed a flash of irritation cross Sam's face before he squelched it. Despite his effort, the tension between the two men bothered Marie. She knew her husband hated being bossed around by anyone and could almost feel his resentment vibrating from him. "I'll get the blankets, just in case."

"Mrs. Warren, please excuse me, duty calls," Sam said as he turned and left.

Once certain he was out of earshot of them, Charles said, "Humor him my ass."

Did her ears deceive her? Marie strove to keep her voice low. "Pardon?"

"You heard me." He stopped watching Sam walk away to peer at her. "All the doomsday muck that man shovels on us on a daily basis, I get tired of listening to it."

Wanting to know what mental bee was stinging him, Marie ventured, "He does seem to be overly cautious."

"You don't know the half of it." He settled in by the fire, grabbing a plate to fill. "Be careful here, watch out there, make sure everywhere. Between him and Hester parroting him to me, I'm going mad."

Marie wasn't surprised her sister in law hung on Sam's every word. But to ease her husband's mood she said, "Hester does that often?"

"Yes, and I'm sick to death of it," he said in between bites.

Working on filling her own plate, she asked, "Come to think of it, where is she?"

"She'll be along any minute." Charles went back to eating.

Hester walked up to them, smiling. "Am I your 'she,' Chas?"

He looked up at her, then to his empty plate. "Yes, you're the she soon to arrive, just as I leave."

"Oh, don't be a fuss. I just wanted to freshen up a little before the air turned colder." She warmed her hands at the fire. "Mr. Granville said we might get snow tonight and will need more blankets than usual."

Marie glanced at her husband and saw his irritated expression. She grinned at him when he looked at her. "He did?" she asked, hoping Charles saw how right he'd been about his sister.

"I just said he did." She paused in dishing up her food to say to him, "Did you have to marry the stupidest woman in Louisiana?"

Trying to keep calm, Marie said, "Your inability to speak clearly is not my fault." She turned to Charles. "I might have been having some fun at her expense, but I'm in no way stupid, and she needs to apologize to me."

"Don't drag me into this." He stood tossing his dishes into the pail. "Both of you have nothing new to say about anything. Hester, you wash up. Marie, get those blankets all of you must have. I'm finding somewhere else to be this evening."

CHAPTER 5

Ice Slough gave them a reason to take a midmorning break. Sam steered them around the area as best he and his men could. Prior settlers digging in the peat-like grasses had left holes in the surface. When seeing Arnold, he hollered, "See that the Winslows stay clear of here. The old man tends to forget where he is."

The younger man tipped his hat and rode out to complete his orders. Ellen's father had a bad habit of ignoring the road ahead. Sam didn't feel like putting down an animal today due to the man's carelessness. He helped dig ice from under the matted grasses. His favorite part was where everyone marveled at the clear blocks chopped out from the earth. He grinned at the children watching with big eyes. They'd all enjoy Soda Springs even more. Wanting to help his hands, Sam ambled over to his own wagon at the edge of the slough.

As he dismounted, Lucky walked up to him. "Hey, boss, just in time. We ain't started working yet."

"Too bad, I was hoping to miss all the fun." He watched as Uncle Joe and Arnold pulled back the covering. Lucky ran off to help Lefty with the shovels. "We'll need a couple of small barrels, too, men."

"I'll get them," Uncle Joe volunteered.

Sam nodded and soon they all dug up ice and layered it with the pulled peat. With both barrels full, it took two men to put them in the wagon. A quick check of the other families showed some needed help. He and the boys helped so they could all start moving again.

Rolling alongside the river as it twisted and turned held annoying consequences. Sam's patience ebbed low as the day wore on. Wagon drivers who ignored his warnings about the sand soon found themselves creeping along. The soil's pull wore out oxen already undernourished and overworked. The sun overhead worsened his mood as he gave the order to halt. Both the sun and his hunger told him it was midday. He led Scamp to the river for a drink. While the animal slurped up the water, he dug around in his saddlebag for some jerky and cornbread.

As he chewed, Sam looked at the ground for curiosity's sake. Rain, or more likely a dusting of snow must have dampened the earth in the past few days. Wildflowers bloomed in among the grasses. He recognized the blue flowers, but not the white or yellow ones. Kneeling, Sam picked an orange colored flower. This one he'd seen before now. The leaves were thick, almost like a cactus with no spines.

"Hello, Mr. Granville," Hester called out, walking towards him with a bouquet in her hands. She had them in a jar too small for all the stems.

He looked down at his single bloom, then back at her. "You've been a busy lady, ma'am."

"Oh, these?" She lifted them to her nose and breathed in deep. "My brother found these while walking the oxen and picked them for me. Aren't they lovely? He's so thoughtful."

Sam put a smile on his face. If this is what Warren gave his sister, what must he have given Marie? A stab of jealousy hit his chest. Feelings he had no right to feel. "Quite lovely, Miss Warren."

"Hester? You forgot the bucket." Marie held up the pail for her.

"No, I didn't. I couldn't carry both my flowers and that." She smiled. "You don't mind getting the water for us, do you? Thank you, sweetie!"

Triumph rang in the older woman's voice, and Sam looked to Scamp as the animal pulled at the grasses. Hearing the sounds of Marie stepping through the tall grasses lining the river, he glanced over at her as she filled their bucket. He wanted to say anything to start a conversation with her but wasn't sure what. Off the top of his head, Sam said, "I'm betting your bouquet is bigger than Hester's."

"How much would you bet?" She turned to him, her expression sly. "Do you have a dollar amount in mind?"

"No, just a lot. The man probably had to make two trips for all your flowers." His heart felt odd, but he continued, "Is that what your water is for?

"Oh no, not at all. This is for us to drink." She shrugged. "Hester got flowers, but I've not received any from Charles just yet. He hasn't had the chance, I'm sure."

"I'm sure he will make time later."

89

"Maybe, er, probably." She twisted grass blades in one hand. "He knows Hester likes those sorts of things."

"You don't?"

"I do, but honestly, flowers die anyway. It's all so sad and just as well if he forgets to pick any for me." She glanced up from the blades at him, smiled, then went back to braiding the greenery. "I don't need flowers."

He stared at her, examining her face. She sounded to him as if she wanted to believe her own words. Marie's eyes betrayed her sadness. "Once you pick them, yes, they die. Perhaps when you reach your home in Oregon, he'll plant you a flower garden."

Marie laughed. "You do tend to see the good side of things, don't you?" Pink tinged her cheeks. "I find that to be one of your best traits."

"One of? Why, thank you, ma'am."

"You're welcome." She abandoned her nervous playing with the grass. "They're expecting a drink, so excuse me."

He tipped his hat in response. As she walked away, he retrieved a cup from his saddlebag. Sam dipped up some water and drank, his mind still on her. She'd not fooled him. Marie liked getting flowers, even if they were temporary. He led Scamp away from the river, then paused. He couldn't give her the bouquet she deserved outright. But, he could give every woman in their group a flower or two. Grinning, Sam took out his little pocket knife and began cutting the prettiest flowers he saw.

His horse followed, ambling behind until Sam held more than enough for every woman and man. He laughed, thinking of Lucky's face at getting flowers from him. Maybe not every man, he thought. Sam swung up on Scamp without dropping the bouquet. He galloped at a slow pace until reaching the front of the wagon train. Once there, he worked his way across and back. Each girl and woman received a flower or two. Sam explained away the small gifts as a rare rainy summer occurrence. The children charmed him the most, the girls graciously accepting while the little boys frowned at why anyone would want such a stinky flower.

Each family visited meant he drew one more wagon closer to the Warrens. He suppressed a grin, seeing Ellen's family between him and Marie. For his plan to work, she had to be the very last. Sam rode up to the wagon. "Miss Ellen, good day."

"Good day Mr. Granville." Her eyes widened. "Oh my

goodness! Those are lovely!"

"I think so, too." He pulled off a couple of blossoms. "These are for you." Leaning down to her, he held his horse still as she walked up to take them.

"Are you sure? They're so lovely." She smelled the fragrance, the petals ruffling with her breath.

He pulled off a few more blooms and bent down again to Ellen. "Could you give these to your mother, too?"

She took the flowers, smiling. "Yes, she'll love them, too. We may put these in one water jar if that's all right with you."

Straightening in the saddle, Sam replied, "I don't mind at all."

"I'll give these to her, Mr. Granville. Thank you."

Sam tipped his hat as she went to their wagon. He turned to the Warrens', his heart thudding in his chest from nerves. Wanting and doing were two different things. He'd not counted on feeling shy at giving her what seemed to be a huge bouquet. She wasn't his to give anything to, and yet, a small kindness couldn't hurt, he thought. Sam shook his head of worries and clicked Scamp forward. Reaching Marie's wagon, he saw Hester and Charles on the front seat. "Good afternoon!" He felt transparent under Warren's squinted eyes and ignored his feelings by pulling out a small bunch of flowers from the larger group. "Miss Warren, you inspired me to collect wildflowers this afternoon." He gave her the nosegay. "I've given every lady their own flowers and can't forget you."

"Oh, Mr. Granville, this is an unexpected treat!" She breathed in deep the aroma, sneezing from the pollen. "Thank you!" Her eyelashes fluttered at him. "I'd not expected such a thing from a man like you."

"Yeah, Granville." Charles frowned at him. "Flowers are a bit forward, don't you think?"

Hester gave her brother a playful slap on the arm. "Don't be silly, Chas. It's a wonderful gesture." She tilted her head and asked Sam, "What do you intend to do with the leftovers?"

He shrugged in a casual way. "I suppose give a few to Mrs. Warren since I've not seen her yet."

Hester winked at him. "You don't need to bother with her. I'll be glad to take what you have and add them to my others."

Sam caught the scowl Charles gave her. Not wanting to cause trouble between the Warrens, he grinned and pulled a couple of more flowers from the larger bouquet. He gave the blossoms to Hester. "I might do that if Mrs. Warren doesn't want any for herself. If doing so is acceptable to you, sir."

The comment seemed to surprise Warren. "Of course, it is."

"Good luck, Mr. Granville. If you can't find her, I'll be glad to take all the flowers."

He gave her a smile he didn't feel. "I'll keep that in mind, ma'am." He tipped his hat, needing to get away from the simpering woman. Scanning the area, Sam saw Marie walking upwind from the group and away from the dust. She wasn't too far from the wagon, so he and the horse trotted over to her. Dismounting as he neared, Sam, said, "Hello, Mrs. Warren."

"Hello again, Mr. Granville." She nodded at his flowers. "Don't tell me those are for Hester."

He held out the gift. "They're not. She has more than enough. I gave every other lady their bouquet, and I didn't want to discard these."

She took the flowers and smiled, burying her face in the fragrance. "Thank you, I think, for the leftovers."

"These aren't left..." he began and caught himself. His plan to keep this unobjectionable worked too well. She began strolling in the wagons' direction, a slight smile on her face. Sam fell into step beside her. As they walked along, Sam checked to see how close anyone else might be. Satisfied they were out of earshot, he cleared his throat.

"That sounds like the beginning of something important." She smiled at him and went back to admiring her flowers.

"It might be." He paused before saying, "Yes, these are what's left. They're what I made sure I had saved just for you."

Marie glanced over at him. "Just for me?"

He stared ahead after seeing her face. Her pleased expression made his heart beat hard in his chest. "Yes. I wanted you to have a bigger bouquet than Hester."

"I don't think this is, though."

Hearing the amusement in her voice, he grinned. "It's not, despite what I'd planned. Some of the littler girls wanted flowers too. I might have given them more than expected."

She stared at her blossoms for a while before saying, "I love these. They're beautiful and perfect." Without looking at him, Marie asked, "You saw through my fib, didn't you? About how I love flowers, I mean?"

"Afraid so, Mrs. Warren."

Her cheeks reddened. "You might be getting to know me too well, Mr. Granville."

"I agree." They neared the others, and he wanted to say more before rejoining the group. "I could compare every other woman's beauty to the flowers I gave them. But I can't say the same to you."

"Oh? I'm not sure how to feel about that." She picked a crumpled blossom from the middle. "You couldn't compare me to even the most windblown of them?"

He shook his head. "You are lovely beyond any words I can use without a well-deserved beating from Mr. Warren."

Marie laughed. "We wouldn't want that, would we?"

Her beautiful face turned up to him, the wind blowing around dark hair loosened from her bun. Marie's dark eyes sparkling with amusement, Sam forgot himself, losing any amount of self-control as desire raced along his nerves. Before he could reply, her expression turned serious, and her eyes widened. Time seemed to stop as they halted, staring into each other's eyes. In that instant Sam knew anything Warren did to him would be worth making love to Marie. Her face reflected the hunger he felt. "I'm not sure…." he began.

"They're leaving us behind, Samuel."

A glance ahead confirmed her statement. He smiled at her. "I have a solution for that." Sam swung onto his horse, holding out his hand. "Don't be shy."

"Very well." She placed her right foot into the vacant left stirrup. After her hop and his pull, she sat sidesaddle like before. This time, she held the flowers close to her. Sam nudged Scamp into a trot. Marie yelped and wrapped her arm around Sam's waist to hold onto him, too.

Putting a hand on her arm, he shouted "Hyah!" and they galloped to the Warren's wagon. He leaned forward, her holding on for dear life and him enjoying every inch of their contact. They soon arrived in the midst of the group and slowed. "I enjoyed that."

Her face still pressed against his back, she said, "I need the ground." She shuddered. "My feet on terra firma seems best at the moment, not holding on for dear life."

He looked back at her, grinning. "Admit it, you enjoyed the

speed."

Cheeks blushing, she stared at his shoulder. "I enjoyed the hugging part more."

"Why, Mrs. Warren! I'm shocked to hear such a thing from you." He teased her, trying to ignore how his heart skipped a beat from her admission.

She gave him a sly glance and a smile. "It was either that or landing on my rump."

Sam laughed and held out his hand for her as Marie slid from his horse. Before he could give a retort about her backside, her husband strolled up to them.

"There you are, my dear." His eyes narrowed when seeing the bouquet she held. "My goodness, Mr. Granville had a lot of posies left over, didn't he?"

She shrugged, smiling. "I suppose so. He was kind enough to let me have them instead of letting them go to waste."

Sam didn't want to cause a fuss and figured under explaining his motives would be best. "If you'll excuse me."

"Of course, Granville. I assume you have work to do this afternoon instead of romancing my wife and sister."

"In fact, I do." Sam grinned as if Warren meant to be humorous and tipped his hat to both of them. He rode up to the front, his body still feeling warm from Marie's touch, and he smiled. Any contact with her brightened his day and outlook. She'd held on so tight, the side of her face resting against his back. Rubbing his stomach, his skin seemed branded by her despite how the shirt's fabric separated them. More and more, everything he saw or smelled called her to mind. The warm brown of Scamp's coat matched her eyes, the animal's main and tail matched Marie's hair. Sam grinned. Not that he'd tell her all this. He would bet she'd rather hear how she smelled sweeter than any flowers she carried.

He spent the afternoon daydreaming while trailing the stragglers. Deep blue mountains in the distance accented the bright azure of the sky. Gray-green sage dotted with near lime-hued grass and cactus colored the land. He grinned, appreciating the beauty despite the vast emptiness. Being here always helped him appreciate his family's home in Oregon Territory among the rich vegetation there. He watched as wagons rolled single file to the river crossing. Each inched their way down the hill. The others backed up while waiting their turn. Loud voices, angry, caught his attention and he grimaced. He and his brother Nick rarely fought while out here, but other families seemed to thrive on conflict. Sam nudged Scamp forward to see what the problem was.

While easing his horse to the river along a slender path cut into the cliff, he heard a crash followed by women's screams. He tasted the metallic tang of fear. Sam turned his horse up the incline and back towards his party. Others gathered around an overturned wagon, and he dismounted once reaching them. Not until seeing Marie unharmed and tending to Ellen did he realize how much he dreaded a chance of seeing her injured.

Before he could ask, Lucky said, "The axel broke, then the yoke, and the whole thing toppled over before anyone could think."

Sam noticed Ellen was cradling her arm. "Who else is hurt?"

Indicating the young woman, Lucky replied, "We think Miss Winslow broke her arm. Her little brother and sister weren't in the wagon."

"And her parents?" As soon as he asked, Sam watched as Ellen's mother was freed from under the spilled contents and pulled clear by Mr. Winslow and Arnold. They helped her to lean against one of the ladies.

"Her father is looking for the youngest two now," Lucky said.

"Very well." He nodded, glad to see Mrs. Winslow feebly walking with Ellen's and Marie's assistance. "You all get the wagon righted. We'll take an axle from one of the abandoned rigs around here, and a yoke, too."

The young man shrugged, "What if we can't find any?"

"We can. I saw some back a ways." Sam turned to Uncle Joe and asked, "Ellen's father built this wagon himself, didn't he?"

Joe replied, "Yes, he did, but not very well. Mr. Winslow made it out of old wood instead of buying new. He saved his money, wanting a chance to use the timber in the Territory he had heard about."

Sam nodded. "Then Lucky and Arnold, get him what he needs to fix this. Meanwhile, let's see what we can do for the injured." Uncle Joe followed as Sam went to Ellen where she stood among a large group. "Miss Ellen?"

"Yes?" she sobbed.

"Let me check your arm, see if how badly broken it is." At her nod, he took her hand and supported her arm under the elbow. "Can you bend your wrist?"

She tried, wincing. "A little, but it really hurts." A tear escaped and rolled down her cheek.

"I'm sorry to hurt you. Now, can you bend your elbow?"

Ellen did as he asked. "It doesn't hurt as bad as my wrist."

"That's good." He held her arm, palm up, and supported her with a hand underneath. "Tell me when the pressure hurts." Sam gingerly pressed from her elbow to her wrist on the underside of Ellen's forearm. Halfway to her hand, she winced. "There?"

"Yes, very much right there."

"All right." Knowing where the break was, Sam put her uninjured hand under her own arm to brace it. "I have bandages and a splint in the camp wagon. Come with me and we'll get you set." Seeing Lefty helping Ellen's mother walk toward them, he asked, "How is she?"

"She's favoring her right leg, sir," he replied and shrugged.

"I see." Sam said, "Mrs. Winslow, if you'll wait here for a moment I'll get what you need for your leg." After the woman had nodded, he addressed Marie and Jenny. "If you two will watch while I fix up Miss Ellen's arm, you can do the same for Mrs. Winslow." The two paid attention as he placed a splint under Ellen's palm running to near her elbow. Sam then wrapped a bandage snug but not tight around her forearm.

Uncle Joe retrieved a small laudanum pill. "Take this, it'll help the pain."

As Ellen swallowed the medicine, Sam turned to Marie and Jenny. "Do you remember how I found where the bone was broken?"

They both nodded, Marie saying, "Yes, I'm sure we can do this."

"Good. If you need help, let one of us know, and we'll retrieve Mrs. Norman or one of the other ladies." He gave Jenny the bandage and a leg splint and gave Marie the laudanum bottle. He said to Joe, "Let's go and fix up the Winslow's and their wagon."

An ashen Mr. Winslow had the wagon propped up on stacked boxes, most of their possessions on the ground outside. The ladies shielded Mrs. Winslow with their skirts as Marie and Jenny doctored her leg. Lefty, Arnold, and Lucky escorted the other wagons on to the next clear spring.

By late afternoon, the Winslows were ready to rejoin the group. Most of the others had gone ahead and were out of sight. Sam, Winslow, and Uncle Joe lifted Mrs. Winslow onto a thick pile of bedding the women had fixed for her. The two youngest crawled into the wagon with her, soon falling asleep.

Marie broke away from Jenny and Ellen, coming up to Sam. "Here's your laudanum."

He took it while asking, "You gave her only one?"

"Only one, the same as you gave Ellen."

"Good. I've seen a lot of people addicted to this. The last thing I want is a fight over the stuff." He slipped the medicine into his saddle bag.

Before she could say anything else, Lucky galloped up to them. "Hey, boss, we've camped up a ways. The grass ain't so bad, and there's some wood. It's not too far from here if you start soon."

Giving him a wave, Marie left and joined the other women. Turning to Lucky, he said, "Sounds good. We're ready to go." He mounted his horse, whistled, and Winslow started the oxen moving. He turned to see the children still on the seat, somber from the accident. Sam noticed Lucky stayed put and addressed the young man. "Mr. Martin?"

"Boss, maybe I should walk with Miss Jenny and the ladies. In case they get scared." The young man shrugged a second too late to be casual.

Grinning at the obvious ploy Sam retorted, "You can see danger better from horseback. I think the ladies will feel much safer with you up here rather than down there." He grinned at his employee's grimace. The young man didn't know Sam had the same idea to remain near Marie. He'd not mind her seated behind him on Scamp again. Even on a warm afternoon like this, he'd liked her pressed against him again during a gallop.

He glanced over at Lucky. The young man was silent, something out of the ordinary for him. Sam grinned. He probably daydreamed about Jenny. The girl had caught his eye the first day they rolled west, as he'd caught hers. Sam didn't think he and Marie could say the same. Later, he could dwell on when he first fell in love with her. Right now, he needed to get them to a good camp.

The last two families lagged behind at the last ridge. He

needed to get them over what would be the final incline for a while. He forded a shallow part of the river on his way back to them. Once across, he leaned forward as his horse climbed the steep incline. Sam gritted his teeth when hearing how Mr. Winslow hollered at Ellen. He couldn't make out the words from this distance, just the angry tone of the man's voice.

He wiped sweat from his forehead with the back of his hand. While Sam didn't care for how her father talked to Ellen, he knew Jack's yelling lacked any abusive action behind it. He stayed back as Uncle Joe and Arnold helped Winslow ease the wagon down the embankment. The rest of the family stayed up on the ridge, waiting until it was safe to follow. His men knew the drill. Soon they all rolled or walked through the water to their camp for the night.

They didn't have far to go and caught up in an hour or so. The latecomers pulled their wagons into the familiar circle. With the Winslows finding their own place, Sam looked back at the ridge in the distance they'd traveled. The accident, heat, and wind took the starch out of him. He'd noticed how even Lucky lacked his usual energy. If not at such a distance, he'd send someone to the snow laced mountaintops to the north. He shook his head at the idea. The snow would be melted and warm by the time it reached them here in the lower elevations.

To the south, he saw women bringing back full pails. He knew nearby lakes held bad water, but the river ran half a mile south. Sam saw how almost everyone filled their water barrels upon reaching their own wagons.

He rode Scamp to the river, hoping to find decent grass for the animal. The north wind brought aromas that made his stomach growl. A few had dinner cooking already. He dismounted, his horse trotting to the water as soon as Sam's boots hit the dirt. Following, he noticed how the women took advantage of the early stop to wash clothes. He hoped the men saw the chance to hunt. Catching sight of Lefty downstream, he led a reluctant Scamp over to the younger man.

Lefty paused in staking out their oxen to greet him. "Hello, boss. I don't think Uncle Joe and me are ready for the second watch tonight."

Sam suppressed a yawn. "Can't say I blame you. Lucky and I aren't ready for first."

Lefty added, "One thing's for sure, I'm never complaining

about a bed ever again."

Sam smiled. "Me neither." They watched Scamp drink until full. They followed as the animal pulled toward new grass growing along the bank. He shook his head. If he'd been thinking, he'd have taken his horse's saddle off back at camp.

After a little while, Lefty said, "I reckon the ladies have the right idea, washing clothes and all."

"Is that an offer to do our wash?"

"Nope!" The young man shook his head. "Just an observation, boss."

"It's a good idea. We'll all pitch in so none of us spend all day and night scrubbing."

"Don't tell them I thought of it."

Sam laughed instead of replying. He tied off his horse at a sagebrush near the grass and oxen. Making a motion for Lefty to follow, he walked back to camp. "We'll bring back the animals later on this evening. They deserve the chance to eat as much as they want."

At camp, Uncle Joe coaxed a fire out of the sagebrush. He looked up as they approached and nodded. "I did some scouting around for game already. Didn't see anything."

Lucky rustled around in the wagon, adding, "We still have meat from that pronghorn you shot day before, Joe."

"That's right," said Sam. "That'll take care of this evening, and we'll keep an eye out tomorrow. Until then, let's wash up our clothes." The three men groaned, but each went to gather their worst laundry. They took turns carrying all of it sacked up in a sheet. The half mile seemed longer to the one loaded down.

Once at the water's edge, each took a garment and began scrubbing. Lefty had the most difficulty but managed to keep up with the others. All of them had to pause every so often and warm their hands back to near body temperature. The cold, clear water numbed them too soon.

Lefty took a pair of pants from under the water. "How close are we to those hot springs again?"

Sam shook his head. "Not close enough to get warm anytime soon."

"I've seen how some can boil you alive," said Joe.

"After killing and plucking a chicken, we cooked it in one." Lucky grinned at the memory. "The meat was real tender."

Joe nodded. "If you find a spring warm enough for a bath but not too hot, keep hold of your soap. The currents can pull it out of your hand."

"Especially soap," Lucky added.

Spying Lefty's alarmed expression, Sam added, "Don't worry. There are a few hot springs that are warm and mild. You'll see."

The boy frowned as if not quite believing him. "I'm not partial to being stewed alive."

Sam and the others laughed, and Lefty grinned. Wanting to reassure the young man, he said, "We'll tie a rope to you. If we see you get near boiling water, one of us will reel you back in like a fish."

"Don't know if that's necessary," he retorted.

Lucky wrung out his own clothes and loosely folded them. "I'll keep an eye on you tonight. If you try to jump into the cook pot, we'll know for sure what to do."

He paused while placing the folded clothes in the sack. "You reckon that's possible?"

All three of the other men laughed. Sam patted him on the back. "No, we're just funning with you. You can lead the animals to camp while we trade off carrying the clothes." The wet and dripping cloth made staying dry tricky. Trudging up an incline didn't help. They handed off the load a lot more often now than before due to the difficulty. He caught sight of Marie and nodded, enjoying how she smiled back at him. The boost in his mood didn't last long. Back at camp, each minute ticking by made staying awake challenging. He noticed even Lucky looked tired as he began cooking supper.

While Lefty and Joe hung up the laundry to dry, Sam unsaddled Scamp for the night. He gave the animal a good brushing before staking him out near the wagon. Returning to the campfire, bedrolls had been laid out, and the men sat warming their hands with the campfire. He grinned and joined them, liking how the heat spread through his fingers.

They ate, quiet from hunger and fatigue. Sam envied Arnold and Joe their sleep for the moment, knowing in a few hours, they'd be envying him and Lucky. He glanced over at the other man keeping watch. Lucky snored sometimes, and Sam hoped to fall asleep before hearing it. They stayed at opposite ends of the wagon circle, trading off to keep awake. His feelings tugged at him whenever walking past Marie's family. This time of night, he didn't look in on each family, wanting to give everyone their privacy.

He glanced up at a sky brimming with stars. With no full moon to guide him, Sam needed to take care with each step. A couple times around the circle and he knew where most of the bigger rocks lay. The starlight, though lovely and reminding him of Marie's eyes, didn't illuminate much of his path. He passed by the Warrens again. Every night, they'd been the quietest family of the group. With some, he'd worked to not hear the giggles or rustles of bedding. The silence every night in Marie's camp made it far easier to consider Mr. Warren more like her father than anything else.

Remembering when she'd asked him for a kiss at Fort Laramie broke his heart. How her fool of a husband disregarded her continued to anger him. He shook his head. Every day, he saw how she looked at Warren as if waiting for more. Sam knew one day she'd stop expecting the man to live up to his vow. He paused, licking his now dry lips. What would a passionate, giving woman like her do then? He wouldn't be so low as to steal a man's wife but couldn't blame a man for trying.

Sam heard Lucky before seeing him and nodded when they met and continued on their routes. By now, he noticed, all the various groups' campfires had faded to dull red or black. A couple more rounds and it'd be time to wake up Arnold and Joe. His oldest employee's voice stopped Sam.

"Mornin', boss. Arnie and I are ready to take over now."

Returning Uncle Joe's yawn interrupted Sam's grin at Arnold's nickname. "Try to stay awake."

"Always do, sir." Joe tipped his hat, strolling to his post for the remainder of the night.

Sam settled into his cold bedroll, shivering. While doing dishes, he'd retrieved water for the morning. He'd be surprised if the pail didn't have ice in it by dawn. A poke at the embers stirred the campfire a little, warming him and Lucky. The next thing he knew, the smell of breakfast, morning sun, and rustling people woke him.

He sat up, rubbing sleep from his eyes. Seeing Lefty at the fire, he asked, "Has the coffee melted yet?"

The young man laughed. "Yeah, looks like it, boss." Without being asked, Lefty poured Sam a cup and handed it to him.

He hugged the mug, soaking up the warmth. Still too hot to

drink, Sam instead put his lips to the brim, hoping the smell worked as well as the drink. "We'll need to stop at Pacific Springs for noon."

Lefty nodded. "I've wanted to see them for myself."

Uncle Joe joined them. "Pacific Springs? It's a low, boggy spot. Not a lot there except it all goes west from here on out."

Sam agreed and added, "It'll give the animals a chance for water and maybe decent grass." He shrugged off the blankets. "Is the food nearly ready?"

"Yes, sir, in a few minutes or so."

He nodded, standing and stretching. "Good, it's making me hungry." Going to check on Scamp and the other horses, he ran straight into Marie. "Why, hello, ma'am."

"Oh! Please excuse me, Mr. Granville."

He smiled at her disarray. Her hair looked messy as if she'd not had time to fix it when waking. The more Sam tried to walk away, the more put his feet stayed. He didn't have a chance to stare at her like a besotted calf. Judging by the bucket she held, Marie came here for a reason as well.

She frowned. "You're making me a little uncomfortable. Is there a bug on me?"

Sam laughed, "No, I'm just admiring how you're a little darker skinned each day."

"I know." She exhaled in exasperation. "I've neglected my bonnet too much recently. Charles warns me I'll resemble shoe leather by the time we reach Oregon."

"Your skin is a beautiful ecru, not too brown and not too spotty. Does that help?" Sam offered.

She smiled at him. "A little, yes."

"If I were any more honest with you, your husband would tan my hide, and that's if he'd let me keep it in the first place."

"You're so foolish; Charles isn't the possessive type at all." She turned, leading the way to the water's edge.

Sam couldn't admit how jealous Warren should be towards him. Changing the subject so he didn't confess anything to her, he said, "Rest up tonight. We'll be crossing a thirty-mile desert tomorrow evening." Her eyebrows raised and before she could ask, he answered, "There's nothing between the Little Sandy and Big Sandy rivers except dirt. We can carry some water, but not so much the animals are killed pulling the loads."

She went to fill her pail and paused. "I've not read that far in the guidebook."

"Take your time with it. I know reading and walking is difficult to do at the same time. Especially in this terrain."

"All right, I'll tell the Warrens to be prepared." While Marie retrieved water, she continued saying, "I appreciate how much you know about life out here. We'll hear of other misfortunes befalling those traveling alongside us. You keep us both out of danger and out of trouble as much as you and your men can."

Her compliment both pleased and embarrassed him. He loved how she held him in such high esteem. "Do you know how I'm so knowledgeable?"

"I never thought about how someone becomes a trail guide. Do tell."

Sam leaned over to her and said, "I've been in all the dangers and trouble a man can find out here. If you've made every mistake, you learn how to fix or avoid them. Excluding the deadly mistakes, of course. I've managed to avoid them so far." When she laughed, Sam straightened and smiled. He scoured his brain for an excuse to tarry here with her but had none. "Now, if you'll please excuse me, I'm neglecting my morning chores."

"By all means, you're excused," she said and went back to her camp.

He walked away, grinning like a fool. Getting the animals and their gear ready distracted him from dwelling on Marie. Once on the road, he followed upwind of the group. Arnie and Lucky rode on the other side of the long line of wagons. They stayed ahead, scouting the way. The morning wore on. A midday sun warmed him even as gusts from the north brought air chilled from the snowcapped mountains. Reaching Pacific Springs for noon his own goal, Sam resisted the urge to encourage a faster pace. He took a deep breath of the high desert air. The animals needed the slow walk over the difficult road.

Glancing over the people in front of the group, he saw how most of the ladies wore shawls and children had dressed in winter clothes. A wave from Ellen caught Sam's attention. She motioned to him, and he rode over to where she stood with Jennie and Marie.

"Good morning, Mr. Granville," Ellen said. "Tell me, will we ever reach South Pass today?"

Marie retrieved his guidebook from her pocket, saying, "I've been pouring through the guide and found little about the Pass."

He laughed before catching himself. Sliding off Scamp, he said, "We're crossing the pass now."

As if one person, the ladies paused and then laughed. Jenny spoke first. "Mr. Granville, we're not the foolish sort. Maybe the children will believe you, but us?" She looked at the other two. "We've seen nothing resembling a pass today."

Knowing what they'd expected, he grinned at her disbelief. No signs marked the Continental Divide, yet, all of them had crossed it sometime this morning. "This pass just happens to be wide, not a narrow crevice like you'd expect." He turned and looked where they'd been. "See those two hills opposite each other, like posts for a large gate?" The three said yes in unison. "When we went through there, we rolled over the middle of the Pass. Not including the various ravines, we'll be going downhill from here to the Green River."

"That was it?" asked Ellen.

Before he could reply, Marie said, "You could have warned us."

Jenny nodded. "Yes, we wanted to hop over the halfway point."

Sam gave Marie a curious look, and she replied to his silent question. "Those two, mostly. I just wanted to cheer for them."

"I see." He resumed walking west, and they joined him. "My explanations have been lacking, and it's an easy correction. Either I or one of my men will inform you of the landmarks we pass from now until Oregon City."

Ellen peered at him through her glasses as if not quite believing him. Marie seemed a little shamed, while Jenny replied, "That sounds perfect. Thank you, Mr. Granville."

"You're welcome. In fact, in about a mile or so, we'll be reaching Pacific Springs."

"The Pacific? That can't be, of course," Marie protested.

"No, just the springs." The flicker of sadness on her face led him to continue. "It's the first water we've reached that flows to the Pacific."

"Will we be stopping there for noon?" asked Ellen.

"Yes, I'm expecting we will," he replied.

Ellen nodded, saying, "My family will need my help before

then, please excuse me."

"I'm not sure if mine does." Jenny bit her lip. "I'll need to find them and ask. Excuse me as well."

Sam and Marie strolled for a while until he asked, "Am I keeping you from anything?"

She smiled at him. "No, but you're on foot and don't have to be."

"Walking suits me just fine at the moment." He grinned at her. "We'll reach the springs soon enough and separate to do our various chores. Right now, I'm just enjoying this." He glanced over at her, liking how her face glowed with a blush.

"I am, too. The idea of being so close to the ocean thrills me. I can't wait to hear seagulls again, smell the salt in the air instead of crunching it on the ground, and feel the wet sand under my feet." She looked at him. "Everywhere we've been so far has a wild, rugged beauty of its own. I'll just be glad to reach the Pacific soon."

Seeing the familiar dip in the landscape, he nudged her shoulder with his. "Soon, huh? The best I can do in that short time is this up ahead. The water there isn't bad. It meanders toward the Pacific, and probably tastes stagnant most of the time."

"Oh. That doesn't sound promising."

Ahead of them, Uncle Joe signaled him. Sam swung up onto Scamp. "It's not poisonous, or shouldn't be." He stared down at her, not wanting to leave. "I'm being summoned. If you'll excuse me?"

"By all means, sir."

He returned her smile before riding over to Joe. "We need to make our next stop short if we're to reach Little Sandy before dark."

"We'll lay by at Big Sandy?"

"Yes, early tomorrow. It'll make crossing the desert to Green more bearable for us. You tell Lucky, and I'll find Arnie." Waiting until Joe nodded his assent, Sam rode off in Arnold's direction.

"Boss, we got a problem." He tilted his head toward their supply wagon. "One of the oxen is lame, and the other three aren't faring too well."

Sam shook his head, not liking the news. One weak animal meant the other three worked more to catch up the slack. This increased the odds of every ox being unable to pull themselves, never mind supplies for at least four men. "Any others?"

"No one's complained, but I've noticed a couple of the families moving slower than usual." At the questioning look, Arnie explained, "The Allens mostly, even more than the Winslows."

Sam failed to keep the sarcasm from his voice. "That's a surprise."

Arnie grinned at the tone. "Yeah, that's why I thought you should know."

"Very well. We'll overnight at Pacific Springs instead of Little Sandy."

"I'll tell the others." He nudged his horse and galloped to the far end of the line.

Watching him leave, Sam began to inform everyone of the decision. He didn't stay long after talking to each head of a family. With some, chatting led to arguing and he'd prefer to avoid a heated discussion. Soon he reached Jenny Allen's family. A quick examination showed him just how injured their ox was. He slid down from Scamp and led the horse to their wagon. "Good afternoon, Mr. Allen. I see you've got a problem."

Mr. Allen pulled back on the reins, stopping them all. "Aye, he's not walking the best. I was hoping he'd improved over the course of today, but no such luck."

"If you all can make it to Pacific Springs, we'll be staying for the night."

Jenny peeked out from inside the wagon. "It's not on account of us, is it?"

"No. This road is tough on feet, human or animal. The trading posts between here and Fort Hall do a good business in boots and shoes."

Mr. Allen peered at Sam. "I've noticed our clothes are fast wearing out from the hard water since Fort Caspar."

He nodded. "That happens, too." Patting the hurt ox's back, he said to all of them, "We can use rags to wrap feet of all kinds once we reach camp. We don't have far to go, a half mile or so." Convinced the animals would last for a little while longer, Sam got up on his horse. "Let's go. The sooner we start, the sooner we'll be done." The wagon began rolling.

Sam scanned the group for the Winslows to tell them. He wanted the excuse to see Marie but spotted Lucky talking to Hester and Charles. They already knew, then. Disappointed, he trotted far up front, scouting for the springs.

Not until far into the night did Sam slide into his bedroll, exhausted from the day's work. Everything from animal hooves to wagon wheels had needed his attention today. Everyone too, from Allens to Winslows, excluding Marie, the one person he wanted to spend time with today. He turned to the waning fire, wishing she lay between him and the warmth.

He must have slept as soon as his eyelashes brushed his cheek. Opening his eyes, Sam saw his breath as he exhaled into the frosty morning air. He looked over to see the campfire embers burned to ash. Frost coated the vegetation surrounding them. Lefty glanced up at him from where he sat. The young man gave a nod and went back to reading his bible. Lucky's snoring almost drowned out Uncle Joe's and Arnold's footsteps crunching through the grasses. "Good morning."

"Good morning, sir," Arnold replied first. He and Joe began building up the fire. "All we could find was this scrub brush."

Joe added, "Works fine, though, doesn't it? Smells good, too."

Propped up on his elbows, Lucky said, "I'm missing the piney smells of home."

"I am, too," Sam admitted. He sat, rubbing his eyes free of sleep. The sun's rays still hid behind the eastern horizon. The chill lingered in the still morning air. As the fire roared to life, the five men held their hands out as if doing a familiar dance.

Lucky hopped to his feet and slid on his boots. "I'll get water for the coffee."

"And I'll get the coffee." More slowly than his employee, Sam also got to his feet and put on boots. He frowned at the three amused expressions staring back at him. "I'm just cold."

Arnold snickered outright. "Of course, sir."

"Has nothing to do with your age, I reckon," Joe joined in with a chuckle.

Lefty added his opinion while sliding his book into a pillow case. "Nothing with age and everything with the cold ground."

Unsure if they meant what they said, Sam decided not to press the issue. Instead, he brought out the coffee pot and beans from the back of the wagon. He shivered, already missing the fire's warmth. They'd planned on staying put today, he realized, and everyone could rest for a while longer. Good, he thought. No need for Lucky to play that infernal bugle this morning. He'd like to have the chance to miss the sound. Rubbing the stubble on his face reminded him a shave would be nice. He and the others might hunt for where the water bubbled up through the ground.

Lucky returned, frowning at the bucket he carried. As he approached, he said, "It's not the best water I've ever seen. We need to find the wellhead to the springs."

Having the solution in mind, Sam went back and scooped up another handful of coffee beans. "I thought we'd dig around this morning and find a better source for later today. It'd be a good idea to store some for later. Little Sandy may be drier than we'd thought."

Joe nodded, adding, "When was the last time we caught rain, before Sweetwater?" He stood up and went to the wagon. They heard rattles as the man dug around for breakfast and cookware.

"It seems so long, I don't remember," replied Arnold.

After he had placed the full coffee pot on the fire, Lucky said, "Prospect Hill is the last I remember. Since then there's been a few flakes, nothing serious."

Sam shrugged. "I'm not surprised, considering the lack of vegetation. The dry makes me appreciate my home that much more."

They all chimed in with their agreements, talking over each other as Arnold poured coffee. Each ate their meal without much chatter, hunger keeping them quiet. After Sam had swallowed his last bite, he said, "I can wash up."

Feminine voices caught everyone's attention. Lucky was the first to stand, dropping his dishes in the bucket for washing. "You know, boss, I can clean up if you want to stake out the animals for better grass."

He joined in with Joe, Lefty, and Arnie in grinning at the young man's eagerness. "That's a good idea. Arnold, you can bring the shovel to dig out fresh water from a spring or two. Joe, you and Lefty can bring our laundry, and Lucky can get the dishes."

"Sure thing, boss," Lefty replied and followed the older man to the back of the wagon.

Sam took the horses first to the first spring dug. Others from their group were there, already washing everything but themselves. He grinned at the thought of bathing in the frigid water. A spit bath of heated water sounded much better. Bringing the oxen down to drink next, he saw that Scamp already munched on the reedy grass growing in the mushy soil.

As Sam approached the springs, he saw the Warrens, all three of them, doing their chores. Marie washed dishes, while the twins seemed to wash clothes. How long had they been on the trail? Yet, those two acted like they'd never scrubbed laundry before now. He'd seen Marie with the other ladies on washday. She seemed competent enough.

He nodded a greeting to them as he walked past and upstream. After all the recriminations he'd heard them give her, they acted more like children than Marie ever did. Sam turned his back on them while letting his horse drink and staking out the oxen. An idea coming to mind, he acted as if he were a little frustrated, then eased his way back to the Warrens.

"Good day, sir!" boomed Charles. "Lovely morning."

Hester threw the end of a sheet at him saying, "Help me wring out this mess." He gave her a frown and began twisting the cloth in the opposite direction from her.

Sam smiled as he settled down near Marie to wash their dishes. "Good morning, Mrs. Warren."

"Good morning." She stopped scrubbing the pan long enough to smile at him. "The decision to rest a day has improved everyone's mood."

Before he could reply, Charles interjected, "What you need, Granville, is a woman." Not even looking at Sam, he reached down and threw the end of a sheet at Hester. The wet cloth smacked against her, splattering water everywhere. Over her laugh, he added, "You'd never have to wash dishes again, my man."

Marie gave Sam a weak smile and glance before returning to her chores. He knew she'd learned of his prior engagement. Her hair unkempt from last night's sleep and her focus on the task both stirred him as he stared at her. "You're right. I do need a woman, don't I?"

Charles winked at him. "My advice is to get a gal from a poor family. She'll know how to care for you."

A flash of anger crossed Marie's face at Hester's laugh. Sam felt as if he was missing a key piece of information. Wanting to know more, he asked, "Oh? I'd always had my sights set on a woman of means." He glanced at Mrs. Warren and saw how the expression on her face didn't change.

"Ha! No, you don't, young man." Charles barked, giving the folded sheet to his sister. "Don't get me wrong, a woman of means is a wonderful thing. I love my wife." He turned to Sam and Marie. "But even she will tell you, losing our servants left her helpless as a babe."

She stopped washing dishes long enough to glare at him. "I'm hardly helpless, Charles."

"Don't be silly, my dear." He shook the water from a dripping shirt. "Maybe not now, but at first I thought we'd all starve from your cooking."

"You're right about that; I did need to learn." She straightened while holding the bucket of clean dishes. "We've yet to starve, so maybe there's hope for me, yet." Giving Sam a smile that didn't reach her eyes, she added, "My husband is right. Find a woman who is better than I am in taking care of her man. If you'll excuse me."

Marie walked to the camp, her steps seeming measured. Sam frowned as his eyes followed her over part of the distance, knowing she was angry just from the set of her shoulders.

Hester said, "Oh look, Chas, you've angered the poor little thing." Her voice seemed to carry more amusement than censure.

"She'll get over it and will be pawing at me again to –" he stopped, looking at Sam. To him, he said, "My wife is temperamental. Furious one minute, loving the next. I'm not worried. She's a good woman."

He eased back as if going to care for the animals. "I'm certain she is. Excuse me, please. I have stock to tend."

Hester held out her arm for him to take with his free hand. "We'll walk back with you, Mr. Granville, and you can tell me what you're looking for in a wife."

Pushing aside his desire to flinch away, Sam intertwined arms with Miss Warren. "You flatter me, ma'am, in thinking a woman would tolerate me."

"Oh, silly." She smacked his bicep in a playful way. "I'm sure any girl would love your attentions."

He gave her Scamp's reins, glad she let go of his arm long enough to take them. She followed him to the oxen as he double-checked their ties. Hester's interest in him worried Sam. Did she have scurvy? Maybe mountain fever or some other insanity causing illness led her to believe he'd welcome her flirting. He didn't protest, not wanting to start an argument, and gave her a wan smile. "Thank you. I appreciate your confidence in me."

Frowning and loaded down with their laundry, Charles went to the opposite side of Sam. "Tell me. What do you think of all this prospecting in the gold fields down south?"

"You mean California?" Sam glanced at Hester, her expression seeming sly to him. They neared the Warrens' wagon, and Sam wanted nothing more than to be free of the older woman's cloying grip.

She tapped his arm. "Of course, silly. There's lots of money to be made there. We'd have servants again and not have to rely on ourselves and Marie to do everything."

The Warrens rolling hundreds of miles away from him? He smiled at her, hoping to hide the dread in his heart. "Haven't you heard by now? The gold is about gone. It's been, what, nearly ten years since word first reached the states. It's all been mined out by now." Looking ahead, he saw Marie at their wagon and fear spread through his insides. If they branched off, he'd likely never see her again. Sam couldn't let that happen. "You're too late to make any real money." Now within earshot of her, he fought the urge to take her in his arms and never let her go. "Oregon Territory is set to take off; the money is there instead."

Marie looked from one man to the other and Hester let go of Sam's arm. As Charles set the dripping laundry on the tailgate, he said, "I know you're biased, being from there and all. That's excusable. We've changed our minds about Oregon, however, and will take any advice you have on getting us to California. I'd like to split off at the Parting of Ways unless you're going to Fort Bridger for supplies."

CHAPTER 6

Marie's heart thudded hard in her chest. She looked at her husband to Sam and back again. "California? But, I thought we'd all settled on Oregon. You had plans for a shop and everything."

Excitement evident on his face, Charles said, "Have you heard the latest numbers? Far more people live-"

"Six times the amount," Hester interrupted.

He nodded to his sister. "Six times more live in California. Think of the money to be made there."

"You intend to mine for a living?" Marie ranked panning for gold equal to digging and refilling a hole in the ground repeatedly.

Hester laughed. "No, of course he doesn't."

Charles joined in with his twin, the scorn evident in his tone. "Me, a miner? Don't be stupid."

"Now look here…" Sam stepped forward. "Considering the vast number of gold hungry settlers to California, it's a legitimate question."

"Not when it's my wife doing the asking, young man. She should know better than to assume I'd be grubbing around in the dirt like a common laborer."

"Enough!" Marie raised her hands. "It's not stupid to suppose you'll be digging during a gold rush, Charles. I'm just now hearing of this and am more than a little surprised, that's all." The lie slipped easily from her lips. She prayed her face didn't betray the horror she felt at leaving Sam and her friends. Before she could stop it, her lower lip quivered a bit. "What you're saying makes sense, of course."

"Makes sense," Hester snorted. "That's rich."

"Hessy," her brother interjected, holding up a hand to quiet her.

She paid him no mind and put her hands on hips. "Do you understand how six times the population means six times the amount of money to be made there rather than in Oregon? California is close to being a state, too. It could be decades before Oregon follows."

"I'd like to make as much as I can." Charles smiled, giving

Marie's upper arm a reassuring squeeze. "Maybe one day, after we're wealthy again, we can move north."

"Why would we do that?" Hester interrupted. "She's been complaining the entire way about how cold it's been. I doubt moving north will solve her problems."

Marie patted Charles' hand, pulling it from her arm and giving him a squeeze. "We'll do what you think best, dearest. No need to quarrel, Hester." She struggled to ignore the ache in her throat. "You just took me by surprise is all. I'll be fine." Marie smiled at Sam. "I suppose I'm the only one caught unaware?"

"No, this is news to me, too." Addressing Mr. Warren, he asked, "If you had said something earlier, I could have put the word out you needed guides there. As it is, I don't know anyone going that direction."

Charles shrugged as if unconcerned. "We could go on ourselves."

His face grim, Sam said, "It's possible. You've all had enough experience out here to know some of the dangers." He looked at the ground, kicking a rock with the toe of his boot. "I'm not fond of the idea. You'd be out there alone." He glanced at Marie before staring at Charles. "If something happened, it might be a while before anyone came by to help."

"That's a foolish thing to say." Charles stretched out his arms as if to embrace the empty plains. "Since when have we ever been alone? I've seen a plethora of people we passed and pass by us every single day since we left Missouri." He shook his head, smirking. "I think we'll be just fine without your so called protection."

"Even if the worst happened, my brother can handle it. He can handle anything." Hester retorted.

"Thank you, dearest," the older man said to his sister. "I appreciate your confidence in me. Too bad Mr. Granville and my wife don't agree with you."

"Your abilities aren't being called into question, sir." Sam crossed his arms.

"Oh no?" Charles retorted.

Sam gave them a tight smile. "No, sir. There's a reason for the phrase 'Safety in numbers.' Accidents, illness, attacks by animals or humans are all dangers best dealt with by a group."

"I suppose you and your group are the only people able to

keep any of us safe. I guess we've learned nothing in these past few months."

"No one's saying that," Sam countered.

Charles' voice grew louder with each word. "Yes, you are. You think I can't care for my own wife and sister."

"Fine. I can see I'm wasting my time in arguing with you all." He tipped his hat. "I have chores to do. Excuse me, please."

Waving him away, Charles turned to Marie. "He's a hotheaded young man, isn't he?" Before she could answer, he continued, "Never mind that. We'll do fine on our own and link up with another and better group going south."

"I'm certain you're right, dearest." She rubbed at a corner of her eye. "I'm rather thirsty, so if you'll excuse me as well."

"Of course, sweetheart." He leaned over and kissed her forehead. "Thank you for being agreeable."

"You're welcome." She felt anything but agreeable. To leave her friends in a few days broke her heart. She'd had plans on living in the same community as Ellen and Jenny. Marie helped Hester with draping clothes over the rope stretched across a couple of wagons. Keeping busy, she poured her energy from anger into the chores. Her sister in law chatted about the change in plans, but Marie couldn't listen. Instead, she mused over her reluctance to leave Sam.

She nodded at something Hester said while leaving and letting Marie do the rest of the work. After picking up each item, she twisted, uncurled, and draped the last few dresses. She straightened her back, stretching. On the other side of the camp, her friends also hung their washing out to dry. She smiled and returned Jenny's wave, wanting to visit but not wanting to cry in front of her and Ellen. Instead, she found the pail and made a pretense of visiting the springs.

Taking a detour, Marie climbed up an embankment and sat. She watched the activity in the various camps. Each group tended to keep to themselves. For a while, she tried to avoid searching for Sam but gave up after spotting him talking to someone from another group. He drew her attention like a lighthouse on a foggy night. She smiled at him wearing a clean shirt even on a laundry day when no one else did so. How he kept it white in the camp's dust was a mystery. Maybe he had a gaggle of washerwomen obeying his every order. She smiled when imagining a herd of females all batting eyelashes at the man while scrubbing his clothes. It's a wonder he wasn't already married several times over. Sam glanced up at her, and she averted her eyes in case he saw her staring at him. She'd taken living near him in Oregon City for granted. The thought of never seeing him again bothered her in a way that hurt her stomach.

Even while staring at the mountainous horizon, she saw Sam leave the group and walk toward her. She smiled, hoping for a chance to talk with him. Smoothing her skirt, she glanced down in time to see him distracted by Uncle Joe's greeting. He spoke with the older man for a little while before following him to camp. Disappointed at the missed opportunity, she sighed. Marie picked at the graveled ground beside her. Every so often she'd find a small rock and toss it, idly wondering how to change Charles' mind. Only one thing worked in convincing him of anything. She had to find a way to persuade him of how Oregon seemed prosperous.

"Good afternoon!" Ellen said, easing her way up the slight incline, Jenny following her.

"Hello, how are you both? Finished washing?"

"For now." Ellen sat down beside her.

"Me too." Jenny settled in on Marie's other side. "We heard you're going south instead of with us."

Marie swallowed the growing lump in her throat. "Yes, I heard that, too."

"You can't!" exclaimed Jenny. When Ellen nodded her agreement, she continued, "I'd planned on having you both over for sewing and church."

Blinking back tears, Marie said, "Charles has figured California is more profitable."

Ellen hugged her. "Doesn't he know land is free in Oregon, and the territory is on the brink of statehood?"

Jenny patted Marie's back to comfort her. "Wouldn't we have heard by now?"

"I'm not sure. Anything not from one of the forts would probably be a rumor," said Ellen as she let Marie go, allowing Jenny to step in to hug her.

"Lucky told me Mr. Granville was, how did he put it, acting like a horse with a burr under his saddle." Jenny let go of Marie and patted her back a couple of more times.

Ellen leaned forward to ask Jenny, "Did he say why?"

"Only that Mr. Warren brushed off his advice and laughed at him." The ladies both looked at Marie before Jenny added, "Or so Lucky overheard. He didn't mean to eavesdrop, I'm sure."

"In a group this small, it's difficult to not overhear everything," Marie reassured her. "Most men think their way is the only way."

The other two women nodded. The three sat for a moment, watching the activity below them. In the quiet, she struggled to find a way to enlist the other girls' help. "I'd prefer to go north with everyone else, not south, and need to help Charles change his mind."

"You've been married long enough to know how to tell him what to think, haven't you?" Ellen said with a wink.

"His latest plan has been such a surprise, I'm not sure how to convince him." Marie shrugged. "Yelling never works, threats don't, and a favorite dinner might at times."

Jenny frowned and picked up some small stones to throw. "That doesn't leave us much else."

"Maybe some feminine wiles?" Ellen began skimming rocks, too.

"Not with my husband." Seeing their disbelieving looks, Marie added, "After a certain age, those wiles cease working so much. Trust me, it's a problem for wives everywhere." Shadows from the wagons stretched toward the east since they'd sat down. She suppressed a sigh. "I suppose everything is dry, considering the heat and wind today."

Smiling at her, Ellen said, "This isn't too bad. We wouldn't have sat here so long on a rainy day."

Jenny laughed and also got up as the other ladies stood. "We would be clean, too. I so miss the rain, don't you?"

Marie retorted while leading the way back to camp, "Very much. I've had as much wild desert beauty as I can stand."

Simmering beans and rice greeted her as she neared the Warren campsite. Her sister in law sat nearby, stirring the pot.

Without looking up, Hester said, "Good, you're here and can watch this for me. I have mending to do."

Marie sat as the other woman moved away. She heard her rustling around in the wagon before leaving the area. After giving the dinner another stir, she went to the cart and retrieved Sam's guidebook. It was where she'd left it, in her pillowcase, safe. She went to the pot and checked the simmering. Satisfied, she sat to read everything possible about California. She rechecked every road to the gold fields then reached over to stir the food again. Seeing it ready so soon, she slipped the guidebook in her pocket and stood to find the others.

Fifteen minutes of searching near the livestock and at the Springs, she found Hester and Charles at the campsite eating dinner.

Before Marie could say anything, Hester said, "You let the meal scald."

"Looking for you two took longer than I'd planned." She knelt and scraped her food from the bottom of the pan.

"Granville is having the usual get together tonight." Charles stood and put his dishes in the wash pail. "I'm not going. Instead, I want to visit with someone who is going south."

"We can go, and you meet us there when finished," Hester offered.

"Sounds good, Hessy."

She wrinkled her nose at Marie. "You can wash up before dark, can't you?" Standing, she added her dish and spoon to her brother's. "Maybe you'll be done before Charles finds another group for us."

The other woman left before giving her a chance to retort. The thought of leaving everyone behind loomed too real all of a sudden, and her dinner turned flavorless in her mouth. Marie put down her spoon, no longer hungry. She picked up the washing on the way to the water. Her least favorite chore, she did the dishes as fast as possible to be through sooner. Clothes still hung from every clean surface of the wagon. She frowned, not wanting to fold them later on this evening. Putting away the dishes, she then folded laundry. Marie imagined conversations she'd need to have with Hester and maybe Charles about the division of labor between them. Including those two's shares to her fair share was beginning to anger her. She put the last of the clothing away, shaking her head. Bottling up fury until it exploded did no good. Hester laughed at her while her yelling drove Charles out of the house.

She felt Sam's guidebook in her pocket where it rested against her leg. He'd want it back before they parted. Marie's breath caught in her throat. She'd never thought of never seeing him again. Had her feelings for him always been strong but hidden, she wondered.

Or was the thought of separation creating new emotions? She straightened her skirt. Either way, time with Sam ebbed to a close, and she wanted each second possible until they left the Granville party.

Marie made her way to the larger group, smiling when seeing her friends already there. Jenny waved to her, not interrupting Lefty's talking. Ellen shared a blanket near the fire with Arnold, both unaware of her approach. Hester sat beside Sam while everyone listened as Lefty told a story. Arriving too late to catch anything of the tale, she settled on a scrap of blanket next to Uncle Joe.

Without a pause, Lefty concluded, "When I opened the door, my cat walked inside the house with its head in its mouth."

She smiled at how the men laughed while the ladies shuddered. She told Lefty, "You must tell me this story later when the others aren't around. It sounds incredible."

"Why sure, ma'am."

His face turning ruddy, Marie wanted to ease his shyness around her. "We don't have to be too much alone, just enough to not bore the others with hearing it again."

"Of course, ma'am."

The boy was relentless in his polite formality. She gave him a smile and looked up when a movement caught her eye. Charles approached, and Marie waved. He saw and shook his head, instead going to a spot near Sam. Sitting next to his sister, Warren addressed Sam. "So, Granville, I've found a group headed south."

"I see. Will you be joining them tomorrow, or going with us until they leave our path?"

"A little bit of both. Staying with you will give my wife a chance to say goodbye to her friends."

"That's considerate of you."

Charles laughed. "I do have an ulterior motive. Letting her have a little of her way keeps the peace around here."

"Do you know where exactly this group will go?"

"Some. They drew a map in the dirt for me. We're to head south into Utah after Fort Bridger, supply at Salt Lake City, and head out to Humboldt River."

Sam nodded. "I've heard that route takes miles and days off the travel time. It would be the best way to go."

"We agree? Mark this day down as a first, Hessy! Granville

and I agree on something."

Marie disliked her husband's disingenuous laugh, the one he gave now. She'd heard it many times at dinner parties where he'd later confessed he was "suffering fools." When he leaned back to chat with his sister, Marie glanced at Sam. She froze, having not seen the expression on his face since Jimmy's death. His sorrow reached to her across the way and felt like a physical thing in her heart. Stunned, she felt her mouth gape open a little before recovering enough to look away, close her lips, and force a placid expression. He'd been staring at her, hadn't he? Marie snuck a peek at him. He stared into the fire, lowered eyelashes covering his eyes. His mouth set in a grim line showed his mood.

After seeing his anguish, she felt like an automaton at a State Fair sideshow. She was able to move and pretend, but nothing else. The conversations went on around her. Marie tried to listen, but inside, her stomach churned. She didn't want him upset over her leaving. Recognizing her own conceit made her smile. Of course, his mood had nothing to do with her. They were friends, true. Even families parted ways out here, doomed to communicate through letters for the rest of their lives. If dissuading her husband from California didn't work, perhaps she and Sam could keep up a respectable amount of correspondence themselves. Lost in thoughts of how to get his address in Oregon City, she startled when Sam began speaking.

"Tomorrow isn't coming any later than usual, everyone. We have a rough week ahead of us and need to rest." He stood and helped Hester to her feet while Charles still struggled to gain a footing. "Lucky, you and I have first watch."

Not wanting to leave, she hesitated before joining the Warrens on their way back to the wagon. Sam disappeared before she could talk with him, so Marie said her good nights to everyone as they dispersed.

Seeing how the twins readied the beds for sleeping, she took the bucket to fill with water. She and other groups had made a well-worn path, easily seen in the gibbous moon's light. At the spring's edge, she scooped up half of the pail. She made her way back to the wagon circle, stopping short at someone blocking the path.

Marie looked up into Sam's face as he said, "We need to talk."
She nodded. "All right."

"Now and in private." He took her hand, leading her back to the group.

His fingers warmed hers. She liked his body heat and shivered in the night air. "Where are we going? Shouldn't we be walking away from everyone for the privacy?"

"We will." He turned right just before the camp, taking her toward the rising moon. "I didn't want to cut across the shrubbery." Steadying her as she slipped down the steep decline, he added, "I found this last night while on watch. We're far enough to be alone but not so much we're vulnerable."

She nodded then realized he probably couldn't see her very well. "You planned this?"

"Yes, since I first heard Warren's change in plans." He turned to face Marie, pulling her close. "Tomorrow, we'll be reaching a good place for you all to leave our group." Holding her in his arms, he said, "Don't go with him, please. I know this is wrong, and I hate myself for saying anything to you, but I can't stand the idea of you leaving us."

"We could write," she offered.

"Marie…"

"That won't be enough, will it." She'd phrased it as a question, but her tone came out as a statement.

"No, not for me." Sam leaned closer to her. "I should have kissed you when I had the chance."

She leaned back, afraid of what would happen if their lips touched. "It might be best if you didn't since you seem to feel strongly about my leaving."

"There's nothing halfway about my feelings for you." He pulled her into his arms. "Marie, I love you. What can I do to keep you with me?"

"Sam! You can't say such things." She put her hands on his chest, trying to keep him at a distance. "How we feel doesn't matter in the least. I'm married, and if Charles wants me to go, I have to follow."

"You have feelings for me?"

"It doesn't matter-" She squeezed her eyes shut to block out his earnest face.

He tilted up her chin, caressing her face. "Say you don't love me, and I'll walk you back to your husband right now."

She opened her mouth, trying to say the words. Unable to lie,

Marie replied, "I can't. You deserve honesty. Yet, I can't tell you I love you."

"Yes, you can. In fact, please do." He pressed his mouth to her ear and whispered, "You've told me with your eyes more than once. I'd love to hear it from your lips in a kiss or two. Aren't you still wanting an appraisal?"

"No," she lied

"Are you sure? Because I'm more than willing." He kissed from her ear to the middle of her forehead.

"Oh dear, Sam. Before was an experiment to help me with Charles. Now, it's more. It'll mean everything now."

"Marie," he growled, his lips claiming hers.

The breath caught in her throat at his touch. Desire overtook her as a hunger for more raced along her skin and into Marie's heart. The last sane portion of her mind gave up resisting as she melted into him. Sam's mouth was the only soft part of him. He felt long and lean against Marie's curves. She shuddered as his kiss deepened. One of them moaned, she couldn't tell who. Her heart skipped a beat when his hands slipped to her lower back. He'd been right. Now might be the last moments they'd have alone together. She ran her fingers through his hair, wanting every inch of contact possible. Desire tingled through her like static, especially after feeling his arousal for her. She broke the kiss first. "Sam, I need…"

"Enough," he hissed, putting her at arm's length. "If we continue…"

"We can't." She stepped back, missing his touch too soon. "We'll already regret this much in the morning."

Sam ran a hand through his hair. "You need to get back to camp. If Warren notices you gone, there will be hell to pay."

"And rightly so. " She followed him as he led the way through the brush. "I'm sorry for encouraging you this way."

He paused, sighed, and continued to her wagon. They neared her family, and he squeezed her arm. "Good night, Mrs. Warren."

"Until tomorrow." Marie left him, concentrating on not making a sound. She placed the water next to the wagon, then went to her bedroll and slipped in next to her husband.

Charles turned over, cuddling her. "You took a while. Longer than I expected."

Guilt settled in her stomach like a cold stone. "I'm sure. It's so dark, one of the men helped me to the springs and back."

He chuckled, "Should I be worried?"

She winced, glad she faced away from him. "Of course not. I'm a married woman."

"That's my girl." He held her close, his leg thrown over both of hers.

Eyes wide, Marie stared at the orange glow of the last few embers. In ten years of marriage, she'd told her first lie to him. Her lips still felt Sam's and she ran her tongue over them, fighting her hunger for him. She closed her eyes, wanting to forget this betrayal.

Marie awoke in almost the same position in which she fell asleep. Thinking a silent thank you to whoever started the coffee, she sat upright. Memories of last night and knowledge of today flooded her mind. She bit her lip, unsure if Sam's kiss had been real or a dream. A cracking stalk of sage caught her attention. Noises all around her told of how others readied for traveling. Resigned, she stood and retrieved three coffee cups from their place. She poured and drank a cup by herself. The disappearance of her husband and his sister had alarmed her the first few times it happened. Now, though, she realized how commonplace their morning absence was. One or the other gave a different reason every time as to why she woke up alone. Most of their excuses blamed her laziness in caring for the animals. The fire burned low, and she decided to let it die for a change. Unwilling to wait on the Warrens, she folded up the bedrolls. Some water remained in the bucket, so she poured the cleaner part of the liquid into a canning jar for later today.

Lucky's bugle notes sounded. Still, the Warrens weren't there. Marie swallowed down panic. Instead, she rechecked that everything had been packed. She went to where the oxen were staked and brought them to the wagon. People to the east of them rolled past her to the west as she struggled to fasten the yokes. She frowned at the irony of being left here, never to see Sam again, instead of being pulled from him by Charles.

"Darling!" Warren ran up, holding Hester's hand and almost dragging her behind him. "You've hitched the team! Great work!" He hoisted himself up on the seat, helping his sister up as well.

"Thank you." So relieved as to be out of breath, Marie hadn't realized how afraid she'd been. Looking back at their camp, she saw the coffee pot still on the embers, waiting for the twins to drink. She heard Charles' whistle and instinctively looked towards him as the Warrens' wagon began to roll away. She raced back to the camp, grabbed up the pot, and emptied it onto the dying embers. Walking fast at first to catch up, she began a slight run as they gained speed and continued down the smooth road with the others. When at last she reached the wagon, Marie dropped the cooled pot in the back, glad it was empty.

Task completed, Marie paused to catch her breath. She smiled at her family's hurry. When the same thing happened last week, they confessed to feeling shamed over the late hour. Charles had said he wanted to catch up with everyone else. The dust made her cough a little. She trailed behind, and a little upwind so the stiff breeze kept her out of the dirty air.

Being at the end of the line meant Arnold and Lefty brought up the tail. She saw them when looking back, as they ambled along and kept guard. Most mornings she didn't look for Sam like she did today. Their kiss last night seemed more of a dream than real. Her stomach gave a slight clench from the memory. He'd been wise to refuse her at Laramie. She'd drunk enough whiskey to know intoxication. Just his touch warmed her blood and shut down her good sense in much the same way as liquor did. Seeing others walking a little ahead of her, Marie slowed. She wanted more time to think about Sam.

What felt like love and desire last night seemed more like foolishness in the harsh light of day. She'd chatted enough with the soiled ladies to know all men lost interest in a woman after a while. Charles had, and so would Sam. Mr. Granville, though a good reason, couldn't be the only one for her wanting to go to Oregon.

"Hey, little filly!" Sam hopped down from his horse. "Looks like I need to rope you in with the rest of the herd."

She laughed. "You're right!" Looking up into his eyes as he fell into step beside her, Marie saw affection shining back. Shyness, an odd feeling for her, took over, and she didn't know what to say.

"It's a beautiful day."

"It is."

"I should apologize for taking liberties with you last night."

"No need. You were merely tardy in granting my request."

He grinned at her. "I deeply regret passing up such a chance. Just think of how helpful I could have been in evaluating your kisses every night since Fort Laramie."

"Oh dear."

"I remember you'd asked for any criticisms." He shrugged. "There are none I can give. I imagined how your lips would feel, but the reality far surpasses my dreams."

She choked a little while saying, "You are a charmer."

"Yes, I am, and I'm also honest." Sam gave her a slight smile. "Which is why I need to tell you something. We're reaching a fork in the road sometime near noon. You'll possibly be headed south, and I meant what I said last night. I love you."

His declaration in the clear morning air alarmed her. "Sam! You can't say such things!"

"Judging how far we are from those up ahead, I can say anything I want for the next few minutes or so. So I'm using the time to tell you how much I've grown to care for you. I know it's wrong, that you'll go wherever your husband leads, but you need to know if you're invisible to him, it has everything to do with his blindness, not your blinding beauty."

"If I can't convince Charles to stay with your group, I'll miss your flattery. Maybe it's best if we head south. You and I are too infatuated with each other." Her heart clenched at the fib. She ignored her feelings and continued. "I blame myself. I propositioned you and haven't done much to discourage feelings between us."

Close enough for others to hear, he gave her a glare. "I'm glad it's mutual, though I seem to be the only one suffering."

Marie laughed at his boyishly stubborn face. "You are. Now go and be our leader while I visit with my friends."

He gave her a wink before getting back on Scamp. "As you wish, ma'am." Sam rode ahead, tipping his hat at the ladies he passed.

She caught up to Jenny as the girl walked with Ellen and her stepmother. Marie said, "Good morning."

"Did you know? It's awful." Jenny hugged her. "We're to be at the Parting of the Ways today."

"Will you and your family leave us there?" asked Mrs. Winslow

Jenny pleaded, "Say no, please."

Ellen shook her head. "She can't do that."

Marie glanced from one to the other of the girls. They'd shared trials and stories these past few weeks, making them lifetime friends. "I don't want to go, either."

"Once Oregon gets statehood, more people will move there. All of them will need goods," said Ellen. "It might be nice if your family had a shop set up and waiting for them."

Marie smiled at the argument. "Exactly. I may have to remind him of this being his original and best idea."

"Do you think it will work?" asked Jenny.

The breeze chilled Marie. "I hope so." The flat road, barren of sagebrush, gave them an easy surface to cross. She listened to her friends, distracted whenever spotting Sam riding past them. Her step felt light and happiness seemed to radiate from her like smoke from a chimney. Guilt over last night's kiss tugged at her a little. She shook her head as if to erase the memory from her mind.

"Are you well?" Ellen asked, frowning a little.

"Yes, very well! I just had a little ugly thought about Hester."

"I so understand!" As if realizing she spoke too loudly, Jenny placed a hand over her mouth in shock.

Ellen grinned before asking Marie, "Did you know her before you married Mr. Warren?"

"I'd met her, but never imagined having to live with her. I do remember being glad the two weren't more alike."

"Did you have a grand wedding? If Lucky would propose, I could start planning ours. He's so shy. Gosh, I may just ask him myself." Jenny's cheeks still blushed from her gaffe.

"Ours was very grand. However, you'll most likely have a wild frontier wedding. Not many women can say such a thing."

Ellen nodded ahead of them. "You could tell us how you met and married your husband."

Jenny added, "I'll bet it was a grand event."

Marie glanced over to see her husband and Hester waiting for them. She said, "Yes, let's do that. Maybe this afternoon."

Once within earshot, Charles grinned and hollered, "Dearest, time to say goodbye to your friends."

She stated in a quiet voice to the girls, "Let me have one last chance at convincing him to stay with everyone here. We can catch up later." They left, Jenny with an audible sniff and Marie began, "Charles, I feel I must say something to you first."

"Oh?"

"Yes." She wrung her hands at his scowl. "Your idea of going north to settle was the best one you've ever had. I've heard how

Oregon's statehood is all but official, and they're granting land to homesteaders. Think of all the people needing to buy lumber and dry goods once they arrive there when the territory is a part of the United States."

"No." Charles shook his head. "Nothing up there is guaranteed. California is already a state and has the population to make me rich. They have all this gold and money, and I intend to give them a place to spend it."

"You make a good point, however, I think…"

"Enough!" he bellowed. "I have decided we're to leave the group today and that's final."

"Very well." To her embarrassment, tears began rolling down her face. "I'll go say goodbye."

"Is there a problem?" asked Sam, leading Scamp behind him. He smacked his thigh with the riding gloves he held.

"Yes, sir, a huge one." Charles gave Marie a glare. "But I think she's back in line."

"Oh?" He looked at her. "You don't seem well."

"I am and am being foolish in not wanting to leave my friends today." She wiped her face dry and sniffed.

He turned back to her husband, "So you've decided to head south. It's a valid choice, one several have made."

Charles crossed his arms. "I'm so glad you approve. That was so important to me."

Sam's head snapped up at the sarcastic tone. "Actually, I don't approve. You'll be traversing a difficult route, I assume without a guide."

"I'll hire one before we leave Fort Bridger." Charles grinned. "Problem solved. Now do I have your all important blessing to go?"

"By leaving now, you'd be heading across Mormon country," said Sam

"I don't care," Charles interjected.

Sam's eyebrows raised. "You've not heard of last year's massacre, I assume?"

Hester gave an unladylike snort. "The Indians did the worst of it, everyone knows that," the older woman snapped at him.

Sam ignored her and addressed Marie. "The Mormons used the Indians to take the blame, but they actually did very little violence. The whites divided up the spoils. I'm not sure if the

Indians got much out of the deal." He paused before telling Charles, "Getting a guide at Fort Bridger is an option, but it's not the only way to the gold. I can think of two others that I'm certain are safer and faster. Any expert worth his skin will take your money and lead you to one of the other roads headed south. You've already paid me. At least let me get you to Fort Hall or even the next cutoff after that."

In what Marie considered was his imperial voice, Charles said, "Very well. We'll stay on until Fort Hall at the least. I didn't come all this way and make this much of an investment to end up in a shallow grave."

"Glad to hear it." Sam nodded. "There's a dry stretch before we reach tonight's camp at Big Sandy River. If you'll excuse me."

Marie watched him walk to Scamp and swing himself into the saddle. A little flutter of happiness tickled her heart. She'd need to read up on how much time they had between here and Fort Hall. He tipped his hat at her before riding away, and she grinned at how this wouldn't be the last time she'd see him. Catching a glimpse of Jenny and Ellen, she hurried to catch up to them.

Jenny spoke first. "You convinced him?"

Marie laughed. "I did! Charles has decided we'll stay on until Fort Hall."

"How wonderful!" Ellen clapped her hands. "We were already missing you."

"We'd also planned on kidnapping you sometime today," Jenny added.

Her eyebrows raised at such an idea. "As much as a plan?"

The girls had exchanged a look before Ellen said, "There were a few details we needed to work out, but yes. Kidnap."

Nodding at the wagons rolling further ahead, Marie said, "I may be more interested in your ideas as we get closer to Fort Hall." She linked arms with them and began walking. "In the meantime, I'd much rather talk about Jenny's romance with Lucky."

The girl's eyes sparkled, "I agree!"

Marie smiled, half listening as the other two women discussed the young man's possible interest in settling on his own land. The day grew warmer as they descended into the vast desert basin. Bones of large animals and weathered belongings littered the trail. They passed over the Little Sandy River. Parts of the riverbed were just damp sand with no standing water. The day wore on with no cooling relief. In the afternoon heat, gusts increased until sand grains stung exposed skin. Marie and her friends didn't talk. They kept their bonnet brims low over their eyes. Occasionally, one or the other risked the grit to peer ahead for the others.

"Oh no! Look!"

Ellen pointed west, and Marie saw the leading wagons increase in speed. Those on horseback galloped to the runaway teams. Hearing distant screams, she held her breath. The wagons in front pushed their animals into the water. Those running close behind crashed into those wheel deep in the river. The decline too gentle to justify their pace, she knew the animals stampeded when smelling the Big Sandy River. Shaking free her shock at the chaos ahead, Marie said, "Let's hurry. I'm sure people have been hurt."

Her friends nodded in unison and hurried to the accident. When close, she saw teams still axle deep in the water. The Marshall wagon had overturned. She'd not seen when it happened, the dust obscuring her view. Three of the oxen, still yoked, pulled and tugged at their restraints. The fourth lay on the ground, crying whenever one of the others stepped on him. She saw how its leg twisted, showing tendons and bone. At another jostle, Marie shuddered at the pain the animal must feel.

"What can we do?" Jenny cried to a passing Arnold.

The young man pulled his horse to a halt. He ran a hand through his pale hair, frowning. "Nothing for now."

Marie looked behind them as Arnold rode off to assist others. People now wiser from viewing the disaster in front of them held firm on their own animals. One man from another group leaned far back, almost lying down to keep his team from bolting. She was torn between her urge to help and the need to stay out of the way. Turning to Ellen and Jenny, she said, "Let's split up to check our own families, then see if others need our help."

The fairer girl nodded and hurried to her parents. Ellen stayed only long enough to say, "I'm sure mine will need me. It may be tonight before I'm able to do anything else but tend to them."

"I understand," Marie said and gave her a smile as Ellen left. With a sketchy father, wilting stepmother, and two rambunctious little brothers, the tall and slender girl found little free time, especially with the wagons halted like now. Marie sought out the twins, not seeing them anywhere nearby. She frowned, looking to the east, then west.

"They're not around here, Mrs. Warren."

Sam's voice caught her unawares, and she startled. Looking up at him as he sat astride, she felt her face heat. "Oh? Since you have the ability to read minds, maybe you can read theirs and tell me where they are."

He grinned at her teasing before going back to frowning. "They wandered off the main trail a while ago. I'd been keeping an eye on them. I rode over to let them know where the rest of us were."

She could imagine how Charles took the advice, judging by Sam's current scowl. "Very well. It's up to them to comply." She nodded in the direction of Uncle Joe and Lucky unhitching the injured oxen from the yoke. "In the meantime, how can I help?"

Tipping his hat, he said, "You can stay out of the way for now. No one is hurt." He glanced around before adding, "I'd like to keep it that way, more so where you're concerned."

"Keep yourself safe as well." She stopped just short of adding more and hoped that he read her feelings in her eyes.

How could cold blue eyes be so warm when they looked at her? Marie shook herself. The man turned her into a dreamy schoolgirl. Determined to act her age, she went to help the unfortunate family. She saw an empty bucket hanging from their wagon. Knowing they'd be thirsty, she hurried to her family's wagon. Neither of the Warren twins was nearby. Marie wondered why they'd leave, but dismissed the thought when finding their own water jar. The Marshall children needed this far more than they did.

She knocked on the Marshalls' wagon where Mrs. Marshall and Ruby, their baby girl, lay inside. Marie hoped the woman was already awake. "Eliza?"

"Yes?"

Marie climbed up to where Mrs. Marshall laid, Ruby asleep beside her. "I have something to drink for you. Why don't you try a little sip?" She knew where the family kept their dishes and found a cup. After dipping out a drink, she handed it to the woman, now seated.

"I'll try a little. Are you sure it's fine?"

"Yes, it's better than anything in the past two days. The livestock and other animals are on down from here, already getting their fill."

A gunshot cracked through the air as it killed the wounded ox. The noise stirred little Ruby. Her eyes popped open; she saw her mother and began to whimper. Mrs. Marshall picked up her infant daughter. "I need to feed her, would you mind washing some of her diapers?"

Marie smiled. She didn't want to do such a chore at all. However, doing such a thing would help the woman and the child even more so. "Yes, of course." She refilled Mrs. Marshall's cup. "Here you go. Drink as much as you can, and I'll be back soon."

She took the bundle of diapers and tried not to choke. Ruby was a little angel, but the smell proved her more earthly than heavenly. Marie walked back toward the Big Sandy. Once downstream from where the animals were staked, she stopped. She unwrapped the bundle there, believing the beasts deserved better than to drink wash water from diapers. When the last cloth rectangle was cleaned, wrung out, and folded, she sat back on her heels. The task became easier with practice. Marie gathered up the damp clothes and headed back to the family.

After a while, her arms shook from the extra weight trapped in the fibers. She stopped holding the bundle away from her, allowing her dress to become even wetter. Marie pushed aside her annoyance, remembering how the baby needed her help. At the Marshall's wagon, she peered in, her eyes struggling to adjust to the darkness. Mrs. Marshall was asleep again, while the child cooed and chewed on a rag doll. She decided to leave the pair alone for the moment and went to hang each diaper to dry on the wheels' spokes.

Mr. Marshall turned the corner as she finished. He nodded at the dripping diapers. "Much obliged for all your help, Mrs. Warren."

She smiled at him. "I'm glad to help. Your wife is resting right now, though Ruby is still awake." The young man, shoulders bent from hardship, stood taller than Marie's husband and far thinner than Charles had ever been. "The baby might need watching. She's already good at crawling."

Mr. Marshall indicated the small cut of beef in his hands. "Do you mind staying until I can get this dressed and in the pot? Won't take long."

"Yes, of course. I'll take the baby with me to tell Charles where I am if he needs anything."

"Thank you, ma'am, I appreciate it."

Marie picked up Ruby and held the baby against her shoulder while patting the infant's back. The child nuzzled Marie, her little face shielded against the wind and dirt. She hoped one of the Warrens was at their own camp. As she approached, she saw Samuel talking with Charles. The two stopped when seeing her with Ruby.

Samuel walked up to her. "Hello, Mrs. Warren. Is this a new friend?"

"It is! This is Ruby Marshall."

He took the baby's hand, "How do you do? It's a pleasure meeting such a beautiful young lady."

When Ruby cooed and reached her arms out to him, Marie laughed. "You are such the ladies' man!"

"I can't help it." He looked her square in the eyes. "Name the man able to resist such a beautiful face."

Charles cleared his throat. "Granville, if you don't mind I'd like to continue our discussion."

Not breaking eye contact, Samuel replied, "Of course, Warren, I'll be right there."

"Charles," Marie said and paused, grinning at Samuel. He smiled back at her. "I'd like to ask you-"

"Marie," he interrupted, "I'm hungry. Stop wasting time and give the child back to her mother so you can start our dinner, please."

"Very well," she said, trying to keep her tone from being sharp with him. "I'll be back soon."

Samuel winked at Marie and tickled Ruby's chin. "Good night, ladies."

"Good evening, sir." She walked back to the Marshall's, struggling and failing to keep a silly grin off of her face.

Mr. Marshall took the baby, a stew cooking on the fire. "Thank you for helping me and my family. I don't know what we would have done without you and the other ladies."

"You're welcome. We're glad to help," she replied. "I see and smell supper is started. Do you need help with the beds?"

Bouncing Ruby on his knee and smiling at her giggles, he quietly answered, "If you don't mind, I'd appreciate it. My wife is still resting." He stood, holding his daughter close. "I'll get the bedding if you'll spread them out for us."

She took the material he pulled from their wagon. "I'm glad Mrs. Marshall is resting, she needs her strength." Marie laid out the bedrolls. "She might want some broth later. It'll do her good." While smoothing the blankets, she added, "That will do it. You all have a good night."

"Thank you, ma'am. Have a good one yourself."

Marie left the small camp, her heart still broken over Jimmy's death. The Marshalls never spoke of him, but the pain showed in their manners and appearance. She hoped Ruby would comfort them both.

At their camp, Charles glanced up from his Bible. "It took you long enough. Were they camped back in Missouri?"

She preferred being given the silent treatment far better than his sarcasm. "Mrs. Marshall has cholera, and I wanted to make sure the Marshall baby was settled for the night."

"Doesn't she have parents?"

She didn't want to argue or discuss this with him in a bad mood. "Yes, and neither are doing well, either."

"I suppose it is better you help them than adopt various children around here if their parents die." He closed his book and stood.

"Heavens, yes. Charles has enough of a child on his hands in you without you adding more." She smiled at Marie. "Despite what you say, you being barren has been a blessing for us all."

"I'm glad you approve." Judging by Hester's frown, Marie had failed to keep the sarcasm out of her tone. The pulse pounded in her head as she stood, holding out her hands for everyone else's dishes. "I'll wash." She ignored the glance passing between the siblings while taking their plates. The cook pot would need a soak, so she took a bucket with her to the Big Sandy. Every blood vessel, still full of anger, seemed too large in her body. She ran through all the retorts she could have said to Hester and even Charles. Passing Sam's men around their own campfire, she kept her head down, not wanting to stop and chat until her mood improved.

She knelt at the river's edge; glad others had worn down the tall grasses to a dense matt. The sandy bank lay far under the water's surface. Marie grimaced at her lack of foresight to bring a washrag. With a sigh, she used the end of her sleeve to scrub the most stubborn food.

Soon finished, she dipped the pail half full and placed the

clean dishes in the water. Marie carried everything back to camp, again passing the Granville camp along the way. The water and work had helped dissipate her irritation, so when Sam smiled at her, she felt able to smile back at him. Marie made a point of giving a nod to those who noticed her passing by. She'd much rather stay with them. Their group seemed much more amicable. She repressed a sigh and instead went back to her own wagon.

A quick search turned up no one else at her camp. Marie shrugged and poured water into the cook pot, extracting each dish and utensil as she could. The pail empty and the drying dishes on the wagon's tailgate, she retrieved her sewing. She tried to focus on every little stitch, instead of how her hands still shook. After a couple of needle sticks, Marie quit. She exchanged her sewing kit for bedrolls. Soon, she had everyone's beds turned down and was reading Sam's guidebook.

Her head began to ache as the sky darkened. Neither of the Warrens had returned, and she didn't want to go looking for them. Marie relaxed into her bed, lying on her side while reading the book.

She woke up warm and against Charles. Anger still clung to her like a thin sheet of frost on the prairie. Marie swallowed, wanting to be away from him, but not away from the blankets. She squeezed her eyes shut, not wanting to dwell on conflict so early in the day. Last night's argument had been nothing new; yet, Marie's attitude had changed. When the dawn spread across the sky, she knew the day would start with or without her. She eased herself from under her husband's arm, careful to bring the guidebook with her. After exchanging the book for the coffee pot in the back of the wagon, she made her way to the river.

Marie passed by Sam's camp. She at first fought the urge to look for him. Her efforts lasted until seeing him asleep. She stopped, staring. He looked younger, almost like a little boy. Thinking of how it'd feel to wake up in his arms, she shuddered. Marie longed to kneel beside him, kissing his face. She smiled, not even minding if he had scratchy stubble. The desire to touch him compelled her a step forward. The movement shook her out her trance. She turned and continued on to the water, needing the coffee to clear her mind of all these daydreams.

By the time she returned to where Sam and his men slept,

they were all awake. She nodded a greeting at Uncle Joe when he smiled at her. Once past Sam, Marie struggled to not look back at him. She hurried to camp. Careful to step around Hester and Charles, she stoked the embers, adding the dried brush stacked nearby. She exchanged the cook pot with the coffee pot and started the coffee brewing.

She peered inside the pan. No one had cleaned it. Last night's sludge grayed the contents, and her stomach churned a little at the mess. She wanted to leave it for Hester. Unwilling to listen to the other woman's complaints, Marie grabbed the handle, a spoon, and went to the river. Sam and his men had left their camp. She saw ahead how Arnold washed dishes, and Uncle Joe folded blankets with Lucky. Lefty and Sam weren't in view. Not that she was hoping to see anyone in particular, Marie thought. She neared the bank, suppressing a smile at her foolishness.

Even from here, Marie could tell how Sam kneeled next to the river in among the tall grasses. She went to his right and scooped up some water so the pan could soak. Placing the pot down on the riverbank and settling in nearby, she began using a spoon to chisel off the food.

He paused in his shaving to say, "Good morning."

"Good morning."

He shaved for a while before adding, "There's not a lot of people up and around just yet."

"No, most are slow from the chill." She stood up and poured the water away from where they sat. Not quite satisfied, Marie refilled the pot and sat.

"You seem fine."

She paused in her work and smiled at him. "I am, thank you, as do you."

"So you're not leaving us until later."

"Not until Fort Hall, it seems."

"We're taking the long way, now. The plan is to follow this stream until it joins with the Big Sandy. It adds a few days to the trip and shortens the desert we have to cross." He glanced at her, "I'm confident taking our time until Fort Hall won't doom any of us."

"Maybe we should have gone south after all."

He glanced at her with a mixed expression of fear and sorrow. "No. You can't do that." As if embarrassed from his outburst, Sam took his small towel and wiped the traces of foam from his chin. He smiled and leaned into her. "Feel my face, to see if it's smooth enough."

She put a hand to his cheek. His face seemed cool under her palm. Before she could stop herself, she gave him a slight caress. "You feel perfect to me."

In a sudden movement, Sam turned his head to press his lips against her skin. He kissed her, taking a little nibble of the fleshy part near her thumb. She gasped at the feeling, and he looked into her eyes. Marie lost herself in those clear blue eyes. "Sam." He held her one hand in both of his as if unwilling to let her go. She bit her lip as he kissed each of her knuckles. Neither had broken their gaze and in as quiet of a voice as possible, she said, "I love you."

CHAPTER 7

Her words both thrilled and scared Sam. He stared at her for a few seconds. "Did I hear you correctly?"

"Oh dear." She put a hand to her mouth. "I suppose, a little."

He grinned at her blush. "It feels like a lot to my heart."

After a quick glance around to see if anyone listened in, she said, "I've thought the words so much about you, they've become natural to say aloud."

Fort Hall suddenly seemed much too close, the time and distance too short. "Marie, you can't leave me."

"No, I can't. Not yet, anyway." She patted his arm. "We're infatuated now, which will soon pass." Standing, she tossed out and refilled the pan while saying, "By the time we reach the fort, all this could amount to nothing more than friendship."

He searched his feelings like a tongue searches for a missing tooth. Getting to his feet, Sam looked into her eyes to see if she believed her words. He smiled. She didn't and the earnestness he saw there telegraphed how much she wanted to do so. Very well, he'd let her think whatever she wanted. He had a couple of months until Hall to convince her otherwise. "I agree."

She frowned at him. "You do?"

"Yep. I'm good with seeing if familiarity does breed contempt." He winked at Marie's blush. "I'd like to see just how contemptuous we could be together."

Her face grew redder. "Mr. Granville, you are an awful man."

"Thank you, ma'am." He tipped the brim of an imaginary hat to tease her. "I can't stay so you can tell me more. We have a long day ahead and need to get going."

"Too bad. Maybe this evening?"

"As soon as possible." He turned to his own wagon, feeling lighter than air. For whatever reason, she'd said she loved him. Infatuation tingled like soda bubbles in his blood. He stowed the breakfast dishes he had washed and left on the tailgate in back. Latching up the wagon, he found Scamp waiting for him with the other horses. Spotting Lefty, he asked, "All accounted for?"

"Yes, sir. Lucky's getting ready…" The bugle interrupted the young man, and Lefty waited until the noise stopped. "Never mind."

Sam laughed at his scrunched up face. "Think they heard that on the other side of the world?"

Putting a hand to his ear, Lefty retorted, "What's that? I can't hear anymore."

Lucky turned the corner just then. "You didn't hear me? Do I need to give the signal again?"

As Lucky raised his bugle, Lefty yelped and clamped his hands over his ears. Sam hollered, "No!" and the man's dismayed expression led him to add, "We all caught your order the first time." He nodded as Allen's wagon passed them. "See? Miss Jenny and her family heard you just fine. Come on men, let's get rolling. Can't let our charges beat us to Green River today."

The early morning sun bathed the gray buttes in golden light. The air held a heavy cold, causing a shiver to course through him. Scamp's body heat warmed his legs. Sam hoped the saddle's blanket also warmed his horse. He passed the first wagon and nodded a greeting to Mr. Allen. Once leading the way, he and his animal settled into an easy walk.

He kept a watch on those traveling ahead of them, those following behind, and the Indians to either side. The natives kept their distance so far. Camping in the middle of the various groups was a long-standing rule with Sam. The extra layers of people prevented Indians from stealing. He grinned. There'd be enough time to think about safety. Right now, he wanted to dwell on how Marie said she loved him.

What had possessed the woman to confess such a thing? Probably the same feeling that had also overwhelmed him. Away from Marie, he felt like a normal, moral person. But close up? Staring into her deep, dark eyes, full of affection and mystery? Sam shook his head. He didn't stand a chance of resisting her in person.

Looking up at the lightening sky, he marveled at how his brother had avoided spending time with the married woman he'd fallen in love with out here. Their circumstances were different, true. Nick had interfered in a sham marriage, not a true one like the Warren's. The memory sobered up Sam, and his lovesickness faded. He and Marie would have no such tidy resolution brought about by a confession. He swallowed, his throat dry.

Every day he resolved to avoid falling more in love with her, and every day he failed. Sam turned, watching how oxen pulling the first wagon struggled up the hill to him. They drew up close, and he led the way down the slight decline to the river. A quick glance at the ground showed he and his horse had little shadow under them. He waved to Uncle Joe, the older man behind and to the east of him. Joe nudged his horse into a trot and approached.

At his questioning look, Sam said, "We'll stop here for noon."

"Green River is nearby."

"I'd like to press on, but it'll be a hurry up and wait. Might as well take our time and make it easy for the working animals."

"Sounds good, sir." Uncle Joe gave a flick of his spurs and headed back east.

Sam took the western side of his group, meeting Arnold at the end. He and the younger man rode together, bringing up the rear with Lefty. The party fanned out along the riverbank, the animals drinking their fill. Thinking aloud, he said, "We will likely stay at Green River for a couple of days, waiting for the ferry."

Arnold asked, "There's nowhere to ford it ourselves?"

The other two slid off their horses when Sam did. "Not this time of year. The snow runoff from the mountains raises the water levels. It's usually safer to wait and take the ferry."

"How close are we to the Green?" Arnold dug around in his saddlebag, getting his lunch.

Sam interrupted his own hunt to reply, "Close enough to have gone on without stopping if it had been just us."

Lefty nodded. His animal finished with drinking, he retrieved his cup and some jerky from a saddlebag. "We'd be home by now, I reckon."

Sam used his own up to scoop up some drinking water. "Maybe, but without our supply wagon, it'd be a tough trip." He drank between each bite of the dry biscuit left over from breakfast.

Brushing crumbs from his chest, Lefty dunked his canteen, topping it off with fresh water. "I used to not need supplies so often. The older I get, the more I like the comforts of civilization. Hunting has thinned out in the past few years, too. Less to eat for everyone."

They all agreed with the older man and hopped back up on their horses. Lefty and Sam ambled back to their position at the front of the party. If he remembered correctly, a large stretch of nothing lay between them and the next water. Heat from the sun penetrated his shirt, pressing against him as if the rays had physical mass. He fidgeted in the saddle.

They inched west, and the air shimmered in the distance. He removed his hat and wiped his forehead in one move. The brown felt trapped heat too well in the desert lowlands. He put it on the saddle pommel and ran his hand through his hair. Even warm, air flowing between the strands gave a small relief.

The river ahead cut a green path through the grayish beige desert. Away from the water, people and animals kicked up dust as they went about their business. He spotted the ferry, a little north of their approach. The long line waiting to cross snaked a half mile east. He could estimate how long they'd wait for their own turn, but wanted solid confirmation. The wagons moved slowly enough. He'd have time to go ask and get back. Sam waved to Lefty before kicking Scamp into a trot. "Would you go see how long the wait is?" He looked at their approaching party. "I'll lead everyone north to camp 'til then."

"Sure, boss." The young man galloped over to the ferry, dust billowing after him.

Sam rode up to Winslow's wagon, and when spotting Jack, said, "Follow me." At Mr. Winslow's nod, he ambled to the right and upstream to an opening along the riverbank. Everyone else trailed behind in a slow, graceful arc.

Lefty trotted up to him. "Sir, the ferryman said a day but others have been waiting for two."

"What the hell?" exclaimed Charles.

Warren's shout behind him got Sam's attention. He turned to the man. "Excuse me?"

Charles hopped down from his perch. "Did I hear right? Two damn days before we cross?"

From the corner of his eyes, he saw Lefty back away and ride to the first wagon. "You did," Sam replied. "I assume this bothers you?"

"Hell yes, it does! I don't have time to lollygag at every drop of water in this country."

"Lollygag?" Sam grit his teeth to keep from saying anything else that might betray his anger to the client.

"I hired you to get us to Oregon promptly, not slowly lope through the land. I expect you and your men to do your jobs every day."

Sam took a deep breath, resisting the urge to slide down and punch Warren. Ignoring the irritation, he continued, "It's a shame you feel that way. Let's discuss this later, when everyone is settled for the night."

Warren's jaw jutted forward. "Good. I have some things to say about how you run things around here, and it's about time you listened."

He watched through narrowed eyes as Warren got back on his wagon. They rejoined the others who'd had to move around him, stopped there in their way. Hate and fury in Sam mixed so strongly he could almost taste it. Later, he resolved. He'd allow all this anger later when chores were done. Animals needed tending, bacon needed cutting, and they'd have time for a cobbler tonight. Planning on slow cooked beans and cornmeal biscuits cheered him as much as the idea of dessert. He ignored his hunger pains, concentrating on seeing everyone else settled. Satisfied each family had found a campsite, he found his wagon and rode over to it.

Uncle Joe held the cook pot in one hand and the Dutch oven in the other. "I reckon today's as good as any for a Sunday dinner."

Sam laughed. "You've been reading my mind."

"Sir?"

He turned to see Lucky there, holding out his hand. "What? It's not payday, yet."

"I know that." The younger man grinned. "I'm staking out the animals, horses included."

Handing over the reins, Sam said, "Let me take off his livery first." He set the saddle next to the wagon wheel, placing the blanket over it. "So you're letting us find something to burn, huh?"

"Yep! Good luck finding anything." Lucky led away the horse, grabbing Lefty's and Uncle Joe's mounts, too.

Sam didn't bother to reply. He'd watched for campfire fuel all afternoon. Everyone else had, too. He said to his last two hands, "Lefty, Arnold, let's go see what we can scavenge." They walked along side each other, stopping at a discarded wagon. Ox bones lay scattered on the ground, bleaching in the bright sun. Everything useful had been stripped, wheel spokes, axils, the canvas top. The seat and long boards making up the bottom remained. A few other metal parts, half buried in the drifting soil, rusted. "Let's take a couple of these boards each. We can cut them up at our wagon."

The wood pulled free from the metal frame without much

force. Sam always wondered about the people involved with this sort of defeat. No one ever left their home with the intention of failing, and yet, he didn't know how they'd succeed with no transportation.

The three reached camp, and Uncle Joe looked up from building the fire pit. "That's a lot of wood. How much food do you want me to cook?"

Lefty grinned while Sam and Arnold chuckled. They propped their spoils against the wagon while Sam dug around the back for their saws. Finding both of them, he handed one to Arnold. "We can do the cutting, Lefty, while you do the stacking. Some outside, some in the pit, and the rest will need a place in the back here." As the two of them worked, the other two built a fire.

It took them a while to finish. Arnold wiped the sweat from his face, asking, "Are we washing today or tomorrow?"

Sam glanced at the sky. "Tomorrow. First thing, so our bedding has time to dry."

"Granville, we need to talk."

He winced when hearing Warren's voice. Turning to face him, Sam replied, "All right. I have time. What do you want to discuss?"

"Our slow crawl." He held up his hands to stop any protest. "I already talked to the ferryman, offered him some financial incentive, and he refused."

"He did?" Sam had a tough time believing someone turned down cash. He wondered what the catch was.

"In a way. More like he wanted too much for one crossing."

"I'm surprised people waiting in line didn't protest your cutting in ahead of them."

"They did. So, to foster goodwill among potential customers, I stepped aside." Warren grinned. "I've decided a day or two resting won't hurt anything. It'll give the women a chance to catch up on their housekeeping and me a much-needed rest." He followed Sam to the front of the Granville wagon. "All this responsibility is exhausting. You're fortunate to have so many men helping you."

Sam shrugged, not thinking he'd hired too many for the job. "I pay them enough, and they're good people."

"Yes, well, I'm sure they are." Warren tipped his hat. "If you'll excuse me. I have several things to do this afternoon and not a lot of hired help."

"Of course." He motioned an after-you to him, and he left. Glancing back at Uncle Joe and Lucky, he saw their guarded expressions. "What's up with you two?"

"He's beggin' for an ass kickin', boss," said Lucky.

Sam grinned. "He is, but he isn't going to get one from me."

Uncle Joe snickered. "Not even after asking so nicely?"

He shook his head. "No, I have a rule about scrapping with my clients. We can find more productive ways to spend the day."

Arnold walked up with Lefty, saying, "My rifle could use a cleaning."

"Mine, too," the other man chimed in. "One of my reins is fraying at the bit and needs repair, too."

"Do the rest of you all have things to do?" Sam asked. Seeing everyone else nod, he added, "All right, we'll take it easy this afternoon." He dug around in the wagon for a couple of blankets and his journal. With a comfortable seat, he settled in to update his notes on their journey. Time passed, the food smelling better every hour it simmered. He finished writing at last. After capping the inkwell, Sam flexed his cramped fingers. The others had wandered around doing their chores, he'd noticed, but so focused for so long, he felt as if just waking up from a nap.

Uncle Joe sat upwind from the fire on his own bedroll like Sam, reading a book. He paused every few minutes to stir the beans and check the cobbler.

Sam stood up to put his journal and pen back into the wagon. "Dinner smells great, Joe. Tell me it's ready."

"It's ready." He chuckled at his boss's laugh. "It really is, no lie."

Since he was already nearby, Sam brought out the usual plates and utensils. Everyone else in the group appeared as if his rattling the metal items was a dinner bell. He grinned when seeing how fast they sat around the fire. Without a pause, he handed everyone a plate and fork. Keeping one for him and one for Uncle Joe, he waited his turn for the baked beans and cornbread. Hunger and eating kept them all quiet for a while.

"That peach cobbler is looking good," said Arnold.

"Hand over your plate, Arnie, and I'll set you up." Joe held a big scoop of fruit and crust, plopping it on the younger man's empty dish.

In one motion, everyone else did the same, ready for dessert.

Sam's eating slowed, his stomach almost too full. Unwilling to waste the least crumb, he ate the last couple of bites. "Joe, you've outdone yourself."

Lucky stood. "I'd be willing to knock off early every day for a meal like this."

They all said their agreements over each other, but Sam knew better. He also stood, getting the water bucket. "I'd give you three days before you were all itching to make real tracks."

Shrugging, Lefty added, "We'd be out of canned peaches in a week. Might as well get home sooner rather than later."

The pail loaded down with dishes, Sam picked up the empty cook pot and made his way to the river. Seeing Marie seated on the graveled bank and wrapped in a blanket, he hesitated. No one else was close to her. She might want her privacy, but a small greeting before he cleaned up might not bother her. He didn't like the idea of scaring her, so he made extra noise on his way to the water's edge.

As he approached, Marie turned her face to him and said, "Hello."

He settled beside her. "Hello."

"The mosquitoes are horrible. They're why I'm wearing this," she said and held up her arms a little.

"I figured as much." He paused in washing the cook pot and leaned on her. "You're too sweet to be out here unprotected."

Laughing, she pushed him back upright. "You don't seem bothered by them. I suppose they find you sour?"

He shrugged, going back to work. "Maybe, most likely I'm salty."

"You can't be serious!" She glanced at him and gave his arm a playful pinch. "Oh, you aren't!"

Her statement stirred his curiosity. "I must be. Since our kiss, I've thought of nothing else." Sam looked at her while putting the silverware in the pail. Even in the dim light, her face glowed with a blush.

"I'm not sure that's good."

Unsure of what else to say, he continued washing dishes. Sam enjoyed the time to just be near her. The last dish washed, he searched for and could find no good excuse to stay when other chores needed doing. "I suppose I'd better head back to camp for the night. May I escort you there?"

"You could in a little while if you stayed a minute or so more. I want to be away from the Warrens for a few moments." After a slight pause, she said, "Going back to the campsite and listening to the Warrens go on about their own concerns, well, it's unbearable tonight."

Her reluctance to join her family bothered him. If she made a habit of avoiding others then somehow got lost, he'd never forgive himself. To stop a problem before it started, he asked, "Why tonight? You seem happy most times. Warren doesn't speak to you as I would to my own wife, but seems respectful most times."

Marie turned from him for just a moment. Facing forward, she replied, "They act as if this is some grand adventure and on a holiday when it isn't." She stared up at the stars. "He's made a lot of changes in our lives in the past few months. I've gone from plantation to wagon in that time with no influence over my own fate. Hester has had more input than I have in all this. Which is galling when I consider it's my life, too. I feel as if I should have had more say-so over everything in the past year." She gave him a watery smile, eyes brimming with tears. "I'm sure this is a common complaint among the women on this journey."

His mind reeled. Plantation to wagon? He imagined living in a southern mansion and then trying to share an oversized cart with two other people. The change had to be overwhelming. Before thinking of the impropriety of his question, he blurted, "Marie, why did he give up his home and land? As much as such a sale would make a man, why are you three traveling across the country? A steamer ship to Panama and then to Oregon is so much faster. It's how I go in the winter to get to Missouri."

She didn't reply, instead wrapping the blanket closer around herself. After a while, she said, "As forward as I've been with you before now, I suppose there's no reason to not answer. It's just too difficult for me to say aloud at the moment. Suffice it to say, a steamer ship was not an option."

Her tone was sweet, but he felt chastised just the same. "I'm sorry, my question was too personal."

"It's getting late, so I'm tired and out of sorts." She took off the blanket and patted his knee. "Before we leave, let's agree no apologies are necessary." Marie stood and began folding the cover.

He also stood. "I'll walk you back, Mrs. Warren."

"Thank you." She gave him an ornery glance. "Some of the

ladies, me included, want to visit the Indian trading post tomorrow. It's the closest a few have ever been to the natives. Even Hester mentioned rising from her deathbed to go."

"Has she been ill?"

"Very. The further we go, the more she's allergic to chores." She waited until Sam quit laughing. "When Ellen suggested you might escort us there, Hester improved substantially."

The idea of such a woman hankering for him disgusted Sam. He struggled to keep his face from showing his feelings. "The poor woman; she'll be so disappointed at having to stay behind for whatever reason I can invent."

Marie stared at him openmouthed then laughed. "I'm glad your eyesight is perfect. Besides, Ellen is much prettier and likes you. Jenny is taken, I'm afraid. The other girls, well, they are a little young.

He smiled, enjoying how a lovely woman like Ellen fancied him. "Has Miss Winslow said anything to you specifically about me?"

"Oh my! You are the charmer, aren't you?" She lowered her voice as they passed a group of people hosting a church service. "She's not been overt, no, but has mentioned a few nice things about you."

He caught the tremble in her smile and wanted to reassure her of his feelings. A raucous bunch nearby kept him quiet until they walked a little further. Once clear of the music and shouts, Sam said, "I like Ellen, too. She's a sweet, smart, and quiet lady."

"Opposites attract and that's surely why we're such good friends."

They arrived at her campsite. Sam smiled, aware he couldn't object too much, especially when her husband slept nearby. Instead, he said, "I consider you two, three with Miss Jenny included, as lovely and charming birds of a feather." When she opened her mouth to argue, he said, "Case closed and good night, Mrs. Warren."

Closing her mouth with a snap, she stepped back and said, "Good night, Mr. Granville. Sleep well."

He strolled back to his camp. One of the men had spread out his bedroll, and he gave a silent thank you to whoever had been so thoughtful. A quiet settled over the area. Even the boisterous simmered down to muted conversation. All of his hands had bedded down already. Lucky laid face up, his mouth agape. Sam struggled to not laugh aloud at his snores. Joe stretched out on his side, Arnold nearby and echoing the position. Lefty slept curled up as if to protect his mangled right arm. He'd had his concerns about the crew when Claude, Larry, and Chuck couldn't return for this trip. These past few months proved he had chosen a team of decent and good men.

Sam kicked off his boots and slid into his bedroll. His conversation with Marie stayed in his mind. She'd been wealthy, yet he'd never heard her voice a rich woman's complaint. He grinned. She didn't seem to enjoy talking about Ellen and him. That little flash of jealousy in her eyes warmed his heart. The woman needed a taste of what he got every time Warren touched her.

Sounds of people talking and bacon frying woke Sam. He smiled before opening his eyes. No get-up, hurry-up sounds of a bugle. The cold morning air hung heavy with moisture from the nearby body of water. He nodded. Yep, right about now was when he started getting homesick. Nowhere else but home did the rolling hills combine with evergreens while Mount Hood stood watch in the distance.

"Playing possum, boss?"

Sam sat up and grinned at Uncle Joe. "Yes, and not very well, I suppose."

"Nope. Good thing I'm not a coyote." The older man flipped the bacon. "Coffee's ready."

"Great." He stood, legs a little stiff from the cold. "Where is everyone?"

"Not far. Checking the animals, changing their grazing stakes."

Cup in hand, Sam poured some coffee. "You could have shaken me awake to help. Though I'm glad you didn't."

"I reckoned so. It'll take some time for you to get used to the second watch."

He nodded, drinking the hot liquid. The warmth seeped into him, waking him with each sip. "Lucky's up running around here?"

"Yep. He'll be dead asleep by dinner."

Sam laughed. "I'm sure." Glancing over the fine clothes Joe wore, he asked, "Are the others wearing their Sunday best, too?"

"Yep." He indicated the trio behind Sam. "And they know

when to show for breakfast."

Lefty settled in next to Sam. "We'd have been here sooner, but Lucky made us take the long way."

"Past Allen's wagon?" He took plates from Joe, passing each dish full of food to his men.

"Yeah," the young man replied with a grin. "Though I'd rather wander around like that after breakfast."

Full plates soon became empty. He and the others didn't talk; the bacon and cornbread had their attention. In between bites, Sam said, "Let me change clothes after this so we can get started washing."

Done first, Lucky stood. "I vote you wash dishes, boss, while we get started on the bedding and such."

Sam grinned, wanting to dispute the idea this was a democracy. Resigned to dishpan hands, he also got to his feet. "All right. I'll throw wash out of the wagon to you all, then change into my best." He put his dishes into the pail with Joe's and Lucky's. To Arnold and Lefty, he said, "No need to rush. The last man to the river gets to wash the frying pan, and I don't want to be him." He got into the back of the wagon and began tossing out the dirty bedding and clothes onto a sheet. By the time he found a clean shirt and pants, all of his men had left with the dishes and laundry. Sam laughed, seeing them gone. He secured the front and back flaps of the canvas wagon top before changing clothes. Sam emerged wearing his best with the worst wrapped in a bundle.

He followed a straight line to the river but didn't see anyone in his employ. Frowning, Sam scanned the landscape. He spotted them at a distance, walking toward him. Predictable, he thought. They'd taken the long way for Lucky's sake. He resisted the urge to put his hands on his hips like a schoolmarm and struggled to suppress a smile. Everyone but Lefty carried laundry. The young man held the pail in his good hand, frying pan sticking out of the top. As they neared, Sam chided Lucky, "How many times in a day are you going to say hello to that girl?"

He had the good sense to turn red. Dropping the dirty clothes next to the water, he admitted, "Probably not much more today, sir."

"They're coming over here later to wash up, too," Arnold added, handing Lefty a spoon.

Sam pulled off his boots and socks, getting ready to wade out into the water. "That sounds interesting. Does your 'they' mean all of the Allens?"

Joe said, "More like the three ladies."

Sam nodded, trying to not smile at the prospect of seeing Marie this morning. "Let's get all this over with, and whoever wants to stay here and help the ladies can do so."

Frowning, Arnold said, "I don't know if I like any woman enough for double duty."

They laughed at the young man's sullen face. Uncle Joe assured him with, "It'll happen, one of these days."

Taking the kidding as well as he took the dishes from Lefty, Arnold replied, "It could happen today if she scrubs these for me." He held up the frying pan and picked at some of the burned fat inside. "I'll need a knife to cut off all this mess."

Bent over and raising his pants cuffs, Sam said, "Whatever it takes to get them clean for noon is fine with me." He glanced over and saw Lucky was ready, too. "Sooner we start, sooner we're done." They both waded into the river, the water cold. "Damn."

"Should we fill up a wash tub for boiling?" Joe asked, handing over shirts to each of them.

"Let's see how this works." Sam started scrubbing the fabric with the soap Joe gave him. "It's cleaning up pretty well."

Arnold took off his boots and rolled up his cuffs as the other had. He grabbed up a couple of shirts and soap, giving Lucky his own bar of lye. As the three of them washed the laundry, Joe carried the damp clothes to their wagon for drying. Meanwhile, Lefty cleaned up the dishes, taking them to the cart when finished.

Sam wrung out the last of the pants. He stretched, his back stiff from being bent over while dredging the blankets. Lucky carried one sodden mass to the edge. Uncle Joe took the bundle while Arnold stepped up to take Sam's load. Lefty's arrival caught Sam's attention, and he kidded, "Welcome back, stranger! Glad you could help us."

"Don't blame him, Mr. Granville," said Jenny.

"No, don't," added Marie. "He told us where to find you. Otherwise, he'd still be working on your wagon."

"What happened there?" asked Sam while giving Lucky another wrung dry shirt.

"Nothing, boss," Lefty replied. "Just making sure the wind didn't blow away everything."

"Good idea." He grinned at the three women. "We're not at our best right now, ladies."

Ellen stepped up and picked up a fallen part of the fabric before it hit the ground. "We'd hoped you could escort us to the Indian trading post this afternoon."

"Please say you will," said Jenny, her hands in a prayer pose.

He grinned at the girl's pleading. Sam stepped out of the creek and onto the dry soil. Using his socks to brush the sand from his feet, he looked up at Marie while unrolling his cuff. "Are you in on this, too?"

She smiled at him. "Of course."

With a sigh as if he carried the weight of the world on his shoulders, Sam said, "Fine." He pulled on his boots then picked up a bundle of wet laundry. "Help us get this set up to dry and we'll go."

They worked in pairs, the women giving the men various items, which they draped over every possible part of the wagons. In a short while, Lucky offered, "I should go with you, just to help keep everyone safe."

"I agree," said Jenny in a tone louder than her usual. She turned pink. "If you approve, Mr. Granville."

Sam grinned at her apparent preference for the young man. "Good idea." He turned to ask Arnold, "Are you with us as well?" Looking past him and at the older man, he added, "How about you, Uncle Joe?"

Arnold shook his head. "I'll stay and keep watch over our wash."

Uncle Joe shrugged. "I can go see if there're any supplies worth the money they're charging."

"Lefty?" Sam asked.

The young man glanced at Ellen before staring at his feet. "I might."

"Good." He draped a sheet they'd used to carry clothes over the wagon's tailgate. That's the last of it. Ladies, if you're ready?" Their faces gave him the answer. "Then let's go."

Jenny hurried and linked arms with Lucky. She asked him, "How will we know if they're honest with the trades?"

"I've never known them to lie." He indicated Sam with a nod, "Our boss here knows Sioux."

Marie clapped her hands a couple of times in applause. "Mr.

Granville, I'm impressed."

Feeling shy, Sam replied, "Don't be. People around here speak Shoshone. I might know a few words, but not much more." He led them along the river, walking around the various groups of people parked along the bank.

Jenny and Lucky stopped talking to listen to him after Ellen asked, "Was the Indians' language difficult to learn?"

"More so than Latin and French," Sam admitted with a shrug. The trading post was a few yards ahead, and he looked over at Marie. Getting lost in the crowd with her appealed to him.

"Who taught Indian to you?" asked Jenny.

Ellen also asked, "Have any books on their language been written?"

Sam saw various people he'd met, approaching them as if going back to the pioneers' camps. Remembering the women's questions, he replied, "None that I know of. When my family went across the country in the 30's, we had a guide. I thought his words were interesting and asked him to teach me as we went."

"How remarkable you are!" Jenny said. "You can speak to any savage we encounter."

He disliked the description she'd used of the people and tried to ignore his ire. "Thank you, but not as much as you'd think. I've forgotten as much as I've learned."

Marie smiled at him. "I like how you can communicate with them. Do they all speak the same language, or do different groups have different dialects?"

Grinning back, he replied, "A very good observation! They have separate languages and even their own dialects like the whites."

"Would you know what to say to those who massacred the Whitmans?" asked Ellen.

Her question took him aback. Shocked, he first said, "Probably the same thing I'd say to a group of whites who massacred an Indian village of women and children. Controversy aside, I know some Sioux, and my brother married a Nez Pierce. She taught me a little before she died. They're both different from Cayuse."

"Was your sister in law on the warpath?" Ellen asked, her eyes wide.

He shook his head, amazed at the foolishness of what she'd

said. "No, women don't go on the warpath. Sally died in childbirth."

She looked contrite. "Oh, I'm sorry. Not even an Indian deserves that sort of death."

Jenny added, "You'll have to excuse her, Mr. Granville. My theory is an Indian once bit her as a child, and she's not been the same since."

A familiar language reached Sam's ears. The young brave speaking sat to the right, grinning. Sam looked at him, eyes narrowed. "Excuse me?" he asked in the Sioux language, and the man repeated his suggestion. He shook his head, not wanting to trade Marie or the other women for a war pony. Glancing at the ladies, he grimaced, not wanting to explain. He replied in Sioux, "No trade."

""I'll give two ponies," he replied.

Shaking his head, Sam replied, "No, they are all mine and far more valuable than any horses you have."

The brave laughed. "The women are more valuable? They have tricked you."

He grinned. "Yes, they have. If I reconsider, I will come to you."

The man gave a go on gesture, knowing he'd failed. Taking the hint, Sam took Ellen's elbow and Jenny's hand. "Jenny, could you link arms with Marie, please? We need to look at the other items away from this gentleman."

"Why would we do that?" asked Jenny. "He seemed very nice."

"He thought you were nice, too."

Ellen's expression was sour. "Don't tell me, he wanted to trade for one of us." She crossed her arms. "I've read about this. You said no, I assume?"

"I did," Sam assured her.

Hands on her hips, Ellen scolded him as if she were the guide instead of him. "That cinches it. He'll be following after us, kidnapping us in the middle of the night to go live as a savage. You know how they are, always just taking what they want."

He noticed how Marie and Jenny gave each other a glance as if used to Ellen's strong opinions and shook his head. "We are on their land, and we take what we want, too."

She frowned, not budging in her stance. "Maybe so, but we

don't take people or scalps like they do! You told him no trade and your saying so should be enough."

"For the scrupulous ones, it is." Ellen was starting to anger Sam, and he didn't want to argue with someone with a closed mind. "There's a criminal element in every culture. Indians are no different."

She crossed her arms, still frowning. "Well, in this culture, there's more criminal than not."

He watched Marie admire a string of turquoise beads. "It's been my experience, personally, that the natives are more honest than whites." When Ellen glared at him, he couldn't help adding, "You have to concede I might be an expert."

"That is an excellent point." Her expression softened as they walked along. "Fine, I do concede you are an expert, and I can sleep safe tonight."

Grinning at her, he said, "I'm glad you think so."

Ellen smiled at him, but before she could say anything, Lucky said, "Boss, Miss Jenny wants me to look at something further down the line."

"Sure." Sam leaned in so only Lucky heard. "Just keep her safe, even from you."

Giving him the nod, Lucky said, "You got it."

Whites and Indians mingled all around them. A few black freedmen had offers for customers or themselves shopped for good deals. Sam looked over the available items. Some seemed new, fresh off of a wagon. Others had signs of being scavenged. Once past a stack of weathered and new books, he turned to look at him. Sure enough, they had drawn in Lefty. Sam waited a little while, watching as the boy picked up one blank journal then another half full of scribbles. "Should we move on and let you stay for a while?"

"I suppose so, sir." The young man didn't glance up from the book. "This might take a while."

"Sounds good." Sam grinned at Ellen and Marie. "I don't mind being with two beautiful women."

The younger girl's expression showed her disbelief, while Marie only laughed. "Thank you. I'd been wondering what happened to all your excessive charm."

"Excessive?" He winked at Ellen. Rewarded with a smile, he added, "I'm just honest, dearest."

"I'm sure." She paused at a selection of quilts. "Do you suppose we should trade for a few? The guidebook mentioned something about cold mountain air at night."

Before he could answer, a tall, lanky man tapped him on the shoulder. "Samuel! How are you?" They shook hands. "You're out here again so soon after your wedding?"

"I'm doing well, leading another group west." Sam looked at his friend's clothes. Indian buckskins, long braided hair, and moccasins meant he'd embraced the Shoshone side of his family tree. He grinned at the change, more used to seeing Adelard as a French man.

With an intense focus, the man's gaze fixed on Marie. Seeming a little shy under his scrutiny, she smiled. Del took her hand and kissed it as if in Europe or the nation's capital. "Is this the beautiful Anne you've described to me?"

Sam shook his head. "The wedding didn't happen. This is Marie." He paused, unable to take back his faux pas. "I mean, Mrs. Charles Warren."

"Bonjour, Madame Warren." He kissed her hand yet again.

"She's very married, so mind your manners," Sam retorted. "Ma'am, this is Mr. Du Boise."

"Adelard, to you, ma copine." The man released her hand as if reluctant to do so.

A blush crept over her face. "Thank you, though copine is a bit much. You must call me Marie, instead."

Sam shifted from one foot to the other, uneasy at the attention his friend paid Marie. He expected his friend to use some form of the French word for dear, but copine sounded suspiciously like more than an endearment. Many other women walked around them, yet Adelard focused solely on Marie. Sam needed to distract him with another pretty face. He stepped over to where Ellen browsed through a selection of discarded shoes. Taking her elbow, he grinned at her puzzled expression and led her to the other two. "This is Miss Ellen Winslow. Miss Winslow, this is Adelard Du Boise."

"Mademoiselle, is it?" He took her hand and kissed it as he'd done Marie's. "I'm very charmed and pleased there's no Mr. Winslow."

A smile belied his friend's words. Sam muttered to Marie, "Not as pleased as all those broken hearts in his wake."

Ignoring Del, Ellen said, "Mr. Granville, I'm not like a lot of the other women. I'm sure this, um, gentleman, will find me far too fussy for his tastes and will soon go on his way."

"Qu'est que c'est?" Del stared at Ellen for a few seconds. "Fussy?"

She gave him a tight grin. "Hmm, maybe picky is the word." Ellen pulled her hand from his. "So are you from this area?"

"Yes. I live with my mother's people, as you can see, but still appreciate my father's society very much. I've had adventures in both cultures."

"How interesting," Ellen said.

"It is, actually," said Sam, winking at the young woman's sour face. "However, I've heard this story before and need to get supplies."

"So do I, Mr. Granville," Ellen interjected. "I'll accompany you while Marie might keep your friend company."

Adelard held out his arm for Marie to take. "Excellent idea! I'll escort Madame Warren while you work."

She took his offered support, saying, "I wouldn't want you to be troubled."

"Bah! It's no trouble for you. If Samuel is agreeable, I'll bring today's hunt to tonight's dinner at your camp and share. Maybe then he can tell me how he let his Anne get away."

"Dinner tonight will be good. There are plenty of other ladies for you there." Sam smiled at Marie and tipped his hat. "Beware, his tales can be taller than he is."

"Shh, Samuel, let me tell the lady my secrets myself." He put his arm around her, leading Marie down to look at the handcrafted items. "Monsieur Granville exaggerates my faults instead of my charms. He's misguided."

Ellen waited until they walked out of earshot. "Do you think he will be back this evening early, or very late?"

"I'm counting on early, since he's bringing us dinner." He paused at a knife display. The blades gleamed in the sunlight, and he admired the craftsmanship in the ornate handles.

"Him? Bringing us dinner? Should we have him taste it first to see if it's safe to eat?"

He straightened, not knowing how to respond in a calm way and walked on down the row. A long silence stretched between them as he tried to concentrate on the items in front of them. A long time had passed since the last time he and Del had been around Americans together. Sam had forgotten how people from the States thought little of the natives they'd displaced. When they'd studied together in Europe, his friend had been the toast of the continent. Sam remembered that attitude far more than the discrimination here. At last, he said, "Du Boise is one of the finest men I've ever met. One of the bravest and trustworthy friends I've known."

Ellen crossed her arms. "He's a brave, certainly."

He glanced over at her, seeing the mulish expression and a little bit of a sneer. Some natives deserved her scorn, but not this one. He strove to hide his irritation at her attitude by looking at the shoes to see if any might fit some of the faster-growing children in their group. Sam made note of a couple pairs, feeling calm enough to tell Ellen, "I don't doubt there are some Indians who have earned your harsh judgment of them. This particular one does not. Your opinion of Del is very wrong."

"You're probably right. He's rather fair-complected and speaks French," she acknowledged.

"His father is French."

"Oh! So he's not all bad."

Her grasping onto his European heritage bothered Sam. The man had more redeeming qualities than Ellen gave him credit for. "No, just half, and I already disagree with you on which half that is."

"You must admit, newspapers and other first-hand accounts haven't painted savag-, um, natives, in the best of light. I might be forgiven for thinking they're a deplorable race of people."

"Have you ever considered a legal career? You're persistent in a debate." He saw Marie glance at him from a few vendors away and smiled. She returned his grin and went back to looking at the jewelry in front of her.

"I've been told that by those who know me." Ellen followed his line of sight and added, "Mrs. Warren is a lovely person, isn't she?"

"What?" The young woman had caught him off guard and red handed. "I suppose so." He added, "She's kind to others."

Ellen gazed at various goods as they strolled. "She is. Her husband is very charming. Marie has a huge blind spot where he is concerned. Most do, I've seen."

His heart dropped. Despite admitting they loved each other, Sam knew she'd go wherever Charles went. He just didn't want to hear the same thing from someone else and make Marie's leaving more real. "What do you mean by blind spot?"

"A lot of people think he's a wonderful man."

Sam kept his own counsel on Warren's personality. She didn't need to know he had the same opinion. "I see."

"You don't right now, but keep your eyes open and you will."

"Is there something you need to tell me? As captain of the wagon party, I need to know when it affects the group."

"That's a fair question. It's not my place to tell you, and if I did, it wouldn't affect everyone." She reiterated, "Keep your eyes open and you'll see soon enough."

Sam had no idea what she went on about and stated, "I'd prefer if you just told me flat out."

"So would I, trust me, but it's not for me to say you." She sighed, frustrated. "When you learn for yourself, remember that I did want to tell you but…"

"It's not for you to say."

"Exactly! Please believe that." She linked arms with him. "Come on, let's catch up with the others. You'll find out soon enough, and it'll most likely end up well for you."

Sam pondered her meaning while walking back to camp with her. As they talked about the various goods and people they'd seen, he went over his experiences with Warren's behavior in his mind. Ellen's allusion had been too vague. He didn't like surprises and made a mental note to keep an eye on the man.

The Indians had begun packing with the first hint of sunset. He looked back to see most of them gone. Clouds hovered above the western mountain range. The sun dipped below to give them a golden lining. He glanced back at the trading post again, glad to see no one following and insisting on a trade for the women.

Arriving at Winslow's wagon, Sam realized he had not heard a word she'd said in their walk. He didn't remember his responses, either. Trying to keep his expression more neutral than shameful over his lack of attention, he tipped his hat in goodbye. At his own camp, Lefty sat on his bedroll with a stack of books beside him. Sam had caught Uncle Joe before he began cooking. "Joe, we're having a guest tonight who is bringing the meat."

"Just that? Cooked?"

The question amused Sam. He'd not thought about that aspect. "I'm assuming raw."

He nodded. "Fine. I can start the biscuits and an apple cobbler until then."

Sam's stomach growled in response. "Let me know if I can help!" He reached out to feel the heavier blankets. Now dry, he pulled one from the wagon's ribbing and started folding. Lefty jumped up to help, while Joe dug around in the back for food.

"You mentioned us having a guest tonight?" asked Joe, his voice muffled as he searched.

"I did," replied Sam. He walked forward, taking the blanket ends from Lefty. "He's French Indian, and I've known him since we were children."

"So, he's more French than Indian?" asked Lefty.

The other men set out tonight's bedding for them to sit on during dinner. As he put away the stack of spare blankets, Sam replied, "He's an equal mix of both."

"Excellent answer, my friend!"

Sam turned at Del's voice and said, "Merely the truth." Indicating the slab of meat held in the other man's hand, he teased, "You walked through my camp carrying that?"

"Voilà." He held up the raw beef. "Yes, as promised, I brought dinner." Glancing at the fire, Del smiled when seeing the Dutch oven. "Dessert?"

Joe said, "It's apple cobbler."

"*Merci*, I appreciate you adding such a treat." He turned to Sam. "If I could use a pan, a plate, and some whiskey, you can continue being a gossipy hen about me."

Lucky and Arnold walked up to camp. Seeing the wary expressions on both, Sam let them know, "Gentlemen, meet a good friend of mine, Adelard Du Boise. We met at the trading post today, and we agreed he'd fix dinner for us."

"Mostly," added Uncle Joe.

Del stood and held out his palms, blood stained from cutting the flank into smaller portions for them. "We can shake hands later, agreed?"

The younger men nodded, Lucky adding, "Agreed."

Arnold came over, pausing at the apple cinnamon smell. Distracted by dessert, he said, "Boss, the stock is settled in for the night."

"Thank you." Sam was last as they settled in around the fire. Lefty and Arnold talked about the books Lefty had acquired. Everyone else watched as Del poured a cup of whiskey in the pan and placed it on the fire. One by one, he positioned the fillets in the hot liquor. The aroma released as the meat simmered made Sam's mouth water. The cobbler bubbled in the pan.

"Hello, there, Granville."

Sam recognized the voice as Ellen's father and glanced up at him. "Hello, Mr. Winslow. Are you joining us for dinner?"

He stopped in his approach when seeing Del at the fire. Mrs. Winslow bumped into him from behind as a result. "Yes."

The one clipped word and the expression on his face echoing his daughter's told Sam all he needed to know. An understanding man might let Winslow make a graceful exit so as not to socialize with an Indian. Sam didn't feel like being understanding at the moment. "Good! You and your wife join us. I see you brought your youngest. Will your daughter and other son be joining us?"

"Yes. They're on their way now." Jack Winslow sat first, taking up most of the blanket his wife spread out for them. Lucy Winslow claimed her portion, and Little Buster sat on her lap.

Sam saw Winslow fidget as if retrieving a flask from an inner vest pocket. That explained the liquor smell radiating from him. "Good evening, Jack. Missus."

Mr. Winslow cleared his throat. "I see we have a guest or sorts."

"We do. This is Adelard Du Boise, a longtime friend of mine."

Del held out his hand. "Pleased to make your acquaintance, sir."

Winslow ignored Del and turned to Sam. "Young man, if I were in charge of this operation, I'd do a lot of things on the journey different."

"Is that a fact?" Sam shook his head. First Warren and now Winslow questioning his abilities?

"Absolutely. From start to finish, there have been things I'd change for the better."

"So you've said." Sam bit back a retort suggesting Winslow take the lead and see how easy being responsible really is.

"You know, I've often wondered how many people have perished under your watch. Oh, not as a direct result of your actions, but very close."

"Dearest, please." Lucy patted his arm.

"You're not a stupid man; I'm not saying such. Still, there are a lot more precautions you could be taking." He gestured to Del at the fire. "This savage, for instance, working on our meal. You trust him too much with our provisions this evening. Has he poisoned our dinner? Shouldn't we have him taste our food, first?"

With a hard glare, Del growled, "How about you testing this first. If poisoned, I shall be distressed to see you die."

Mr. Winslow's murderous expression matched the native's. He stood, turned on his heel and left the group. While bumping into Ellen as she and Skeeter walked up to the group, Jack barked, "Family, follow."

His wife jumped up, following without hesitation. Lucy held their youngest son's hand and gave him no chance to rebel.

Ellen moved to obey out of habit and paused. Sam saw her look from her exiting family to the food cooking. She licked her lips before glancing back at them as they disappeared among the camps.

"Ellie, I don't want to go," her younger brother Skeeter whispered. He clung to her arm.

Winking at her, Del said, "I did say distressed, didn't I?"

"I think it's the insincerity of your tone, my friend." Sam tapped his fork against his tin plate. "What counts is that the remaining Winlows are in for a treat."

"My father has a bit of a temper. I'm sure he's already regretting his actions, and I'd like to apologize on his behalf."

"Apology accepted, Miss. Winslow is entitled to his opinion. This is a free country, after all." Del glanced at her, then behind her. "Bonjour, ladies. Did you bring your appetites this evening?"

Sam stood to greet Marie and Jenny.

"We did, Mr. Du Boise." Marie gave him her hand.

Jenny held back, turning his greeting from a kiss to a handshake. "Mr. Du Boise. I have to admit, the aroma led us here."

The small group settled in around the fire. Lucky sat next to Jenny, who handed Del her plate for her. Del motioned for Skeeter's plate. He gave the full dish back to the youngster then motioned for hers. Her brother ate, all the while staring with big eyes at the older man. When done distributing his cooking, Del sat next to Ellen and Sam with an effortless grace.

Marie paused in eating. "This is wonderful, Mr. Du Boise. Thank you for cooking tonight."

"The pleasure is mine, ma coup-, Marie."

As if difficult to admit, Jenny added, "It's delicious. Much better than I expected." She blushed as if realizing she'd been rude. "I mean, cooked on a campfire in such a remote place." She stirred her dinner as if her life depended on it. "Of course, you'd be good at doing so; I'm sure you could give us all lessons."

"I might have to give lessons to you in particular. A woman with your beauty would dazzle any man so much as to forget his stomach."

Mr. Lucky laughed as Jenny blushed. "That's right! Why, when I first saw this little lady, I near forgot who I was. I ain't even thought of food since she showed up, except if I thought she was hungry or something."

His enthusiasm amused everyone. They ate in silence until Del asked Marie, "We'll have to find the opportunity to talk more in French than is polite at the moment. I look forward to hearing your unique accent in one of my languages."

Marie laughed. "My accent isn't unique where I was born, but that sounds lovely, Mr. Du Boise. I should look forward to it as well."

Finished with her meal, Ellen patted her little brother on the back. "Did you get enough, Skeeter?"

"Yeah, and it was good." He whispered, "Do you think we should bring some back for everyone else?"

Hearing the question, their host interjected, "Yes, but of course you should. It will waste if you don't."

Sam added, "It's a moral imperative. I'll find a bowl."

"She could take the cook pot, yes?" Del stood, took the handle, and set the dish in front of them. "Since this is my friend's, please keep it as long as you like."

Sam glared at him, not liking the easy way Del gave away his belongings, "Which, I hope isn't too long of a time. Otherwise, I'll be dining with the Winslows."

"You're always welcome to join us." Ellen smiled at him. "But, I'll make sure you're able to cook in this first thing tomorrow morning."

"I'm certain of that, Miss Ellen," Sam said, knowing he'd have the pan back before bedtime tonight. "Skeeter? Can you help your sister take the food back to your family?"

"Sure, Mr. Granville." The young boy stood tall. "I'd be glad to."

He grinned at the serious tone. "Which chore is everyone willing to do tonight? I can stake out the animals."

"I'll help you," said Joe.

Lucky shrugged. "I can go with Lefty to wash dishes."

"That leaves me to set up bedding," Arnold volunteered.

"With my help," Del added.

Each man got to his feet and set off to get their work finished. Sam laughed and addressed Del, "Who asked you to spend the night with us?"

"Who said I couldn't?" he retorted. "Besides, we've not visited in how many years? I might stay for a while on my way back home. Or not, if you prefer." Del shrugged. "I have no plans."

"You do now. Tag along and we can catch up on what you've been doing since university." Sam saw Jenny seem uncertain what to do next. "Miss, would you like me to walk you back to camp?"

"Oh my, no. We're just across there." She smiled at him and gave a wave. "Tell Mr. Lucky goodnight for me, please. He was a bit eager to get his chores done, I suppose."

"I will and goodnight to you as well." He reached for a hat that wasn't there and tipped an imaginary brim. She giggled and left for her own family. Sam liked the young lady. She seemed a good match for Lucky. He stepped around Del and Arnold as they set out the bedrolls and took the animals for a drink and some fresh grass. Used to the routine, both men and animals soon settled in for sleep.

A loud thud jolted Sam from dozing. He shrugged out of his blankets. The sound seemed to come from the opposite side of camp. He ran to the noise's origin, picking up his rifle on the way.

"Git outta here, you dirty red Injun!" Mr. Norman, brandishing a shovel, stood over an unconscious brave.

"I think you got him, Mr. Norman," said Sam. As the night watch, Lucky and Arnold came up on horseback, he said, "We'll take care of him."

"You sure? 'Cause I kin whack him a coupla times more." He brandished the shovel like one of those baseball bats.

"We're sure." He examined the man, who wore a long-sleeved

shirt and boots but wore his hair long and braided. Sam felt for a pulse. Finding none, he stood, facing Mr. Norman. "He's dead."

CHAPTER 8

A tinny whump sound shook Marie awake. She'd never heard the sound of metal against a body before now. Taking a deep breath while sliding out of bed, she wanted to see what had happened. She took care in not waking Charles. If the noise had been something serious, they'd have all been awakened by an alarm. Quiet as she could, Marie tiptoed in the odd sound's direction. She stopped when hearing Sam declare someone dead. Afraid he was speaking about someone she knew, she pressed on and halted when seeing him and the Granville men standing around a body.

Mr. Norman looked up at her, then back at his victim before saying, "I cain't have hit him that hard."

"Hard enough to kill him, certainly." Sam shook his head and began patting down the dead man. No one spoke until he straightened. "I didn't feel a knife or gun."

Searching the ground, Mr. Norman said, "He had a gun. I saw it fall when I hit him."

"Tell me what happened. How did you avoid getting shot?"

He scratched his forehead while thinking. "I saw him stealin' my horse, got my shovel. When I made a noise, he jumped an' drew his gun. I froze 'till he started off with my horse. Soon as he did that, I smacked him hard to teach him a lesson." He stooped, picking up the gun. "Here ya' go! Right where he left it."

Sam took the weapon, asking, "Why didn't you use your shotgun?"

Mr. Norman shrugged. "I don't keep it loaded on account of my children. Loadin' it takes too much time when a man's ridin' away with your horse."

After a few moments, Lucky asked Sam, "What do you think, boss?"

"A lot of things. First, it was self-defense since Mr. Norman had a gun drawn on him. Second, the man is a horse thief. Or rather, was. Third, he's white, trying to pass as Indian." Sam knelt and pushed the sleeve up the dead man's arm. Marie saw from where she stood how the bandit had painted his face and hands, leaving his arms pale. Sam continued, "His act could have started a war with the Indians."

"Should we strip and bury him?" asked Lefty.

"Yes, with Mr. Norman getting the gun and money for his trouble." He turned to Marie and the small crowd of other light sleepers who'd gathered behind her. "Back to sleep, everyone. Morning won't get here any later than usual because of this."

Marie turned to the others to go back to their beds. She tried not to stare after Sam and yawned while returning to her own camp. Charles was sitting up as she approached, while Hester still slept. He held open the blankets for her, and Marie slid in beside him.

"What happened?" he whispered. "I heard the commotion."

"Someone dressed like an Indian tried to steal a horse. One of the men hit him in the head with a shovel and killed him."

"With what? Who is digging around at this time of night so a shovel is handy?" He snuggled in against her. "Though, I suppose hitting him with a pillow would be less effective."

She stifled a chuckle at her husband's quip. "Should you go help bury him?"

"No, I can't. I'm asleep."

Her last thought before dozing was of wondering when Charles had become so lazy and uncharitable. She couldn't remember if he'd always been this way or not.

Early morning rustling woke Marie. She shivered and breathed in the desert air still heavy with dew Marie sat up with a smile, not realizing until now how much she'd missed the moisture. Easing out of bed, she was careful to not disturb her husband's sleep. The siren song of fresh coffee called to her, so she grabbed up a bucket and went to the river.

She smiled and nodded greetings at others as she passed them, both going to and coming from the water. Rebuilding the fire took some work. She assembled the ingredients for biscuits in a hurry, eager to get the day started. A chill swept through her. Why be eager when each step carried her closer to a separation from Sam? In the clear sunlight of morning, seeing the last of him didn't seem possible. Marie continued stirring, now not ready to start cooking.

"Hmm," Charles sat up, rubbing his eyes. "Smells good."

His voice snapped her out of her thoughts. "So will breakfast, darling."

"Biscuits again?"

"I'm afraid so." She placed scoops of dough into the pan. "I'll cut some bacon in a minute. Help yourself to the coffee." A glance over at Hester showed the older woman still slept. Marie shook her head, amazed at how her sister in law could still doze when the camp hummed to life around her. Getting the bacon and a jar of preserves to placate her husband, she returned to the campfire. "Should we wake her?"

"Not yet. She needs the rest."

Marie refrained from the retort concerning rest from what, exactly, coming to mind. She handed him a cup and filled one for herself. "You're probably right. She seems to have been a bit terse lately."

"It's this country. It takes a lot out of a woman like her." He glanced over at his wife. "I mean, she's not like you. Hester is more highly strung. Like an exquisite mare, really."

She looked at him from over the rim of her cup. Asking him what sort of animal he'd compare her to might not end the morning on a positive note. As she was much shorter than the twins, they probably thought of her as something small and rodent-like. Better to stay quiet and think on what creature he most closely resembled. If Hester was a mare, then it seemed to reason Charles was a stallion. Or more likely, a gelding. The two talked as Marie suppressed a wicked grin and flipped the biscuits. The comparison seemed a little wrong. Maybe he resembled something less gallant than a horse, yet nobler than a jackass.

The sun peeked over the eastern horizon, spreading light over all of them. She watched as Hester stirred to life, blinking and rubbing her eyes much as her brother had earlier. Not needing to be asked, Marie dished out the breakfast. She saved back some for lunch and set aside the pan to cool as she ate her own meal. Glancing up to see Hester's frown when staring at her own plate, she couldn't blame the woman for showing dissatisfaction. Marie dreamed of a return to the days of banquets and feasts. Without interrupting the siblings as they talked, she stood and took their empty plates. They needed to be ready for the ferry today. She hoped the twins would have everything ready with the bedrolls put away and animals tended by the time she returned from washing.

She cleaned up, a little grin on her face when realizing how much she'd been searching for Sam in the walk back to camp. In a group as small as theirs camped in one spot, they met up at least once a day. She gazed out across the wide river. Already the air held a promise of the day's desert heat. She breathed in deep, enjoying how the warmth amplified the smells. If she stared straight ahead and ignored the sounds around her, she'd be the only person in the world. An appealing thought when either Warren loitered nearby, not so much if Sam was absent. Shaking off the reluctance to return, Marie broke her reverie and headed back to the wagon.

A welcome sight greeted her. Their belongings had been packed away, and the animals weren't there. She presumed Charles and less likely Hester was seeing to them before they started for the ferry. Feeling an odd mix of impatience and reluctance, she put the dinner pail full of drying dishes into the wagon. Angry chatter from first Charles, then his sister, grew louder as the two approached.

"Easy for you to say. It's not your six dollars they're wanting."

"No, but it's my life if this topples over and I drown."

"You're not going to drown. Don't you have more faith in me than that?"

"I do, but sometimes…"

A piercing scream interrupted Hester. Marie and the Warrens ran to the source, leaving the animals half hitched. Following the sound and continuing shouts led them to the river's edge. Marie watched in horror as the Winslows and Granville's men struggled to pull the wagon and animals back to shore. She tried to count people as they bobbed and swam. Feeling someone grab her arm, she turned to see Jenny clinging to her.

"Oh no! Mr. Granville warned them and now look!"

Marie put her arm around the distraught girl. "They'll be fine. Samuel and Lucky are there." She pointed. "Look! Mr. Du Boise has Ellen, and the boys are on shore. They're all fine."

"Damn," said Charles from behind the women.

She turned to see her husband squinting at the incident and asked him, "I suppose we're paying to cross?"

"Looks like it." He stepped forward when a bundle of clothes floated towards them. Reaching into the river and scooping it up, he said, "I suppose they'll need this." He held the soggy bundle out to Marie, water pouring from it. "You can give them their bedding, if that is what this is, while I get us ready for the ferry."

She took the bundle, holding it away from her dress. "Of course." In the meantime, Jenny had let go of her, and Marie saw the girl hugging Ellen. She walked over to the group gathering around the Winslows.

Jenny let go of her friend while saying, "You disappeared, then Mr. Du Boise, then Mr. Granville. After seeing the wagon, we just knew the worst had happened."

Smiling when seeing a soaked Del standing in front of her, Marie said to him, "I'll hug you for saving our friend's life after you're dry."

"I'll take you up on that, ma chère." He said to Ellen, "We should both find other clothes soon."

Marie spoke before her friend could reply. "Everything in your wagon is probably drenched. You can help me search our things for something dry." She crooked her finger for Ellen to follow her. "Your hems will be a little high due to our height difference."

"I'll be happy with whatever you find. Anything is better than this cold feeling for the rest of the day."

"Good. Jenny, your mother and Mrs. Winslow are similar. She and the boys might be able to borrow some clothes from your family, too."

"I'll take them to Ma and see what she can find them." The girl hurried off to escort the rest of the family to the Allens' wagon.

Marie took Ellen's hand, alarmed at how chilled it was. "Mercy! You're near frozen. Let's go get started."

Del tapped her on the shoulder. "Madame, please excuse me while I'm finding other clothes. I prefer trousers to dresses."

Her first impulse was to help Del by offering Charles' clothes. She frowned, imagining her husband's adverse reaction and nodded without saying anything. Even the idea of the tall, dark man in a dress too short for him didn't cheer her. They watched as he walked toward Sam's wagon.

Ellen spoke first, "He is a good-looking man for an Indian."

"I think so, too," Marie said.

Ellen shrugged. "He didn't have to save us. If we died, there would be fewer white people for his people to kill later."

The outrageous statement first took Marie's breath. She stared at the younger woman. "Good heaven above, why would you say such a thing?" As she saw shame sweep Ellen's face, she added,

"Not all the natives want to kill us. A lot of them who do are retaliating for wars started by us." During her speech, Marie saw how Ellen stared at her father on the other side of the river. She followed her friend's gaze and watched as Mr. Winslow talked with a group of men. The family wagon, oxen still connected, continued to drain water even while on the opposite bank. When Marie looked back at Ellen, the girl still staring down at her soaked clothes and shoes.

Ellen coughed and stated in a quiet voice, "If not for a damned Indian, as my father calls them, he'd be the only one of us alive now. I think I can stop pretending and admit I'm extremely fond of Mr. Du Boise."

"He seems to be a fine man and a kind person." Marie smiled when seeing the softening of Ellen's expression.

The younger woman blushed. "If I weren't forbidden by my father, I would be thrilled to learn everything about him. He's handsome, seems educated, and speaks several languages. As if all that weren't enough, he thinks I'm beautiful and has said so more than once." She shrugged, adding, "Clearly, the man isn't perfect. He needs glasses as strong as mine. Still, I do like him very much."

Marie felt compelled to dispute Ellen's comment. Not wanting to argue at the moment, she said instead, "Then, I suppose it's settled. Mr. Du Boise is not only very wise, but is also very tolerable. We shall be kind to him from now on, but not too much. He's still a man we've only just met."

Her face glowed when Ellen admitted, "I might need to be less kind than I have been in the past day or so."

With a wicked grin, Marie motioned for her to follow. "You'll have to tell me why exactly as you sort through my longest dresses."

"I don't know if I should even say aloud what happened."

She laughed when seeing a deep red blush begin on her friend's face. "Goodness! That much?"

"No, not much. Although anything is too much since he's not white."

"Oh." Ellen's crude statements, an echo of her father's prejudice, still rang in Marie's mind. She nodded. "Yes, that would be a problem."

"I don't think my father would even see the European part of Adelard."

Marie let down the tailgate and climbed inside the wagon. "Maybe if Del wore clothes from France, your father might see him differently." She opened a trunk, found just the right dress for Ellen, and held it up. "I'd loan you this, but it's Hester's. She'd protest."

"Best not to start a fight, then. I'd rather wear one of yours, even if my knees showed."

Marie snorted a laugh before stopping herself. "Now, now, I'm not so tall. You're just a lovely young sapling." She searched through the dresses, pulling a pale blue calico of her own from the trunk. "This is perfect! Yes, it's not long enough, but everyone will be looking at how bright gray your eyes are. No one will see your ankles."

Taking the dress, Ellen held it against her. "It's so lovely, I'm not sure I should take it."

"Yes, you should." She dug around in the trunk, thinking of another she could loan her friend. "Here, you'll want this as well. It's one of my Sunday dresses and is a little too tight, or has been. I don't even want to try this on again and stretch the seams."

"You don't think you've slimmed since we left Missouri?"

Marie paused, knowing Ellen was right. Still, the light green would look so pretty on the young woman. "I might have. It doesn't matter. I want you to have this. Charles has been complaining about how many dresses I packed. You'll be doing all of us a favor by taking this. He won't need to complain, and I won't need to hear him." She closed the trunk and went to another one. "I have some leftover fabric in here. Enough to make a couple of ruffles to lengthen the skirts."

The woman took a step back. "I don't know; that's awfully generous of you."

"Not so much generous as necessary." She found the folded cloth. "The oxen will like the lighter load, and Charles will be happy." Giving the fabric to Ellen, she said, "See? I'm entirely selfish in this."

"I'm not sure about that, but thank you." Ellen shook her head. "This is like a birthday and Christmas in one day."

Charles knocked on the wagon. "Ladies? We're the next to cross on the ferry."

"Thank you, dear. We'll be out in a moment." Marie turned to her friend. "Jenny's family is behind us. I'm sure you can change in their wagon without the rush."

Ellen nodded, holding the dresses close to her. "Thank you again, Marie. You're a true friend."

The compliment left her feeling shy. "It takes one to know one."

Nodding at the young woman, Charles said, "Miss Winslow. Looks like you're set."

"Thank you, too, Mr. Warren, for helping us."

"You're welcome." He said to Marie, "Are you ready, yet?"

"I am." She looked at Ellen, who nodded, and turned back to her husband. "Ready whenever you are. Where's Hester?"

"She's on the ferry already with the fare." He sat on the wagon seat. "Come on up and let's go."

Marie hoisted herself up and settled in next to her husband. Charles clicked and snapped the reins. The oxen pulled them over to where the ferry and Hester waited. They rolled onto the conveyance with a jounce. The wood underneath their wheels swayed a little under their combined weight. She held onto the seat with the motion. As soon as the ferry started across, Charles hopped down and went to Hester. Marie looked back at them for a moment before turning ahead to watch the opposite bank approach.

River crossings both scared and thrilled her. Each time, the possibility of tipping over and drowning loomed. Reaching solid ground meant one more landmark lay behind them. Marie smiled as the ferry bumped its way onto the bank. Charles helped Hester up before seating himself beside his sister. They continued on, catching up with others in the Granville party. All of them rolled slow enough for those behind them to catch up. Before too long, Marie grew tired of being jostled. "Charles? I'd like to step down now."

He heaved a sigh as if bothered by the request. "Very well." The animals eased to a stop when he pulled the reins, giving Marie the chance to jump down. The instant her hemline brushed the ground; Charles clicked the oxen back into motion. Marie looked away to hide her scowl from him. She disliked his quiet punishments almost more than his louder temper tantrums. She frowned when thinking of joining Jenny or Ellen for noon. No sense in inflicting her sour disposition on them. A long day of dwelling on California loomed ahead of her. The incline Marie walked up winded her. She stopped to catch her breath, already missing her friends' distracting chatter.

The gravel under her feet rolled. She caught herself, halting a tumble to the ground. Marie looked down the road, wanting a steady ridge to follow. This struggling uphill and bracing herself downhill grew tiresome fast. At a distance, the hills looked easy to traverse. Going up one side and down the other worked the men and animals hard. They followed a dry creek bed for what seem like days before finding a small pool of spring water.

When hearing the signal to stop, she sighed, grateful for the day's milestone. Marie shivered with cold, though a rivulet of sweat ran down her back. She frowned at the sensation. Shaking her head, she tried to think of an illness with such symptoms and couldn't remember any. She went to her family's wagon, now hot and wanting a drink of water.

She found a cup and went to the front of the wagon. Charles had their animals there. The oxen slurped at the thin stream. Marie smiled at her husband. "I don't blame them."

He gave her a grin. "Nor do I. When the sun isn't roasting us alive, the cold winds are freezing us."

"I'm glad to hear that." She knelt a little upstream from the animals' noses. "I've been feeling feverish all morning."

Charles walked over to her, pressing the back of his hand against her forehead. "No, you're not sick."

His smile and touch warmed her heart. Marie looked up at him, seeing a glimpse of the man she'd married. "I'm glad. Thank you for checking."

"My pleasure." He smoothed a stray lock of hair back behind her ear. "We've not been alone like this in a while, have we?" Looking up and around him, he added, "Alone as much as we can be while traveling in the group, of course. You and I will spend much more time together in California. We'll keep a shop, have our home above the store, and will be very successful, I promise." He caressed her cheek.

Her heart skipped when she heard his plans. Charles' loving kindness to Marie just now made leaving Sam almost bearable. She glanced away from her husband's brown eyes and into the western horizon. Soon, the days would run out, and she'd have to leave Sam and the others.

"You seem troubled, my love."

Her eyebrows raised and Marie struggled to keep an even temper. "Your love? I've not heard that from you in a long time, I think," she blurted, her voice angry to even her own ears. She stopped just short of asking why all the affectionate words now after pushing her away for months. He'd only give the reason as respecting her privacy, something she didn't quite believe anymore.

He frowned. "I've thought such words were understood."

She followed as he led the oxen to a patch of short grass. "They are, but I enjoy hearing them once in a while from you."

"I suppose you want me to go on and on about love and such."

"No, I'm all right with hearing the occasional word."

He stared past her shoulder and frowned. "Are you? I don't think so. I give you one romantic sentiment, and you're acting like I've been neglectful."

"What? No, not at all. You're a good husband…."

Bumping her a little, Hester brushed past Marie. "You're right. My brother is the best husband a woman could want."

Like a dog with a bone, Charles picked up on his wife's admission and didn't let go. "You think I'm good? I suppose I should be grateful for that much." He glanced up from watching the animals eat. "You have never been happy with anything I've given you."

Marie clenched her hands. "I have so."

"No, you haven't. I know what you meant by thanking me, how I've not been paying enough attention to you or saying lovely things to you often enough." He jerked on the oxen, pulling them away from their grazing. "You think I'm neglectful and don't coddle you enough."

"I don't mean that at all."

"Yes, you do. You think, well, it doesn't matter what you think. I'll never be enough of a lapdog for you. I'm too busy trying to get us across the country and into a better life. You're just too spoiled to notice my hard work."

"Why, Charles! Of course, I appreciate what you do…"

"No, you sure as hell don't." He turned and stomped away without taking the animals with him.

Hester smirked at her before following Charles. Marie stood frozen, wondering what had happened to them. After a moment, she closed her mouth and shook her head. Somehow in the conversation, she'd offended him. Seeing others moseying back to the wagons, she bent and took the oxen's reins in her hands. Neither Charles nor Hester said anything to her as Marie gave the reins to her husband. She glanced up at Hester, perched on the seat. The other woman gave a nod before staring ahead. Marie didn't like the smirk her sister in law failed to hide.

They all moved as one when the bugle's notes drifted across the land. Her stomach growled, reminding Marie she missed eating. A long afternoon stretched out in front of her. Unwilling to beg for scraps from others, and not wanting to stop the Warrens, she knelt by the water and scooped up a handful to drink. Several sips later, she began following the wagon train.

At the top of a steep incline, she paused. If the climb hadn't left her breathless, the vista in front of Marie would have. Gray-green hills spread out in all directions, low mountains in the distance. Bright yellow splashes of wildflowers broke up the sage, brightening the landscape. She breathed in as the north breeze flowed against her face. The vastness stretched endlessly with the westward march of emigrants being the only sign of humanity. The sound of a horse's hooves caught her attention. Marie smiled, hoping Sam was checking on her. She turned to see Del as he approached.

"*Bonjour, madam.*" He dismounted a few feet away from her. "*Comment allez vous?*"

"*Tres bien, merci. Et vous?*"

"*Bien, d'accord.*"

"Penny for your thoughts, Adelard, as if I didn't already know," Marie said.

Del smiled and shook his head. "I can't admit to thinking of a particular woman."

She smiled. "Good, because I'd hate to see my friend hurt."

"Hurt? How could I do that?"

"Probably in the same way she could hurt you."

"Not possible." Del shook his head "I don't regard her as a savage and subhuman."

She nodded. "It is possible. She's beginning to care a lot for you." Marie smiled at him, "She said a lot of complimentary things about you after the rescue. I'm not sure if she wanted me to say anything, though. She ought to give her opinion to you herself."

"This discussion is somewhat futile. Her father has forbidden us to talk."

"Do you think she'll abide by his decision?" she asked.

He smiled. "As much as she can, despite my tempting her."

Marie stared hard at him. "Are you sure doing so is a good idea? I'd hate to see her punished for your actions."

"As would I." He held his hand out for her to hold, steadying her as she inched down a steep decline. "She's in no danger, I can promise."

She waited until he and his horse clambered down as well. "Thank you for the reassurance."

Del opened his mouth just as Lucky rode up to them. He smiled at her. "We can continue this later?"

"Oui." She returned his grin. "I'd like that."

Lucky spoke first. "Ma'am, Mr. Du Boise, we're stopping at Emigrant Springs up ahead. Mr. Granville wants to make camp there tonight. He thinks it might be the last good water until Smith's Fork."

Del turned to Marie. "Madame, I see your family up ahead." He swung up onto his horse and nodded. "Au revoir."

She watched as Lucky tipped his hat in farewell and they rode toward the back of the train. Both men had warm brown eyes similar to Charles'. She smiled, thinking of how their young lives stretched out in front of them. Looking ahead, Marie sighed. The lead wagons pulled around in the usual circle. Jenny caught her eye, and she waved at the girl who returned her greeting.

Another wagon party pulled in just behind them, forming their own circle. Marie found her family's wagon. Used to their chores, she noticed the other Warrens had unhitched the oxen. Charles took care of them, and Hester gathered firewood most evenings. Retrieving the pail, she snuck glances at the various people when scooping water for dinner. No one looked familiar, so she didn't stop to chat with anyone. A sudden faint feeling reminded her of missing the noon meal.

Getting dinner together took her no time. Marie set out the blankets to sit on and settled in to wait. She drummed her fingers, hunger nagging her into action. Standing, she went off in search of sage to burn.

With the fuel gathered and the campfire ready for cooking, she placed cut up chunks of bacon in to fry. Beans needed more time than she had. Marie mixed up some cornbread, putting in a handful of dried currants to give it some taste. The food smelled better with each passing minute. Satisfied the meat was ready, she moved the pans to the side of the fire and dished up her own meal. The Warrens walked up just as she finished her last bite.

Charles spoke first while bending down to kiss the top of her head. "Hello, dearest. Dinner is ready, I see."

Before she could reply to her husband, Hester said, "And you kept it warm for us. Astounding."

Marie frowned, sensing censure in her sister in law's tone. "I did, in fact. Everything is close enough to keep warm without burning."

"Oh, certainly it is." Hester settled in and started getting food. "I'm pleased to see such common sense from you, dear sister."

She stopped just short of frowning at the older woman. Charles blocked her view for a moment, getting his own dinner. He leaned back and Marie took the opportunity to ask, "Would one of you be willing to do dishes tonight?"

Grinning at her, Charles replied, "I'd be glad to wash dishes. Hessy can help."

Hester's face wrinkled in disagreement. "I can?"

"For a meal like this, you can."

Her expression didn't change. "I suppose so."

Marie was tempted to tell them that the dinner was no better cooked than any other night but only seemed so because they'd come on time rather than letting it scorch and dry while they tarried doing God knows what. She summoned the good grace to refrain, however, mostly to avoid involvement. Wanting to just let them fight it out among themselves, Marie ignored the banter and added, "Then I might go see what's happening at the main camp, see if there's any entertainment tonight."

"Oh, goodness. You think the music that man plays is enjoyable?"

Charles patted his sister's hand. "Now, Hess, she's entitled to her own preferences."

Marie took the chance in their pause to ask, "Do I need to do any chores?"

"No, dearest," said Charles. "We took the animals for a long graze."

"Thank you both." She slipped away, taking a deep breath once out of earshot. As if shedding a second skin, Marie's tension eased with each step towards Sam's campsite.

She stepped around a wagon, saw him in the firelight, and stopped in her tracks. He'd taken off his hat. His dark hair stood up from where he'd run a hand through it. He laughed after Del said something she couldn't hear. Marie loved how warm his skin looked, his smile creasing his face. He glanced at her, his expression skipping her heart a beat. His eyes warmed her soul like the flames shimmering in the night air between them. Staring at the handsome and scruffy man appealed so much to her right now. Del waving at her caught Marie's attention, breaking the spell between her and Sam. "Good evening, gentlemen," she said while taking a step forward. "Is there room for me?"

"Always, ma chère. Have a seat between us." The cinnamon-skinned man scooted further away from Sam.

Embarrassed at being caught staring, she didn't look at Sam as she settled in between him and his friend. She looked around the fire, seeing Lucky polish his bugle, Arnold writing in a journal, and Uncle Joe sewing closed a tear in some clothing.

Sam leaned over, bumping her shoulder with his. "Lefty is checking on the animals, Jenny is staying at her family's camp this evening, and Ellen said she'd try to be here later."

"Thank you for answering my question before I asked." She smiled at him, her breath catching at the affection in his clear blue eyes. Afraid to seem calf-eyed over him, Marie cleared her throat and turned to Del. "Do you plan on staying here if Ellen joins us tonight?"

He scooped up another handful of pebbles and tossed them into the fire one by one. "I try to stay away, yet always find a reason to see her." Again throwing little rocks, he asked no one in particular, "Why do I do this when there are more pressing matters in my life?"

Marie smiled at him, "Such as?"

Del crossed his legs at the ankles, watching the flames flickering beyond his feet. "Such as anything else except convincing Mr. Winslow I don't have designs on his daughter."

"Ah," Sam said. "But don't you?"

He shrugged. "I might or might not."

"More like you do and you do." Sam laughed at Del's scornful look and asked, "Or are you interested in her as more than a temporary lady friend?"

"Every woman interests me more than as a temporary friend." He grinned at Marie. "Including you, ma coupin."

"Are you sure I'm yours?" she asked. "Or has the meaning of coupin changed in Canada to mean something less than a girlfriend?"

"Girlfriend?" Sam's eyebrows rose. "But you call every woman that. Which isn't a surprise now that I think about it."

Ignoring his friend's remark, Del responded, "Forgive me, I've been too familiar with you. I'm not so much Canadian but French."

When seeing Ellen approach, Marie said, "Ellen! Hello!" She patted the blanket next to her. "Please join us! Mr. Du Boise was just explaining his citizenship in our two countries."

"Canada and the United States are the two countries?" Still in Marie's dress, Ellen settled in.

"More as in France and the United States," said Sam

Settled in, Ellen gave him her full attention. "You're truly a French citizen?"

"Yes, I am. The United States won't grant automatic citizenship to native people. Being born on its soil doesn't matter. Only if a person is lighter than my buckskins are they given such an honor."

Her brow furrowed, she said, "I should think the native peoples would automatically be citizens if they chose."

"Non." Del shook his head, "Not of the US. France is more inclusive, so, I claim its citizenship, and it claims me."

Ellen smiled at him. "Have you ever been to France, or is it a distant thought and land?"

"I have been and lived, ma coeur." He glanced at Sam to quell any remarks. "Then came back home."

"Did you like it there?" asked Marie. "I've never been, though my father was born there and came here soon after. He didn't remember anything, and you must tell me everything."

Sam laughed. "If he tells you everything, every conquest, we'll be here all night. He's not had as many conquests here in the Territories. Unlike overseas, he's a face in the crowd instead of a face to crowd."

"You are so right, but you are leaving out your own escapades with the fairer gender." Addressing Marie, Del went on, "Our Samuel snuck out of many, many windows in the predawn." The other man stopped smiling. "There were a few he did not have to pay to enter."

"My goodness, Sam! You'd told me you'd never had need of…" She glanced at Ellen. "Need of a saloon."

At Ellen's confused expression, Del reassured Marie, "It is all in jest. The girls liked the idea of Sam being an uncouth American and found his accent appealing. Our friend here was the novelty all the ladies loved."

"I see. Well, I suppose we've established the women there are very friendly. What was the countryside like, or did you see any while lurking around at night?"

Sam laughed, "She has you there, Del."

Smiling, he responded, "The country is beautiful in a tame way. The mountains seem to hold up the sky, while every city's streets follow the curve of its river. Row after row of grapes hung from fence-like structures." He looked at Sam, "What are they called?" Back to Ellen, "No matter. The fruit hangs from the vine, begging to be picked, but you don't take a single one."

"You did," Sam chided.

Del laughed, "Yes, and an angry grower's pellet gun is why now I don't."

"How long were you there?"

Marie smiled at the lowered tones of the couple and stared into the fire. She welcomed the warmth against the chilly night air. Feeling Sam's gaze on her, she said, "Does it ever feel like Oregon is closer to China than to Independence?"

He laughed. "Yes, more times than I care to admit." He leaned back on his hands, staring at the stars. "I believe the moon is easier to reach some days."

She followed his movements, also leaning back on her hands to look at the twinkling canopy above them. "Lately, though, Fort Hall seems distressingly close." She peeked at him without turning her head. "I'm not sure if I'm feeling fear or dread at the idea of going south from there."

Sam closed his eyes for several long moments. "Mine is dread." He sat up, looking at the fire. "I won't be able…" Interrupting himself, he shook his head. "I can continue on afterward, even though able to and willing to are very different." He turned to look at her. "If I can't keep going after the fort, I'll learn how to pan gold."

Sitting up, she stared at him. He would follow them? Did she want him to do so? She swallowed the rising lump in her throat, wanting to ask him a dozen personal questions. Before Marie could say anything, he stood and held out his hand to help her up as well.

He smiled at Ellen while saying, "Miss Winslow, I hate to break up what seems to be an intense chat. It's getting late, however, and I think your father would be happiest if you camped with them tonight."

Ellen got to her feet. "I know he would. And after today's events, I'm exhausted."

Marie took Sam's arm. "If you'll see me back to my wagon, Adelard can walk Ellen to her camp."

Ellen looked from Marie to Del. "Maybe only halfway."

Nodding, Del said, "Halfway, then."

The quartet separated, and once out of earshot of anyone else, Sam whispered in Marie's ear, "I'm glad he's distracted with Ellen."

She covered her mouth with a hand to muffle her laugh. "You're just now telling me this?"

"You are always your own person. I'm rational enough to know such a thing. However, when a man like Du Bois is attentive to you, I can't stand it." He caressed her face. "I didn't like him talking to you that day at the trading post."

"He was a bit overwhelming to me. His height was one aspect, but his attention left no doubt as to Adelard's intentions."

Sam's expression darkened, and his eyes narrowed. "He had intentions?"

Marie tried to hide a smile. "More like he seemed to have them that day until he met Ellen. Once Adelard saw her, well, he was still very nice to Jenny and me, but you saw how he was with Ellen."

"All I saw was how he acted with you."

While she liked his jealousy, Marie couldn't let him suffer. "It doesn't matter how he acted with me. I'm not your responsibility."

He shook his head. "No, you're much more than that to me." Sam glanced at the night sky. "We can argue this at a later date. Time for bed."

Though hidden from the campfire's light in the wagon's shadow, Marie saw Sam's face. She knew his expressions well enough to see the love there, and her heart thudded. Facing away from a sleeping Charles and an alert Hester, Marie let her face betray her emotions. She wanted to caress the stubble on his face, kiss his lips until he begged for more. The idea of doing anything so bold left her lightheaded. To stem the rising tide of desire, she turned without waiting for him to go. "Until later, then. Good night." Marie nodded at her sister in law while slipping off her shoes. She glanced up to see Hester's demeanor change from pleasant to sour.

When Sam was out of earshot, Hester said, "I suppose you think you're special, don't you?"

"Excuse me?" asked Marie.

"Don't think I can't see what you're doing."

"And that would be?"

She shook her finger at the younger woman. "You're lining up a new husband in case something happens to our dear Charles."

"I'm not!"

Hester's eyes narrowed even more. "You heard me. Don't get any funny ideas about running off with Granville. He's too good for you."

Anger at the insult cloaked Marie like a second skin. "Oh? He's also too good for you as well, yet, that's not stopped you from flirting."

Giving her a mean little smile, Hester said, "I'm not serious. Not as much as you are."

Marie opened her mouth to deny everything and stopped. She had been flirting, although not too sincerely. She couldn't lie. "I have no ideas about running off with anyone. I'm also not planning on Charles' death. Thus, there is no list of future husbands I'm cultivating."

Hester looked down her nose at Marie. "I'll pretend to believe you for now."

"It doesn't matter what you believe. The truth is the truth."

Her sister in law rolled over to face away from Marie. A weight settled in the pit of her stomach. She settled in beside her husband and slipped her hand between his arm and waist to hold him. Had she been overtly flirtatious with Sam in front of anyone? She grimaced. One of the problems already apparent was thinking of him as someone more familiar than Mr. Granville. When she added in the kissing and other intimacies? Marie shook her head. She'd been desperate for touch and let that drive her actions.

Charles' body heat warmed her as she snuggled in closer. He

smelled like sunshine and his own sweat. The trip had been grueling on all of them. She pressed her forehead against his back. He had all the responsibility. No wonder he'd been short with her. Most men had behaved far worse than he ever did. Guilt took a solid hold of her. She needed to be a much better wife to Charles and dwell a lot less on Mr. Granville.

Marie greeted the morning with good intentions. Yes, she loved Sam, adored him, even. If not for her marriage, loving him as more than a friend would be so easy for her. She sat up, seeing the empty space where Charles had laid. When ignoring his sometimes cranky and distracted treatment, she enjoyed his loving care and fatherly protection of her. She sighed, pushing down the feelings within her for Sam, struggling to be acknowledged. After a glance at the stone cold embers, she eased her chilled limbs into standing. The still morning air managed to smell of coffee, despite the lack of a breeze. She placed a hand on Charles' side of the bedding. Judging by the warmth, he'd not been gone long.

No one had gathered more fuel in her absence last night. Marie stretched, hoping that's what the Warrens were doing at the moment. She searched for and found the water pail. The sight of crusted dinner dishes greeted her, and she gritted her teeth. Blood pounded in her ears as she stifled a curse. She took a deep, calming breath while picking up the pail. A second examination of the plates showed the food might wash off easier than she'd expected. She walked to the water's edge, keeping her jaw clamped against anger.

She managed to smile at others as they fetched water for their breakfasts. It seemed no one else cleaned up dinner dishes as she did. Having her hands in the stream felt oddly comforting. Marie's temper cooled while she worked. Setting the pans on soil more rock than dirt, she put the plates and silverware on top. She eased from her knees to her feet, balancing the dishes in one hand and carrying the half-full pail in the other.

By the time she reached the camp, a fire burned in the pit. No coffee boiled since they'd relied on her to bring the water, she supposed. "Good morning." She smiled as both nodded a greeting. Filling the coffee pot took no time, and she placed the frying pan on the small grill. After a quick mix of the batter ingredients, Marie began cooking the biscuits.

Hester sighed as if weighted by the world's problems before she stood and started gathering the beds. Charles stood up as she came over to him to put away his and Marie's beds as well. "Let me help you shake these," he said. She gave him the opposite ends of a blanket, and they shook the fabric clean. Marie smiled, watching them almost dance as they folded until everything was stored in the wagon.

After eating and drinking, she and Hester washed up while Charles tended the animals and yoked them to the cart for the day. The bugle sounded to travel with them ready to go. Marie took their preparedness as a good omen for the day. Various head of families chirped to their beasts, and they all started moving north along the valley.

Before she could begin looking for her friends, fresh gusts brought the heavy smell of rain. Moisture in the air pressed back against her as she walked forward. Soon enough sprinkles fell, followed by larger, hail like drops of water. Huge splashes pelted Marie, and she ran to the back of their wagon. The animals pulled slow enough; climbing aboard wasn't difficult, even with slippery shoes. She crawled over the cargo to the front. Hester waited there while Charles sat, tipping his hat against the wind. Both women stared out the opening. Marie wanted to suggest they stop until the storm ended, but all the other wagons continued inching forward.

She went to the back of the wagon. Closer to light, Marie pulled a book she'd not read in a while from her trunk and began reading. She'd forgone reading on sunny days just for this reason. The rough road made a necessity of keeping a finger on the line of text as she read. The morning passed with her in another world and unaware when the rain stopped.

The motion easing to a stop caught her attention. Marie looked out to see a line of their party following them. She placed a marker in the book and set it aside. She hopped out of the wagon and walked around to the front. A few other families remained in front of them. They all faced a huge spiny hill. The sharp ridges rising vertically from the stone reminded her of shark fins placed in rows. She marveled at how the layers of rock lay vertically instead of the usual horizontal. Thinking ahead to lunch or even dinner led her to look around for wood before she shook her head. No trees dotted any of the landscape, and any wood would be too wet to use right now. Even the trusty sage seemed absent. All that lay between her and the various foothills was grass and Smith's Fork.

The ground squished under her feet as she went to the front of the wagon train. Several people stood around Sam. He nodded when seeing Marie. "Everyone going to the village can head over with me and Del. Otherwise, we'll spend noon here before heading up the fork for the best camping.

Hearing someone step up behind her, Marie turned to see Charles and Hester. Marie asked, "Do you want to go to the trading post with us?"

"No, we don't need anything over there. In fact, I think it's best if you stay here and help me reorganize our belongings."

"Oh?" She turned to see Sam, Del, Jenny, Ellen, and Lucky walk toward the village. Marie frowned at being left there. "They might have something we need."

"In that case, I'll go," said Hester. "I personally don't think there'll be much of value there, but would like the chance to see for myself."

"Splendid, Hessy." He turned to Marie. "Come along then, and we'll get better organized. He turned toward the wagon and began walking, Marie following. "I've heard talk of steep mountains, worse than what we've seen so far." He let down the wagon's tailgate. "I want you to help me double check what we have with an eye toward getting rid of excess."

"We've done this twice already!"

"Yes, and we'll do it as many times more as needed."

Marie kept quiet as she climbed in after her husband. Arguing, while appealing, was useless with his jaw set so firm. "Finding fresh clothes to wear might be a good idea."

"Hmm, I suppose so."

"What we're wearing now is threadbare."

"Fine."

By working together, they rearranged foodstuffs, putting dry goods into smaller containers when possible. Halfway along the trail meant half of their original stores remained. Not for the first time did Marie wish Charles were a better hunter.

"I'll set this to the back for Hester. I'm sure she'll want fresh clothes, too."

Marie nodded as he did just that. She took his offered hand to help her out of the wagon, smiling at the thoughtfulness. "We should have a bite to eat and let the animals drink, too."

"Agreed." He took the pail. "I'll get water for all of us. You can locate our lunch biscuits."

She smiled her assent and reached into the back for their lunch wrapped in a napkin. Away from the wagon, she saw their group return from the Indian village. No one smiled as they approached. The men scattered to their horses as Jenny, Hester, and Ellen came up to Marie. "What's wrong?"

"Ellen almost started a war."

"Miss Allen is overstating the issue," Hester retorted. At Marie's raised eyebrow, she went on, saying, "It's all so foolish. This young savage saw Miss Winslow and offered for her."

"To marry her? This soon?" Marie looked at her friend. "What did you say?"

Crossing her arms, Ellen tapped her foot. "I'm not going to be the slave of some animal."

"Ellen!" The sentiment shocked Marie. The natives might live in a primitive manner, but they were still human. She looked past Ellen to see Del. "I know you don't think that."

"You don't know what I think. No one does," Ellen snapped.

Jenny gave the other two women a weak smile. Wringing her hands, she said, "I think she's just scared. I know I am. They started yelling, and Mr. Du Boise pushed the chief's son to the ground."

Marie shook her head, unable to see the calm Del as a violent man. "Why would he do that?"

"Because they're all animals, and fighting is the only way they solve anything," Hester snapped. She looked down at the biscuits. "Is this lunch, such as it is?"

"Yes," said Marie.

"I'm starving. Otherwise, I'd not give this a second look." Hester took four of the biscuits. "Some of these are for Charles. Carry on, ladies."

Her sister in law's absence took the heavy air with her. Marie turned to Ellen, asking, "The tribe leader's son and Del were fighting over you, fisticuffs and everything?"

Ellen sighed. "Yes, after the chief offered for me. When Del said no, the son hopped up and started pushing at him."

Nodding, Jenny added, "They were yelling so loudly that I thought everyone here could hear."

Marie shook her head. "I didn't notice, but then I was busy in our wagon helping Charles. How did you dissuade him?"

"I didn't. Sam and Del did all the talking. They told the chief that I'm married." She crossed her arms as if chilled. "Sam stepped next to me and held my hand, claiming me in front of everyone there."

A warm rose color spread across Jenny's face. "Lucky and I had to pretend to be married as well."

The signal to continue forward drifted to the trio. Marie scooped up a couple of biscuits for herself and latched the tailgate into place. "Do you think the son is convinced you're not for sale?"

As Charles snapped the reins and the wheels turned, all three women fell in step together. Ellen shrugged. "I hope so. I hugged Sam as if we were together. He even kissed my forehead and the chief laughed."

An ugly little tendril of jealousy wound its way around her heart. Marie shook off the feeling, determined to press onward. "Did you get a chance to trade for anything before the incident?"

"No. Their town was so small, we only had time to look at a few things."

Jenny added, "The jewelry looked lovely. Primitive, of course, but so pretty."

Marie half listened as the two discussed the various semi-precious stones the tribe offered. She'd seen similar items in places before this. How Sam had kissed Ellen stuck in her mind like a broken off splinter. She glanced over at her friend. The girl smiled at something Jenny said. She was so lovely. Marie preferred to ignore how Sam probably enjoyed the pretense. For the rest of the afternoon, the younger girls talked while Marie pretended not to stew.

So caught up in her own thoughts, Marie didn't realize they'd reached camp for the night. The bugle's noise startled all three, with the other girls laughing with how they jumped at the sound. "How are we surprised at something that happens every day?" she asked.

"His bugle always surprises me," Ellen confessed. "I'm not scared, but can never seem to remember when he's going to use it."

Sighing, Jenny said, "I love when he plays at night. He's such a talented musician."

Marie and Ellen's gaze met and they both smiled. Good, yes,

she thought, but talented? "I'll agree. His playing has been a pleasant part of all this." She paused, as did her friends, waiting for the wagons to move into their usual circle. Several trees grew near camp. Some even had dead branches under them ready for use. With plenty of grass, the cattle and other stock had already stopped to graze. Excited at the prospect of burning wood instead of sage, she stepped away from her friends. "Until tonight?"

The girls nodded and Marie smiled, headed for her wagon. Charles and the oxen were absent, as was Hester. Hands on hips, she tapped her foot. Could she count on Hester being out there, gathering firewood? She shook her head and started toward the small grove of trees to the west. Getting ever closer, Marie grinned. She'd not realized how much she missed trees until just now.

Gathering wood hadn't taken long. She'd smelled every new wildflower each time she bent down to pick up a stick or branch. Arms full, she came back to camp to see both Warrens there.

"Good job, sweetheart!" Charles said. "You've saved us a lot of time."

She smiled, feeling warmed from his compliment. "I hope so. It's early, yet. I wonder if there are fish in the river over there."

He shrugged. "I didn't notice any."

Dreams of a crispy fish fillet with firm white meat for supper faded from her mind but not her stomach. "That's a shame."

"Still, I could try. Hessy, how do you feel about fishing with me until dinner?"

Giving her brother a slight smile, she said, "I suppose I could."

"Excellent. Marie, you are on your own until this evening, when we'll have fish to eat."

"I could go fishing with you."

"You'll talk too much and scare the fish," said Hester, already climbing into the wagon for fishing poles.

"Yes, dearest, it might be best if you stayed here." He leaned forward and kissed her forehead. "Find something relaxing and productive, and we'll be back before you know it."

When his lips touched her skin, a thought made the back of her throat ache as if she'd been chewing metal. Sam kissed Ellen in the same way. Marie pushed the feeling away for later consideration. She watched, mute, as her husband and his sister headed off to the river's edge. Still lost in thought, she said, "Good luck. I'll start some dinner in the meantime."

"Wonderful, sweetheart." He arranged his string and hook, putting them over his shoulder as he linked arms with Hester.

She watched them walk to the river's edge. After starting a fire, she'd have to follow them to get water for dinner. Marie bit her lip. Maybe not, if her being near them scared away all the fish. She arranged the sticks and tinder. After the fire had blazed, she took the pail for water. She kept a watch for her family, seeing nearly everyone else but them in the meantime. Uncle Joe nodded at her while leading the horses to better grazing. Arnold tipped his hat, as did Lefty when they brought water for their own meals. By the time she returned to camp, the fire burned at a gentle heat. Putting a pot of beans on took little effort. Soon, she had blankets folded into seats and began cutting her rags into quilt squares.

A few hours later, Marie stood and stretched. She'd filled her quilting box with new squares and dinner was ready. Checking the beans, they mashed easily under her wooden spoon. Her stomach growled. She straightened, her back stiff from being crouched so long while working. As if her insides boiled, too, bubbles of anger kept trying to rise within her. She took a deep, calming breath. They were late to dinner more often than on time. She knew this, and yet their being late irritated her every time. She saw two choices for the evening. One was to stay mad and eat when they got there. The other, which Marie preferred, was to eat now and let them eat later.

Dishing up a bowl of food, her stomach growled. Marie settled in and stirred her beans and ham. The aroma smelled heavenly, and she ate fast, burning her tongue in her haste. Soon she sighed, full and happy. Thinking of the Warrens, she put a plate over the cook pot to keep the food warm. Rinsing off her dishes in the nearby stream took a little time. She placed the bowl and spoon in the wagon. Was now too soon to visit Sam's campsite? The sun dipped below the western mountains. She followed the mountain range to the south as if trying to see the Californian route. She had a fleeting image of Sam and Ellen ending up married in Oregon. Marie swallowed the lump in her throat. For right now, she needed all the time she could spend with him.

She approached their campsite, a little nervous. All the Granville hands sat round the fire, some eating, others finished and working on their own projects. Del and Sam sat with Ellen between them as if guarding her. If not for their welcoming expressions, she'd have turned around and not intruded.

"Mrs. Warren!" Lucky waved to her. "Come over and sit with us." Uncle Joe leaned over and said something in his ear. Lucky grinned, "If you're free to, of course."

"I am free, thank you for asking." She settled in next to Uncle Joe and opposite the fire from Sam, Del, Ellen, and Arnold. "Thank you, too, Joe, for assuming my dance card is full."

The elder man grinned at her. "You're welcome, little lady."

"There you are, dearest! Thank you for cooking dinner. There's none left, it was so good." Charles settled in beside her. "Hester is washing up and might join us later."

She turned to her husband, almost glad for his company. His expression seemed a lot more chipper. Glad he didn't have his usual dour one, she asked, "Did you catch anything?"

"No. The closest we came was when Hessy lost her footing and almost fell into the water." He winked at Marie. "I had to remind her we wanted to catch fish, not a chill."

Marie chuckled. "I'll bet she didn't like hearing that," she said and happened to glance across the campfire. Her heart skipped a beat, seeing Sam looking at her. He scowled, only stopping when Ellen patted his arm.

"Whew! Isn't this a lovely night?" asked Hester, sitting down on Charles' side.

She smiled, "Yes it is." Marie bit back a retort along the lines of it was until she arrived.

"The river was so beautiful, moonlight glinting off of it as if someone had thrown pearls." Hester sighed. "I could have stayed there on the bank all night."

Charles laughed, and leaned back on his elbows, legs stretched out in front. "It was a sight."

Looking at Hester, Marie had a little knot in her stomach. Her sister-in-law was staring at Charles the same as Jenny did Lucky. When they lapsed into their own language, she frowned. Of course, she'd look at her brother like that, Marie reasoned with herself. They were twins and closer than most siblings. She was silly. First, she'd been jealous over Sam, now Charles. Marie looked up through her lashes at the other hired hands, smiling. Next, she'd be jealous of Uncle Joe, Lucky, Larry, and Lefty.

Sam and Ellen caught her attention when the young woman

whispered in his ear. He continued to stare at Marie; she noticed and tried to still her shaking hands. The two were her friends. Would they fall in love after she left with the Warrens? Remembering her husband and his sister, she wanted to see for herself if the river was as lovely as the Mississippi in the moonlight. She considered everyone too wrapped up in his or her own conversations to notice as she slipped away into the darkness.

In a few moments, Marie stood on the bank of Smith's Fork. Her eyes soon adjusted to the silvery light around her. The river's current ran differently here. Now, the water flowed so swiftly, no one dared swim across for fear of being swept away. The waning moon sent shimmers across the waves. She stepped closer to the water, homesick for the ocean and entranced by the silvery sparkles. Her shoe slipped a little on the rock from her sole worn smooth. As Marie steadied herself, the other foot gave way. She yelped, toppling into the inky black water.

CHAPTER 9

His blood froze at Marie's scream and the sound of a splash. Sam ran to the water's edge. Moonlight did little to illuminate her dark hair. Only her fair skin gave away her location further downstream. He dove in, unwilling to wait for the water to carry him to her. He swam as hard and fast as he could. Feeling fabric, he held onto her arm. "I've got you!" His voice rasped even to his own ears.

"Sam! What are you doing?" She held onto first one reed then another. Each tore away from the soaked earth as the river pulled her. "I can get out of here just fine."

Like the icy water held him, he wrapped his arm around her. "Come on. Let's get to shore." His heart pounded hard in his chest as he struggled to regain his footing and hold up both of them.

"You shouldn't have jumped in here." As she gripped his arm with one hand and clung to a handful of vegetation with the other, her teeth began chattering. "It's not deep, just cold, and I can't move properly."

"I've got you. Let go of the grass."

"No." The last root gave way, and she laughed when the current took them further downstream. "All right, I'll let go." Her body warmed his, her skirt getting tangled with his legs.

Her amusement angered him. They were in a dire situation, not a humorous one. They needed to get back on dry land before she drowned. "This isn't funny, Marie."

"I'm sorry. You're right, it isn't." She reached behind her and pulled the skirt free from both of them. "Hold this and let go of me so we can swim to the side."

Sam did as she asked, gripping the fabric to keep her with him. He wanted to keep her safe even if they ended up miles away from camp. She swam toward the bank, surprising him by pulling them both through the water. By the time he recovered from the shock at her strength, they had washed up onto rocks jutting above the water. He glanced down at the water to see the river had widened and become shallow.

Marie laughed again. "So much for my heroic rescue of you."

She climbed onto a rock and out of the water. Holding a hand out for him, she added, "If we'd known about this, you'd not have needed to jump in after me."

"What the hell was that?" His tone came out harsher than he'd expected.

She frowned while struggling to stand. "I'm not sure. An accident?"

"Dear God, Marie. You could have drowned. Animals and men have tried crossing this and failed." He got to his knees and started to stand until his hand slipped on the slick rock. An electric current of fear went through him. Easing his way after her, he sighed in relief when seeing her on solid ground ahead of him.

"Sam, you're worrying too much. I've been swimming since I was a baby."

The bank, still warm from the daytime heat, comforted him once he reached where Marie sat. "What if you'd hit your head on a rock, got caught on some weeds, or anything else?"

"None of it matters; we're both safe. I'll admit, I don't like swimming at night, but knew I'd reach the bank eventually."

He didn't know what to say. Everything coming to mind sounded too intimate. Yet, in the sparse moonlight, anything seemed possible. He brushed her cheek with the back of his hand. "I've been scheming ways of getting you alone for days."

She leaned into his caress. "Could we be less cold and wet next time?"

Her lower lip trembled, and he heard her teeth clicking. "My poor darling." Sam took her in his arms, her body small and shivering against his. "Do you mind me warming you before we walk back?"

"No, I don't mind." She looked up at him, their lips closer now. "Sam," she whispered.

He felt the warmth of her breath as she said his name. He shook his head in a silent no to himself, but doing so didn't work. Sam leaned down just a little, brushing his lips against hers. The small groan from her ignited hunger in him. He deepened the kiss when she wrapped her arms around him to bury her fingers in his hair. Doing so trapped him against her. He left off kissing her mouth to nibble a path to the soft and still damp skin of her neck. Smiling at how quickly this changed from a rescue to a seduction, he asked, "Do you want to sleep here tonight?"

"If you kept me warm I would."

"Sweetheart, I'd keep you so hot, you'd start a prairie fire."

She chuckled. "We need to join the others."

"So soon?"

She stopped caressing him. "The others are probably on their way. I want one last taste of you." Marie straddled him as he sat there. "One last memory before we leave."

He suppressed a whimper as her hips contacted his. With their bodies so close, Sam knew Marie felt how ready he was. She leaned forward and licked his lips. He wrapped his arms around her, imprisoning her against him. Running his hand from her back to her butt, he ran his tongue along the front of her teeth.

She shuddered and leaned back. "We can't continue, or we'll go too far."

"I know." He hugged her close, taking the chance for one last kiss before letting her go. When their lips parted, he glanced toward the camp. Sure enough, lanterns in the distance loomed closer. "Our search party awaits."

"I don't want to leave."

"Nor do I."

"Honestly? You enjoy, um…" Marie moved away, using his offered hand to steady herself as she got to her feet.

He grinned despite the cold air chilling him where her warmth had been. "Couldn't you tell?" Sam asked as he stood up.

She laughed. "A little, yes."

"Only a little?" He leaned in to whisper in her ear. "That makes me sad."

"Oh dear. From what I could tell, you need never be sad."

Sam enjoyed how he could see how much she blushed even in the darkness. "You can tell me more."

Nodding ahead at the approaching group, she said, "Not while we have company, dearest."

Followed by Ellen and Mr. Norman, Charles ran up to them. "What the hell were you doing, Marie?"

"I accidentally fell into the river." She took the blanket Ellen gave her. "Thank you."

Giving her a withering glare, Charles retorted, "I know accidentally, I didn't think you did this on purpose." Charles snorted, "Good thing you were headed northwest. No way am I backtracking just for you."

She glanced at Sam and tried to smile. "There's no need to worry about it. I'm here safe and sound." Before her husband could say anything else, she added, "You're tired and cranky. Why don't we get some sleep before tomorrow?"

Charles reached out his hand to Sam. "Thanks for saving her worthless hide."

Sam wrapped the blanket Ellen gave him around his chilled body before shaking Warren's hand. He glanced from Marie to her husband. How could the man not know he had no choice in rescuing her? "Keeping her alive is my job." He saw the slight look of surprise on Marie's face and wondered why she didn't catch his underlying meaning. "Mrs. Warren, you might consider putting on dry clothes and getting warm before catching your death."

She nodded. "I will, and I appreciate you saving me tonight. It might have been the Pacific before I could reach shore without your help."

He shook his head, disagreeing with how far she'd get before he'd find her. Her sudden smile let him know she'd seen the thought from his expression. His transparency worried him, more so since the crowd still stood around them. Not wanting to broadcast his feelings through body language, he said, "If you all will excuse me, I'm exhausted and am going to bed."

As he walked away, Sam heard a few of his men fall into step behind him. He knew without looking that Joe and Lefty had first watch tonight. Seeing the fire, Sam began shivering. The excitement had kept him warm, he figured.

Arnold waited for them at the campfire, all their beds laid out for them. Looking up from his journal, he said, "Leaned too far over for a drink, sir?"

Sam grinned. "Something like that." He headed to the wagon for some dry clothes. "Lucky, you can fill him in on my heroics. I'm far too modest to go bragging." After climbing up and pulling the canvas opening closed, he heard his men talking about the rescue. Concealed inside the wagon, he sagged like an airless balloon. Sighing, the energizing fear left him as he exhaled. Tonight might have gone much differently if Marie had been less of a swimmer or inadvertently breathed in the water. He shook his head, not wanting to entertain any other thought besides the current outcome.

He gritted his teeth to keep them from chattering in the night air. The heavy, wet clothes clung to him as he tried peeling them off his arms and legs. His fresh clothes in a trunk still kept the day's heat, and he held them close. The warmth lulled him into sleepiness, so he made quick work of getting them on. He exchanged one pair of soaked wool socks for a much dryer pair his sister in law had made him last year.

Now comfortable, Sam hopped down and went to his bedroll. He'd listened with half an ear to Lucky's recounting of the night's adventure. "Thank you for turning out our beds tonight, Arnie."

"It's my job, sir."

He gave a slight smile to the young man, but snug in his blankets, Sam struggled to keep his eyes open. He tried to talk to the other two, but couldn't stay conscious long enough to say anything.

The day began bright, and Sam rubbed his eyes. What had happened to him being on the second watch? Seeing Uncle Joe getting a cup of coffee, Sam asked, "Who took second last night?"

"Lucky and Arnold volunteered. Figured it was the least they could do for a bona fide hero." Handing him a cup, Joe went on to say, "It was that or carry you around on our shoulders, and no one wanted that."

Sam laughed at the idea. The coffee tasted rich, hot and thawing him from the chilly morning air. A few more drinks and he smiled at Joe. "You have that look on your face, so go ahead and tell me."

With a wide grin, Joe nodded. "Very well. One of the Winslow boys is sick, probably mosquitoes. Everyone's been having problems with them."

As Arnold and Lucky passed between Joe and him, Sam waited for a second before saying, "To be expected. Go on."

Joe dished out bacon and biscuits to the two new arrivals. "The mother seems ill, but I think that's her usual constitution." Lefty came over, sitting next to Joe. Without a word, the older man gave the boy his breakfast.

When seeing everyone had food, Sam asked, "Has Del been hanging around them still, trying to help?"

"Yes, he has," said Del.

Sam laughed, a little startled by his friend answering from behind him. "You know better."

"No, I don't." Del settled in, reaching for some food. "I'm in love and know nothing for sure."

A questioning look in Joe's expression led Sam to nod, "Yes, do go on."

"The Normans and Allens are good, as are everyone else."

Sam held out his cup for more coffee. As Joe filled it for him, he saw a look pass between Joe and Del. He took a drink then asked, "What about the Warrens? I assume Mrs. Warren is doing well after last night's swim."

"They are."

The two-word answer frustrated Sam. He refrained from asking anything more pointedly about Marie. The men suspecting something between them didn't bother him as much as them knowing he and Marie were involved. "Very well. Might as well get started."

At that, the men began their usual morning duties. Lucky made quick work of cleaning dishes. Uncle Joe and Arnold hitched up the horses and gathered their few head of cattle. Sam and Lefty rolled up the bedding, placing everything in the wagon. Lucky came in behind them with the dishes and gave Sam a questioning look. At his nod, the younger man took out his bugle and sounded the call to move.

This morning, he let himself fall back to the rear, keeping an eye on any stragglers. The fresh new day seemed extra bright. The sunlight glimmered off the nearby Bear River. He took every opportunity of its closeness to let Scamp eat and drink to his heart's content. Memories of how Marie's lips felt against his, the warmth of her body, and how she sighed as he kissed her neck wouldn't leave his mind. He stared up at the clear blue sky as he and Scamp ambled along. As the sun climbed higher over the horizon, the air warmed with the breezes staying crisp. He smiled at the thought of how the weather here blew hot and cold like he and Marie. She'd been distant and polite with him around anyone else. Last night, her skin's warmth rivaled any hot springs.

He spent the next few hours ambling along, keeping an eye out for anything out of the ordinary. As much as he'd prefer to swell on Marie. The run in they'd had with the chief's son kept him unnerved. The young man's vow to take Ellen as his wife nagged at Sam. Del and all his men pledged to keep her and the others safe. He scanned along the mountain ridge. A few more days might need to pass before he felt comfortable again.

"Noon?" Sam asked when Del came over to him.

"Yes." They rode on for a while. "They all think of you as a hero after last night."

Sam laughed. "They think wrong. Mrs. Warren is an excellent swimmer. Good enough to have saved me, instead." The signal to stop rippled its way to them. "She didn't need my help after all."

The other man gave him a sly glance. "I'd disagree."

"I would argue, but would rather eat." He nudged Scamp into a trot and went to his wagon for grub. He and his men each grabbed their own biscuit and hunk of meat. Seeing Lefty, Sam said, "Left, let me take the flank this afternoon."

Lefty nodded and hitched up the wagon's tailgate. "Sure thing, sir. Don't mind keeping an eye out for the stragglers today."

He patted him on the back, saying, "Good man." They all went in their own direction, ready to start the day's second half of traveling. Uncle Joe went to the front of the wagon and clicked for the oxen to move as Lucky sounded the bugle.

Sam rode over to the right middle of the group, easing Scamp into a walk. He smiled when spotting Marie. After cantering over to her, he said, "Hello, ma'am." He slid off of Scamp and fell into step beside her. "Lovely day for a walk."

"It is. I appreciate you joining me."

"My pleasure." He glanced over at her. A small smile played around her lips, and she looked up at him through her lashes. The slightest of gasps escaped him when seeing the warm dark brown of her eyes. While staring at each other, she stumbled over a rock. He reached out and grabbed her arm. "Whoa there, little lady."

"Oh dear!" She found her footing, placing a hand over his. "I saved your life last night, and you kept my dignity just now."

"Pardon me? I saved you, remember?" He grinned when she laughed. "Or maybe not. You are an excellent swimmer, surprisingly strong."

"How very kind of you to say so, sir."

They walked for a while, neither saying anything. Sam's thoughts ran at a hundred miles an hour, wanting to talk about their closeness last night. He tried to find the words to say that kept her with him for the rest of their lives. "Fort Hall is closer with every step."

"It is. Do you think we could walk backward instead?"

He laughed at the idea. "If I knew it'd work, I'd walk backward all the way to Independence." He glanced at her and saw her cheeks redden. "And then to California to fetch you for myself."

"Sam, I don't know…"

"That's fine. I do know." Touching her shoulder, he added, "I would do whatever you needed of me."

She chuckled. "I learned exactly what you'd do last night after you jumped into that icy cold river. You could have caught your death."

Shrugging off her concern, he said, "I'm tougher than that. It'll take a little more than a cold bath to kill me."

"Good."

He looked over at her, the one-word spreading joy through him. After a quick scan to see who might overhear, he leaned a little closer to her. "I wonder if last night's kiss was a dream? If I didn't need to find a place to camp, I'd lure you to the nearest copse."

"If I weren't sure sunlight kisses with you would lead to moonlight kisses, I'd let you take me anywhere."

Sam climbed on Scamp and grinned down at her. Tipping his hat, he said, "Such big talk for a little woman."

She laughed. "You know it's true."

"Until later, ma'am." He waited until she nodded before trotting to the head of the line. Her letting him take her anywhere sentence still rung in his ears. Sam shook his head at her boldness. He'd like to think she wasn't joking with him. Accidental kisses were one thing, intentional lovemaking quite another. He kept an eye open for an ideal camp.

Resisting the urge to see what lay beyond the next bend in the river, Sam tallied up the current location's benefits. Good water, plenty of grass, and several groves made for a good place to stop. He looked back at the wagons far behind him. The others would reach here by late afternoon. Scanning ahead, he saw no significant trees ahead of them. Soda Springs would have to wait until tomorrow.

He turned Scamp back to the others, nudging him into a gallop. In no time, he reached Arnold out in front. "I've found a camp for the night."

"So soon?"

"I'm afraid so."

Arnold shrugged. "Just as well, some of the animals have turned up lame from the larger rocks."

He nodded. "We're a little ahead of schedule." Sam guided his horse to fall in step next to Arnold's. "Even allowing for future trouble, we'll be home by September."

"I won't know what to do with that much time in one space."

Not wanting to admit what he'd most want to happen, Sam replied, "Me neither." He stared ahead at the horizon. The valley curved enough to make it seem as if they'd have to climb mountains to continue. He grinned to himself, wondering whether any of the others had noticed and despaired. Sam made a mental note to tell everyone about the bend in the Bear River. "Anywhere along here should be good, Arnie. What do you think?"

"I reckon a little past the tree thicket. Makes me feel like we're getting somewhere today."

"I agree. Scout ahead for the exact place, and I'll ride back to tell the others." At Arnold's nod, Sam urged Scamp into a gallop. Seeing Uncle Joe, he rode over to him. "Arnie's found our camp for tonight, tell Lucky."

"Will do." With that, Joe cut across to the other flank.

Sam continued on to the back of the party, resisting the urge to slow down and catch a glimpse of Marie. Lefty brought up the very rear and grinned as Sam approached. "Hey, Lefty. We're stopping early this afternoon." He pulled his horse in line with the younger man's.

"Just as well, sir. Several have fallen back 'cause one ox or another's come up lame." He pointed to one of the families. "The Normans wanted to stop sooner. Had to remind them policy is we don't leave anyone behind."

"Good." Sam looked behind them, scanning the hilltops for signs of Indian ponies. Maybe he could breathe easier now with no sign of the chief's son in the past couple of days. Up ahead, the families pulled their wagons in a semicircle around the oxbow bend of the river. With the Bear being a couple dozen feet or so wide, he hoped the depth deterred any curious livestock.

The next couple of hours passed in a hurry as he and his men settled themselves and everyone else in for the night. Animals received their care, campfires burned, and the few dirty clothes they washed hung out in the sun. Fresh meat sounded good, and with an hour or so until dinner, Sam decided to try hunting in the area. Before leaving camp, he hollered at Lucky, "Mr. Lucky, I'm heading out to hunt. I'll be back in a couple of hours or so."

The young man nodded and went back to building a fire. "I'll be ready to cook whatever you bring back."

Sam laughed, "You might want to be ready for salt pork."

"I'm not worried. If you don't get something, Joe or Larry will."

His other men were hunting as well. "What directions did they go?"

"Both went south; a few went north."

"I'll try west, then." The west face of the canyon was the steepest, but he didn't mind. Sam enjoyed the challenge of a climb, especially now. Later, hiking a vertical surface wasn't a necessity as it would be near Snake River. The effort rewarded him once he reached the canyon's rim. His view of the wide green valley was beautiful. He could see the road they'd take tomorrow as it wound around, following the river. Sam took a deep breath and started descending on the west side. The land leveled some, becoming heavily wooded.

As he crept deeper into the forest, Sam was sure he heard a bear's call from within the pines. He took quiet, easy steps. Any twigs underfoot kept quiet with his careful movements. There, he heard the call again, closer this time. He was closing the gap between him and the animal. He'd eaten bear once or twice. Others in his camp may not like it as much, but it was fresh meat. This early in the year meant the meat would keep some of its sweetness.

Hearing the call again, Sam stopped. He didn't see a bear in the underbrush because that was no bear. Damn it all, he'd intruded on a couple making love. He grinned, a little embarrassed but also envious. Not wanting to interrupt, he backtracked almost as quietly as he'd arrived. Making a little noise in his retreat didn't bother him. He felt sure the two wouldn't notice anything, even though they should. Sam almost laughed, wondering what if he'd been the bear instead.

At a safe distance from the couple, he relaxed. It was too close to sunset to continue hunting, anyway. A lot of mistakes in shooting were made this time of day. He'd already lost a few to illness and accident, damned if he were going to accidentally kill others. Most of the berry pickers had gone east of the river, the hunters west.

He reached the camp, enjoying the smell. Someone else had been lucky in their hunt, judging by the aromas. His stomach growled. If not for the romantic two in the bushes, he'd be dressing an animal himself. At his wagon, the hands were already cooking up dinner.

"Hello, boss!" greeted Uncle Joe as he scooped another spoonful of stew into a bowl. "Has Mrs. Warren reached you?"

Lucky added, "She acted worried, asked if we'd seen the Warrens, then asked if we'd seen you." He took the ladle from Joe. "I think the Warrens must not be back because why else would she be looking for them? She asked about you, too. But then I believe it was because we didn't know where her family was. You might have seen them out hunting or picking berries or whatnot."

He laughed, "Lucky, calm down a little. I'll go and make sure the Warrens are back. Save me some of that, would you?"

"Sure thing, boss, it's good. Arnold shot a deer, a tender one, so this is going fast."

Arnold just nodded, too busy chewing to be talking. Sam said, "Thank you, I look forward to having some later."

He started for the Warrens' wagon. From the corner of his eye, Sam saw Charles and Hester strolling in from the west, buckets in hand. He recognized the voices, now seeing the persons connected to the moans. "No," he whispered, wanting to be sick. "Not them." Sam had a live and let live attitude, but this? He stepped behind a wagon, not wanting to greet the duo. Questions raced through his mind. Was it really them he'd heard in the woods? Were they really twins? How long had the two been intimate? He held the back of his hand to his mouth, lastly wondering, did Marie know?

Ellen had warned him. She'd known all this time and said next to nothing. Sam went to find her at the Winslows' wagon. As he approached, she looked up from her cooking at him. He nodded at her grim expression. "Yes, I know, and we're going to talk."

She glanced around for her parents, seeming nervous to be alone with him. "Pa is out hunting, and Lucy is washing Skeeter and Buster. Sit nearby and we can talk about what I'm assuming are the Warrens."

He sat next to her. For once, the smell of food so late in the day turned his stomach. "How long have you known about the two?"

She didn't look at him. "Since the Black Hills."

Before thinking, he blurted, "That was two months ago, and you said nothing to Marie."

"What would you have me tell her? What could I say that she'd believe without seeing with her own eyes?"

He swallowed, knowing she was right. Bile rose in his throat. Sam tried to imagine how a man might prefer his own sister to Marie. He shuddered.

"I know. It's deplorable and against anything decent." Ellen leaned forward to stir the pot of beans and rice. "As much as I've heard Mr. Warren call Del a savage, well, he has no room to talk."

"We need to let Marie know. She can't go to California with them."

"Especially if she finds out about their affair once there. She'd be alone, knowing everything, and have nowhere to turn."

"I can't let that happen." Sam stood. Seeing her questioning expression, he said, "No, I don't know what to say, but I'll have to think of something before Fort Hall."

"That would be best for her."

"Thank you for the talk. See you after dinner?"

"I'll try."

"Good." He tipped his hat and went back to his own campsite. Keeping the disgust and anger from his face proved more difficult as he approached his men. They knew him too well, would see the emotions he struggled to hide. He paused, took a deep breath and exhaled, thinking of a placid lake's smooth surface. He would be that lake. Ready now to be calm around his men, Sam walked up to the group. "Game is scarce around here boys. I'm glad you went ahead with cooking, Joe."

"I figured as much. We're rolling over ruts too recent for there to be much around here."

Sam picked up the last plate. "I'm glad I got here when I did."

"We're not. We'd had plans to split your share."

He settled for giving Arnold a mock glare, making the younger man laugh. Hunger made for a good sauce. Joe's beans and ham tasted better than usual. White flour biscuits cooked on the embers. Sam presumed they'd be for tomorrow. Would then be the day Marie learned the terrible secret of her husband and his sister? If so, who'd tell her? Would their own actions betray them, or would he and Ellen? As he ate, the food began tasting more like mush. He had guessed at her and Charles' relationship so far. He worried about her reaction, not knowing if discovering the truth would break her heart or merely infuriate her. He shifted in his seat, uneasy at the idea of her being devastated by the news.

"Something bothering ya?" asked Joe. "I reckon from your frown something's off with the beans."

Sam looked up, catching Del's concerned expression as well. To reassure them both, he said, "No, nothing like that." He tried to keep his expression even and thought up the most likely reason for a bad mood. "Damn mosquitoes are getting to me."

"I heard one of the Winslow boys has it bad. All swollen from the bites," Lucky said, taking Sam's empty plate.

Sam exchanged looks with the younger man. "I hope he doesn't get any worse." They both remembered burying the sickly little Calhoon boy not too far from here.

"Miss Winslow and I spoke earlier this afternoon," Del said. "Buster is doing better. She sends her regrets about attending any festivities tonight." He gave Lucky his plate and utensil. "She also mentioned I might want to stay until Fort Hall at least."

Sam saw how his men all looked everywhere but at his friend. They probably all thought that Ellen and Del were sweet on each other. While most likely true, he figured she wanted his friend in on the plans to help Marie, when or if the Warrens stopped hiding their affair. A glance at the man's face confirmed it for Sam. He saw a flicker of pity cross his expression. After raising an eyebrow, he gave Del a slight frown. Sam didn't need sympathy. He needed a reliable solution for helping Marie. "I'll take first watch."

"I'll get the bedding ready for the rest of us." Uncle Joe stood with a little difficulty. "Reckon you'll want me and Lucky to take second?"

"Sure. Lefty or Arnie can help with first, whoever feels up to it."

"I will," said Lefty.

Arnold stood. "I can help Joe with seeing to the stock."

Sam nodded and went to the river, intending to help Lucky with the washing. As he walked down the slight decline, the air grew cooler. He met the younger man coming back to the camp. "Done already?"

"Yes, sir."

"Good job." At the camp, he saw how chores were done, and Lefty already lay in his bed, scribbling in his journal. Even though Sam tried not to pry, he saw drawings on the page opposite Lefty's notes. He'd noticed the young man's drawings before now, but hadn't commented. Seeing how the picture resembled today's landscape so much, Sam had to say something. "Looks nice, Lefty. I mean, from this distance and all. I can't read what you're writing or anything."

The boy looked up with a slight grin. "Thank you, Mr. Granville. I appreciate you saying so. It's not so important, just the day's events."

"They're your thoughts, so that makes them valuable. I didn't mean to be rude, just the mountains look familiar."

"I'm glad. They're supposed to."

He grinned at the happy tone of Lefty's voice. "Keep drawing, then, and any time you want to share, I'd like to see. My brother is an excellent artist, and this is as fine as any work of his."

"Oh?" Lefty sat up. "I'll keep that in mind." He went back to writing, flipping the page, and began sketching.

Sam let him have his privacy and went to get his rifle for tonight's watch. He met Arnold going to the wagon, too. "Remember, ask first and shoot later. I've not seen anything of the chief's son."

"Some other lovely lady might have him distracted."

"Probably so. Still, I'll feel better when we're further down the road." He and Arnold split up, going separate directions. Each man went around the wagons' semi-circle, reached the river, then turned and came back to the center. Sam nodded at his employee and passed by him to retrace Arnold's steps to the river and back. They did this for a couple of hours, scanning the landscape for movement.

He managed to not stop and look at Marie each time he walked by her and the sleeping Warrens. Sam refused to think of them as a family. People you love didn't do such despicable things as Charles had done to her. Maybe Hester had a pass, not being a blood relative or spouse to Marie. Sam gritted his teeth, angry at Warren's deception. His teeth began to hurt, and he took in a deep breath. Emotions might distract him from keeping watch. No need to be furious at the moment. Marie might know all about the

Warrens and condone it. He choked back a laugh at the thought, certain his mind was too tired to think properly. She didn't know at all. He paused at her family's campsite, straining to see her face in the campfire embers dull glow. Too dark, so he went on to the main camp. Joe and Lucky waited there, ready to take their shift. They changed watch without a word, wanting to let the others sleep. Sam slid into his own bed, grateful for the soft warmth.

Breakfast cooking woke Sam. He opened an eye to see Lefty cooking. Turning to lay on his back, he stared up at a clear blue sky. He sat up, cheered by the clear weather and ready to get started on the day.

"Good morning, sir. Just in time to eat."

"Thank you, Lefty." He looked around to see only Lucky still slept. "Where is everyone?"

Lefty shrugged while handing a cup to Sam. "Out doing things. Some of the ladies wanted fresh berries for their breakfast. A few of the men wanted to try hunting first thing."

He held the cup out as the boy poured coffee. "Before or after chores?"

Grinning, he admitted, "You got 'em there. They left after breakfast and taking care of the stock." He dished out potatoes and ham on the plate Sam held. "Said they'd be back in time to pack up and wash up. If I didn't have it done already, that is."

Sam considered doing their work for them a small price to pay for fresh food. He ate, ignoring how plain the meal now tasted. Something in the air caught his attention. He paused in eating, listening. All the usual sounds from animals, the river, the fire continued. He glanced up at Lefty, knowing the distant chatter, strident, of a group drifted over on the morning breeze. He stood. "I think something's gone wrong."

In the distance, a man screamed, and Lefty's eyes widened as he also got to his feet. "I think you're right."

He turned, and before Sam could say anything, Del came around the wagon to them. The look on his friend's pale face caused his stomach to reject the meal sitting there. "What happened?"

Others crowded around them, including Marie, Lucky, and Uncle Joe. Del was the first to answer. "Mrs. Winslow is dead,

Sam." At the admission, Marie sobbed, and the man put his arm around her to comfort her.

Sam knew the question, but the words stayed stuck in his throat. Something else was wrong, and he had to know. "Is she the only one?" he asked, dreading the answer.

"I'm not sure. Miss Winslow is gone."

CHAPTER 10

Marie's heartbeat pounded in her ears. She struggled to hear over the noise. Everyone seemed in shock, their tones clipped, and faces pale with worry.

"What do you mean gone?" asked Sam.

Uncle Joe answered, "We've searched all the brush around the body."

"I've tried to see if blood stained the bottom of their feet," Del added.

Sam nodded. "We'll need to send out a search party for her. It's been recent enough, we stand a good chance of finding her."

"No. You don't want to do that." Del crossed his arms, shaking his head. "A search party is too slow and cumbersome for this. They took her into the mountains."

"How do you know for sure?" asked Uncle Joe.

Del looked off into the distance, squinting as if to see Ellen herself. "It's what I would do."

Jack Winslow staggered around the wagon yelling, "What the hell happened to my wife?"

He brushed past Marie to the circle of men. The smell of whiskey assaulted her nose. Without thinking, she glanced at the sun to check the time. Midmorning and he reeked of rotgut. She took a deep breath of fresh air as he moved downwind. No wonder his family was so spindly; he carried more drink than food. Whatever faults Charles had, she liked how he stayed sober.

Jack stood in the middle of the circle of men. "I heard she's dead. That can't be true."

"Yes, sir," Sam began. "It's my duty and regret to inform you…"

"No!" Jack lunged for Del. Sam and Lucky grabbed hold of him, keeping him firmly in place as he screamed, "One of you red skinned bastards killed her!" He spat at Del, the gob getting caught in his beard and running down his chin. "I'll see you hang from the nearest tree."

Sam said through gritted teeth, "There's no need for that, Mr. Winslow."

"The hell there isn't! I'll bet the bastard raped her before slitting her throat."

Del's eyes narrowed. "How did you know her throat was cut?"

Jack paled and sagged in Sam's and Lucky's arms. Sam shook the man as he began sobbing. "Answer him. I thought you didn't know how your wife died."

Leaning his head back while still limp, he gave a high, keening wail until out of breath. Before he could inhale, Sam shook him again. Jack made a gurgling sound before replying, "I guessed." He panted a few times. "This animal never carries a tomahawk, just a knife."

Del folded his arms. "So I do. You carry a rifle. Does that mean every person shot in the territory has died by your hand?"

Winslow let his head sag to his chest, his entire body deadweight. Lucky shot Sam an exasperated look, and Sam nodded. They both let Mr. Winslow sag to his knees. When his shins hit the dirt, he began his wailing again. The younger men eased away from him and went to Del. Sam spoke first in a quiet voice. "We can't go on without Ellen."

A moment had passed before Del swallowed as if a lump had formed in his throat. "Yes, you can. Continue and we'll catch up."

"We?" asked Marie.

"Yes. I will find Ellen and bring her back when I do." Del took Sam's offered hand, and the two had a brotherly hug. They separated, and Del stared down at the keening man below him. "Though I'm not sure he deserves a daughter like her." Glancing at Jenny wiping the tears from her eyes, then at Marie, he added, "Ellen's brothers and friends need her, so I go."

"She'll want something familiar when you find her," offered Marie. "It'll comfort her."

Sam nodded in agreement. "We'll go and pack her some food and fresh clothes."

The darker man made an after you motion with his hand. "Let's get started."

Jenny began sobbing as the men went to get Del ready to leave. She went into Marie's open arms. To comfort the young girl, she said, "There, there, Jenny. This is horrible, I know. If anyone can find our dear Ellen, it's Del."

"Poor Mrs. Winslow," cried Jenny.

Mr. Winslow must have quieted while she focused on her friend, Marie noticed because he began his infernal wailing again. Wincing at the racket, she gave her friend a squeeze before letting her go. "We need to think of the boys." Winslow grew louder, and Jenny squinted at the noise. To get away from the man, Marie led her to Winslow's family wagon. "Let's go see Skeeter and Little Buster. They probably need care."

They went to the two children. Marie's first instinct was to quiet the crying Buster. Jenny reached him first, gathering him in her arms. Skeeter sat apart from his little brother. The boy's pale face showed no emotion. He wore pants and an unbuttoned shirt.

When he spotted Marie approaching him, he said, "I got my shirt muddy."

She began buttoning his shirt. "It's all right, dear. We'll get you dressed and back at play very soon." As she helped him off the tailgate, Marie saw Sam and Mr. Winslow approach. The younger man held up the other as he shuffled along. They drew closer, and she heard more of their discussion.

"These women are fine for now, Granville, but I'm going to need someone permanent." He saw Little Buster and cried out before staggering over to the child. "My poor little motherless children."

Skeeter trembled as he clung to Marie's skirt. He leaned against her. She blinked back tears, her heart aching for the children. "We can all help you until Ellen is found."

Jack fixed her with a hard stare. "What makes you think I want that Indian's whore back here?"

His horrible choice of words almost stopped her heart. "Excuse me?"

"You heard me just fine, ma'am. Now that some animal has made her his squaw, I don't want her back here."

Marie's jaw had dropped before she recovered enough to say, "Mr. Winslow! She's your daughter and will need you after she's rescued."

He shook his head. "I don't care. She's been hanging on Granville's friend here. Let him have her."

She glanced over at Jenny, standing to the side and holding Little Buster. The girl stared at Winslow opened jawed until seeing Marie. Jenny shut her mouth into a thin line. Without a word, Marie knew they both agreed at how Winslow had crossed a line with them.

Winslow reached out for Buster, saying, "My baby boy." The child went to his father and Jenny handed him over carefully. "You and your brother are all I have left of my beloved Lucy."

"Mrs. Warren, Miss Allen?" Sam began. "We need to start rolling. Please tell your families to pack up if they've not begun."

She'd been upset and not noticed how Sam still stood behind all of them, watching Mr. Winslow's drama. Marie followed him toward her own wagon with Jenny going to opposite way. Anger radiated from his body as if he'd gotten out of a hot spring on a cold day. "Mr. Granville?"

"Yes?"

Now that she had his attention, she wasn't quite sure what to do with it. "I suppose Mrs. Winslow's body has been interred?"

"Of course. The men are finishing up right now."

"I supposed Mr. Winslow had a difficult time of it."

"Seems so." Sam looked at the head of the wagons, seeing Lucky waving at him. "I need to go. Take care of yourself, will you?"

"I will. You do the same."

After a nod, Sam strode away. She tried not to watch him leave, instead concentrating on getting ready to go. When done, she went to the wagon seat to find Charles. He and his sister sat there, talking. The twins used their own language to speak in hushed, sharp tones. An odd word they used caught her attention. She'd heard it before now, but not often enough to repeat or remember it for long.

"Granville knows about…"

"Has he said anything to you or her?"

"Nothing I'm aware of."

"What happens if she finds out about us?"

Us? She knew everything about the two already. But the use of "us" implied something sinister. She retrieved her sunbonnet. The three of them were together nearly every minute of the day. Charles had full control over her finances. Very little of her worldly possessions remained. Puzzled, she wondered what more did the two have planned without her consult.

The bugle sounded, and they began the day's journey. Being alone gave her time to ponder what the twins meant by the expression "oochegoo." She wondered if it were a new word for the natives. Although, all the Indians they'd seen so far already had a tribal name. She shook her head, making a mental note to ask them about it later at dinner.

A long afternoon of travel alone gave her a lot of time to admire the landscape. Wonderful grass for the livestock carpeted the Bear River Valley. Fir trees along with a few others lined the streams that wound their way down mountains to the main river. Upstream from where they crossed, the water ran clear and freezing cold. She began carrying a cup in her pocket after the first creek she stepped over. Drinking now made up for all those thirsty days behind her. Between the freezing water and cool breezes, she shivered despite the hot afternoon.

She saw Jenny every so often. The girl clung to her family, understandable to Marie. She'd also kept an eye on the Winslow children. The two stayed with the Norman children, leaving their father able to concentrate on driving the wagon. She pursed her lips when thinking of how drunk he'd been this morning. Had he gone to bed intoxicated or started drinking after his morning coffee? She shook her head. Either way was deplorable on his part.

Sam gave the order to halt just as the sun hovered over the western mountain peaks. The late hour didn't give them much time to do chores before dark. Marie hurried to their wagon as it rolled into the nightly semicircle along the riverbank. Being this close to the water meant no romantic meetings for anyone this evening. She smiled. Unless someone wanted to find more of the black currant bushes they'd been passing all afternoon. Most of the bushes had held a scant amount of berries. Maybe she'd find a few off the beaten path. Excited at the chance to eat something besides the usual, Marie grabbed an empty jar.

Her husband turned the corner, almost running into her. "Whoa, little lady! You're not using hat little ole thing instead of the water bucket, are you?"

Hester came up behind him. Marie nodded a greeting to her and answered, "I thought about seeing if there were any more berries. There might be more away from the crowds."

"I see." He turned to his sister. "Hessy, want to go?"

"Let's." She took the jar from Marie. "It makes sense for us to go. A woman alone is not a good idea, and we've seen just this morning it's not safe for two."

Marie shrugged. "Very well. I can care for the animals and

search for wood while you're gone."

"We won't be long."

She called out to them as they walked away from her. "I hope not. Dusk is coming up fast." Charles gave her a wave as if he'd heard. She watched them and shook her head. They didn't even look around for the currants. Dinner would be late and without anything new. The oxen took little time to unhitch. She led them upriver, searching for anything to burn. Sagebrush grew less here, too. Marie watched as their animals ate. She hoped Oregon had everything they'd need. She glanced up, barely seeing the orange gold clouds in the west. California, not Oregon. She needed to remember that.

Leading the animals back to camp, she gathered as many twigs and sticks as possible. The placid oxen made easy work of holding their reins in one hand while holding an apron full of tinder in the other. After securing them, she made a small campfire for dinner. Marie considered searching for more wood, now hungry and growing impatient. The dark purple-black of the sky deterred her from wandering away, and she began cooking cornbread and ham. Just as she retrieved dishes and utensils, she saw her husband and sister in law. Relieved to see them she said, "There you are!" She handed each one their dishes. "Dinner is ready."

"Smells good," said Charles.

"Doesn't it?" She peered into their bucket, disappointed to see it empty. "The berry picking was a bust for you, too? I had a difficult time finding anything for the fire tonight." Marie saw Hester dish up her and Charles' food. They both looked rumpled and dirty. "It appears you two had to climb some hills in your search."

"It wasn't too bad," said Hester while holding out her plate for Marie to fill. "The task ended up being very fun."

"That's good," Marie said.

"Yes, I didn't mind at all." He smiled at her and held out his plate to Marie, too. "I only wish we'd been able to hunt longer."

She forced a smile. "Well, maybe tomorrow there'll be a better chance of finding something tasty. " Marie was glad they were chipper this evening. She preferred this to their glummer moods.

Like a burst dam floods a valley, both Warrens talked non-stop through their supper. Hester asked about everyone in the camp. Charles enquired about the Winslows and how the children were doing after the tragedy. Their sudden kindness left her feeling odd. "I haven't seen much of Mr. Granville or his men."

"They've beefed up security," Charles said in between bites. "I heard from Allen that some of us would be the close guard while the others ride to check for danger further out from us."

"Hello, Mrs. Warren," said Samuel, and nodded to the other two.

His expression worried, almost scared Marie. He seemed furious, pale, and only looked at her. "Well, speak of the devil. Is everything fine, Mr. Granville?"

"It is. I'd noticed the three of you were away from camp a bit late. After this morning, I'd prefer everyone stay within sight."

"Oh, I see." She glanced at her family, now quiet and not eating. "We should have been more security minded."

Charles stood, giving Marie his dirty plate but talking to Sam. "You're a good man for noticing, Granville."

He looked Charles up and down without speaking before staring at Marie. His every word clipped, Sam said, "Mrs. Warren if you need anything outside of camp and after dark, tell me or one of my men. Do you understand?"

"Yes," Marie smiled, hoping to charm some of the hostility from his face. "I do and have been if there were problems."

"Good." He tipped his hat at her, nodded at the Warrens, and walked back to his men's camp.

"Not only did a bee get in his bonnet, the whole hive did and stung him." She turned to her husband, "I've never seen Mr. Granville so angry." Marie took Hester's offered dishes. She looked from one sibling to the other. The mood had been so pleasant before Samuel stopped by. Now, Charles seemed sullen, and Hester looked scared. They didn't even talk in their twin language. Samuel's displeasure must be contagious, Marie thought, because she grew aggravated, too. "I don't suppose we could go back to being cheerful again."

Hester and Charles exchanged looks, him saying, "I don't feel like it."

She struggled to be police while wrapping the leftover cornbread in a napkin. "Fine, what do you feel like?"

"Like sleeping, since it is dark, now." Hester retorted.

"Very well, I'll help get out the mattresses and blankets." She helped set up everything for resting but didn't want to sleep just yet. Not while the fire still burned brightly. After retrieving her own bedding and sewing, Marie hopped down and took the dishes to wash.

A full moon helped her to see the river. She nodded to the watch as she passed. He was a gentleman from a family who kept to themselves. Marie didn't know any of them well. She didn't stop to exchange pleasantries, feeling shy all of a sudden. The moonlight glinted off the flowing water. The river ran fast enough to worry her. She took off her shoes on the sandy bank, sat down, and dangled her feet into the water. As her foot hit the liquid ice, a hand clamped over her mouth and arms pulled her against a man.

"Marie, don't scream."

As soon as he released her, she whirled to face him, "Samuel Granville, what are you doing? All that security nonsense and you do a silly prank like this?"

He held onto her upper arms and drew her closer. "Robert James," he whispered in her ear.

The night wasn't so dark as to hide his smile and she struggled not to grin, also. "Excuse me? Who are you talking about?"

"It's Samuel Robert James Granville when I'm in trouble with my mother." He pressed his lips against her ear.

"I'm not your mother, and I don't care." Now his breath in her ear completely distracted her. "You're still in trouble with me."

"I know and don't care." He settled in beside Marie and held her tight. "I'm going to be in a lot more trouble by the time I'm finished with you."

She shuddered when his lips met hers in a bruising kiss and heard him growl low in his throat. Pulling away, she gasped "You, we can't do this."

"Yes, we can. All night if we want. No one has the right to censor us."

He stopped what she wanted to say next by covering her lips with his own again. She returned his kiss, letting her tongue trace his lips as his did hers. Marie wrapped her arms around him. His breathing quickened. She could feel the pulse in his body as well as her own. Not everyone slept yet, especially the night watch. She couldn't let this continue. "Sam, let's stop. We can't."

He lifted her skirt, tracing his hand along her outer thigh. "From now on, we can do whatever we want, tonight and every night."

"No, we can't, Sam." She put her hand over his, stopping his progress. "Sam! Please!"

He paused, asking, "Is that a please stop, or a please go?" He nipped at Marie's neck, and she moaned. "I think it's a please go."

"It's a please stop because you're not a sinful man." She took his hand from her thigh and brought it up to kiss his knuckles. "In fact, you're a very good man who is tempted by some dangerous ideas."

Sam ceased kissing her and pulled Marie's skirt down modestly below her knees. "You are a very mean woman calling out my conscience like that," he whispered. "On our wedding night, I'm going to punish you for stopping me so soon."

"Pardon me?" Apparently, she'd driven Sam insane by not allowing him to go any further. How else could she explain the wedding night comment? Deciding to leave his error alone for the moment, she instead asked, "Am I to assume by punishment you mean to hurt me, and I won't enjoy it?"

"I could never hurt you, and I hope you would enjoy it very much." He reached over to get her bucket of dirty dishes with a groan. "My idea of teaching you a lesson is pleasing you so many times you lose count. You'll be ruined for any other man, only wanting me as a lover." Sam knelt by the water's edge and took out the plates and cutlery, placing each on the ground.

She realized he meant to wash dishes for her. Marie smiled and kneeled to help him. They cleaned in silence until she could no longer refrain from asking, "Could you please tell me what is wrong tonight? Why you acted so rough?"

He shrugged and placed a clean plate into the pail. "I covered your mouth in case I startled you."

"That explains some of it."

"You were in my arms, and I thought of all you deserved as a wife. I lost control. Today was horrible. I kept thinking what if they'd taken you instead of Ellen? Del can travel light and quick. Plus, he's not responsible for all these other people. If you'd been in her place, I'd have had to let him go get you. It's bad enough waiting to hear about her. I'd not live through losing you." He put the last of the silverware in the pail before continuing. "I'm tired of wanting you so much that I can't sleep and am unable to help the situation." Upon standing, he helped Marie to her feet as well.

She gave him a quick hug, afraid to believe in his feelings for her. "I knew you cared for me, but I don't think it's as much as you're saying."

He held her at arm's length. "Do you think I'm lying?"

"Not at all. I believe that you want someone you can't have."

"I can have you, and I will by the time we reach Fort Hall. I swear it."

His serious tone made her laugh, and without thinking, she said, "I wouldn't be swearing such things. Especially when you have no right to do so."

"All right. I won't promise anything until I hear your answer. Do you love him more than you love me?"

The question bothered her. She couldn't be honest with him and tried giving Sam a feeble laugh. "You know I can't answer that."

After pausing for a moment while examining her face, he said, "Come on." He held out his hand for her to take. "You need your sleep, as do I. Let me walk you back."

A thought from earlier in the day came to mind, and she stopped. "Sam! You'll know the answer, I'm sure. Have you heard of 'oochiegoo'?"

After pondering the question, he answered, "No, where did you hear this?"

She shook her head, disappointed he didn't know. "It's a word Charles and Hester bandy about in conversation."

"How is it used? Like a noun or a verb?"

"Like a verb, as in when will we, or did you enjoy it when we, or…" Much like Eden's snake, the thought wrapped itself in her mind. A verb they do together in secret? "What I think it means isn't possible."

"It might be." He led her outside the wagon semicircle and downstream, nodding to Uncle Joe as they passed him a few feet away.

Marie laughed at her ludicrous idea. "If they weren't siblings, I'd swear they were planning a rendezvous. That's just not possible. He wouldn't be with Hester. Charles has me always available and has no interest. "

"No interest in you?" At her go-ahead, he asked, "Can you pinpoint a time when it ended?"

She shook her head until the memory surfaced. "Hester moved into the guest house and things cooled rapidly between us.

He's a private person. Having her underfoot inhibited him."

"You didn't have servants?"

"Of course, we did, but they weren't family. I suppose he felt comfortable being intimate as if they were invisible." As if they were lightning strikes, a thousand clues hit her consciousness at once. "Sam." Dizzy, Marie reached out for him. He held her hand, steadying her. "I have the strangest idea that Charles and Hester are having an affair, have had one for years now. Isn't that the silliest?" Her nose stung and tears filled her eyes. His face swam in front of her as she requested, "Tell me that can't be true."

He shook his head, "I can't lie to you. I also think they're carrying on together, very together."

"Oh, mercy!" She put a hand to her mouth muffling, "I'm going to be sick!" Marie ran a little way before bending over and dry heaving. Hearing Sam behind her, she cried, "No, please don't follow me. It's not nice. I'm not ladylike right now."

"I can handle it."

Standing, she took a deep breath. An image of the twins being intimate sprang to her mind, and she resumed retching. During a break, she said, "Please, Sam, just leave me here alone. I'm finished with this entire trip."

"That's not going to happen."

She stayed faced away from him, her head bowed. "I don't know that I can be around them, knowing this."

"They're the ones who should be ashamed of themselves. It's disgusting."

Marie looked up at him, appreciating the sympathy without pity she saw in his eyes. "They've probably been laughing at me this whole time. He's probably told her every time I tried to seduce him." She put the back of her hand to her mouth. "You suspected this about them?" When he nodded, she asked, "For how long? Since Independence?"

"Not that long. Maybe a day or so after you fell in the river, then saved my life. I didn't know which couple I'd overheard, not until you were asking after them. I'd thought you knew, too, but only at first."

"You'd think I'd know and condone their actions?" Tears started falling in earnest. "I suppose I deserve your opinion, considering my forward conduct with you."

"You deserve nothing like this!" He reached out and held her upper arms. "How many times do you think they were together before you and I kissed?"

"Excuse me?"

"How many times have they had sex for each one of our kisses?"

"I, I don't..." She pulled away from his grip, wanting to stop the images in her mind.

"No, let's add up the occurrences, shall we?"

Frowning, she sulked, "I'd prefer not to."

"Hester's been stashed in the guest house for how long now? How many years? I also happen to know Warren is a gentleman farmer, meaning he works very little, if at all. His hands were as soft as an infant's when we first met. I'm surprised he lived this long out here. Usually, weak men like him have died before now."

Marie looked at him, blinking. She'd thought he condoned the Warren's activities and wrongly so. "You're every bit as angry as I am, maybe more so, since you're not injured, just indignant."

He stopped, facing her and almost yelling, "I've gone through hell wanting to crush his head like a melon, yet unable to say or do anything." Sam pinched the bridge of his nose and took a deep breath. "I both did and didn't want you to know because of how much hurt you'd endure. That old goat had a vibrant, beautiful woman like you and carries on with another? It's galling. Especially the other goat he's pawing after."

"If she's who Charles wanted, nothing I could try would gain his attention." A wave of nausea hit her. "Sam, I don't know if I can be good with them. Does everyone know?"

"Most don't, but others suspect."

She held her mouth, trying to calm her stomach. Marie had seen no pitying looks from anyone but had noticed how none of the others included either twin in conversations.

He tipped her chin up to see her face. "Marie, don't feel forced into doing anything you'd prefer not doing. I'm here, my men are here, and even your friends will do whatever they can for you."

Sam's expression was so earnest, she smiled at him. "You are a very kind man."

"Sweetheart," he murmured, "you don't have to do anything today. Nor tomorrow, nor ever, if it's what you want." He stood very close to her. "I only want your happiness."

She stared into his eyes. Sam was handsome down to his bones, inside and out. "I didn't know how long I'd been beating a dead horse. Now, I'm aware and can't go back. When I get to Oregon City, maybe you can recommend a good divorce attorney."

Sam grinned, his whole face showing his joy. "I can recommend one right now. A man who can have the document filed by the time we reach Fort Hall."

"I assume you're the man?" she said as they passed Uncle Joe's post.

"Yes. Whatever you need, however you need it, I'm here." He took her hand. "In the meantime, what do you want to do tonight?"

Marie's stomach churned despite being empty. She considered herself no better in the morals department. Eventually, she'd have to face Charles. "Nothing, but I need to do something, I suppose." Marie almost wished she'd been intimate with Sam. She'd have liked to rub her husband's nose in her own infidelity out of spite and to feel less like a throwaway wife. How many times had he crawled out of Hester's bed and straight into theirs? Or maybe Hester had been the one leaving their bedroom after she and Charles. Marie shuddered with revulsion. "Let's go ask them directly."

"Do you expect them to be honest with us?"

She stopped in her tracks. "I had expected them to, yes. Even if they lie, it will show on their faces and in their voices." Pulling him forward, she added, "I need to know either way."

Every family they passed was asleep. Only the night watch still stirred. As they neared the Warrens, Sam gave Marie's hand a squeeze. She said, "Thank you, I need the confidence."

When seeing them, Charles jumped to his feet. "Where the hell have you been? It's far past the time you should take in washing." He saw how the two still held hands before Marie let go of Sam. "Wait, I think I can guess what you two were doing in the dark, alone, for God knows how long." He stepped up to his wife as the younger man put the bucket in the wagon. "You disgusting little trollop. I knew you lusted for someone around here and should have guessed it was Granville. Should I ask how far have you two gone, or rather how many times?"

Marie swallowed the lump in her throat. She clenched her fists, forcing her voice to be calm. "Neither one is as much as you have with your sister."

He paled and looked at Hester, then back at his wife. "That's different. I love her. You're just a mare in heat for him, as you are for every man."

Stepping up to Charles, Sam said, "Excuse me?"

She blocked the younger man's progress, angry tears stinging her eyes. "Well, at least the men I'm in heat for aren't my blood relatives. Your family tree doesn't branch much, does it?"

Charles grabbed her arm and shook. "I ought to beat the sass out of you, young lady."

She winced from the pain, trying to pull away from his grip. When Sam tapped his shoulder, Charles let her go. The older man whirled around, both fists up and ready to fight.

Sam shook his head, smiling. "You don't want to do that. You also don't want to threaten or even touch Marie. Do so again and I'll either punch you into the next territory or leave you and your sister behind and on your own."

His fists lowered, and he sneered. "You wouldn't leave us here alone with the Shoshones around here. You care too much for Marie."

"Was I unclear in saying you and your sister? Because I distinctly remember meaning only you two when I spoke."

Charles threw a punch at Sam. The younger man grabbed his arm, twisting it behind his back and lifting up to immobilize him. "That wasn't a wise move, Mr. Warren."

"Go to hell!"

"I guess you didn't have a brother." When he looked over at Marie, she smiled and shook her head. "No? I did, and he taught me a lot about fighting, more than I wanted. Not only that but if I whistle, my men will know I need help." Lifting Charles' arm higher and getting a squeal for the effort, he laughed. "What you're going to do is sign any paper I give you tomorrow without protest or hesitation. When done, I'll not say a word about your sexual relationship with Miss Warren to anyone here. Am I clear?"

"Yes," he gasped.

"Clear enough to let go of you? I'd hate to damage your writing hand, after all."

"Yes, yes! I'll sign anything, just don't break my arm."

After looking at Marie for an approving nod, Sam released him go with a shove. "I'll have divorce papers written up tomorrow at daybreak. You will sign them, and if Mrs. Warren so chooses, when she signs, they'll be official. I have legal authority in Oregon Territory, which lucky for you, we're in at the moment."

Still rubbing his upper arm, Charles muttered, "Only barely in the territory."

"We're across the border well enough for Marie to move her belongings out of your wagon and into anyone else's."

Stepping away and into Hester's arms, he snarled, "I suppose you mean yours. She's nothing but a whore for you and your men."

Marie gasped in horror. "Charles! I'm not! You take that back this instant."

Sam grabbed the older man's shirt. "You heard her."

"Fine, get your stuff and get out of my way. I'll sign anything that gets me rid of you. You've been an albatross around my neck for long enough. Now that your Daddy's money is gone, I don't need you. Hester and I can go somewhere and live like we've always wanted without having to coddle you every minute. We're well rid of you."

She took a deep breath and stepped back. "Samuel, could you draw up a document of divorce, please? I'll want my former name back. Also, he's to have no say in my future or future income."

Charles snorted and then spit on the ground. "As if I'd want anything you earned on your back."

Pushing Charles backward and letting go of his shirt in the process, Sam growled, "One more insult from you and not even the wolves will find enough of you to eat when I'm done."

Marie wanted to smile when her husband turned white with fear for the second time that evening. She knew Sam loved her, but his deadly expression even scared her a little. She put a hand on his arm. "Don't, Sam. He's not worth it."

Sam turned to her saying, "You're right. I'll start working on your paper as requested." He glanced around as the small crowd of the first night watch gathered. "We can discuss the details later, agreed, Mr. Warren?"

"Agreed."

"Mrs. Warren, I'll send my men over to help you." He turned on a heel and went to his camp.

She glanced at Charles, who didn't look at her. Unsure of what to say after hearing all his insults, she went to the back of the wagon. After climbing in, Marie began sorting her clothes and other items.

Hester's scowling face appeared at the tailgate. "You're going to need watching, so you don't steal anything from us. You could take anything in the moonlight, and we'd not see."

"Steal? From you?" she retorted. "I wouldn't bother. Neither one of you has anything worth taking." As she sorted items, Hester examined everything Marie touched. She gave the older woman a surreptitious glare. She'd meant her sarcasm and took only family heirlooms Charles had earlier deemed unsalable. She handed her belongings down to Arnold, who waited below. He left, and Lucky turned up in his place, so she gave him a few of her things, too. When he was gone, Uncle Joe appeared. After he had disappeared with another bundle, she peered out to see where they went.

The men carried her things directly to Sam's wagon. In any other situation, she'd have laughed at how antlike they looked. Now, all this just saddened her.

"Chazzy told me about the saloon gal dresses you had made specially to seduce him," Hester said loud enough for an approaching Lefty to hear.

Marie handed the blushing man her sewing and smiled. "These are my quilt supplies, I promise." He nodded and hurried away with the bundle.

"I didn't see those dresses in what you packed. Are you leaving them for me? I'm sure you'll need them in your new career."

"Charles considered my wearing them foolish early on, so they were discarded." Marie shrugged. "Besides, they never worked for me. You'll have to find your own way of keeping him interested. Especially now, seeing as you're no longer forbidden fruit."

Hands on hips, the older woman replied, "You're not either, dear former sister. Remember that when Mr. Granville starts wishing he had a sister to love instead of you."

"You think this is normal? This bedding between siblings?" She climbed down from the wagon. "No, Hester, this is very abnormal. Otherwise, Charles and you wouldn't have kept it secret for so long."

"You're the reason we kept quiet. We needed your money."

"Congratulations, then. You've taken everything, liquidated it, spent the profit, and now what do you have? A wagon, four tired ole oxen, and now no one to do your chores for you." Hester opened her mouth to say something and Marie interrupted her. "No, I'm not interested in anything else you have to say. I'm done here, and you two can go on as you please." She turned on her heel and started walking, following Sam's men.

"Ma'am? We put your things in the back of our second wagon. Most of our day to day belongings are there, too." Lucky led her over to the second wagon. "I reckon you should get some sleep tonight. Boss is hoping to reach Soda Springs tomorrow."

"Very well." She peeked over the tailgate. "I suppose my bedroll is here, too?"

"Yes, ma'am." He indicated the other empty beds around the dying campfire. "Most of us are out keeping the area safe. We take a couple hour naps, one man at a time."

"That sounds difficult." She began spreading out her blankets for the night.

"It is, but if we can keep anyone else from being murdered and kidnapped, it's worth the effort."

Marie sat on her bed, staring up at the young man. "Thank you for watching over us. I'll be sure to make coffee extra strong for y'all tomorrow."

"We'd appreciate that, ma'am." He went to his own bed and took off his boots. "If you don't mind, I'd like to get some shut eye." At her nod, he settled in for his rest.

"Of course, Mr. Lucky. Sleep well." Marie undid her boots, setting them to the side. She slid in under the covers and laid down face up.

How long had those two been together? Since they were old enough to "oochiegoo"? Her stomach churned with nausea. Had they carried on during Charles' first marriage, too? She glanced over at a softly snoring Lucky, envying him his ability to sleep. Combing through her life with Charles for what she should have seen, Marie sighed. Saloon gals, one of the ladies in their current wagon party, some woman in New Orleans were all possible partners for her husband's affairs. But his own sister? She turned to her side, away from the fire's light. The woman had no redeeming qualities to Marie, not even in personality or demeanor.

She struggled to sleep until at last the night eased its way into the day. Each man had taken his turn napping in his bedroll before going back to his duty post. She didn't stir to see which one, not even if the man could have been Sam. As the sky grew brighter, she sat up to see Arnold asleep across the fire pit. She looked around for the water pail, wanting to make good on her promise to Lucky. It hung from the wagon, so she grabbed it and headed for the river.

No one else in camp stirred, not even when she returned. Marie looked in the back of the wagon holding her things. With two wagons, they might not have food and bedding in both. Or maybe they would if one caught fire. She sighed. Rummaging through their belongings would be both rude and noisy. She didn't want to disturb everyone with her ignorance.

"Up so early?" Sam's voice startled her in the quiet morning air.

She smiled at him. "Lucky had me promise to make strong coffee first thing. It's the least I can do."

"Great. Let me help you find everything, and coffee can be your job with us."

"I don't know about…"

He held up a bag. "The beans are kept here." Reaching further into the back, he said, "And here's the pot. There are cups in this area as well. Makes everything easy and fast."

"Would you want me to start breakfast?"

"Always, if you'd like. You doing for us what you did for the Warrens would help all of us. We could keep you on for the cooking and cleaning, allowing us to keep more men on security."

"How long would you need my help for?"

"For as long as you're willing. I'd like for you to stay until after we reach Oregon City, but it's your choice."

"I see." She saw the Warrens approach from behind Sam. "Oh dear."

Sam turned to see them, too. "Good morning, Mr. Warren, Miss. What brings you both to my side of the camp so early?"

"I think you know. Marie, pack up your things and get back to our camp."

She looked at Sam when he laughed. As he quieted, she said, "This isn't funny."

He swallowed as if he'd been caught with his hand in the cookie jar. "No, I don't suppose it is."

Each word of Charles' was clipped as he said, "Did I stutter? Because my wife isn't getting her tail back to our camp after I distinctly told her to do just that."

Addressing Marie, Sam said, "You have to admit, he really is rather humorous. The man still thinks you belong to him."

Warren went to stand between Sam and Marie. "That's because she does. No matter what you two might have done last night, she's still my wife, and I still need her to go with us to California."

Sam smiled, taking a step back and away from the couple. "Very well. You two have a few things to discuss."

"Yes we do," said Marie. She kept her glare on Charles; silently wishing Sam would leave already and let her give the Warrens a talking to.

Sam grinned. "Excuse me while I tend to an overdue task. Marie, I expect you to continue with coffee and breakfast. Warren, you and your sister are welcome to join us."

Marie watched as the younger man climbed into one of the company wagons. Before she could begin talking to him, Charles grabbed her arm and said, "What the hell is this breakfast thing you've agreed to?" He shoved her away from him. "Never mind. Just do as he said, so we can eat and get back on our way. This hanging on to Granville is over."

"Hanging on to?" She saw red as much as any bull in the matador's arena. "You think I'm going to return to your camp and live as your servant while you and Hester carry on your affair?"

"Lower your voice," Hester whispered. "I don't want anyone hearing this and thinking I'm as much a tart as you are."

Aghast at what the woman dared to say, Marie had no useful retort. She closed her open mouth. "Excuse me while I begin cooking for everyone. I suppose you're included at Granville's insistence." She ignored them as if the two were fence posts. She poured water into the coffee pot and put in a healthy portion of beans. Most of the men, Lefty, Uncle Joe, and Lucky gathered around. Each carried a couple of handfuls of twigs and other brush. They threw the kindling onto the fire, avoiding the pot. After moving around the Warrens a couple of times, she said, "Please. Have a seat out of the way."

Hester leaned over to her brother, but said loud enough for everyone to hear, "I wouldn't worry, Charles. Marie is a smart woman who knows where her bread is buttered. You're a good husband. You've never beat her and have always provided." She looked at Marie. "Better the devil you know than the devil you don't."

Before she could reply to Hester, Sam walked over to them with a piece of paper. "Mrs. Warren?" He continued, "I have the paper drying. It'll be ready whenever you are." He took her hand and helped Marie to her feet. "I'd have blotted the ink already, but I want no smudges or mistakes to mar the intent."

She glanced over the neat script, seeing "Divorce Decree" large across the top. "I appreciate that, Mr. Granville."

"Arnold is keeping guard over the pen, paper, and ink over there at the tailgate." Sam grinned at her. He called out to Charles, saying, "Mr. Warren? I have an official document for you to sign."

"What?" He stood with difficulty and walked to where the three of them were waiting. Seeing the paper, Charles stopped. "Hell no. I'm not divorcing her. Not while she's still able bodied and can help us get to California."

Sam's eyes narrowed. "You will sign and with a smile on your face."

"Or?" Charles laughed.

Leaning in to say in a quieter voice, Sam added, "Or, I will tell everyone I ever see again about the man who preferred bedding his sister over his own wife."

Charles' demeanor changed from amused to rage. "You wouldn't dare. No one would believe you."

"Not only would I, but I'd also write a story for every newspaper between here, Mexico City, and Boston. Every single one, about you and Hester, and I will name names."

"Sam, you can't. I couldn't take the notoriety."

"I wouldn't mention you, of course. Besides, once they read Charles, Hester, lovers, and siblings, no one would talk about anything else." He glared at Warren. "So? Don't you think you and your sister might be just fine without Marie?"

He looked back at Hester, now as pale as he was. She nodded, and he turned back to Sam. "You win. Where do I sign?"

"Here, please." Sam pointed to the first line and handed him the quill. When the man hesitated, Sam added, "Don't you want to be rid of such an albatross of a wife, Mr. Warren? Don't you prefer someone else?"

Grabbing the pen, Charles jabbed it in the inkwell and signed his name with a flourish. "There. We're done, and it's about time."

Marie watched while holding her breath. No one moved. The

air hung so still, she could hear the pen tip scratch the paper's surface. He straightened, handing her the pen. She walked up to the document and dipped the tip in ink. Her hand shook as she tapped off the excess ink.

Before she could sign her name, Charles stepped forward and hissed in her ear, "I wonder which of these men you'll take first? My money's on Granville."

CHAPTER 11

Marie's hand shook, getting a drop of ink on her dress. "Oh." Her vision blurred from the tears, and she took a step back. "Could you take the pen for a moment, Mr. Granville?"

"Certainly," said Sam, taking back the pen. "Thank you, Mr. Warren. When we get to Oregon City, I'll submit a copy there for the record."

"It's not official now?" asked Hester.

He smiled. "It will be as soon as Mrs. Warren and a couple of witnesses sign. Misters Lefty and Joe have already volunteered since they can both read and write." He'd kept the language simple intentionally. No need in him letting things bog down by lengthy legal scribbles. He wanted this signed as soon as possible. Her face pale and hands shaky, Marie stepped back while giving Sam the pen. He swallowed, trying to ignore the flips his heart did in joy. "Thank you, Miss?"

"Renaud."

She didn't meet his gaze. He glanced over at the Warrens. Charles scowled while Hester still wore the same smug smile she'd arrived with. "It's a pleasure, Miss Renaud." Sam moved over so Joe and Lefty had access to the paper. "The marriage is dissolved, and you're as free as any other unmarried woman in the party."

"All right," Marie nodded. "I'm sorry to be so obtuse. This is my first and only divorce so far." Thinking for a moment, she added, "I don't even know of anyone else who's had one. I don't owe him anything, nor does he owe me anything? Is it truly as easy as a signature?"

Sam gave her question some consideration and answered, "No, not usually. Divorce is granted by the Territory's legislature. While the decree itself is general, I'll include a letter with more detail to a discreet friend of mine. Had there been children, custody and support would have been addressed in the main document. Being none, it's a non-issue and not included in the decree. You also own no land together, am I right?"

"Not yet, not until California."

"Very well, then. You're completely your own person."

"I see." She glanced around at the scattering crowd. Lefty, being the last to sign, still held the pen and weighed down the drying paper. "I think he's done."

Sam took the pen and paper. "Thank you, sir. I appreciate your help with the matter."

"My pleasure, boss." He tipped his hat. "Miss."

Warren looked Marie up and down, saying, "Goodbye, Marie. I'll leave you with your payment, then." He said to Sam, "Granville." After motioning to his sister, the two walked away.

Tears gathered in Marie's eyes as she said, "I might find some chores that need doing. If you don't mind, I'd prefer to be alone for a while."

"Of course. This is a sad day for you, and I'm sorry for all of it." He wanted to reach out to her, but she wore a don't-touch feeling like a cloak. "We're a little late in getting started. So double check everything is packed, and we'll be moving shortly."

She nodded, wiping away the tears dripping down her face. He resisted giving her a hug, not easy when every part of him wanted to console her. Sam went to saddle Scamp and see where the other men in his party were. Riding a little to the north, he saw Lucky sitting astride, bugle ready. Sam nodded, and the young man sounded the order to move.

Wheels began rolling along the broad, scenic valley. The fresh morning air, a beautiful ribbon of river, and the smell of fresh grass being crushed underfoot brightened his day. Out of her sight, he allowed himself a grin over Marie's freedom. He'd expected her to mourn the loss of her marriage. While aware of his selfishness, he enjoyed the chance to court her openly. Which called for a solid plan. He kept up in front with Lucky, admiring the landscape and calculating how long to wait until proposing to her.

"Boss?" Lucky asked.

The young man appearing at his side startled Sam a little. A sliver of fear slid down his spine to his naval. He needed to pay attention to the surroundings a lot better in Shoshone country. Too many tit for tat killings had happened for his comfort. "Yes?"

"We'll lunch at Soda Springs?"

"That's the plan."

"Good. I'll ride back and tell the others."

Sam resisted the urge to have Lucky stay up front while he went himself. He scanned the low mountains to the sides, knowing he just wanted the excuse to see Marie. Enough time had passed since this morning, and his elation faded to worry. He fretted over how she must now feel about the sudden upheaval in her life. Would she find him attractive even if he were no longer the forbidden fruit? Sam shook his head at the thought. She said she loved him. His heart thudded heavy in his chest. He'd see her to wherever she wanted to go, even if the place ended up being far from him. Hearing hoofbeats behind him, he turned to see who approached.

"Sir," Lucky began. "They're all set to stop at Soda Springs."

"Thank you. It'll be a treat."

"Mrs., er, Miss Marie is fine. She's with our wagons."

He nodded, resisting the need to ask any more about her. Realizing she was free for him to talk with any time he wanted smacked his thoughts. "You know, Lucky, I think you can lead us to the springs. I need to check on Marie myself."

Lucky gave his boss a sly grin. "I was wondering how long you'd be up here this morning."

Turning Scamp around to backtrack, Sam trotted to the company wagons. He eased up, letting his horse slow when seeing her off to the side. His heart hurt at how forlorn and lovely she looked. She'd let her sunbonnet fall down behind her while walking. When she caught sight of him, he waved, grinned at her return greeting, and trotted over to her. "Hello, ma'am."

As he swung off his horse, she asked, "Hello, Sam. Is everything all right so far?"

He fell into step beside her. Her hair glistened in the sunlight, but her eyes seemed clouded. Sam kept his tone bright, hoping a good mood was contagious. "So far, yes. How about you?"

"Oh, I'm still sorrowful and extremely shocked. I feel horribly foolish, too." She tugged at her sleeve. "They'd been carrying on under my nose for who knows how long. I never suspected."

Sam disliked how she didn't share his joy at her freedom. He patted her shoulder in an attempt to comfort her. "Of course, you didn't, sweetheart. Who would suspect those two? No one."

She gave him a sideways glance. "I'm not just ignorant for believing Charles was only with me?"

"No, you're not." He shook his head, adding, "No more so than any other woman with a philandering husband."

"I suppose we're all stupid, then."

Anytime she was less than kind to herself, Sam didn't like it. Bad enough he'd had to endure the Warrens' attitude toward Marie. He hated her echoing their words, and said, "No, I'd not say so. Trusting your spouse isn't a test of intelligence."

She laughed. "Good thing it isn't. Though maybe as close as you and I have been, I'm as guilty as Charles is."

He squelched his first impulse to loudly deny anything could be wrong with her. Taking a breath, Sam stalled for time, saying, "Hmm. I'd have to think about that."

"There's no need. I'm terribly guilty. We've kissed. I've said I love you, and both are enough. Charles and Hester's actions are my just rewards."

This entire conversation irritated him. He didn't like thinking of Marie as anything other than an angel. "I disagree. If they'd behaved as a proper brother and sister, you'd not be the third wheel in your own marriage. Their romance left you alone enough to fall for the next handsome man you saw." He glanced over to see her grin.

"I suppose so, Mr. Handsome." They walked for a bit. After a while, she sighed and said, "This may take a while for me to get through, Sam. I'm happy to be free, since I do care about you, but my heart still hurts."

Seeing her eyes well up with tears, he put an arm around her. "I'm certain it does, sweetheart. It has to. Even if you hated him, and who could tolerate her…?"

"Do I need to answer?" He put his face close to her hair and breathed in, enjoying her scent.

"No, but I do wonder how a man could ever look at another woman after seeing you. Knowing you has been like being bit by a mosquito."

"How romantic," she said, her voice indicating it was anything but.

Sam stopped her, putting a hand to her chin and having her look into his eyes. She needed to know he was serious. "It is. You're in my blood like a fever that won't let go."

She choked back a laugh before saying, "I appreciate you not calling me an illness. Fever sounds much better."

He chuckled and resisted caressing her face. Up ahead, the first of their party eased to a stop. Sam judged he had another ten minutes alone with her and wanted to make the time count. He let his arm around her shoulders fall and resumed walking. Summoning up his best casual tone, he said, "My love for you is a condition I never want to cure."

She laughed. "It took only a few steps for you to think up such a pretty line."

"Just think what I could say between here and Oregon City."

"Oh dear. I consider myself warned."

Glancing over, he grinned when seeing the twinkle in her eyes. "I'll make Shakespeare's sonnets pale in comparison."

Her eyebrows lifted in surprise before she laughed. "I'm sure you will, Mr. Granville."

The wagons followed close enough to one another that the oxen knew to slow as those ahead of them slowed to a stop. His face heated as he thought of what he'd promised. Words to rival the Bard's? Sam went to the wagon and retrieved a glass jar. "I have a treat for you. Just follow me and you'll see."

She nodded. "That sounds like a fun idea. Could we care for the animals at the same time?"

"Sure." He continued to lead Scamp. Catching sight of Lefty, Sam said, "Lefty, I'm getting some soda water for Miss Renaud and the rest of us. Can you and the other men lead the animals to a fresh pond?"

"You bet, boss." Lefty nudged his horse on to find the others.

Grinning at Marie, Sam said, "You'll like this." He led her to a bubbling spring he was familiar with and knelt to scoop up some water. "It's a little lukewarm, but fizzy."

After giving him a dubious look, she tipped up the glass and drank a couple of sips. She stopped, chuckling. "It tickles! How fun! The water tastes plain, but doesn't feel plain." She handed him the jar. "Here, the rest is for you."

"I'll take it. We can get more for later." He refilled the container and stood.

Following him back to camp, she asked, "Do the bubbles last very long?"

"Some. They gradually decrease over time."

"What happens then?"

Sam dug around in the wagon for whiskey and sugar. "It turns into ordinary water." He added a splash of the liquor to the water and a dash of sugar. Swirling it until most of the sugar dissolved, he handed the jar to Marie.

"Oh. No explosions or poison?" She tried a sip at first, and a surprised expression crossed her face before she took a longer drink.

He laughed and eased the mix away from her. "No, none of that," Sam said before trying the drink himself. It tasted better than he'd remembered.

With a small grin, she asked, "May I have some more?"

"Of course." He gave her what was left of the sweet whiskey water. "I'd tried putting a lid on the whiskey jug last time, but it didn't work. The bouncing of the wagon shook the bubbles right out of the water. The drink wasn't bad, just not what I'd expected."

"That's a shame. I'd have liked mixing a strong wine with the bubbles and make a sparkling rosé."

"I like that idea." At the wagon, they waited until his men got their lunches from a napkin covered cook pot. Everyone spent more time chewing than talking, eager to get back to the soda water. He grinned when seeing how fast Lucky, Lefty, and Arnold left for the springs with Uncle Joe strolling behind them. "They're going to have it all drank by the time we get there."

"No, they can't."

Chuckling at her dismay, he reassured her with a pat on the back. "No, I don't think it's possible, sweetheart. We can go help them. The springs past here aren't as good."

She nodded, following him as he went to the best watering hole. Most of the others, including Sam's men, stored some for later. He hoped the fizz lasted longer for them than it had for him during earlier trips. The shadows lengthened, showing the time past noon. "All right, gentlemen. Let's get moving." As they all went to get ready for moving, Sam turned to Marie. "Would you like to ride on Scamp with me? I promise to behave."

"Maybe later," she said. He must have betrayed some dismay at her answer because she put her hand on his arm. "Right now, I need time alone to think. Ask me again some other time, and I might say yes."

"I'll hold you to that."

"Please do."

Lucky's bugle sounded, and the wheels began their slow roll. Most times the noise didn't bother him as much as it did now. Sam reckoned he must be irritated. The man picked the instrument up on their last trip west and never put down the blasted thing. Sam shook his head. No doubt about it. Marie's refusal stuck in his craw. His own irritation bothered him, too. The woman needed time, he scolded himself, not some man pawing at her. He sat up straighter in the saddle. They still had a third of the journey ahead of them. In that time, he could think of the best arguments for her marrying him. Besides, arguing was his specialty. He grinned. She didn't stand a chance of refusing him.

Lost in his thoughts and scanning the horizon, he led them ten miles down the road. Sam saw a few people letting their animals drink from some of the creeks they encountered despite him telling them distinctly not to do so. He made a mental note to mix up some molasses and vinegar. It'd help ease stomach aches the poison water might cause.

Seeing the sun dip under the horizon, he sighed. Sure, the mountains helped the day seem shorter. They still needed to find a good spot to camp for the night. They had another day's travel before reaching better water. He led Scamp to the sliver of a creek they followed. Once there, he hopped down and tasted the water. Taking another drink to be sure, he found nothing wrong. It might have a bit of alkali, but not enough to immediately detect. He looked north, searching for anything able to give them fuel to dinner's fire. A few scrub brush thickets followed the canyons down from the mountains to the east.

He straightened. The dead twigs and branches might be enough for them tonight. As Lucky trotted up to him, Sam said, "That next clump of shrubby trees? That can be camp."

"I'll let everyone know." The young man nudged his horse into a gallop, kicking up white powdery dust.

Sam shook his head. He'd need a dose of his own vinegar tonic this evening, judging by the soil. Hopping up on Scamp, he trotted ahead to the potential campsite. Getting there didn't take long. Once there, the water seemed good and he saw plenty of grass for the animals. What looked like scrub brush from far away turned out to be a thicket of stunted trees.

The first of the wagons caught up to him. Mr. Allen and his wife sat up front, with Jenny strolling beside. She carried a handful of yellow wildflowers. He tipped his hat at the Allens and called out to Jenny. "Good afternoon, Miss."

She didn't meet his eyes. "Good afternoon, Mr. Granville."

Her frown puzzled him, but other concerns needed his

attention more at the moment. "Mr. Allen, we'll camp here. Stopping anywhere is fine."

The other man nodded while Mrs. Allen smiled at him. Sam rode on down the line certain what bothered Jenny didn't concern the rest of her family. He checked over everyone in the group. They all settled in for the evening as smooth as ever. His men scattered to do their chores. Sam removed Scamp's saddle and staked him out for the evening. Seeing the others tend to the oxen and their own horses, he went to the clump of trees. Not a lot of wood lay ready on the ground, but a few branches had snapped in the afternoon winds. He picked up an armload full. Lucky passed by him with the same idea. By the time the young man returned with another bunch of wood, Sam had a good campfire burning.

Marie walked up to him. "How nice. I don't think I'll ever take wood for granted again. Clean water, either."

He leaned back on his bedroll and patted the blanket. "Just wait until your first night in a real bed."

She went to the nearby wagon, saying. "Oh, goodness! Such heaven. I can't even imagine."

He laughed. "Surely you remember beds."

She paused in fixing the meal as if trying to recall. "I've not even touched a bed since…"

"Fort Laramie. I remember a bed there."

"My. Yes, there might have been something like that." She glanced up at him, and his body temperature spiked. "I might have regretted not taking advantage of what I had at the time."

He'd suspected Marie had the same desires as him. She'd hinted as much before now. He said, "I know I wish every night I'd spent the night at the fort."

"Every night since?"

"Absolutely." He glanced over at her, smiling at the blush staining her cheeks. She glowed like an autumn sunset, and he almost laughed. Wanting to see how bright of a red she could get, he added, "Though I've often imagined not even needing a bed. The back of the wagon, in warm hot springs, against a tree, or even on top of Independence Rock. A man could sleep anywhere if the circumstances allowed."

Her face brighter than the campfire, she put food on to cook. The crew came in one by one and sat, waiting for dinner. In a transparent attempt to change the subject, Marie said, "This friend of yours, Adelard. Do you trust him?"

He glanced around at the assembled group. "Of course, I do, as much as I trust anyone here."

"All right then, I trust him, too."

"Good. He's been nothing but a decent man since I've known him. Plus, he's the only one who could go get Ellen back for us." He paused, staring into the fire. "I've trusted him with my life before and know I can trust him with hers. If she's still alive, he'll bring her back to us."

"He needs to get a move on. I'm missing the fresh game he hunted for us." Arnold's comment broke the somber atmosphere, and everyone laughed.

Dinner passed quickly and without much talking. The meal was the usual salt pork with cornbread biscuits. The first finished, Sam stood up, stretching his legs. "Miss Renaud cooked. I can clean." He gathered plates and forks from everyone after each ate the last few bites. "Unless someone else besides her wants to volunteer?" he joked. Their chorus of no's answered his question, and he laughed. Other chores would keep them busy while he washed up from dinner. He waited while Marie wrapped the extra biscuits in a clean cloth. "We probably need a few napkins washed for tomorrow and maybe the next day. We should reach Fort Hall by then."

"All right. I can clean these and the wash rags while you're doing dishes." She stood up with the bundle of food. Going to the back of the wagon, Marie placed the leftovers in a basket. She gathered up the used napkins and dishcloths. "I'm assuming there's a lot more clean water at the fort than here?"

"Yes. If you wanted to wait and make a day of it, we can." He made a motion with his head for her to follow him to the creek. "I don't like putting off the wash until then, but a couple of days won't hurt." He saw her nod, but she didn't respond otherwise. Waiting until reaching the water, he asked, "What's bothering you, sweetheart? Tell me and I'll fix it."

"You can't fix this." She knelt and began scrubbing the cloth squares with a bar of soap.

He joined her, downstream so the food wouldn't wash back on her clean fabric. "How do you know I can't fix it? I'm pretty handy, plus I have a crew of men. If none of us can fix it, maybe it isn't broken."

She coughed out a little laugh. "You can't fix society, Sam."

"When I'm leading a society through the mountains, I can." He saw in the orange light reflected by the clouds overhead how her eyes filled with tears. Resisting the need to put a wet hand on her shoulder, he asked, "Can you at least tell me? A sorrow shared is a sorrow lessened. Or so my mother says."

Marie's chin trembled, and she stopped scrubbing. "It's nothing, really. I just can't associate with Jenny and probably Ellen anymore." She glanced up at him. "A divorcee isn't a good influence on young women."

He didn't know what to say. Sam wanted to kiss her until she smiled again, but that wouldn't solve her problem. He sighed while scrubbing a particularly stubborn crust. Kissing her would prove everyone right. A divorced woman was a loose woman. "You're a lady, Marie, by anyone's standards. I'm certain Miss Jenny will see she's very wrong in allowing a civilization hundreds of miles away to dictate who she can be friends with."

"I'd like to believe you."

"So? Trust me. It's not that difficult."

She laughed. "Very well, I believe Jenny will regret not being my friend in this space of time."

"See how easy that was?"

They walked into the camp, finding it empty except for Lefty. The young man glanced up from his journaling. "You just missed Mr. Warren. He told us his oxen are sick. Uncle Joe, Lucky, and Arnie are all caring for the others' livestock. Their animals are doing poorly, too."

"What are you still doing here?"

"I took care of our livestock already and put out our bedrolls." He nodded at Marie's blankets. "Hope you don't mind, ma'am. I thought I might help you, too."

"Not at all, Mr. Lefty."

Sam said, "I'll go double check on how the boys are doing. You can put everything away, Miss Renaud."

"Certainly."

He turned on his heel and went down the line. All the oxen and most of the horses already smelled like vinegar. Sam couldn't detect the molasses, but knew his men had used a mix of the two. At the last wagon, the Warrens', he paused, not wanting to see either one of the twins. Before Sam could slip past, Charles turned the corner and saw him standing there.

Warren strolled up to him. "Well, Mr. Granville. How very kind of you to visit. Especially since that tart you've been sniffing after isn't here anymore."

"Excuse me? Marie is nothing but a respectable woman, and you'd best remember to keep a civil tongue."

Charles laughed. "You're a fool. She's lovely enough at first but turns into a sow-eared nag after a year. "

"Maybe it was the company she kept that helped her become a nag, sir."

"Her life was perfect, except for her being in it. Besides, nothing I say matters. You can't be interested in keeping a useless female like her past Fort Hall. She isn't worth the trouble."

Fury swept through him like a dust devil on a summer's day. As if in reflex, he swung up and his right fist connected with Warren's chin. Sam's left punched him just as fast. One more hit and Warren woke up, punching Sam in the gut. Seeing the blow approach, he tensed his abdomen before Charles connected. Fighting with Nick all these years taught Sam the best times to hit and the best to block. Soon, he had Charles in a headlock with the older man struggling to get free. Sam laughed. Nick would have been stomping his shins or pinching his upper leg to bruising.

"What on earth is going on here?" Hester's voice screeched out in the quiet evening air, halting both men.

Charles took the chance to slip out of the chokehold and Sam let him. While he checked his jaw for injury, Sam said, "It's a fight, Miss Warren."

"I can see that." She stepped up to her brother. "Charles, really. I expected better of you than this street urchin behavior."

"He started it," Charles said, rubbing the back of his neck.

"Dear God, Chas, it doesn't matter who started it. You're supposed to be the adult." She put her arm around him. "Come on now, and I'll fix up those horrible wounds."

Sam's brows rose as he took a couple of steps back. If those were wounds, he sincerely hoped Warren never saw the harsh realities of war. Or Indian attacks. Either way, they'd both learn about how fast a person could bleed out. He looked around him to see Lucky, Arnold, and Joe standing behind the Warrens.

Joe spoke first. "Your animals are all dosed, sir."

"Thank you," muttered Charles. "Good night."

"Good evening," replied Joe.

Without another word, the four went back to their own camp. His stomach and face hurt more with each step he took. He breathed in to see how much doing so would hurt and only inhaled so much before stopping. His eye ached from where Warren's fist connected. Judging by Marie's expression when he entered the firelight's glow, his face looked as bad as it felt.

"Oh, Sam." She rushed over to him. Putting cool hands to his face, she asked, "What happened? I heard Hester screeching. Tell me she didn't do this to you."

Sam laughed, even though doing so hurt. "No, I could handle her."

"You fought Charles? That was foolish."

"Maybe." He lifted up his chin so she could attend to him. "I might have thrown the first punch, but he started it."

"Oh, dear." She brushed a lock of hair from his forehead. Dabbing a little more whiskey on a scrape, Marie added, "Why would you punch him, anyway?"

He winced at the alcohol's sting. "He said something I didn't like, something rude, and needed to know his words had consequences."

"I see." Pouring a little more onto the cloth, Marie resumed her doctoring. "What did he say?"

"Don't know if I want to say."

She paused. "What was it?"

"He was saying rude things about you."

"Ah, so you took it upon yourself to defend my honor."

He didn't care for the scornful tone of her voice. "Yes, I did. He says one more word about you being useless, and I'll fight him again."

Marie laughed, and Sam remembered how much he loved the sound. She shook her head. "I've heard him say that very thing many times. Did he tell you how I was a useless, sow-eared nag? It's one of his favorites when he's angry." She picked up one of his hands, examining for and finding the broken skin on his knuckles. "Either I've been pretty good for a long while, or he's been distracted. Otherwise, he'd have called me that, and you'd have heard him before now."

Her touches and holding his hand left his chest feeling as if he'd been breathing soda water. He loved how soft her skin felt against his fingertips. "If I'd heard him even then, I wouldn't have hit him tonight." Sam turned his hand palm up and tickled her wrist. "Traded him to the Indians, indeed, but not hit."

She grabbed his fingertips to stop the teasing. "Right now, I'd let you trade him to anyone for anything." Standing and storing the supplies back in the wagon, she added, "They could take Hester, too. She's quiet in front of others, but she's horrible, too." She nodded at Lucky as he strolled by while on watch. "Let's try to get some sleep. They're not worth keeping us awake tonight."

He smiled. The embers burned low, so much that they gave her face a dim glow. By firelight or sunlight, Sam thought she was beautiful. He leaned in closer and said, "You're everything a woman should be, what other women aspire to be."

"Oh, my, thank you. I suppose you have had time to be poetic." She settled into her bedroll with a sigh.

"That's just a small sample. I'm planning on us being married by the time we get home." He smiled when hearing her chuckle and snuggled deeper into his own blankets.

"Planning. So funny."

Sam waited for her to continue until hearing her soft snore. He closed his eyes, too, and fell asleep.

He stood in the middle of town. Noisy, smelly, and everything civilization flowed around Sam. He breathed in, puzzled at how the cooking odors made his stomach growl in what seemed like midday. None of this seemed real. They'd not even reached the Columbia River. Opening his eyes, Sam groaned. Still heading west, still eating campfire food. He sat up, looking at the fire. Coffee and breakfast appeared ready.

"Good morning, sir." Arnold held up a cornbread biscuit. "You're the last one awake."

"I see that."

"We made the usual amount of noise. Lucky offered to play a tune. Miss Renaud suggested we see how long it took before your stomach woke you."

Sam laughed. "Too long, it seems." He went to the fire, accepting the cup Marie offered. She poured him coffee and handed him a plate. "Thank you, ma'am."

"My pleasure. The sooner you eat, the sooner I can start washing."

Arnold snickered. Sam put down his coffee and placed a hand over his heart. "Your concern for my hunger touches my very soul."

"I'm sure." She wrapped up the leftovers. "Arnie, did you want more coffee? There's about a cupful left."

"Naw, ma'am. I need to help the others with getting ready." He stood, handing her his cup and dish. "Looks like my boss here needs it more than I do."

Sam scowled at the kid as if greatly insulted. He took a sip, ignoring Arnie's grin as he left. The cornbread biscuits tasted great. Marie had mixed in currants, giving the food a hint of sweetness. He wanted to savor every bite, but hunger took over, and he quickly finished. "Miss Renaud, you cooked a fine meal. Thank you."

Taking his plate while pouring him more coffee, she said, "My pleasure. You're doing me a great favor by allowing me to tag along with your crew."

"I could hardly leave you at the side of the road."

"True, and I'm forever grateful you didn't."

Sam didn't like how seriously she took his joking. "I misspoke. I'd never leave you alone anywhere. A man did just that once before out here, and I guess I'm still angry about it." He finished up his drink. "Also, I'm more than a little unhappy at how Warren seemed to think you'd continue with him after their secret was revealed."

"Well, he is quite a man." She held out her hand for his cup.

He gave it to her, frowning until she winked at him. "Do you need any help?"

"No, and it seems the boys left picking up the beds to you." She turned to go, saying over her shoulder, "You don't want to wait too long. Lucky's bugle will catch you lollygagging."

Grinning, he did just as she suggested. Sam shook the dust and debris from each blanket before folding and stacking them.

He nodded at Uncle Joe and Lefty. "Good morning." Both greeted him and continued hitching up the oxen to their wagons. Sam walked to the water and saw Marie walking toward him. He saw how pale her skin was under the slight tan. Her chin trembled, and he asked, "What's wrong?"

She didn't hesitate, sidestepping past him to the back of the wagon. "Nothing at all."

Following, he said, "I can tell something is bothering you." He watched her hand shake as she put the bucket of dishes in their place. "Did you see a snake, an Indian? A Snake Indian?"

"No, nothing like that." The sound to move blasted through the cold air, interrupting her. "There's no time for you to ask again."

He hated knowing she was right. "Fine. We can always talk later." Sam saddled his horse in a hurry. He got on and led Scamp to the water for a quick drink before leaving. One good day of traveling and they'd reach Fort Hall. There, he could send on the Warrens' divorce, and military couriers could take it from there. He'd not feel right about planning a future with her until the act was official. He grinned. Until then, he'd fix whatever was bothering Marie and enjoy the beautiful day.

By noon, most of the animals struggled, sick. Some were lame, but most acted poorly. Sam knew from the alkaline dust that they'd need a dose of vinegar and molasses for each. He rode his horse to their wagons, glad to see Marie, and made medicine for everyone. After the sickest of humans each had a tablespoon, he and his men made sure all the animals had a portion. They continued on after an hour, rolling down good roads. The gradual incline became steeper with each passing minute.

He had his eye on reaching the summit of the ridge dividing the Columbia and Bear rivers. If he remembered correctly, a healthy creek ran from a spring. They'd have to go a couple of miles past the summit. Up so high, they'd all have a good view of the sunset and any dangers approaching. He didn't expect to see Del and Ellen, hoping both waited at Fort Hall for them.

They reached the summit creek later than Sam had planned. He'd resisted the urge to gallop ahead, staying with the middle of the group. Lucky knew where tonight's campsite was, and Sam allowed him to lead the way.

They did their chores as usual. Marie helped with theirs first, Sam noticed, and then went to help Mr. Winslow with the boys. Uncle Joe cooked dinner, having it ready just as she got back to them. She ate without talking much. Sam fretted a little over her silence. But with everyone talking about Ellen and whether or not Del had found her yet, Marie couldn't have gotten a word in edgewise anyway, he supposed.

When she began gathering their empty plates, Sam stood too,

saying, "I'll help with washing." He walked with her, not giving Marie any choice in the matter. She didn't say anything on their way to the creek. Sam struggled to stay quiet, intending to let her talk to him when she was ready. He knelt on the bank when she did. Sam took all the dishes and silverware from the bucket so she could rinse it. When she set the pail down, he gave her a plate. They washed up this way, her putting the clean item into the bucket as she finished.

Her reserve worried him. Sam needed to hear her happy voice, not this lingering silence. "Please, Marie. There's something wrong. You've been quiet all day." He caressed her face with the back of his hand. "I've not seen any hint of a smile since breakfast."

"How are your knuckles?" She held his hand and examined the wet skin. "Still looks painful."

"Never mind that." He tipped her chin up to look into her eyes. "Tell me what's troubling you."

She blinked a couple of times before saying, "I need to mention an issue you might find necessary. It'll probably determine how much you would want to help me get to Oregon."

He frowned. "There's nothing able to sway me from helping you do whatever it is you want unless it's remarrying Warren. Even then, if your heart were set, I'd help you."

"No, this is another issue. I have no children because I'm barren. Charles has two sons with his first wife, so we know he does not lack in any way." She paused, looking away from him. "I figured if any man were to offer for me, he'd like to be aware of my inability."

Keeping his expression neutral, Sam nodded. "I understand and remember you telling me this a while back. I also appreciate your candor. My offer of getting you to Oregon is unchanged, of course."

"Thank you."

"You're welcome. It's my job." He looked back at the camp for a moment. No one approached them. "And my pleasure."

She smiled up at him before continuing to clean. After returning her grin, he also kept washing, his mind occupied. Now that marrying her seemed possible, his feelings about being a father someday now mattered. Sam had always assumed he'd have children. He slowed, wanting to be near her as long as possible.

Marie placed her last dish in the bucket. "I'd always thought that if orphans arrived in Oregon, Charles and I could adopt and care for them." She stood. "We'd talked about it. Maybe he and Hester could carry on if a child needs help."

Getting to his feet and picking up the dinner pail, he said, "As much as you've cared for Winslow's children, I'd think you'd taken them to raise."

"No, but they are good boys."

He kept quiet on what he'd seen of Winslow's actions in the past. The drinking, the mean attitude, his siding with Warren and going against Sam's orders all added up to reckless behavior. The man had been quiet since his wife died and daughter disappeared. As he and Marie approached the camp, Sam realized thinking of the devil made him materialize. Winslow stomped his way to them.

"Ma'am. You need to help me with the boys. Miss Jenny has helped out today, not hiding around like you."

"Excuse me?" asked Sam. His voice came out harsher than he'd intended and he cleared his throat.

Marie patted Mr. Winslow on the arm. "It's all right."

"Yeah, everyone was all sympathetic. Now everyone has gone back to their lives, leaving me alone to deal with two rascals. You promised to help, and now you need to make right with it," grumbled Winslow.

"Very well. Have they had their dinner?"

"Yes, Miss Jenny did that. You need to wash dishes and set up the bedrolls for us."

Sam didn't like the man's condescending tone. The way he ordered around Marie led him to wonder how much of Jenny's help had been voluntary instead of forced. Thinking Winslow was a grown man and capable of caring for two little boys, Sam asked, "You can't do all that yourself?"

"I can and have been. Warren is having a little get-together, and I want to attend. I work hard and deserve a night to relax."

He saw the conflict of emotions wash over Marie's face before she said, "Go on, then, and I'll tuck the boys in and wash up for you."

The man's bad attitude melted like shaved ice in an oven. "Thank you kindly ma'am." Winslow walked off without a backward glance, not toward his own wagon, but the Warrens'.

She stared at him, her mouth set. "Before you say anything,

Sam, the children need someone more than he needs the help. I've been self-centered with my own problems. It will do me some good to help someone else with theirs."

As he watched, she walked away in the same direction as Winslow. The boys all sat around the fire. Some read. Lucky and Joe sewed up tears in their clothing. Sam grinned every time one of them made a grunt from poking themselves with the needle. He went to the wagon, putting up the dish pail and wondering what to do next. Weariness settled in his bones. He picked up his trail book, determined to be as productive as his men. After kicking off his boots, Sam laid down in his bedroll and began to read. He must have fallen asleep. When Arnold shook him awake, Sam looked over to see Marie sleeping in her own bedroll. He slipped on his boots and began the night watch.

He paused each time when passing Marie as she slept. She talked in her sleep once. He listened just to hear her voice. When Arnold met up with him, he grinned and continued his round. The first of the sun's rays for the day didn't come fast enough for Sam. Fort Hall meant civilization, which also meant Marie would be truly free. He intended on being the first and only in line to win her hand.

In an irritable mood, Sam rushed through caring for the stock. Breakfast, too, passed in a blur. He ate, helped Lefty wash, and double-checked that Marie packed up everything they owned before letting Lucky give the signal to move.

Midmorning, they exited a shallow canyon. A vast plain stretched out before them with a ribbon of river cutting the landscape in half. As the group approached, the white adobe walls of Fort Hall gleamed in the noon sunlight. Dark storm clouds loomed behind the brightness of civilization, enhancing the fort's glow. As fast as the rain moved east, they'd soon be rolling through a downpour. This area needed every drop of rain squeezed from the sky above. This meant the road would soon turn to a sticky mud and slow their progress.

Though hoping for a noontime arrival, Sam knew a dinner at the fort was more likely. He fidgeted in the saddle. Sam kept his heels still against Scamp's flanks. He resisted the urge to gallop ahead with the divorce decree in his saddlebag.

Sam looked behind him at the group following him. He'd noticed how bare soil replaced grass as they neared the fort. For the animals' sake, they should put down stakes here for the night. He couldn't give the order. Del and Ellen might be waiting for them. He also knew a courier could take documents to the territory capital, and that kept him moving forward.

A slight gust front hit, threatening to lift his hat away. Sam pushed it back down on his head and tilted the broad side forward to keep on the hat. Though the clouds overhead reflected sunlight, small droplets of rain turned to huge in a hurry. He didn't want to stop. After the initial blast, he turned back and motioned for them to continue. He grinned, almost hearing their groans even at this distance. The fort lay a mile ahead. They'd miss a lot of the sticky mud if they kept a constant pace.

The rain grew colder. He shivered, the cotton shirt thin cover against the wet. Sam looked behind him, making sure all those who had walked earlier were now in their own wagons. Satisfied no one was still on foot, he settled in for the remaining half mile. He glanced up and saw the gate stood open for them and anyone else on the trail. Sam realized they'd not have to keep watch tonight. He and his men could enjoy their first full night's sleep since leaving Missouri.

Impatient, he nudged Scamp into a trot and entered the enclosed walls. When seeing an officer, he called out, "Excuse me, sir?" The man's attention caught, Sam dismounted and went to him. "We had a young lady kidnapped near Soda Springs."

"That's a shame."

"It is, and one of my men, a Métis, went to retrieve her and meet us here."

"A half-breed and a woman how old?"

Sam wanted to correct the man. Métis was the best term for Del, not the derogatory "half-breed." Under the circumstances, he decided to let it slide. "Youngish, old enough to marry, but too young to be a spinster."

"I'd remember a gal like that. Every other lady fitting your description is with her family, not some half breed."

Instead of giving the officer a lesson in manners, Sam said, "I see. It's important that she's found, so I'd like to check in with your commander as well."

"Of course, sir."

Sam smelled Winslow behind him. Before he could turn to face him, the sloppy drunk let out a blood-curdling wail. "You lied to me! My daughter is gone! Gone with that damned Indian!"

CHAPTER 12

Marie buttoned Skeeter's shirt. She looked down to see Little Buster leaning against her, struggling to put on his boot. "Give me a moment, Buster, and I'll help you." Helping the older boy down, she turned to the youngest and held his boot steady while he slipped his foot inside. "Good! Now the other." As she readied his other shoe, she heard shouting above the fort's usual noises. Recognizing Sam's and Jack's yells, she concluded Ellen hadn't been here waiting for them to arrive. "Boys, play in the wagon or nearby for a while." Distracted, she noticed how they ran off as if late to their next adventure.

Arnold stepped up from behind her. "I reckon boss is in trouble, ma'am."

"Should we go help him?" asked Marie.

"He can probably handle old Jack himself." The young man shrugged. "Still, it'd be worth the effort going over there to see if Miss Ellen is back."

Lucky strolled up in dry clothes. "My bet is she's not. Otherwise, Mr. Winslow would be a lot quieter."

Laughing, Arnold said, "I'll take that bet. Lefty, you in?"

Still in his wet gear, Lefty laughed. "Hearing him from here? Naw, I like my silver."

A group of men left the commander's building, stopping their banter. Marie bit her lip when seeing how angry Sam looked as he stood talking with one of the soldiers. After examining the other men's faces, they appeared to share his mood. All of them watched as Winslow approached with only the commander. Marie asked, "Ellen isn't here?"

"No, she ain't come back to us." Winslow crooked his head in Sam's direction. "Granville was wrong about his friend. That half-breed probably slitted her throat himself."

The very thought of Ellen dead brought tears to Marie's eyes. "Don't say such things, Mr. Winslow. Mr. Du Boise cares for Ellen." Her chin trembled just before she began sobbing. As she buried her face in her hands, she felt one of the men pat her on the back in comfort.

"Here, here, ma'am," said Lucky. "No need for that."

Lefty leaned closer to say in a quiet tone, "I agree with the boss. We'll find her."

Marie sniffed, glancing up at the boys' earnest expressions. "How can you be sure? It's been several days."

"Two weeks," said Lucky. Arnold punched him in the arm as if to quiet him. "What? It's been that long, hasn't it?"

"Seems like," added Lefty.

The commander raised his gloved hands to get their attention and stop the conversation. "Nevertheless. With Granville's assurances and a group of my finest beginning their search for her, we will find Miss Winslow."

Giving Sam a sneering glare as he approached, Jack said to the commander, "I'm mighty glad to have your help."

"Now then, you folks settle in for the rest of the day. We'll find your missing woman." The commander tipped his hat and turned to where his soldiers waited as Sam left the group.

When Sam joined Marie and the others, Jack spat out, "And no thanks to you." He turned on his heel, going back among the wagons.

Narrowing his eyes at the man, Sam remained silent until addressing his men. "Gentlemen, let's get settled. They have fresher horses, and if the two are anywhere near here, they'll find them." As his employees left to carry out his orders, he put his hand on Marie's shoulder, saying, "Would you please walk a moment with me? I have news for you."

Marie wiped her face with a clean part of her sleeve. His serious tone worried her. "Is everything well?"

"For me, it's very well." He let his hand slide down her upper arm until it broke contact at her elbow. "I'm not sure how you'll take this, but your paperwork has been filed."

"I see." She stopped walking. She truly was alone, now. Her nose began itching and her eyes stung with tears. "So, Charles and I are no longer married?"

He shook his head. "I'd like to say you're not officially wed. I can't until the paperwork is filed at the territory courthouse."

"So, I have to be Charles' wife until then?" Marie asked. Sam laughed, but she didn't hear humor in the sound. "I feel ill." At the group's wagon, she used it for support.

"Don't. The courier leaves in the morning, and my letter is in there. The decree has an effective date, which has already passed." He turned her to face him, and at her questioning look, he answered, "Yes, I'd feel better when the paper is securely in the courthouse."

His response didn't reassure her. Anything could happen between here and Oregon City. "I have witnesses who saw both of us sign. We can't still be…I'm not going back to him, Sam. I can't."

"What?" He held her by the shoulders. "No, dearest, you're not going back to him. Not now, not ever. Even if we find the decree floating back to us on the river, I'll write up a new document. None of my men will mind signing as witnesses again."

She liked how he was quick with a solution to her potential problem. The warmth of his touch steadied the pounding in her chest. "If a new document needs to be written, so be it." Marie thought a moment before suggesting, "I do know how to write Charles' signature."

He hugged her close, and she felt his lips pressed against her head. "I can't condone that, sweetheart."

Under his chin with her face against his chest, she breathed in deep, loving his scent. She felt every inch of their contact as if a static charge of electricity lurked underneath her skin. "You wouldn't let me?"

"Let's say I'd prefer to not know if you did." He released her, still holding onto her arms. "No conflict of interest and no hindrance to our marriage."

"No hindrance to our what?" Her hair stood on end, and Marie swore she tasted metal at the back of her throat. "Sam, are you suggesting we get married?"

"Suggesting is such a mild word for it, sweetheart." He smoothed a loose strand of her hair back into place. "I'm expecting you to marry me as soon as possible."

She stepped back from him, swallowing before protesting, "Love is one thing, but marriage?" Marie shook her head, saying, "We can't. It's too soon."

He stepped forward as she stepped back into the tailgate of the supply wagon. "No, it's not. We love each other, and I'm tired of waiting." Sam frowned and pointed toward Charles and Hester's wagon. "You're not leaving me to go with those two. What else can you do besides marry someone?" Crossing his arms, he gave her an arrogant look. "I expect that someone to be me, no exceptions."

Marie laughed at his arrogance but knew he was right. What single woman traveled with a trunk and the clothes on her back? She looked up into his eyes, the clear blue shining with love and a large dose of triumph. "Samuel, I don't want to marry someone in desperation."

"You wouldn't be." He waved his hand toward the fort's log cabin headquarters. "Any man there or even here in our own party would jump at the chance to marry you. Wink at any of them, and you'll see how much desperate doesn't apply here."

She echoed his previous stance by crossing her arms, not believing him and not wanting to argue. "Don't be absurd. After my father had died, he left me with a plantation to run. I didn't know the first thing about what to do, and if not for Charles, I'd have been destitute within a year. Besides, you've seen him. He was even more handsome when we met, and I was lucky he married me."

He stared at her for a moment before laughing. "You can't be serious." When she nodded, he ran a hand through his hair. "How does he have anything to do with me? I love and desire you more than I do my next breath. I can think of nothing other than your smile and live to hear your voice. Us marrying isn't an option; it's a necessity."

The more he spoke, the harder her pulse knocked in her chest. His words sounded sincere and eerily familiar. "Stop. Please. I've heard this before, you know. Not from you, no, but from him." She turned from Sam, hands trembling as she gathered the washing from the back of the wagon. "It's all the same now as it was then. What will happen in five, ten years time? I'll learn my lesson when you've found another, someone younger than I am and able to have children. You'll tell me it's not going to happen, but then I'd have never imagined Charles and Hester could…" Marie paused and faced him, her stomach churning. "I'd rather die alone on my way to civilization than be betrayed again."

"I've made a mistake. You're having doubts about leaving him. I'd not realized how much you still cared for Warren." Before she could argue, he went on. "All this has been a huge change for you, sweetheart. You found out about those two and divorced in an instant. Now, I'm asking you to jump back into something new before you've properly mourned the old." He exhaled, staring up at the sky. "I need to apologize. Impatience has clouded my manners, and I've pressured you into something too much, too soon."

"Sam." She held onto his arm. "Let's give this more time. When we get to Oregon City, and if you still care for me, I'll let you propose."

"You'll let me, hmm?" He shook his head. "You have no choice in if I ask, only in what you reply." Sam walked around to the side of the wagon and reached in, retrieving a fishing pole. "I'll be gone until dinner, trying to catch us some salmon. Send out a search party if I'm not back by dark."

"Of course. Is there anything you want me to do until then?" she asked, and he shook his head while walking away. As he went farther downstream, Marie smiled at the sudden thought of how this absence wasn't permanent. She had the chance to see his home at the journey's end. No spending her days in a gold rush boomtown store from dawn to dusk. Marie almost laughed with joy, happiness crowding out any worries. Even if Sam grew disinterested in her later, she'd have the choice now and later to see if their relationship had legs.

Shaking her head to better focus on the afternoon chores, she went to the wagon, wondering what to do with her afternoon in the Fort. Maybe cleaning up and rearranging items could keep her busy. She had the laundry gathered, what few items there were. She sighed, thinking. Taking care of the Winslow boys always needed doing. Glancing around, she saw Skeeter playing with other boys as they rolled a hoop with a stick. Little Buster hung back, sucking his thumb as he watched. They seemed fine for now.

Before Marie could decide what to do first, the gates to Fort Hall opened. A contingent of soldiers rode in, followed by Del and Ellen riding on the same horse. Seeing her friend, Marie cheered. She hurried to the group, stopping just shy of them. Hearing a boy's cry, she turned to see Skeeter run toward his sister.

The child had noticed Ellen before she saw him. He yelled, and she turned as he barreled toward her. "Ellie! You're here!" He jumped up into her arms as soon as her feet touched the ground. "You're here. Mama's gone, did you know?" He started crying.

Ellen's gaze met Marie's. "Yes, sweetheart, I know and I'm so sorry."

His voice muffled, he cried, "I miss her! Little Buster don't know, but I do. Pa's been sick this whole time, too." He squeezed her even more. "I'm glad you're here with us."

She held him, returning his hug. "I am, too, baby boy."

Marie felt the youngest brother take her hand, and she looked down at him. He still sucked his thumb, but held on to her and leaned against her leg. She told Ellen, "Skeeter has been the best boy I've ever met. He's polite, is kind to other children, and has helped me with Little Buster's care. He's already such a little man."

"He's always been the best brother ever," Ellen said. Addressing him, she added, "Thank you, Skeeter, for helping with Little Buster. I know this can't have been easy for you, and you've been so brave."

"Thank you, Ellie." He sagged against her as if absorbing her comfort. "They buried Ma way back there. I didn't want to leave her, but Pa made me."

Brushing away her tears, Ellen said, "I know, sweetheart. Ma would have wanted you to stay with Pa while she went with the angels."

"But she was with us, and then we put her in the ground. Pa didn't even wrap her in a blanket. She's probably cold."

Ellen glanced at Marie, worry etched on her face. She wanted to reassure the young woman and said, "The men made a box from scrap lumber. It worked very well for her. We ladies put her in a Sunday dress with a lovely wrap for her neck." Ellen nodded as if understanding what Marie didn't want to say in front of the children.

"That sounds perfect. Thank you for taking such good care of Lucy." Ellen pulled away a little from her brother. "Everyone here did very well for our mother. Her body is in the earth, but her spirit is in heaven, I'm sure."

The boy nodded, seeming happier now. "Ma doesn't know she's in the ground, I suppose."

"She doesn't," Ellen assured him. "She's somewhere else much nicer."

He sniffed. "Probably she's already at where we'll be living, but as a ghost. Ma will be a good ghost, not one that scares me or anything."

"Of course not. She'll keep watch over you every day. You and Little Buster both." Ellen let him slide out of her grip and nodded at their youngest brother.

"All right," Skeeter wiped his nose on his sleeve. "I can keep an eye out for Ma's ghost, just in case she's not there yet."

"You could do that, yes."

"Can I go tell the other boys to help me watch for her?"

"Of course, but keep in mind her ghost might be at our new home waiting for us, all right?" Ellen patted his back, but the boy was already distracted when seeing the other children playing.

"All right!" Skeeter ran off, headed toward his friends.

When the boy was out of earshot, she asked Marie, "How else was I supposed to handle that? He thinks his mother is around here as a ghost. Pa is going to be so angry with me."

Marie tried to be diplomatic, keeping her voice free from the hostility she felt for the oldest Warren. "Then, maybe your father should have taken care of this himself. Instead, he has drunk himself sick every day and ignored his sons." As soon as she'd said the words aloud, she covered her mouth with her hand. "I'm sorry. I tried to not say that."

Ellen reached out to Litter Buster, who ran into her arms. "Good to know he's not changed. I was worried."

Her friend's choice of words reassured Marie and compelled her to ask, "How are you? Really?" Unable to resist comforting her friend, she hugged Ellen and her brother at the same time. "Did they hurt you?"

The girl melted into Marie's arms like a long lost daughter. "No, not at all. Del was there."

"Was he really? I'm so glad. You'll have to tell me what happened. But wait until Jenny is with us because I know she'll want to know as well." She stepped back hoping their friend would forgo her boycott of Marie long enough to properly greet Ellen. Buster whined until she let him down. Once free, the child ran off to join his brother. They both smiled at the little boy, and Marie said, "I'm sure Adelard is telling Sam now. I'm so sorry about Lucy. Did you have to see them...?"

Ellen shuddered at the memory. "Yes. They told us not to scream; she did, and they killed her without hesitation. After that, I was too scared to make a sound."

Imagining the scene gave Marie goose bumps and she shuddered. "You poor dear. How about you wait until you're rested to say anything about this? The main thing is you're safe and here with us. The boys are fine, and your father will sober up someday."

As if hearing them talk about him, Jack's moan and yell for

her rose incoherent above the fort's usual busy sounds. Ellen's voice rang with sarcasm. "It seems like he's already started the process."

Patting her friend's arm, Marie reassured her. "Don't worry about the boys. They're safe with me. Just get him healed up first."

"Thank you, Marie. Both you and Jenny are the best friends ever." She paused at another yell from Jack.

"I hear her! Ellen! Where are you? Get over here!" He stumbled over to her, head bleeding from a cut. "I fell out of the damned wagon. Where were you? My Lucy is dead, and you weren't here to help me. I need a bucket." He staggered away and started retching.

Feeling ill herself, Marie swallowed while telling Ellen, "I need to let you take care of him. Good luck."

Ellen nodded before going for the requested bucket. "Thank you. I need every bit of luck possible."

Walking back to the crew's wagons, Marie stopped in shock. Charles and Hester seemed to be waiting, Charles leaning against the wagon and his sister sitting on the tailgate. She did not want to approach. Moving slowly, she took a step back and caught her former husband's eye. Their gazes met, and she grimaced before catching herself.

"Hello, Marie." He stood up straight as his sister hopped to her feet. "We've come to say goodbye."

"Oh. Had we not done so before now?"

"Yes, but not permanently."

"I see. Very well, Charles, goodbye, and I hope California is all you've hoped it would be." She held out her hand to shake, wanting to keep things formal.

He reached for her hand and pulled her into his arms. "I'll miss you, dearest."

How could words trigger a stomach illness, she wondered. Marie fought the urge to throw up on him. She eased out of his grip and tried to smile. "Well, I'm sure Hester will keep you company."

His sister sidled over and took his hand. "At last, you understand."

"Hess," Charles warned.

"Good-bye, dear former sister, and good luck with Granville or whoever will take you in." She snuggled up to her brother.

"That Joe character seems desperate enough. In case Sam doesn't work out, of course."

The demonstration of affection between the two made the bile bubble up from her stomach. Fighting the bitter taste in her mouth, Marie faked a calm she didn't feel. "We'll see. I'm in no hurry to replace Charles and look forward to being just another part of the crew."

Hester leaned over to her brother. "She can't replace you. Look at her brown skin, and that dress. Sam might use her for a while, but how soon do you think it will be until he passes her off to one of his men? They'll hand her on down until Lefty is the only one left she's not, well, you know."

Her former husband snickered, and Marie saw red. She wasn't that sort of woman, and they knew it. Plus, Lefty was an excellent young man. Certainly not the last pick of any litter he was in. Beyond furious, she gritted her teeth. "You're here to say goodbye, so goodbye and good riddance." She glared at both of them as they exchanged a look. Afraid of what she might say next, she added, "Excuse me, I have chores to do." Marie turned on her heel and went to the supply wagon. Listening for their departure, she reached in for a water jar. Her nose began its familiar sting, warning her about the tears welling in her eyes. She grabbed a dishrag to place across her face when done crying.

Marie made her way out of the fort and down to the water's rocky edge, fighting tears all the way. Others were around but not so close to seeing her cry. She found a steady rock to sit on and dipped the rag into the cool water. Scalding hot tears began running down her cheeks as if the gurgling river called a siren's song to them. All the grief she'd been pushing aside to be cheery welled up in her heart. Losing the plantation, saying goodbye to loyal servants, the humiliation of her marriage, and finally having to rely on the mercy of Sam weighed like stones in her stomach. Her throat hurt with the tightness of silent keening for her former life as she silently sobbed. She folded the rag, not opening her eyes, and placed the cold press against her upper face. Some part of her felt how the hot tears sunk into the cotton. The chill soothed her and eased the sorrow still welling inside Marie. When thinking ahead to her future, all she saw was a black veil clouding the view. Sam loved her, and she wanted to cling to him, but she'd done the same after her father died and married Charles.

"Marie? Are you all right?"

Sam's voice surprised her, and she let the washcloth fall. "Hello, yes, and you? Did you catch anything?" She filled the water jar as an excuse to hide her face.

He walked around to her, tilting his head to better see her. "Something is wrong. You've been crying."

"Everything is fine." She nodded at his string of fish. "You did well today." Struggling to her feet, she accepted his hand for balance. "Let's get back to camp, so we can start dinner."

"You can help me clean these and tell me why you were crying."

Hearing the worry in his voice, she pulled up a distraction for him. "Better that I say how Del and Ellen arrived this afternoon."

"Great! Are they all right? Neither was harmed?"

She smiled, glad her tactic worked. "He looked all right from a distance. Ellen looked good. A little frayed around the edges, but not bad. The boys were happy to see her."

Sam nodded as they entered the fort's walls. "I'll bet. She'll keep them better fed and cleaned." Nearing the wagon area, he held out his fishing pole and day's catch to her. "Take these while I go and learn more from Del and the commander. Don't wait for dinner. We may be a while."

Doing as he requested, she carried everything to the wagons while he went off in the other direction. Seeing Joe starting a fire, Marie held up Sam's fish. "I've never seen this sort of fish before? Are they any good?"

Joe stood, taking them from her. "They're the best you'll ever eat, ma'am. Let me have the pail, and I'll get the boys to help me clean them."

Giving him the bucket, she asked, "What can I do?"

He grinned at her. "Start fixing the rest of the supper."

"Mr. Granville said he and Del would be late."

"I expected as much. The soldiers will want every detail Du Boise can remember about the kidnappers. Make enough for them, but keep it to the side. It might be breakfast for them." He nodded before walking down to the river with the fish and a pail.

Facing the open gate, she stoked the fire. Marie glanced up to see Lucky and Arnold join Joe before he left the courtyard. She marveled at how Sam's men seemed to know when and how to do everything necessary in a wagon party. Though she thought while getting the dry goods together for dinner, she'd learned a few things too. Soon white biscuits cooked in a Dutch oven, and the dried peas she'd soaked overnight simmered in a small cook pan. Knowing three men would make short work of cleaning a few fish, she set out a frying pan to heat.

The men arrived with a bucket full of filets just as the pan caused drops of water to bounce on its surface. Lefty spoke first. "Dinner already smells good, ma'am. I'm partial to peas."

"Good. I didn't know for sure, and I've not had them in a while." She stood. "I can set out some blankets for us to sit on while we cook."

"Thank you, ma'am," said Joe. He began laying out the fish, the meat sizzling when it hit the metal.

Marie started to pull out blankets, Lefty, Arnold, and Lucky beside her, each waiting for their turns. She carried everything closer to the campfire. Lefty followed her with his journal, Arnold his current book, and Lucky brought his bugle and polishing cloth. She smiled at them. Each man waited while she placed their blankets in a stack. One by one they sat and began work on their projects. She settled in next to Joe and checked the biscuits. A quick stir of the peas showed they cooked nicely. The wind brought a scent of the cooking fish, and she smiled.

Glancing up at her, Joe returned her grin. "Smelling good, isn't it?"

She nodded. "Very much."

"Looks like I'm just in time."

They all turned at Sam's voice. "Didn't take as long as I expected. They're more interested in Adelard's statement. I just corroborated his testimony and was a character witness."

"They do believe him, don't they, that he saved Ellen's life?" asked Marie.

"Yes. Him bringing her back alive gave him a lot of credibility."

"Did Du Boise tell you the whole story?" asked Lucky.

Sam shrugged. "I heard most of it before they had me leave." He took a plate from Joe and gave it to Marie.

She wanted to hear everything he knew about what happened to Ellen. Almost getting to her feet, she urged him, "So tell us, if you can."

"It's pretty simple. The chief's son had her taken and would have brought Lucy along as a prize if she'd not screamed. They had Ellen dressed as the bride when Del rode in and claimed her as his own." Each man had food before Sam settled in to eat his own serving.

Her jaw dropped when realizing what that meant. "They're not married, are they?"

"In the Shoshone's eyes, they are now."

Wondering how Ellen might free herself from Del's partnership, she asked, "Is that official in our country?"

"Not legally if the couple doesn't get a license." In between bites, he added, "Plenty of people don't out here. Too much trouble. A piece of paper isn't necessary for two people to work on a homestead together."

Marie raised her eyebrows when he looked at her. She didn't like the gleam in his eye. "I'd still prefer everything be legal. Some day all this will be part of the United States, and I think most women would like the protection a valid marriage provides."

"As would most men, I expect. Don't worry. You're preaching to the choir on this matter." He held out his empty plate for her to take. "A common law marriage is fine, but I'd prefer a legally binding contract saying my wife is mine."

The men snickered or chuckled under their breath. Marie gave him a grin, knowing he tried to get her goat. "Since you're bereft of a wife and I prefer clean breakfast dishes, I'll be glad to wash up this evening. Can't have a big strong man like you doing women's work." She got to her feet, picking up the dinner pail and adding his empty plate to her own. All the others reached over for her to take their empty dishes, too, each one giving her thanks as she piled them in the wash pail. "I'll be back for the pans, Joe."

"No need, ma'am. Mr. Granville and the boys want to help you by taking care of them for you. Good practice for when they get married."

Lefty and Arnold talked over each other, each denying they'd ever be under a woman's thumb. Marie smiled at how Lucky just grinned and shook his head. She couldn't see Sam since he sat with his back facing her. "Very well. I'll get started on this, then."

Sam stood and followed her, saying, "It's almost sunset. Let's all get started, so we're back before they close the gate for the night."

She slowed a little to let him catch up to her. "Thank you for helping. I'd not noticed how late it had become. What happens when they close the gates, and we're outside the walls?"

"They'd let us in, of course. The Army doesn't want to lose civilians to Indian attacks."

"I tend to agree." She saw Ellen walking with Jenny and the Allens. She waved to all of them, Ellen being the only one returning her greeting.

"Did they just snub you?" asked Sam. "How dare they?"

"Sam, it's all right." She put a hand on his arm. "They're just maintaining a distance for Jenny's sake. It's not proper for a single woman to associate with me."

"The hell it is."

When he started towards the Allens, she held onto his arm and pulled him a little away. "Sam! You can't say or do anything. You know they're right. Please, leave it alone for Jenny's sake. Mine too. I'd be mortified if they were forced to acknowledge me."

He stopped resisting and let her lead him to the river. "Since you insist, I'll let it go. This makes a good case for us getting married."

Laughing, she shook her head. "No, I'd like better reasons than that." She gave him a grin, knowing he'd not argue with her so close to his men. They washed as if long used to each other's motions. She smiled when giving him the last clean fork. All the others had washed their one item and left.

"Marie, why were you crying earlier today? Please tell me."

"It was nothing." She straightened, and he stood with her. Continuing before he could begin arguing, she added, "Very much nothing, just Hester being her selfish little self."

His eyes narrowed as they walked back to the camp. "Do I need to talk to both of them?"

She laughed. "You're just spoiling for a fight, aren't you? There's no need. I just needed a good cry and indulged myself. I really do feel much better." They entered the yard as the gates closed behind them. "Let's worry about something more significant, like anything but the Warrens."

The first notes of Taps wafted to them on the late evening air. Sam leaned in and said, "That just leaves everything else in the world."

Marie stifled a giggle as they faced the flag as it was lowered. The entire fort stayed silent except for noises by various animals.

The last notes faded, and activity resumed. She playfully punched Sam on the arm. "So much for us being sober during such a ceremony."

He gave her a little boy grin. "What can I say? I like seeing you smile."

At the wagon, she put the dishes next to the pots and pans already put in there by the others. The fire didn't burn bright enough, and the new moon kept the night dark. She yawned, vowing to pick up her sewing tomorrow or the next day.

Marie straightened out her bedroll, glancing across the campfire to see Sam doing the same. She wanted to sleep in the wagon for propriety's sake, but the air already held a nippy cold to it. She snuggled in under her blanket, almost missing Charles' warmth. Thinking of him led to thinking of Hester. She squeezed her eyes, giving her head a slight shake. No more stewing over either one of them. She took a deep breath and began counting backward from fifty and soon fell asleep.

Revelry played by the fort's bugler woke her, and she stifled a curse at the noise. She'd have to see about helping the young man misplace his bugle for just one morning. She heard angry mutterings, recognized Lucky's voice, and laughed out loud. It served him right for greeting the days with his own bugle as he had for so long. "They always say better to give than receive."

Lucky punched his pillow and growled as the others laughed. "They would be correct, boss."

Sam was the first to sit up. "All right, enough kidding around. Now that everyone is accounted for, I'm eager to get home."

"Sir, are the Warrens going with us?" asked Lefty.

"No. I spoke with Warren early yesterday. They're headed south with another group."

"We're waiting for Adelard, aren't we?"

"I'm checking on that, next." He put his bedding up and left them, headed toward the commander's office.

Marie saw the flag had been raised, and now the gates slid open to allow the day's activities. She put away her own bedding as Joe handed the pail to Arnold for water. She marveled how they all communicated without a word. Familiarity didn't just breed contempt, it bred a routine, too. Not rushing around while waiting on the twins left her idle. She helped Lefty fold his blankets, smiling at the kind young man when they were finished. "Having two makes the work more fun, doesn't it?"

"Yes, ma'am. Sure does."

After a breakfast big enough to feed them again at lunch, they hitched the animals and began rolling out of the fort. Marie caught up to Sam as he saddled Scamp. "I've not seen Del this morning. We're not leaving him here, are we?"

"He has to stay, at the commander's insistence." He paused before resuming his cinching of the saddle. "He wants to catch up to us when he's released."

"How long are they keeping him imprisoned?"

"Not for too long, the commander said, but no, I don't like it, either. He's told them everything; I've vouched for him. There's no reason why he can't go with us."

"Should we be worried about him?"

Sam looked down at her. "More like concerned until he is with us again. In the meantime, I have a job for you. While we're in this part of the country, I'll need you to drive a team of oxen. With one of us scouting ahead for the clearest road and the rest guarding everyone, you being in charge of the oxen would help a great deal. Can you do it?"

"Yes, I've driven our wagon a few times."

"Good enough. Go on up and let Lefty know you're taking over."

She nodded and walked faster to the supply wagon as Sam rode to the front of the train. Lefty grinned as she approached, his green eyes sparkling. "I suppose boss wants me to keep watch?"

"You suppose right." She waited as Lefty pulled the animals to a halt and hopped down.

"Just remember, they've had enough food, water, and rest these past few days and might be ornery," he hollered while walking to the back of the wagon. He untied his horse and quickly mounted. "Be sure to keep a firm grip, and don't let them get by with nothing." With a click, he galloped off toward the river.

As she held the reins in a firm grip, she realized Lefty had been far too correct. The animals kept a quick pace, slowing every so often to rest up. She didn't like the stop and go, so she tried to keep them subdued when they'd rather just hoof it onward. As the morning heated, sweat began beading on her skin. The dry air kept her from feeling soaked. Even so, drops tickled as they rolled down her cleavage and the back of her neck. The infernal sunbonnet didn't help, being in the wagon and not on her head.

Noon approached, and the wind shifted from the north, carrying the smell of river to her. Once the animals caught the water's aroma, they pulled in its direction. Marie hoped that during the noontime, she could eat and relax for a little while.

No order to stop for lunch sounded, though her stomach growled. She didn't feel confident enough to tie up the reins to go into the back to search for leftover biscuits. Still, she kept the oxen on the road until reaching the American Falls late that afternoon. At last, the order to halt sounded and she put on the wagon's brake. She unhitched both animals, intending to lead them to the river if the cliffs allowed access.

A few feet later, a breeze brought in a stronger scent of water. Marie breathed deep, enjoying the smell. The animals perked up and began trotting. She pulled back on them shouting, "Whoa! Whoa!" and digging in her heels. At that, both took off at a full gallop, jerking her from her feet and dragging her behind them. Stunned, she held on as they pulled her over rocks and sagebrush. She let go after what felt like a few miles. Her eyes ached from the dust in them. She blinked a few times to clear them, shock freezing her in place.

"Ma'am! Are you alive?" Lucky asked, jumping down off his horse. He knelt beside her, taking her hand.

"I think so," she answered, holding on to him while pushing up to her knees. Both were skinned and showed through holes in her skirt. "Oh my! This isn't good." Marie glanced up to see the oxen drinking at the water's edge, still hitched together. "I suppose they're fine for the moment."

Sam rode up and dismounted from Scamp in one fluid motion. "What the hell were you thinking, holding on like that?" He pulled Marie from her knees to her feet. "Can you walk? Goodness, woman, why didn't you let go? They weren't going anywhere."

Her chin started trembling, and she tried not to cry. "I didn't know how far they'd run. What if we never saw them again?" She turned toward the wagon. "Since they're fine, I'm going to put on something decent." Her legs ached as she hobbled back to the wagon.

Sam asked, "Lucky, could you see to the team?"

"Yes, boss." The young man tipped his hat and galloped to the wayward animals.

"Thank you." Leading his horse, he caught up to Marie. "Sweetheart, wait a moment, please. We're going to have to clean up your scrapes."

She shrugged. "I can do it."

"I know you can." His voice softened as he leaned in to add, "I'd like to help."

Her dignity still bruised, she had to protest his offer. "You don't have to. I already know how to clean a scrape and change my own clothes."

"I'm sure you do."

Not liking the amusement in his tone, she glanced at him to see a small smile playing about his face. She knew pain made her cranky but couldn't keep from saying, "You can go help someone else. I just didn't know how to stop charging oxen is all."

He laughed. "No one does."

She gave him a sideways glance. "I've never handled those types of animals before today. Charles thought I was too irresponsible, and I didn't want to tell you. I suppose he was right in thinking so."

Sam snorted his disbelief. "No, he was wrong to not teach you how. What if something happened to him out here and you needed to know? I'd say the irresponsibility is his entirely." He helped her up to sit on the tailgate and didn't ask before pulling off her boots and socks. "I've not seen anyone do as well on their first day. So much so, I didn't know it was the first time you'd done anything like this."

She smoothed down her skirt so he saw no more of her legs. "You flatter me."

"I don't." He looked at her, smiling. "While I'd like nothing better than to help you undress and maybe dress again, it's best if you're alone. I'll get some fresh water for you to wash the dirt from your scrapes while you change."

"All right." As he left, she climbed in under the canvas cover. Marie closed the canopy's flaps. She searched her trunk for a dress and waited for a couple of moments before slipping off her torn garment. Her knees and forearms bore the brunt of the landscape, and she winced. Putting on the clean and whole dress, she was already planning on how to fix her torn clothes. She fastened the upper buttons.

Sam's voice filtered in from outside. "Are you still dressed?"

"More like re-dressed, yes."

He peeked in from around the flap. "Should I circle a few more times until you're not?"

Taking the water from him, she chided, "No, it's too late, and we'd both be in trouble if you did such a thing."

As if he weren't leaving, Sam added, "I could stay if you needed help. I don't mind seeing your legs or anything."

She laughed. "Go on already. It won't take me long."

"If you insist." He disappeared.

She raised her skirt to mid thigh and began washing the blood and dirt from her skin. The salt in her sweat stung. Even with the sun bearing down on the canvas top, now that she was still and a little undressed, she shivered from the cold.

"How are you doing in there?" asked Sam. "I'm always ready to help a lady with her clothes."

She laughed. "I'll bet you are, you villain." Opening up the flaps, she stopped smiling when seeing him and his serious expression.

He looked up at her. "I'm sorry about being so angry with you."

His worried face charmed her. Marie shook her head before saying, "Don't apologize, I was foolish. Now that I know what to do, it won't happen again."

He climbed up into the wagon and sat with her on the bedding stacked there. "If they'd trampled you, it could have meant a slow, painful death. I'd have to wait and watch you die." Pinching the bridge of his nose, he said, "I couldn't stand having to do that."

"I'm fine," she whispered, "and know what to do next time." He'd been right about how serious her actions had been. Marie shuddered at what a death by trampling would mean. She'd heard enough stories to have a healthy respect for hooves. "Please, don't worry about me." Marie saw him blink a few times. On impulse, she leaned in and kissed his cheek. He didn't move at first; just let her lips caress him. With a groan, Sam faced and held her, deepening their kiss. He left her mouth to nibble all over Marie's face, and she laughed at the tickles. When his lips touched her closed eyelid, she smiled at how right he seemed for her.

"Damn, woman, you tempt me beyond all reason. People are

out there expecting us to be together like this."

"Oh, mercy. Are they really?" She chuckled.

He lightly kissed her lips and said, "They're placing bets, dearest."

She looked at her hands, pressed against his chest. "I suppose we'd better move about in here, so they know we're not improper."

"We'd better before I say to hell with their bets." A little louder, he said, "Bring it with your other wash tomorrow if you think the dress can be repaired."

"It can," she said as loud as he'd talked. Sam still held her. Marie's skin tingled everywhere they touched. He lowered his head, pressing his lips against hers before tracing their outline with his tongue. She liked the game and did the same to him, making him shudder. "We could slip away tonight and do more in private."

He exhaled and shook his head. "No, I need to marry you first."

Marie smiled at his gasped declaration. How very chivalrous of him. "You don't, not for tonight." She slid her hand down to his belt buckle and tugged. "Married is for later, if ever. You don't have to marry me, not for this."

Taking her hand from his belt, he held it before pulling her so close she had no choice but to hug him. He pressed his lips against her ear and whispered, "I have no choice. Even if I treat you like a wayward saloon gal tonight, I have to marry you."

She shook her head, reconsidering her answer to his proposal. "You might want to wait on hitching yourself to me like that. If you make my heart skip beats later as it is now, I'll be asking you to make love to me every day. In a week, you'll be begging me to leave you alone."

"Is that a threat or a dare?" Sam took her lips with his, kissing her as if a thirsty man in the desert. He paused to say, "I'd like to see you try such a thing with me," before leaning her back to nip at her earlobe and down her neck.

She held on to his shoulders, enjoying the feel of him through the cotton shirt. "You seem like a big, strong man. Why don't you go first?"

He slipped his fingers under each side of her neckline, pulling the two sides a little apart. Speaking against her skin, he said, "Do you know how easy it would be for me to rip this off your body and take you right here?"

Burying her fingers in his dark, untrimmed hair, she said, "You don't know how easy it would be to let you." Marie trembled as his lips drifted down into her cleavage and drew him closer. "Besides, why not just lift my skirt and take me this second?" She put her hands back on his shoulders and gently pushed him away as she whispered, "Pin me down and make me take you."

"Not now, because when I do attack you, I want every inch of your naked skin against every inch of mine." He eased his way to the back of the wagon while continuing to hold her, taking Marie with him. "Every inch for hours upon hours. You know too well what it's like to beg for love. You need to feel what it's like to be so sated, you beg me to stop."

He took her hand, kissing her palm. Chill bumps raced over her skin from his touch. Struggling to breathe, she gasped, "I can't imagine asking such a thing! Must we wait until forever for this? How soon can we marry again?"

Sam gave her a wicked grin as he climbed over the tailgate. "As soon as we can find any sort of a minister, justice of the peace, or boat captain."

She chuckled at the idea of one of the scruffy ferrymen they'd met officiating a wedding. "If wagon captains could do so, I'd ask you to marry us right now and end this torture." Holding his hand for balance, she stepped down onto the ground with him.

"Don't tease me, Marie." He caressed her face. "If you don't marry me, I'll die an old man, an old man confirmed bachelor." Narrowing his eyes for emphasis, he added, "Alone, unloved, wasted away because the one woman I wanted didn't return my love."

She laughed before turning her head to kiss his right palm. "That's not true. You know I care deeply for you."

"How can I be sure you'll always love me?" he asked kissing her forehead.

Unconcerned with who might be watching, she pressed her lips to his. "I do, my darling Sam, and always will."

He picked her up in his arms and twirled her around before kissing her. A few moments later, Sam broke away and said, "Let's get packed. I want us married by this time tomorrow." He took her hand, pulling her toward the others.

Marie laughed at his impatience and teased, "Why the rush, sir?"

"Shall I mosey now, ma'am?" He gave her a wicked grin and walked measurably slower.

"Not on your life, Granville." She grabbed his forearm and pulled. "We need to make up for lost time."

He resisted her efforts, leaning his weight back on his heels. "What if we can't get there tonight and have to stop to sleep? Will you be agreeable?"

She let go of his arm to stand in front of him, her hands on her hips. Marie looked him up one way and down the other as if he were a tasty dessert. She licked her lips for emphasis, and said, "Only if I'm allowed a preview of our wedding night."

Sam stopped as if frozen solid, except for his dropped jaw. His brows furrowed, making his blue eyes dark as any sea. He cleared his throat before hollering, "Hey, Lucky, Joe, Arnold! Anyone want to loan Miss Renaud his horse? Lefty, what about you?"

Seeing his desire at her suggestion took her breath away. He grabbed her hand, nearly dragging her to Scamp. His touch, his eagerness to be truly with her, thrilled Marie. She squeezed his hand, certain that marrying Sam would be the beginning of a whole new life for her.

OTHER BOOKS BY LAURA STAPLETON

The Oregon Trail Series

The Oregon Trail Short Stories
Unavoidable
Undeniable
Unexpected
Undesirable
Unfortunate
Uncivilized
Lucky's Christmas Wish

The Very Manly Series

The Very Best Man
The Very Worst Man
The Very Rich Man

Nova Scotia Murder Mysteries

Imposter
Holidays
Betrayal
Impatience
Pleasure
Surplus
Appearances
Rage
Honeymoon

ABOUT THE AUTHOR

With an overactive imagination and a love for writing, Laura Stapleton decided to type out her daydreams and what-ifs in order to share her lovable characters and their worlds with readers. She currently lives in Kansas City with her husband, daughter, dog, and a few cats. When not at the computer, you'll find her in the park for a jog or at the yarn store's clearance section.

CPSIA information can be obtained
at www.ICGtesting.com
Printed in the USA
LVOW04s2154051216
515893LV00032B/1534/P